Spectra

Joanne Elder

MuseItUp Publishing
www.museituppublishing.com

MuseItUp Publishing
14878 James, Pierrefonds, Quebec, Canada, H9H 1P5
http://www.museituppublishing.com

Cover Art © 2011 by Tiger Matthews
Edited by Natisha LaPierre
Copyedited by Penny Lockwood Ehrenkranz
Layout and Book Production by Lea Schizas

Print ISBN: 978-1-927085-10-3
eBook ISBN: 978-1-926931-83-8
First eBook Edition * July 2011
First Print Edition *July 2011
Production by MuseItUp Publishing

SPECTRA

BY

JOANNE ELDER

Dedication

To my father, William Cavendish Macneill, a World War II veteran. William passed away in 2008 after suffering from Alzheimer's disease. In memory of my father, half of the ebook author royalties will be donated to Alzheimer's research.

Acknowledgements

The author would like to acknowledge the hard work and expertise of the content editor, Natisha LaPierre, the line editor, Penny Ehrenkranz, and the cover artist Tiger Matthews. She would also like to acknowledge the dedication and support of her publisher Lea Schizas.

Many thanks go to the editing help of friends and family.

Preface

"The soul of man is immortal and imperishable."
Plato (427 BC-347 BC), *The Republic*

Do we have a soul? Throughout history, philosophers, spiritualists, and physicists have sought answers to this question. Independent of the belief in a god, the belief in the existence of a soul has given comfort to humans in their quest for eternal life.

Over the past centuries, many cultures have theorized about the existence of a soul. Ancient Indian spiritualists developed the concept of prana as the vital, life-sustaining force of living beings. This spurred the practice of Yoga, which focuses on the energy centers of the body referred to as Chakras to promote health and well-being. The ancient Qigong masters in China later identified *Qi* (pronounced Ch'i) as the vital flow of energy sustaining all life. Other names for this energy include *Ki* (Japan), *Pneuma* (Greece), *Mana* (Polynesia), and Breath of Life (Hebrew). Scientists believe the flow of energy through the body follows specific pathways, a concept inherent in the practice of acupuncture in Chinese medicine.

In modern times, scientists have sought to confirm the existence of a human energy field (HEF). In a more spiritual sense, the HEF is the aura surrounding and penetrating the physical body. In the past century, techniques have been developed in an attempt to photograph the luminous energy emanating from the human body, including gas discharge visualization (the basis of Kirlian photography) and biofeedback aura photography. Whether or not these photographic techniques actually reveal the human aura is controversial.

In the past two decades, improvements in the sensitivity of measuring devices led to the confirmation of minute energy fields around the human body. These electrical impulses have a frequency significantly higher than brain waves and may correspond to the human aura. One day, these research results could be used as a diagnostic technique and possibly lead to medicinal energy healing techniques.

Recently, researchers in Russia demonstrated that plasma (ionized gas composed of ions, free protons, and free electrons) could self-organize into a structure similar to a simple living cell with helical currents resembling DNA. Since plasma is the most common state of matter in the universe, it is conceivable for inorganic living plasma to be the most common form of life in the universe. Perhaps living plasma existed on early Earth and formed the template for biological life. Maybe, the human energy field is comprised of living plasma.

Many scientists now support the possible existence of a human energy field beyond the physical realm. Continued research may one day answer the question: What is this energy and how does it interact with the human body? Once this question is answered, the true human potential may be embraced.

The Consortium of Planets
2273 CE

In 2273, representatives from the governments of Earth and the settled planets Lyra, Draco, and Cygnus came together to form the Consortium of Planets to facilitate collaboration between the individual governments. The Consortium's mandate included control of interplanetary commerce and immigration. Ships fueled by vacuum particle energy enabled space travel between the planets. Incredible speeds were possible by flying along rare defects in the cosmic particle energy structure of space called textures. Freighters as well as passenger ships traveled daily along the texture corridors between the planets. Spaceports located on the three base stations include the Earth Base Station on the moon, the Eagle Base Station at the entrance to Lyra space, and the Lyra Base Station orbiting the planet Lyra.

Chapter One

March 3, 2298

"Are you crazy?"

Dean barely heard the voice over the thunder of the river, his grin wider than the jet of the current. He took a deep breath and prepared to line up his maneuver, his skin tingling. The timing had to be exact, or the churning water at the bottom of the rapids would swallow him whole. He narrowed his eyes only long enough to shield them from the sparkling blast. Caught by the eddy, he set up his angle feeling the kayak slide into place as an extension of himself.

Now!

He leaned forward and dug his paddle into the edge of the white water, his knuckles matching the hue; and he aligned himself with a smooth, strong sweep and a shift of his hips. As he leaned back to lift the bow, the descent began. With drum-tight abs, he brought his knees to his chest. His eyes focused on the whirlpools downstream with the blur of the canyon walls framing his landing. The tilt of the boat hinted just off horizontal, and he adjusted his weight.

Yeah!

A shower of water enveloped him as he popped out of the torrent. One last quick stroke sent him in the direction of the weathered rocks edging the river. He loved the Kicking Horse.

Dean flushed last summer's thrill ride out of his head and focused on the preparations for the impending one. Flying might lack the splash of the Kicking Horse, but there was plenty of *kick*. Both were in his blood.

"Hey Weston! What in God's name are you doing, rewriting history? The pod's been cleared for takeoff, and we're ready to go."

With each spoken word, Dean felt the hint of a moist breeze from Ivan's breath as though a prize bull snorted down the back of his neck. He took a step back, half expecting a set of horns to charge at him, and raised his voice slightly to be heard over the bustling activity in the hangar. "Navigating textures is an exact science. The probe data indicates the texture defect leading to this planet is highly unstable. If I'm going to navigate us through it safely, then you'll have to be patient while I finish. I'm almost done."

"Well hurry up! This is the first planet we've found in months that may actually have decent mineral reserves."

Dean tuned out Ivan's badgering and ran his fingers through his hair, laying them to rest in the patch of thorn bushes starting to germinate on the side of his face. He had extensive data from the probe he launched into the texture defect earlier in the week and couldn't afford to allow Ivan's anxiousness to rush him through it.

It was Ivan's seventh year managing the Consortium Mining Authority's Exploration Division. Their division located planets with minable commodities, preferably inhabitable ones. Two crews of six manned the exploration missions, and there were a total of three pods at their disposal. The costs of the operations were high. Often thrust into danger, crews flew along unstable textures to planets with harsh environments. Pods often returned with extensive damage.

Ivan lost a pod during flight, with no survivors, shortly after he'd joined the Authority. As part of a cost-cutting measure, he made the decision to let go of one of the crew's team leaders and take on the job himself. The leadership position fit in with his management role, although his qualifications for it were questionable. The senior executives in the Mining Authority had frowned at the promotion, but they liked the difference it made to the bottom line.

Dean did some more number crunching before pausing to formulate his final plan of attack. He stifled a yawn, and then he grabbed for his silver travel mug and started to swirl the last bit of coffee dampening the bottom. His wife, Karen, enjoyed tea, particularly green, leaving the ritual of coffee preparation to him. He had stayed up late the previous night to prepare for his early flight, and when the time came to prepare his favorite hot beverage, he did so with bleary eyes. He stumbled to the machine, carelessly stuffed the grounds into the filter, and went to bed.

When he went to reap the rewards of his effort, the whirlpool of grounds looked like the remnants of a melted chocolate mocha dessert.

He lifted the cup and threw back the tepid fluid. It cooled his throat, and he dispensed with the empty mug at the back of the table. In its final resting place, it reflected a caricature of his face. It caught his attention, and for a fleeting moment, he amused himself by watching his elongated eyes roll back and forth like blue-flecked marbles.

Dean often puzzled over how he landed the position of Navigator. He thought about it over the years and decided the incident was similar to an unintentional flip of his kayak. Your course seems planned, and you're speeding along as expected; when all of a sudden, you're making a wet exit, and you can't really recall the events leading up to it. He had graduated from the Lyra Institute of Space Study exactly fourteen years earlier with a degree in Flight Engineering and a minor in Particle Physics. The minor had taken an additional year, but he thought it would give him an edge. His plan backfired. For ten years, he'd been enjoying piloting pods for the Exploration Division when, out of the blue, Ivan decided to switch him to navigation. The position required piloting experience, expertise in particle physics, and keen wit. Dean's education and flight experience along with his two years of military training made him an ideal candidate. Good navigators were in high demand, and Ivan gave him no choice in accepting the position. And so he became a navigator. Although he preferred to be in the driver's seat, he found the challenge rewarding.

"Okay, I've got a good handle on this. We can head out." Dean donned his flight jacket and gave a sturdy tug to its collar. He had that jacket for many years of service, and the unpolished bush pilot appearance it lent him still made him smile.

"It's about time," Ivan mumbled.

The six members of the expedition boarded the pod and locked it down.

The pod was a rather odd-looking spacecraft, exhibiting features of an old war tank with sleekness reminiscent of a stealth fighter. The entire fuselage consisted of a finely polished array of rectangular plates, which had the color and sheen of a black pearl. The plates used to harness the energy of cosmic particles for fuel would luminesce during flight, providing a spectacular light show. The Achilles heel of the handsome ship was the large bulky housing located on its underbelly where the drilling equipment was stowed. The pod had a bow to stern length of twenty-five meters and boasted a girth of thirteen. The cabin would have been considered claustrophobic but for the shiny metallic walls and the flashy instrument panels.

The crew launched into the routine they'd established after flying together for over a year. Dean leaned against the back wall thoughtfully massaging his dimple, watching to see if Kevin still fit into the narrow pilot's seat before moving in to take the seat beside him. Ivan's station was on the other side of Dean's, but he liked to be the last to sit down. Dean figured it made him feel important. Dean's wife, Karen Jenkins, was the expedition medic and biologist. She sat on the port side, just far enough from Dean to keep her seductive mannerisms from luring his attention. Annie Wilson, the flight geologist, sat beside Karen, and stationed across from them on the starboard side was Roger, the communication and computer analyst.

As Kevin engaged the thrusters, the cabin filled with the impressive hum of the engine. The pod emerged from the hangar seeming even less significant than an insect in the vastness of space. The hanger doors closed with a monumental roar, and they were off. A handful of viewports decaled the sides of the vessel, so each crewmember could enjoy the majestic sight that lay ahead in the darkness. In the distance glowed Vega, the powerful blue sun that warmed the planet Lyra. Beyond that, the Herculis Nebula performed a dazzling laser show with the color and sparkle of the finest gems. As the pod set some distance, the backdrop of the Lyra Base Station came into view; it was a small, vibrant, and brilliantly lit city in space.

"The texture structure begins 4550 kilometers from here, on a course twenty-two degrees to the right of our present trajectory. Why don't we stop there, and we can go over the flight plan," Dean suggested.

Kevin adjusted the controls and followed Dean's direction. Within fifteen minutes, they had reached the initiation point.

"Okay, listen up people." Ivan rotated his seat to the right. He adjusted the screen on the monitor to display the region of space they were destined to travel. "The star is called Cryton and is part of a group of eclipsing binaries. It's Class M and is 12.1 light-years from our current position." Ivan scrolled his index finger along the monitor showing the path from their present location to the star. "It has two small planets in its system. Our interest is in the first planet, which is slightly smaller than Earth. As you all know, Annie's geological report suggests this planet may be mineable."

"And we've all heard that one before." Dean relaxed back in his seat and folded his arms across his chest.

"Yeah, don't pull out your bottle of Bordeaux quite yet, Ivan. You know probe data isn't always accurate," Annie said. She raised an eyebrow at Dean. "What kind of a hellish ride are we in for, Flyboy?"

Annie had a way with words that Dean found amusing. *Flyboy* was new, and he grinned. "Let's just say nobody's going to be drinking Bordeaux along the way. Rough waters ahead. And Kevin, you're going to have to be right on track with me, or we're going to get our asses kicked. You understand what I'm telling you?"

Kevin scowled, and before he had a chance to make a defensive rebuttal, Ivan intervened. "How about you stop beating around the bush and get to the point, Dean."

"Fine! The length of the texture is 13 light-years, so it's plenty long enough to get us there, but it's not exactly stable." Dean leaned toward the monitor and spoke the word "grid." A grid pattern appeared on the screen. "The entrance point to catch the best trajectory is sixty-three degrees from normal based on our present location." Dean touched the screen at this coordinate, and a red dot appeared. "The entry should be smooth if Kevin hits it at a velocity in excess of 1200 kilometers per second." Dean looked at Kevin. "Once we're in, you should set a course approximately twenty-five kilometers to the left of the centerline. I'll give you adjustments as we go. There are a significant number of energy sinks, so we can expect some severe turbulence. I'll do my best to navigate around them. The density of energetic particles is well above average for a typical texture, which will give us a bit of a rough ride. On the positive side, they'll provide us with lots of reserve fuel."

"What about the gravitational field?" Ivan asked.

"The gravitational field at the rim of the structure seems to be fairly high and consistent, which should serve to our advantage until we exit the texture. No promises on how close we'll be when we make our break away. I'm more concerned about getting us there in one piece. Ivan, you're going to have to monitor the vibration of the pod closely as it can throw our monitors out of calibration if the frequency gets too high. I don't have to tell you what can happen if I'm not getting accurate readings. Any questions?"

"Sounds like you better not mess up," Ivan stammered.

Dean saw resentment in Ivan's eyes, the petty kind that typically stems from jealousy. Ivan had struggled during his post secondary education and worked hard to get where he was. He scraped by during his undergraduate space science degree before going on to triumph in business. Dean gave him credit for his charisma and strong work ethic but objected to the way he treated underlings by occasionally referring to them as "punk-ass kids." Despite being only five years Ivan's junior, Dean was certain that was how Ivan perceived him.

Having the look of a pampered English gentleman, Ivan's black hair, brown eyes, and average stature did not provide him with Dean's commanding appearance. Any potential for mutual respect disintegrated years ago, and Dean thoroughly enjoyed getting a rise out of Ivan every chance he could.

Dean tightened his seat restraint and signaled the others to do the same. "Whenever you're ready, Ivan. You're the boss."

Looking around the pod, Ivan said, "Everybody ready? Any questions? Okay, then let's do it." Ivan nodded to Kevin. "When you're ready."

Kevin piloted the pod to the coordinates Dean provided, setting the necessary velocity. As expected, the pod entered the texture smoothly, giving the crew a few moments to look out the viewports where charged particles flowed together in pastel waves forming a mosaic of color similar to the Northern Lights of Earth.

* * * *

With a trip as harrowing as flying a biplane through a thunderstorm, the one and a half hours since entering the texture passed like days. Dean continued to monitor the energy surges with sharply focused eyes. With one quarter of a light-year remaining until they reached the planet, he couldn't afford to break his concentration for even a moment, especially considering the increased instability of the texture.

"Kevin, I think we may have to pull out in a hurry. Stand by on my signal." The words barely left Dean's lips when the monitor flashed red, indicating a critical change in the background microwave radiation (BMR).

"I'm going to exhaust a burst of stored particles from the lower collector plate to try to increase the BMR. That will hopefully buy us enough time to reach the planet." Dean's voice sounded choppy with the turbulence. He slowly turned the exhaust control a quarter turn to the right. *This is a hell of a rock to dodge.*

He took a deep breath, savoring the adrenaline but suspected the others weren't sharing his pleasure. Kevin's face looked flushed, exaggerating his cratered complexion, and he sat with his legs tight like a kid about to pee his pants.

"Isn't that a little much," Ivan yelped.

"We have to increase the radiation." In the same moment Dean shot back, Ivan leaned over and dialed down the stored particle exhaust control. "What the hell are you doing?" Dean yelled.

In the presence of such a high gravitational force, Ivan's slight readjustment was enough to stall the exhaust module, triggering an ear-piercing alarm. The pod started to shudder as the gravitational field in the center of the fragment dropped below the level required for sustainable flight. Dean raised his voice to be heard over the engines' wheezing and the creaking hull as the pod pushed against the crushing forces at the texture rim. "The texture has destabilized. We have to pull out! Best exit point is twenty degrees from normal."

Another turbulent wave jolted the pod several hundred meters to the right, sending Kevin's seat restraint deep into his potbelly, and he gasped. He sounded like a panting dog as he reached over to adjust the thrusters. His eyes bulged as he maneuvered the controls with a shaky hand. The vibration of the pod surged, and he pulled the controls toward him as he attempted to make the exit. The pod deflected off the fragment rim with a torque that hurled it into a spin, generating a huge g-force inside the cabin.

Dean started to doubt Kevin's ability to pilot them out of the texture. He looked as though he just rounded the top of a hill on a roller coaster, perhaps one called *Dead in a Minute*. Dean would have howled at the twisted chub of his face on a coaster, but not in the pod— not when his life depended on Kevin's next move. Kevin bit down on his lip and threw a hand over his mouth as though swatting a fly, his other losing its grip of the controls. While he fought off his apparent sudden wave of nausea, Dean readied himself to take control. Just as he was about to, Kevin took the controls and re-established their position in the texture. Adjusting the right thrusters while trimming up the rear spoilers, he stuttered, "Dean, I need a new exit point."

"Ivan can you adjust the coils to compensate for the g-forces; they're throwing off the field monitor." Dean shook his head to clear away the dizziness. The g-forces were starting to affect his peripheral vision, and he tried squinting to compensate. "Damn!"

"Best I can do is to get it down to four g," Ivan stammered.

Moments after adjusting the coils, the pod began to stabilize, and the reading on the monitor became steady enough for Dean to cross-reference it to the exterior energy levels. "Kevin, you've got one more chance at it. Use all of the reserve energy and head sixty-seven degrees from normal."

Kevin adjusted the controls, and with a blinding flash of light, the pod jolted to the left and exited the texture fragment. The trajectory of the pod evened out.

"Head us toward the planet and set an orbit of 1100 kilometers—" Ivan jerked his head toward Karen as she leaped out of her seat and ran toward the washroom. Seconds later, the sound of her vomiting echoed throughout the cabin with perfect acoustics. "Great, a sick medic." Ivan rolled his eyes.

A jolt of concern sent Dean in pursuit. With the tight quarters, he stood at the door to the washroom and cracked a sliver of a smile. "Taste good?"

Karen grunted as she splashed a fountain of water on her pallid face. She wore her long, flowing, black hair smoothed back into a tidy ponytail, and the short curls framing her face were now wet and stringy. "Very funny."

Dean handed her a towel and gently pushed the wet strands to one side whispering, "Hey, you okay?"

Karen nodded and gave him a hint of a smile. The fact that she managed to pass the space motion-sickness test baffled him, especially after the experience on their honeymoon three years earlier. The sailing trip he'd planned ended in disaster with Karen leaning over the side of the boat far too frequently. Added to this was his own sunburn, which came out of shear neglect of his fairish complexion. What he intended to be Karen's introduction to his free-spirited love of the water turned into an assortment of dirty looks shot in his direction.

He watched as Karen finished drying her face, admiring her soft skin, wide brown eyes and petite neckline. Being of Asian and Caucasian descent, Karen possessed the refined beauty of a rare orchid. Dean loved her subtle mannerisms. She made every movement seem sexy leaving him vulnerable—something completely out of character for him.

Dean helped Karen back into her seat and then turned with daggers drawn, locking eyes with Ivan. "What the hell were you doing back there?"

Ivan slammed his hands down on his armrest and swung his chair to face Dean. "You overdid it. We're going to need the excess energy from those particles for the way home. You know that."

"Well that would kind'a be a moot point if we didn't even make it here wouldn't it!" Dean said, trying not to sound too patronizing.

Ivan grumbled something under his breath as he repositioned his seat. Dean sat back down and could see Ivan glaring at him out the corner of his eye like a catty girl who had just announced *I'm not talking to you!* He laughed silently at him.

Moments later, the pod established its orbit around the planet. Its sun, the Cryton star, was a red dwarf with a luminescent value significantly less than Vega's. With a daunting reddish-brown hue, the planet showed signs of significant storm activity in the Polar Regions.

"Annie, please don't tell me you want me to land us there." Kevin's lower lip curled out pleadingly as he pointed to the top of the planet with a sausage-sized finger.

Annie commenced geological scans. The results started to show up on her screen almost instantaneously. "At first glance, the most promising mineralization appears to be in the southern hemisphere. I would suggest the best place to drill would be the lower quadrant, but hold on a sec." Annie paused and tucked her strawberry blond hair behind her ears. "Yeah, there's an area about 300 kilometers south of the equator that looks almost as good. Given the looks of those poles, we may want to head there."

Ivan turned toward Karen and softened his tone. "Well, first of all let's see what we're going to be breathing down there."

Karen, wearing a mousey expression, sat cowered in the back of her seat after listening to the harsh exchange between Dean and Ivan. The anger disappeared from Ivan's face, and Karen gave him a wry smile. "Essentially oxygen and carbon dioxide atmosphere, but I wouldn't suggest a marathon run as the oxygen content is about what you would find halfway up Mount Everest. By the way, I should also mention the temperature at the equator is a balmy two degrees Celsius."

"What about breathing apparatuses, do you think we need them?" Ivan asked.

"I don't think so, but at these levels, we'd be wise to do twenty minute rotations monitoring the drilling equipment."

"So assuming we head to the region near the equator, what can we expect during our descent?" Ivan asked.

Dean leaned over to get a better look at the atmospheric data. "Winds in the upper atmosphere are at forty kilometers per hour gusting to sixty. Looks pretty good to me, but I'm not the one flying this thing."

"Piece of cake," Kevin said.

Chapter Two

After an uneventful flight through a velvety blanket of reddish-orange cloud cover, Kevin piloted the craft into a valley and began to scout the topography for a place to set down. Although stark and desert-like, the panoramic view from the elevation was serene. He slowly carved an arc across the crest of a hill and five minutes later settled the pod safely on the ground.

With anticipation, the crew looked out to survey the landscape. The red sun kissed the horizon, casting huge shadows from the higher ground to the north. In localized areas, small dust devils swirled about. The terrain was dry and desolate. Ridges that had formed from years of blowing dirt were piled up like snow drifts across the plain. The crew disengaged their seat restraints and started moving about the cabin. In the shadows, clouds of multicolored lights flickered like fireflies.

"What the heck is that?" Dean whispered.

"Karen, are those bugs?" Ivan asked.

Karen checked the biological sensor reading. "I'm not picking up any life signs whatsoever. Whatever they are they're beautiful, like a fireworks display."

"Are the sensors working properly?" Ivan asked.

"Yeah, I checked them two days ago. Today is the first time the pod's been out since then."

Ivan, looking rather bewildered, called on Roger's expertise. "Are you picking up any unusual energy readings? Could it be an atmospheric phenomenon?"

Karen responded first. "The conditions here are very stable. No significant temperature variations, this isn't caused by any heat or electrical activity in the atmosphere."

"I've initiated a scan to look for any random energy readings. Whatever it is, it's luminous. I'm checking for electrical, chemical, and BMR," Roger said. He circled his thumbs together while the relentless blur of numbers ran across the transparent crystalline monitor. "I'm picking up a tremendous number of electromagnetic pulses of various frequencies. The pulse wave frequencies are in the range of 200 to 1800 hertz. The atmospheric scanners would have filtered these pulses out as noise. They're brilliant. Whatever they are, they're able to emit light."

"Those frequencies are almost as low as the frequencies of brain waves," Karen said.

Ivan let out a long uninterrupted sigh. "This is a tad puzzling wouldn't you say." He perked his comfort by leaning back in his seat and folding his hands behind his head. "Okay, here's what we're going to do. Dean and Kevin, you help Annie get the drill rig ready. The sooner we start the better. Until we have a better understanding of what those lights are, we'd better wear environmental suits outside. Karen, you and I are going out first. Roger, will our cochlear implants work out there?"

"All clear on the implants, but until we know the nature of those electrical impulses, it would probably be wise to have a backup."

The control panel for the drill rig was located in the aft of the cabin sandwiched between the storage locker and the airlock. In extreme circumstances, drilling could be carried out remotely from inside the pod; however, remote drilling was far from ideal. All six members of the crew had firsthand experience dealing with life threatening problems with the drill rig. Under normal circumstances, the drilling procedure was straight forward, and Annie had done it countless times. The drill footings would be lowered down and locked in place to ensure stability, and then drilling could commence. Depending on the hardness of the core samples, they could complete an entire geological survey in just over one hour.

Dean and Kevin followed Annie to the drill rig control panel. Quarters were tight and Kevin's well-fed girth took up half of it. Dean squeezed to the side nearest the locker, creating his own slender bubble of personal space. Annie prepared to lock the footings for the drill in place as Dean checked the initial topsoil scans. Kevin took the job of peering over Dean's shoulder.

Kevin was the last person Dean wanted infringing on his bubble. He glared at him as if to say *back off or else*. "Aren't you supposed to be helping?"

Kevin grumbled and backed away, still doing nothing.

Dead beat. Dean ignored him and set his attention back to the scans. "Looks like there's a shallow layer of soft sediment, probably debris from wind erosion settling in the valley. We'll be into the rock substrate after about one meter."

"Thanks. I guess we're ready then." Annie pulled firmly on the lever beside the panel locking the footings. She turned to the key pad on the left and clicked open the cover and then with her freckled fingers hammered in the code to open the drill manifold at the base of the ship. The soft hum followed by a clunk confirmed the drill equipment was ready to be lowered into position. Moments later, she had the drill rotated downward, piercing the layer of soft sediment.

"Annie, don't get that thing going until I give you the word," Ivan said, handing Karen an environmental suit.

Karen hung the suit on the side of the locker and removed her jacket, exposing her tight powder blue tank top. Beneath it, Dean noticed the silhouette of the heart drop necklace he had given her for her birthday.

Dean scowled as Ivan ogled Karen's curves, which were irresistibly highlighted by her outfit. "What're you looking at?"

"Re…lax." Karen blushed and lifted her hair to one side, clearly flattered by Ivan's glances.

"Christ," Dean mouthed to himself. He knew Karen was aware of Ivan's reputation of being quite a womanizer.

Karen dressed herself in the confining environmental suit, and when Ivan was ready, she proceeded to the side airlock.

"Once we establish it's safe to commence drilling, I'll give you the word." Ivan fixed his grip around the hatch release lever and gave it a quarter turn clockwise. The door hissed open, and the two of them slipped into the airlock chamber, closing the door behind them.

* * * *

Moments later, Ivan and Karen were outside the pod. Ivan made the first move, stepping with caution toward the cloud of flickering lights. The ground was soft with the texture of ash, its brown hue turning reddish-brown in the glow of the dim sunlight. The red sun had the look of a harvest moon, giving the terrain the appearance of Death Valley at sunset. Subtle berms formed a geometric mosaic extending as far as the eye could see. As Ivan made his way toward the cloud of lights, the lights seemed to descend upon him. He looked back at Karen, who was trailing behind, and the lights gave the illusion of her drifting underwater amidst a sea of sparkling bubbles. They were mesmerizing and difficult to focus on individually, yet the colors were vibrant, consisting of various hues of blue, green, yellow, orange, red, violet, white, and gold.

Ivan felt a tingling sensation in his ear and whispered the word "answer."

Roger's voice sounded. "Ivan, can you hear me?"

The reception over Ivan's cochlear implant sounded perfect. "Yeah, I can hear you loud and clear. I'll set my implant for continued communication." Ivan paused, saying, "open connection."

"Ivan, I've set it up so you can communicate freely with everyone in the pod."

"Thanks, Roger." Ivan paused to survey the surroundings. As he continued walking, the lights came at him. It reminded him of driving into a snowstorm where you have to concentrate on focusing on the road and not the individual flakes of snow. For a moment, he felt dizzy. "From inside the pod, you can't see it as well, but these flickering lights are everywhere, not just in the shadows. As I walked away from the pod, they seemed to become more concentrated around me, Karen, too. Have a look. Karen's bio-scan is indicating no sign of life. Not even microbial. At any rate, they don't look like they have any substance to them; they're just lights. I'm picking up the electrical fields Roger mentioned, but the portable device isn't sensitive enough to pick up the higher frequencies clearly. They come across as noise. Roger, keep monitoring it."

"I'm on it. Actually, I've generated a wave frequency spectrum for the pulses, and it looks nothing like noise. At each frequency, there are distinct peaks occurring at regular intervals."

With excitement in his voice, Ivan continued, "Look at this. The changes in the color of the lights seem to be following a pattern. Roger, run this through the computer and cross-reference it with the wave frequencies. Annie, you can start the drilling."

Ivan and Karen backed away from the pod as the drill created a whining billow of dust as it spun downward.

"Annie, for the time being, I'll keep tabs on the rig out here." As the dust settled, Ivan headed toward the rig to monitor the operation.

"Ivan, the wave frequency of the pulses is changing more rapidly now that the drilling has started," Roger said. "What the heck, there seems to be a—"

* * * *

"Karen! What the hell!" Dean was monitoring the operation from one of the viewports. He rushed to the airlock, grabbing an environmental suit on the way. "Ivan, stop her! She's taking her helmet off."

Dean could feel his heart pounding against his ribcage as he fastened the last connections of his suit. He glanced out the window in time to see Karen's helmet drop to the ground. Immediately, a cloud of lights descended on her. *What the hell is she thinking?* He rushed to the airlock and seconds later, he emerged from the pod, dashing toward Karen. Someone grabbed his arm, and he turned to see Ivan's perplexed face.

"Dean, wait."

Dean's wife stood with her palms to the sky and wondrous amazement lighting her eyes. The hair framing her face had dried to ribbons that were taking flight in the chilling breeze.

"I understand them," she said with hardly a breath. "It's incredible. It's binary code, mathematics, I understand them."

"Roger, can you confirm this?" Ivan sounded anxious.

"Yeah, that's what I was trying to tell you. The wave frequencies of the impulses have started to change in tandem and tend to be in upper ranges above 400 hertz. Each frequency seems to correspond to a specific spectrum of color. The darker blue and greens of the lower frequencies have all but disappeared. What's really amazing is the changes are following a mathematical binary pattern. It seems to be some kind of algorithm."

"Karen, what's going on?" Ivan asked.

The unscrupulous leader strikes again! Dean couldn't believe Ivan wasn't ordering her back into the pod. There was no telling what the lights could be doing to her. He had a mind to throw her over his shoulder and carry her in himself. "Who cares what's going on? We need to get her back to the pod."

Karen inhaled slowly as if savoring a fragrance. "Dean, it's okay. I'm fine. I don't know how to explain it, but I understand them. They're some kind of energy, like intelligent energy, not like anything we've ever seen. They're trying to understand what we are. We're completely foreign to them. Do you understand what this means? The only life that's been found on other planets is plant and insect life, which hardly qualifies as intelligent. This discovery is a first! I don't know exactly what they are, but they're incredibly intelligent."

Dean edged closer to Karen and grabbed the bio-scanner strapped to her suit. He held it up to her and initiated a scan. Her heart rate, blood pressure, and other vitals were stable, but it wasn't enough to alleviate his concern. "You feel okay?"

"I feel great, better than great, as though I've been revitalized."

"Dean, I think I'm starting to feel it, too. She's right. It seems structured and mathematical. I can feel their presence," Ivan said.

A deafening screech like the sound of tearing metal, shot across the valley. Ivan jerked his head toward the pod. "The rig!" He took off with the agility of a clumsy man from the drag of the suit, kicking up dust on the way. "It's jammed!" The drill ground to a halt, and one of the footing straps snapped, lashing into Ivan's suit. "Damn it!" He fell to the ground, wincing.

"Annie, shut the rig down. Ivan's hurt!" Dean rushed to Ivan's side, with Karen a few steps behind.

An immense dust cloud hung in the thin air, and Karen sputtered as she started to speak, "That," she spit some dust, "that looks deep." She cupped her bulky glove over her nose and mouth and raised her voice. "We need to get him inside, so I can take care of the wound."

Dean lifted Ivan to his feet and helped him back inside the airlock.

"Lay him down over here." Karen pointed to the center of the cabin. She removed Ivan's helmet, and Dean handed her the med kit and squatted down to assist. She started to cut away the thick fabric of the suit in the vicinity of his lesion. The wound appeared deep with several shards of metal debris imbedded in it. After administering a local anesthesia, Karen removed the debris with an incredible efficiency, seeming to sense the location of each fragment of metal. When the wound was clean and ready for mending, she pulled the mender out of the med kit and flicked it on. She held onto the shiny handle like it was a soupspoon and waited for the forked electrodes at its tip to charge. A blue arc appeared across the fork. Karen placed the arc over the lesion. "It'll take a few minutes to regenerate the tissue. The cut's deep."

Ivan whisked her hand away. "Don't," he said in a small voice. He looked at her hypnotically as if gazing dreamily across a horizon; then his head fell back, and his body went limp. He shut his eyes, and his breathing became heavy like he was in a deep sleep.

"My God, look," Annie whispered.

The wound on Ivan's leg had stopped bleeding, and the little inflammation that had settled in was rapidly disappearing along with the redness around its periphery. Dean gawked at it, completely befuddled. It started to close up millimeter by millimeter as the cells proliferated at an unimaginable rate. A few minutes passed, and a thin scab had formed.

Kevin stared at the wound. "What the hell's going on out there? What are those things?"

"They're some kind of intelligent energy," Karen said. "I could feel them trying to communicate with me telepathically. It was as though they were placing thoughts in my head. That's why I took my helmet off. They're curious about what we are. I don't believe they mean us any harm. They seem peaceful."

"Intelligent energy? All I picked up was electrical impulses." Roger took another look at the measurements he'd taken.

"Yeah, low frequency pulses! There's no biological component to them. People have always expected if intelligent life were found, it would be like us, some kind of biological creature, like a weird looking humanoid or something. After feeling their presence, I think they may be a type of energy on a level we've never seen before, like living energy. Maybe they're made up of a fifth state of matter we're not familiar with, different from gases, liquids, solids, and plasma. Who knows what they are? There's no substance to them. Each light seems to be an individual spark of intelligent energy!" Karen's eyes beamed with the excitement of a kid at an amusement park.

"Like a spirit," Annie said.

Karen started to theorize, "I hadn't thought of it that way, but yeah maybe. History is full of ghost stories and religious teachings about an afterlife. Is it possible this is what these entities are? Some kind of energy life force without a body, like a spirit?"

Kevin's face scrunched up into a round ball with cheeks that looked like they were about to burst. "Oh give me a break! Enough with all this hocus pocus talk. You're starting to sound like my cousin who's into all that mystical, spiritual crap. In my opinion, she smoked too much wacky tobaccy in college. Why don't we pull out the Tarot cards and a crystal ball and read each other's auras?"

Dean folded his arms across his chest and let out a healthy chuckle. Turning to Karen, he said, "Yeah sweetheart, you're getting pretty heavy here. All of a sudden we're talking to spirits?"

Karen glared at Dean.

Dean had a habit of scoffing at what he affectionately referred to as Karen's *hair brained* ideas, something that likely stemmed from the cultural differences between the two of them. He knew it often infuriated her to the point that her complexion glowed red. He thought he'd hold back any more comments as her face was just starting to show a hint of rose.

Karen huffed and then continued, "It's not all hocus pocus crap you know. As I mentioned when we landed, the frequencies we measured from those lights aren't much higher than human brain waves. Brain waves are electromagnetic and are generated from neurons. Higher frequency energy pulses well beyond those of normal brain waves have also been measured from humans. It's clearly documented in the literature. Some theories suggest our electric fields create a non-physical energy aura that surrounds our bodies. In fact, electromagnetic fields with wave frequencies as high as 1800 hertz have been measured around the human body. They can't be generated internally, or they'd be dampened out by the water content of our body, so you have to ask yourself what these fields correspond to. Maybe it is a soul."

Annie interjected, "You guys need to have an open mind. You're scientists for God's sake."

"Thanks Annie," Karen said. "There's no doubt a human energy field exists, and it's interesting to me that the wave frequencies of the electrical impulses from those lights fall within the range of what's been measured from people. You know, the frequencies of brain waves only go as high as 38 hertz, which is during wakeful stimulated activity. Although, I think perhaps the brain waves of men are likely significantly lower, more along the lines of dozy sleep."

"Oh, here we go," Dean murmured.

"Dean, it's not just communication." Karen's complexion had finally reached its annoyed hue. She picked at her thumbnail, sending a small white flake to the floor. "Did you see the efficiency with which I worked getting the debris out of Ivan's leg? There's something different about me, I feel smarter, more in tune with what I'm doing. In fact, I feel great. You were out there. Don't you feel it a little? Ivan didn't even take his helmet off, and look what he did. That also supports my theory. Higher frequency energy fields have been measured from people who've demonstrated enhanced healing abilities."

"Oh yeah, energy healers. My cousin says their auras beam red. Kind of like Rudolph's nose but their whole body. I bet you that reindeer never caught a cold!" Kevin snickered, sending a ripple across his belly.

Karen shot Kevin a dirty look. "Anyway, as I was saying, their healing ability is reflected in their energy field. One thing's for sure, whatever those things are, they're affecting us for the better. There's a scientific explanation for it, and maybe, Kevin, you should keep your skepticism to yourself. I bet if you went out there you'd change your tune."

Ivan rolled his head sideways and blinked several times as he started to come around. "What's going on, I feel like I just woke up from twelve hours of sleep. How long was I out? Oh yeah, the rig, is it okay?"

"You were only out for a few minutes," Karen informed him.

"I stopped the rig right after it jammed. It's fine, and we already have a few decent core samples," Annie added with a satisfied tone. "Ivan, do you realize what you did?"

"Yeah, I got a hell of a gash on my leg; it hurt!"

"Well, look at it now."

Ivan sat up and scrutinized the wound. "So Karen mended it, big deal."

Karen set a soft hand on Ivan's leg. Dean cleared his throat. She frowned and brought her hand to her side. "I didn't mend it. It healed on its own, very quickly."

Ivan pursed his lips and cocked his head as though he hadn't heard her correctly. After a moment, he simply muttered. "How?"

"I was in the middle of treating it when you pushed my hand away and blacked out. You healed yourself. I think it may have something to do with those lights."

Ivan's expression brightened. "The lights…I remember now. I felt them, too."

Karen stood up, leaned against the locker, and began to fill Ivan in on her theory, while at the same time shaking the dust from her hair. He listened attentively as he slowly got to his feet, favoring the spot on his leg that was injured.

"That's incredible, intelligent energy! This is going to be the most significant discovery in history. The philosophers and spiritualists are going to be all over this. We need to document this discovery, try to determine what these things are exactly."

"The equipment we have is not sufficient for a proper study," Karen confessed. "Apart from the energy readings we've already taken, perhaps the best we can do is to continue communication with them. They seem incredibly docile and inquisitive."

Ivan nodded. "I agree. Why don't we all go out and see what we can learn. Roger, continue to monitor their energy pulses. Hey, let's not forget why we're here. We have to get that rig freed up."

"Core spectroscopy results are in," Annie said. "There are high densities of nickel and titanium with significant traces of chromium and cadmium...definitely minable. Sonic tests should tell us how deep the veins run. No wonder the rig jammed."

With his leg seeming as good as new, Ivan went to Annie's station and glanced over the core analysis. "These results are impressive, quite a windfall." He tilted his head in thought. "I only had a chance to glance at the drill rig before the footing strap snapped, but from what I saw it's pretty jammed. I think we can do away with the environmental suits. Dean, Kevin, Annie...the three of you get to work freeing it up. Roger, Karen, and I will try to learn as much as we can about these intelligent lights. If any of you feel light headed, use a breathing apparatus."

* * * *

A couple of hours had passed since Ivan and his crew emerged from the pod to carry out their tasks. Ivan let the others work to free the rig and retract the drill into its manifold and devoted his time to studying the light entities. He observed the concentration of light entities around them increasing as they worked. One by one, each member of the crew reported they were able to make sense of the complex mathematical code and the thoughts being transmitted to them telepathically. The longer their exposure, the simpler it became. They were able to exchange complex questions and answers with the life forms just with thought, and Ivan instructed them to document everything they learned. Most amazing of all, they discovered the entities, as they had coined them, had a collective personality. Like excited, innocent children, they were bubbly and vivacious, all desiring the same thing while maintaining their own unique spark. Each colorful flickering light beamed its own thoughts and excitement over their new found friends. Adding to the intensity of the amazing discovery was an undeniable fact; a fact Ivan found overwhelming to the point of being intoxicating. All of them were becoming smarter, much smarter.

"Karen, how can they be affecting us like this? They say we only use a fraction of our brain, and now my mind is racing at a speed I never thought possible! Mathematical, theoretical, and philosophical problems are just popping into my head, and they're solved instantly. And the healing. It almost feels like parts of my brain I've never used have somehow come alive." Ivan felt flustered while struggling to keep up with his thoughts, but at the same time, he loved the speed at which they were igniting in his mind. It was a head rush; better than any drug he could imagine. He'd risen to the top of an intellectual pillar where he could look down at the meek and simpleminded, and he embraced it.

"Actually, that's a myth. We use all our brain, or at least I do. It's possible the energy of the entities has somehow stimulated our brains and our bodies in some way. The brain is very complex. For example, take a savant. Although there are many theories, no one really knows what causes that syndrome. As for the healing, for centuries acupuncture has been successfully used as a healing technique and is thought to improve the flow of energy through the body. My grandmother's an acupuncturist. The energy of the body is called the Ch'i, and it contains two polar forces called the yin and the yang. The yin and the yang have to be balanced for good health. She believes healing takes a lot of energy from your energy field, and this energy must be replenished from the universal energy field to keep the yin and yang balanced. She says each organ is associated with a specific point on the skin, and the Ch'i flows along channels linking the points. If you believe in this sort of stuff, maybe our energy fields are becoming heightened by the energy of the entities."

"Whoa! That sounds like a pretty heavy duty theory," Ivan added, while massaging his chin. It was his favorite thought provoking mannerism, and now it had a new meaning. "Not to be a devil's advocate, but I've also heard there's a biological explanation to why acupuncture works."

Karen looked toward Dean as if to check to see if he was listening.

"Is there a problem? You seem guarded," Ivan said.

"It's Dean; he doesn't exactly have an open mind when it comes to this kind of stuff. He thinks it's a bunch of hair brained bull crap. Anyway, he seems busy with Roger. As you were saying, biologically, acupuncture improves the biochemical balance in the body and stimulates the body's natural healing abilities. I was merely putting forth a possible explanation as to how it happens. My grandmother has very traditional beliefs. The bottom line is without monitoring our brain activity and our energy field, it's impossible to know biologically how we've been affected; but without a doubt, we've been affected. The long-term potential of this is mind boggling. Think about it. Increased cognitive ability, psychic abilities, telepathy, telekinesis, energy healing...the possibilities are endless. It's pretty frustrating that we don't have the equipment here to monitor our brain activities and energy fields." The wind picked up, whistling across the valley and rippling the freshly turned dirt around the rig. Karen's shoulders shuddered, and she wrapped her arms around herself. Dean glanced over and started in her direction.

* * * *

"How are things going on your end? You look chilly." Dean rubbed her back to help warm her up. "Roger's energy scans have shown nothing beyond the frequency pulses we initially measured, and all we've been able to conclude is that these entities seem to be comprised of some sort of energy we don't understand. Until we understand the nature of this energy, we have no way of explaining how they generate light. Since there's no substance to them, it's not bioluminescence like fireflies. They are self-aware of their existence and seem to have formed a type of community in which their thoughts can work collectively as one or individually depending on their needs. Their energy is self-sustaining, and they're able to distinguish between the energy fields of each other and that of us. They understand they're located on a planet orbiting a star. They also have a mathematical understanding of the configuration of other stars in their sky, and they have a curiosity about them. They seem to be able to sense the energy of things and tend to think and communicate mathematically with each other. They are attracted to our energy and are inquisitive about what we are. They seem mystified by our biological component."

Dean fell silent for a moment, deep in thought. As a concrete thinker, he abolished anything that couldn't be scientifically proven; however, here he stood with the thought crossing his mind that perhaps there could be some merit to Karen and Annie's spiritual hoo haa. He sighed, knowing his stubbornness could never own up to such a premise. He found it curious how a part of him felt quite comfortable and at home with these entities, yet he couldn't quite put his finger on why. Was it their way of thinking, mathematical and precise? Was it their simple, naive perception of the universe uncluttered by the negative emotions that develop in a world full of greed? The emotions he'd picked up from the entities were only positive, after all, in their realm there was no cause for anything but positive thoughts. He found it unsettling that the entities were becoming aware of the negative emotions of the crew.

Roger cleared his throat, shaking Dean out of his personal moment. Roger stood hunched over, studying the device in his hand, but straightened up as he started to speak. "About the energy…the wave frequency of the pulses in our direct vicinity has dropped significantly since we've been out here. They're down to below 300 hertz, and the amplitudes are lower, too. It looks like they're continuing to decline. An hour ago, they were almost providing more light than the sun. Look around; there are more of them than before, but their brightness has definitely diminished, and the colors are predominately dark blue with a few greens."

"That's odd," Dean said. He glanced around at the entities. They almost looked sickly; like a candle with a stub of a wick.

"And have you noticed the communication has decreased, at least for me it has. I'm going to walk over where they're brighter and take some measurements." Fixing his small pack around his shoulder, Roger walked about fifteen meters away from the pod. With an elevated voice, he continued. "The readings are normal here, yep, just like before. I can feel them communicating with me again, its strong here, hold on."

Roger stood ominously still as a somber expression fell upon his face. "They're communicating, but the message is confusing, vague." He shook his head. It was a slow shake; the kind that only comes with bad news. "I understand now." He spoke softly, sadly. "They want us to leave. We're hurting them, killing them. Their energy force is drawn to our own but not compatible with our biological component. That must have something to do with the radical effects they've had on us. They seem to have remorse as we're a discovery for them, but the message is clear. They're collectively placing these thoughts in my mind over and over. They're telling me we cannot coexist, and we must leave."

Ivan stiffened. "Do you think they are a threat to us if we stay? This planet is mineable."

"What the hell kind of question is that? Didn't you hear what the man said, we're killing them!" Dean threw his arms in the air, flabbergasted.

"Well you need to get the big picture Dean. We're standing on a virtual gold mine here. This planet could be another Draco. You know as well as I do how long we've been looking for a discovery like this. This planet is habitable and mineable. Both Earth and Lyra desperately need the ore, and it's our job to find it; and it seems to me, we've finally had success."

Dean's tone sharpened as he felt a cesspool of rage well up inside him. He knew Ivan was self-absorbed but never took him for a murderer. "Don't give me that," he snapped. "Draco has enough reserves to keep up with the demands of both Earth and Lyra for the next fifty years. You know that as well as I do. The problem is no one wants to work on that crap hole. So if it's a question of supply and demand, then the price will go up. Too damn bad! The economy will survive. Maybe the mining giants will have to push up the wages of their employees, entice more people to move there. There are other ways to increase supply apart from killing these life forms. We'll find another planet. I say we do what they ask and leave and never come back. Then we keep our mouths shut about what we've found here. They should be protected."

"Protected!" Ivan scoffed. "We don't even know what they are."

In unison, Roger and Karen spoke, "Dean's right."

Karen continued in a calmer voice. "Of all the planets explored, all we've ever found are bugs, shrubs and a bit of sea life, nothing intelligent. Maybe we don't understand what they are, but they're some sort of self-aware intelligent life. We can't kill them for our benefit. This shouldn't even be open for discussion."

Ivan switched his attack. "Well perhaps we should let the Consortium of Planets decide. They're the ones screaming for ore, and they're the ones paying for this mission."

"And what do you really think they're going to say. Give your head a shake. Where are your morals?" Dean started packing up the equipment.

"What do you think you're doing?" Ivan growled. As he turned to stop Dean, the wind combed back his hair to reveal a forehead creviced with stress lines.

"I'm packing up, we're leaving. You got a problem with it; then we'll take a vote."

"Vote? I'm the one in charge of this mission. We're finished when I say we're finished."

Dean went to face Ivan and looked deep into his eyes to try and understand his idiocies. There was a coldness to them Dean had never seen before; a conniving coldness like you'd see in the eyes of a sociopath. It left him fighting off the urge to deck his *holier than thou* face. "If the majority of us agree we should leave so that we don't harm these entities, then that's what we're going to do. If you use your authority to go against us, then I promise you I will make sure the top executives at the Mining Authority hear about it to the last detail. Ivan, these life forms are intelligent, and I'm not going to let you kill them."

"Fine, who's with Dean here?" With a piercing glare, Ivan locked eyes with each of the crew, one by one.

Without hesitating, Karen, Roger, and Annie raised their hands.

"Kevin?" Dean sneered.

"Sorry, Dean, you know the pressure back home. We really need this ore."

It came of little surprise to Dean that Kevin didn't stand up to Ivan. He was his sniveling little puppet. Kevin had started his career piloting small passenger spaceliners along the stable texture between Earth and Lyra for Spacejet. After the company went bankrupt, Kevin landed himself a job piloting shuttles between the Earth and its moon. Ivan rescued him from the mundane position just over a year ago to pilot his mining expeditions, and Kevin was so grateful for the promotion he looked up to him like an adopted garbage dog. The two men were complete opposites in every way. Kevin had as much class as beef jerky; he was the beer swilling type who would laugh at the sound of his own belch. When Ivan was growing up, his pompous ass father probably would have beaten him silly for associating with someone from Kevin's side of the tracks. *Caviar and Armani my boy, caviar and Armani.* Despite that Kevin visibly repulsed Ivan, he seemed to love their rapport.

Dean shot Kevin a scathing look. "Christ! Well it doesn't matter. It's four against two; we're out of here." He signaled to Roger, Annie, and Karen. "Come on, give me a hand. Let's pack up and leave."

Like a spoiled child who didn't get enough birthday presents, Ivan stomped back to the pod. Kevin followed his lead.

"Jackass," Dean muttered.

* * * *

Thirty minutes later, they were ready to go. With the effects of the entities, Dean had worked with incredible efficiency. He took on the task of communicating to the entities their decision to leave and assured them they would not return unless they found a way to protect them from exposure to humans. The entities were appreciative and regretful at the same time.

The sun was starting to sink into the horizon, turning the sky the color of a fruity tropical drink. High above, sleepy clouds strolled by, leaving behind them a trail of stars. Before stepping back into the pod, Dean looked beyond his long shadow to the beautiful light show the entities were performing, so full of life and meaning, and reflected on his own enlightening experience. With his newfound cognitive abilities, the thought of navigating the pod back along the texture excited him. He felt as though he could conquer anything. The others seemed to share his feelings, and Dean wondered how long the effects would last, or if they might even be permanent.

Dean had pulled Karen, Annie, and Roger aside to discuss the concern they shared for the entities. He suggested the events of the day should be classified, and the others agreed unanimously. The geological survey showed tremendous concentrations of much desired mineral commodities. If the Consortium knew the extent of the results, there was a chance, although slim, they'd side with Ivan. Annie agreed to downplay the results in her report, and Karen promised to document the environment as harsh and barely compatible with human life. Dean knew Karen got along well with Ivan. Their rapport often left him with a bitter taste, but at the time, he thought he could use it to his advantage and volunteered her to convince Ivan to write his report accordingly.

The crew boarded the pod and locked it down.

With a pensive look, Annie broke the silence. "I wonder how many of them we killed. We picked up some amazing abilities. I think I could score an A+ in advanced calculus right now. Not that I'd enjoy it."

Karen turned her attention toward Ivan who appeared lost in thought. "Despite the magnitude of this discovery, the four of us discussed it, and we think the events of today should be classified. And the mining potential of this planet should be downplayed in our reports."

Fueled by the animosity he felt toward Ivan, Dean said in a stout voice, "This has to be contained. When you submit the final expedition report, give it the highest classified designation, Code Fourteen. That way, in the future, any knowledge of this planet and the entities will be limited. The information will only be available to the planetary dignitaries in the Consortium. It will be up to them what they do with it. If they side with you, it'll be beyond our control, but at least I'll be able to sleep at night." Dean's mind drifted to a few people he knew in the Earth and Lyra governments and felt confident the decision would be to protect the entities.

"Ivan, bear in mind, after an in depth analysis of the energy readings we've measured from the entities, it's possible we may find a way to protect them from us, making it safe to mine the planet," Karen said. "It would be enlightening if we could develop a way of communicating with them safely. What we could learn from each other is staggering, not to mention the insight we could gain about ourselves on a spiritual level."

"Fine, for the time being I'll designate the report Code Fourteen, but I'm very much in favor of your points Karen. We need to find a way around the obstacles. This planet has so much potential on several fronts. I don't consider this case to be closed." He turned toward Kevin. "Get us out of here."

Kevin nodded and immediately engaged the thrusters. With a mounting hum, the pod lifted off the ground. Minutes later, they were gazing back at the planet.

Karen inquired with a solemn tone, "What should we call it, the planet I mean?"

"How about Spectra, after the different spectra of light the entities gave off; they were really quite beautiful," Ivan said.

Kevin set a course into the texture, and Spectra faded into the distance.

Chapter Three

Three weeks had passed since Ivan tasted the magic of Spectra. He sipped his Bordeaux and took a few moments to reflect on his experience before submitting the final expedition report. He swirled the red, full-bodied liquid in the crystal glass, admiring the different colors that appeared as the light refracted through it, remembering the magnificence of the entities. He had gained an insight into the beauty of pure thought, as if every time one of the neurons in his brain fired, a glowing spark of life was born. Brilliance was a masterpiece to behold and to savor. It was a true gift that his fate of genetics had shorted him, and he had always discounted it. He sighed and took a deep breath to capture the full bouquet of the wine, a perfect blend of Merlot and Cabernet Sauvignon.

The effects of the entities were finally wearing off and left him with the same sense of uneasiness a child gets on the first day of school. The last three weeks were the most productive of his life and looking back to some of the notes he'd made, he could hardly understand them. Feeling a wave of insecurity, he gazed out the window and wondered how he ever did his job in his normal state. He fought the knot tightening in his gut and took another sip of Bordeaux then swallowed hard enjoying its crispness. *I guess I'm only human,* he thought to himself with troubled sorrow. It was the first time in his life he truly felt frightened.

He cleared his throat and hesitated a moment before speaking into the computer, "File classification Code Fourteen." Second-guessing his decision, he paused for another minute then with an expression of bitter taste whispered, "Send." With the last sip of his wine, he turned off the light and went to bed.

Chapter Four

Eighteen months later…

Annie replaced the lid on her bottle of cola and tossed it into the garbage bin across the aisle from her. *Two points,* she thought to herself as the cup descended into the container dead center. The last bit of fizz tickled her tongue, and she swirled it around in her mouth, puffing out her cheeks slightly, before swallowing. She adjusted herself in the seat and opened her magazine then pulled up her sleeve to reveal her new watch. On the end of the second hand, a basketball went around and around as though in perpetual motion. As she admired it, the corners of her mouth stretched as far across her cheeks as they could. It was a proud grin and one well worth adding to her smile lines as it brought back the memory of the game that earned her MVP. The coach presented her with the watch two weeks later at the season windup party. *Four o'clock, another thirty minutes to go, and my three days from hell will be over.*

Annie's quick trip to Cygnus to collect half a dozen soil samples for analysis turned chaotic by those she typically coined as morons. The soil she was to sample was home to a particular microbe that was lethal, even with limited exposure. Before arriving, she had given specific instructions to have the collection area thoroughly sprayed with an anti-microbial agent. Of course, upon her arrival she found her instructions had not been carried out. With the annual Harvest Festival in full gear, a web of delays set her back two days before it was safe to collect the soil. To add to the confusion, all the hotels were booked for the Festival, and she had to invite herself to stay at an old friend's house. She hated to intrude on people.

A long awaited announcement startled the alertness back into Annie's heavy eyes. "Flight Ninety-two, destined for the Eagle Base Station is ready for boarding. Now boarding first class passengers through Gate Seven." She tucked her magazine, *The Geologist's Report*, under her arm, grabbed her bag, and then made her way to the gate. She handed the attendant her boarding pass. *Ahh, first class.* The silver lining to the three days of black clouds she'd been wearing like a hat. After her delay, it was the only seat left on the flight; and since the Geology Institute was footing the bill, she didn't care.

The attendant reviewed the documentation and handed it to the marshal standing beside her. The tall, lanky man looked to be in his late twenties. He reached out for the paperwork with a long clumsy arm just about knocking them out of her hand. His eyes tightened into an *I mean business* stare, sending a wave of intimidation through Annie. "What was the purpose of your trip to Cygnus? It says here you were collecting samples of some sort?" His tone sounded abrupt.

Annie nodded blankly. "Yes, that's correct. I work for the Geology Institute. I have soil samples I'm taking back to Lyra for analysis." Annie had to make an effort not to stare at the large mole on the side of the man's nose. It reminded her of one of the connect-the-dot activities in the scrapbooks her mother used to plunk in front of her on a rainy afternoon. They were almost as boring as watching the puddles burst over the border of their garden. She wiped the vision out of her mind since if anyone could make a giraffe or an elephant by connecting the dots on someone's face, it would be on hers. *Land of a thousand freckles,* she often referred to herself.

"Are these samples hazardous?"

"Absolutely not. The soil had been thoroughly sprayed before I sampled it, and the Biological Foundation had to clear them as safe before I was allowed to take them off the planet. If you're concerned, they're sealed in an insulated metal container in my bag. You're welcome to check them."

The man glanced at her identification and handed the documents back. "That's fine Miss Wilson, move along."

Annie snickered at the man's lack of appeal and followed the other passengers down the curved hallway through the airlock chamber to the docking port. Out of the side windows, she could see the dark, reflective side of the never-ending spacecraft she was about to board. It always baffled her why such an enormous vessel would have an entry hatch no bigger than the one on the pods she flew in when she worked for the Mining Authority. She ducked inside like she was climbing into a cave and came face to face with a flight attendant wearing a bowtie and a perma-smile. The woman welcomed her with a well-rehearsed greeting and pointed a slender finger toward her seat. The first class ambience was even more inviting than the woman. Annie's footsteps crushed the freshly vacuumed carpet as she made her way to her seat. She went to put her bag in the overhead bin, when another flight attendant approached her, this time an older man wearing too much aftershave.

"Let me help you with that."

Annie sneezed. "Excuse me! It's okay. I'd rather do it myself."

"If there's anything else I can help you with, just push the overhead page."

The leather seat was large enough to accommodate a fat man, and Annie settled into well over half of it. She liked to think basketball had bulked her up, but she knew that wasn't entirely true. She preferred a sporty image over a girly one, wore her hair just long enough to tuck behind her ears, and never bothered with makeup.

The flight to the Eagle Base Station was almost two hours long, and she thought she'd try to get some sleep so she'd be fresh for her dinner with Dean. She had a two and a half hour layover before her flight home to Lyra...the perfect amount of time to catch up with him since his divorce had settled. After six months, Annie could still remember Dean's call like it was yesterday. He spoke with a wounded voice, one festering with anger, hurt, and betrayal. "I caught Karen fucking some other guy," he'd said. Annie's heart sunk.

She knew the incident had crushed Dean, and she stepped forward as a true friend with moral support and guidance. On her advice, he attempted to work through it for a few months but ended up hitting a wall and putting an end to the marriage. Annie was the first person he called with the news, which flattered her.

Since the day Annie met Dean, five years earlier, Annie had a secret attraction to him. He was already in a relationship with Karen at the time, and Annie became very adept at hiding her feelings. Despite the fact Dean was single again, she knew she definitely wasn't his type. She settled with filing him under the category of *best buds*.

Sleep came easily, and Annie jolted awake by an announcement.

"Attention passengers, we will be docking at The Eagle Base Station in twenty minutes. All passengers not continuing on to Earth must disembark. Local time is six p.m."

With pointed toes, Annie stretched her legs. She rubbed the alertness back into her eyes and then looked out the window. As the ship drew closer to the base station, its brightness intensified into a visual wonderland. Home to over 16,000 residents, the station exhibited the intricacies of a snowflake being made up of a network of immense interconnected domes. Ships docked at the spaceports at opposite ends, which resembled two perfectly shaped teardrops decorated with shimmering black beads. Annie decided the entire structure looked as though it should be picked up and hung prominently on a Christmas tree. The serene view drained the tension from her shoulders, and she smacked her lips thinking about the icy beer she'd soon grip in her hands.

As soon as she walked out of the gate, she felt like she might be swept away by the herd of busy travelers. With the Harvest Festival coming to a close and the Eagle Base Station Physics Symposium underway, the spaceport was bustling. The ten gates of the terminal were spaced evenly along the outside edge of the dome, all exiting into a gigantic concourse. The concourse was dotted with fast food eateries, coffee shops, and gift boutiques, and at the far end was the Spaceport Monorail Station. Annie paused to get her bearings and admired the impressive three-dimensional hologram in the center of the concourse, which provided a spectacular laser show while blazing the words, "Welcome Scientists."

"Hey, you!"

Dean's voice rang with masculinity, and she turned abruptly to find him only a short distance away wearing faded blue jeans, a dark blue shirt, and a sports jacket. The smile on his face made her feel flushed.

* * * *

Dean took a few paces to fill the gap between them. "Hey, how are you?"

"Good, it's great to see you. How are you doing?"

"Just great!" Despite his lengthy calls to Annie, Dean hadn't shared a beer with her in months, and he was looking forward to it immensely. He felt indebted to her. He wrapped his arms around her in a bear hug and kissed her cheek. She hugged him back, which after the last few months felt good.

"How was your flight?" As Dean reached for Annie's bag, he noticed the space between her freckles had turned sunburn red. It put a grin on his face.

"Slept all the way," she said, stumbling over her words.

"Well, I hope you're hungry. I thought we'd grab a burger at the pub across from the terminal. It's close."

"What about Henry's?"

"Craving one of their wood oven pizzas are you? I know how much you like it, but look at the line-up for the monorail. It would take us forever to get there."

Annie loosened her jacket. "Okay, the pub sounds good. I'm starving."

Ten minutes later, they sat at a table, each with a tall, frosted glass of beer in hand. Annie raised her voice in a battle with the band playing in the far corner. "This is well earned." She lifted her glass, clanked it with Dean's and took a gulp. She finished with a sigh and brought Dean up to speed on the events of her past few days. "So how's your new job? Running this base station, that's a hell of a promotion. Are you sure you should be hanging with riff raff like me?"

Eight months earlier, the delegates of the Consortium had offered Dean the Executive Director job at Eagle Base Station. Eagle, the largest of the three base stations in the Consortium, was a hub for imports, exports, and passenger traffic. It was also the location of a Lyra Institute for Space Studies campus, the Texture Monitoring Center, and the Biological Research Institute and Hospital. To top that off, the station was a booming tourist hub with several attractions and museums including the Museum of Space Travel that had opened only two years earlier. The position was an incredible honor he couldn't refuse.

"Job's great. Took a few weeks for things to click, but I think I've got it down now. I feel more like a politician slash business man than I do an engineer. It's non-stop. I eat, sleep, and work."

"Just what exactly are you doing?"

"Too much! Not that I'm complaining. I love it. You know me; I like a fast pace. Basically, it's management. Coordinating the different divisions, making sure things run smoothly, dealing with problems." The excitement in his voice faded, and he leaned forward so he wouldn't have to yell over the band. "It would take me a day to explain."

"So what are you doing for fun, now that you're so busy? Don't tell me this job's mellowing you?"

Dean stiffened at the thought. He was determined age would never lead him down the old fuddy-duddy path, year after year stuffing his shirt full of turgid bull crap until it was bursting at the seams. He put on his bad boy face: narrowed eyes and a crooked grin. "Sue brought home a bichon frise puppy a couple of weeks ago. Matt was just thrilled." His grin widened until he felt his cheeks puff out. "Anyway, last Friday, Matt and I ended our squash night with a few too many beers, and when Sue went to bed we dyed the thing purple."

Dean and Matt roomed together during their first year of engineering on Lyra, and with the dry sense of humor they shared, they became fast friends. To uphold the engineering image, they conspired together to pull off a number of practical jokes, their favorite being the time they bricked up walls across the two roadways leading into the campus.

After graduating, Matt decided to add some military training to his resume and coerced Dean into joining him. Karen, Matt's sister, visited often, and Matt introduced her to Dean. A few months passed, and they were in love. Dean lost interest in the military, but Matt continued his training to the highest level and was now the head of security for the Eagle Base Station. He lived in Dean's neighborhood with Sue, his wife of one year. Dean was his best man.

Annie started with her kooky laugh, the laugh that invariably got Dean going, too. "You're going to rot in hell fire. You didn't hurt that poor puppy did you?"

Dean angled himself toward Annie with a wide smile like a hyena reveling over its kill. "Heck no, and don't worry, it's already worn off. Funniest damn thing I've ever seen though! Sue was a little pissed off, but she has a good sense of humor. She got over it."

"Speaking of Matt, I guess things are cool with the two of you since you and Karen split. That's got to be a political nightmare."

Dean hardened his expression and raised his voice. "Well, what the hell is he going to say? For Christ sake, she cheated on me. That's an image I'll never get out of my head." The harsh vision popped back into his mind like an annoying visitor who refuses to leave. It was as vivid as watching a movie: two lovers with their legs tangled in knots, a bare butt glistened with sweat, surging up and down like it was riding the waves of the incoming tide; maybe not even a tide, maybe a damn tsunami. And there was Dean watching from the shore, cold and wet with bitterness. "It's not like I broke her precious heart. I will say it's a bit complicated now with the group dynamics. Matt and Sue and Karen and I used to do everything together. Of course, I'm working with Matt every day now, which is great. Anyway, everything's cool, and he's done his best not to take sides. He would have liked to have joined us tonight, but he's got his hands full right now with the Symposium. A lot of high profile people means lots of security."

"Have you been attending? I know how much you like the academic scene," Annie said.

Dean appreciated her changing the subject. It had been beaten to death. "Yeah, I helped in the organization of it, and now I have to make sure things run smoothly. Thank God, it's only three days long. It's absorbing all my time between the talks and social functions. I had to dodge a couple of bullets just to make it here tonight."

"So, have you fallen asleep in any of those talks? You know, leaning back in your seat with drool trickling down your chin."

Dean threw his head back with laughter. "Almost! Tomorrow should be better. More up my alley." Dean leaned back and glanced down at the menu. "What're you going to have?"

"Don't know. I decide best under pressure."

"Excuse me, are ya ready to order?" The tall brunette interrupted with a lisp as she fought a battle with her tongue ring.

"Sure...Annie, go ahead."

"Hum, decision time. I'll have the cheese burger, well done, with fries and another beer, please."

"I'll have the same, except with salad instead of fries; thanks." Dean smiled.

The waitress returned a smile, her mouth looking as though it was decorated for Christmas.

"So, you back playing the field? I'm sure there are lots of pretty girls that would be happy to go out with the good-looking director of the base station. That waitress sure gave you a nice smile."

"Oh, yeah; she's just my type. No doubt she has a skull and cross bones tattooed to one of her butt cheeks."

"And your name could go on the other. Just think!" Annie giggled as she tucked her hair behind her ears; then she took another gulp of beer. She set the glass down with a clunk, foaming the top of the golden fluid.

Dean laughed quietly as he wrapped his fingers around his glass. The frost had disappeared leaving a ring of moisture on the table. "Let's turn the conversation to you. Why did you have to haul yourself all the way to Cygnus to get a pail of dirt?"

"They want to expand the crops to the north, and they needed a soil analysis."

"And they couldn't find a local to do it?"

"People are nervous about that microbe; you know, the one that makes you paranoid, hemorrhage, and die."

"I can't imagine why that would bother them," Dean said.

"They're morons. You spray the ground, and they're dead within an hour. I've dealt with contaminated soil before, so I guess that's why they called me. Anyway, I got a first class flight out of it and a dinner with you, so it's not all bad. I've got the lab booked for tomorrow afternoon, so I'll analyze the samples and be finished with it."

"Which one of you had the fries?" The waitress had a plate in each hand, her thumb poking into Dean's salad. Dean cocked his head toward Annie.

"This looks good." Annie picked up a fry and started chewing with great satisfaction. She scrunched her nose as she watched Dean push away the patch of lettuce that had been thumbed. "So that's pretty awful about Roger."

"Yeah, crazy. He never knew when he'd had enough, but he seemed to be able to hold his alcohol all right. I was shocked."

"He was a great guy. I sent the family my condolences."

"What a way to go, drowning in your own vomit. Good thing to talk about over dinner," Dean added. "I would have gone to the funeral, but Earth's a long haul and with this job…"

"Didn't his sister Denise find him?"

"Yeah, I talked to her. Apparently, he'd been out late drinking at his favorite bar and didn't show up for his tee time the next morning. You know how much he liked golf. Anyway, his friend called Denise, and she went over to check on him and found him dead in bed. She's not taking it well." Dean took the last bite of his burger and washed it down with a swig of beer. "I guess we're on a timeline." He looked over to catch the waitress's eye and signaled her to bring the bill.

"Yeah, another two-hour flight," Annie said in a tired voice.

Dean paid the bill and walked Annie back to the terminal.

"When's the next time you're going to be on Lyra?" she asked.

"No clue, but I promise to keep in touch." Dean looked over to see the last few passengers pass through the gate. He would have liked to have had more time to reminisce about good times rather than belly ache about the stormy weather of the past months. Regardless, Annie always managed to lift his spirits, and he was sad to see her go. "I guess you gotta board."

She nodded, glumly. He leaned over and gave her a kiss on the cheek, hoping it would turn her face to its *signature* color. It never seemed to fail, and he smiled at her girlishness.

Annie took her bag from Dean. "Thanks for dinner. I wish we had more time."

"Me, too."

She turned and disappeared through the gate.

* * * *

Annie's flight to the Lyra Base Station arrived on time, but with the volume of travelers, the shuttles running to the planet surface were delayed; and it was well after midnight before she stepped through the door of her townhouse. Without stopping to turn on a light, she went straight to her bedroom, set her bag on the floor, and kicked off her shoes. It was a clear night, and the two moons of Lyra shone through the back window of the room, casting their silvery glow onto the dark blue satin bedspread turning it the color of a lake on a cloudy day. As she headed for the washroom, she heard something scurrying in the next room. *Oh, the hamsters.* She had almost forgotten her little pets, Slam and Dunk. "I'll bet you're hungry."

She fed her hamsters, then threw on her favorite basketball flannel pajamas, and dragged herself into the bathroom. During her second flight, she forced herself to stay awake to watch a movie starring her favorite actor, *the sexy Rod Drake,* and the beers were catching up with her. After brushing her teeth, she yawned wide enough to feel a breeze across her tonsils and went off to bed. She had to be at work by eight a.m., which she figured would give her just over six hours of sleep. Pulling the smooth satin bed spread up to her nose, she drifted off.

* * * *

By two-thirty a.m., the moons of Lyra were sinking into the horizon. The lights of the Lyra Base Station twinkled like a brilliant star in the clear, dark sky. *Perfect,* the man thought to himself as he slipped out of the car. He grabbed the small shoulder pack from the side of his seat and shut the door without making a sound. He strode purposefully toward the townhouse half a block down on the far side of the street, being careful not to pick up any dirt from the edge of the walkway. The air was crisp enough to have doused the grass with fresh beads of dew. When he arrived at his destination, he paused to check the address and confirm there were no signs of activity. A large rock on the front lawn displayed the house number, and the fluorescent paka shrubs planted next to it made it easy to read. When he arrived at the front door, he pulled out a pair of black leather gloves from the side pocket of his pack and put them on. He ran the override card across the door lock scanner and heard a small click when the bolt released.

The man entered the townhouse. He paused for a moment to

survey his surroundings and to listen for any sounds. The kitchen to the immediate right had a walk-through design with the dining room at the far end. Just beyond, a nightlight lit up the cheap catalogue furnishings in the living room. The entranceway had the typical set up: a narrow, waist high table with a tacky mirror hanging above it and a coat closet. He turned on his flashlight and walked to the table. The identification card on it had a picture of an average looking girl, probably in her early thirty's, with short strawberry blond hair. At the top of the card were the words Lyra Geology Institute. He adjusted the position of his shoulder pack so it wouldn't shift.

The man moved from room to room taking great care not to make a sound, but there was no sign of the red and black bag. Something stirred in one of the back rooms. He stopped in his tracks and turned toward the direction of the noise. He held his flashlight up like a weapon and edged down the hallway. The door on the right sat ajar, and he could hear rustling. *What the hell!*

He inched the door open only enough to squeeze through it. The room appeared to be an office of sorts with a desk, loveseat, and a table in the corner where the noise was coming from. He gagged from the pungent smell, like rat urine. He shined his light toward the table and spied a hamster galloping on its exercise wheel, another half buried in wood chips and excrement. The energetic one stopped long enough to give him a vacant stare, its black eyes gleaming like beads of oil and its naked nose quivering. *God damn rodents!* In another place and time, he would have crushed their fury hides into the floor. Enjoying the image he painted for himself, he glanced around for the bag and left the room, leaving the door in its original position.

The only room left to check was the one at the end of the hallway. *Great, the bedroom.* With the door shut, no light could be seen through the crack under the door. He walked to the door and stopped to listen. The only sound was his pulsed breaths struggling to keep up with the throbbing in his neck. *Stupid bitch had to take the bag into her bedroom.* He took a moment to remove one of his gloves and satisfy an itch on his forehead. The perspiration gathering around his receding hairline had pasted his thinning hair to his scalp. Like a sly cat, he took a final step toward the room and inched the door open.

Inside, the last remnants of moonlight blanketed the queen size bed. The woman asleep in the bed was tangled in the sheets with a pillow over her head, the crack between her lips just big enough for a fly to enter. Her breathing sounded deep and raspy. Beside the bed lay a red and black duffle bag. On its side, the words "The Cheetahs" were plastered in bold letters next to the monogram of a basketball. The dim moonlight lit a pathway to the bag, and the man switched off his flashlight and started his approach. He took only two steps and tripped over something on the floor. *Damn!* He struggled to regain his footing without making any sound then froze icy still. The woman rolled over and tossed the pillow to the far side of the bed.

His heart felt like it was pounding its way to the surface as he waited for the woman to settle. He took several seconds to unzip the bag. Inside lay some personal effects, clothing, a toiletries bag, and a tacky Harvest Festival souvenir. He made haste pushing the items aside, searching intently. He reached further into the bag and came across the smooth metal surface of a container. *Bingo.* He grabbed the container with a strong grip and removed it from the bag.

He set the container on the floor and released the two front clamps to open it. Inside, he could see six small vials of soil with labels affixed to the lids. He flipped open the flap of his bag and pulled out a medical grade facemask, diligently placing it over his face and mouth and securing it around the back of his head. The man slipped off his leather gloves and replaced them with tight fitting latex. From the front pocket of his bag, he retrieved a plastic bag containing a vial of soil. He then removed a vial from the container, set it on the floor and peeled off the label stating "Sample Two." With careful attention, he removed the duplicate vial from the plastic bag and secured the label to it. He wasted no time placing the new vial back in the container.

He removed his confining mask and latex gloves and slipped his leather gloves back on. The whole operation had taken three minutes. He flipped the lid back on the metal container, secured the clasps, and returned it to the position he'd found it in. Pinching the zipper pull with his thumb and index finger, he started to close the bag. Each click of the zipper seemed to echo through the room like it was an auditorium. *Almost done.* He got back to his feet and headed to the bedroom door, mindful not to trip over the shoes again. As he slithered through the door, he heard a crash from behind him.

"Crap."

The startled voice shot through the man like a bolt of lightning. It sounded like a glass had fallen. The light immediately went on.

With adrenaline surging through his veins, the man left the bedroom door somewhat ajar, hoping the woman wouldn't notice. He tore down the hall, rounding the corner while trying to stay in the shadows. The woman stomped out of the bedroom and made an abrupt right to the bathroom. Her reflection was caught in the hall mirror as she scurried back with a towel, kicking the door shut behind her. *Good, she didn't notice.*

Standing motionless, he waited until the light disappeared from the bedroom and then hurried toward the front door. Once outside, he enjoyed a calming breath of cool air. With the door locked behind him, he vanished into the pre-dawn mist.

Chapter Five

Dean's apartment on Spruce Road was located in the heart of the nicest residential area on the Eagle Base Station. Each dome on the base station had its own climate control, and in the event of an emergency could be locked down from adjoining domes. The neighborhood was entirely contained within its own dome, and Dean loved its slightly tropical feel and the beautiful atrium at its center that showcased exotic plants, a fountain, a children's playground, and a bike and running trail. Spruce Road was only one of several quaint laneways that extended from the atrium to various residences. With little time on his hands, Dean especially enjoyed the conveniences the community had to offer: a number of small shops, a restaurant, a fitness center, and a monorail station.

"It's six a.m." Dean's computer snapped him awake and then tuned to his favorite radio station. He groaned and pulled the pillow over his head. To his relief, a good song came on, not the *shred* crap with the robot voices the kids were bopping to these days. For the moment, he regretted his decision to book a six-thirty squash game with Matt and decided to play dead for another minute. His last few seconds of peace and quiet were soon shattered by a loud, happy trill in his ear. Dean's cat, Costello, a gray tabby, had her wet nose up against the side of his face, enjoying a sniff followed by a loving lick.

Dean grew up with cats and being an only child, they gave him all of their attention. He had great affection for them. At seven years of age, he decided to build them a cat house. His parents were amused by the thought, which at the time baffled him. With a smirk on his face for the duration of the project, Dean's father helped him plan and construct the structure. With great enthusiasm, Dean worked alongside his father and helped with every phase of his first engineering project. By the time they were finished, the three-story building stood higher than Dean. He beamed with satisfaction and over the front door, he carefully painted the words Cat House along with the names of his cats at the time Hockey, Puck, and his favorite, Hat Trick.

Karen hated cats, often referring to them as "mangy critters," and out of spite, Dean had adopted one the day after she left him. With the kitten population on the base station being rather scarce, Dean ended up with a female. This didn't really bother him, except he had already decided on the name Costello in honor of his favorite classic comedy duo. He figured nobody would notice.

Giving in to the loud purr playing along with the music, Dean whipped the covers aside, sat up, and rubbed his face with both hands. *Coffee,* he thought to himself. Swinging around, he found his footing on the dark hardwood and set off for the kitchen wearing only his light green boxers.

Costello took a flying leap off the bed and obediently followed, overtaking him halfway down the hall. Playing a game of cat and mouse, Dean made a hard right into the kitchen and with a jerky motion, stooped over and swept the cat up under his right arm. "Gotcha." He gave the cat a playful little scratch under her chin then released her and filled his cup with the black steamy liquid. *Ahh, nectar of the gods.* After a large gulp, he muttered, "Lights On."

He squinted as his eyes focused and reached for a bowl, filled it with kibble, and then leaned over and placed it in front of Costello. With the tip of her tail twitching, her nose disappeared into the bowl. He grabbed an apple, and the two of them munched down their breakfast together like an old married couple while Dean admired the view out the window. Framed in its center was the neighboring dome, the Biological Foundation Biosphere where Karen worked. Dean thought it looked like a snowy village full of weeds, a fitting environment for her.

After a couple more sips of coffee, he started to feel more himself, and he moved into high gear. He washed up and threw on his athletic shorts, navy T-shirt, and new Stridefast shoes. Slinging his squash racket over his shoulder, he ran out the door.

Matt and Sue's apartment was only five minutes down the road, and the fitness center was five minutes further on the far side of the atrium. The lights were purposely dim to give the atrium the look of dawn. The air smelled flowery, and the crickets were still singing. When he arrived at Matt's, he rang the bell. In the same instant, he heard the yappy barking of Matt's new puppy, Huggy. Dean snickered to himself when Matt cursed as the door opened. The little dog ran out and tried to climb Dean's legs.

"I think he looked better purple, don't you?" Dean gave the dog a gentle nudge to release its grip on his leg.

Matt stood in the door threshold with his thick black hair almost rubbing against the top of the frame. With an energized grin, big enough to distort the strapping features of his face, he let out a hearty laugh. "You don't know the half of it. How about we paint a blue dot on it and use it as a squash ball?"

The sound of Sue's voice echoed from down the hall, "How about we paint a blue dot on you?" Seconds later, she emerged from behind the door with a leash in her hand. Sporting her jogging clothes and a big smile, she gave Dean a cheery greeting. "Good morning, you evil dog hater."

Dean cocked his head and with a mischievous laugh looked up at Matt. "Come on, we have to hustle; our court time's in seven minutes."

Dean and Matt set off across the atrium, laughing at the sound of Sue corralling her little dog.

"You should've gotten a cat," Dean muttered.

"Not bloody likely, you crazy cat man. When you're fifty, you'll probably have twenty of them, and they'll have to call me in for security violations." Matt scoffed. "Who the hell likes cats? By the way, how was your dinner with Annie last night?"

"Great, it was good to see her. She asked about you. I guess you were busy with symposium security?"

"You could say that. An argument erupted in a restaurant between two physicists. It got pretty heated to the point they called me in. It was like a bad domestic dispute. They were arguing about the energy state of some supersymmetric particle. Get a life! What a waste of my time."

"That's why we pay you the big bucks. Who won...I mean the argument?"

"The one with the thicker glasses."

"Very funny," Dean said.

The two men arrived at the fitness center turning the five-minute walk into four.

"Good morning, Mr. Jenkins, you're in Court Two this morning. Have a good game." The receptionist handed Matt a squash ball.

Dean grabbed a couple of waters off the counter. "I'm going to kick your ass!"

"Fat chance."

Dean knew Matt held the upper hand in squash, and the statistics were there to prove it; his win rate ranked about one in four. Matt had fast reflexes from over two decades of martial arts training.

The forty minutes went by quickly, giving them enough time for only three games. At the end, Dean smiled smugly as he'd beaten the statistics and taken two of the games. As they walked toward the atrium, he decided to rub it in. "Starting to lose it old man?"

"Try not to get too excited, you might wet yourself."

Dean laughed and gave Matt a pat on the back. "Good game!"

"What's next on your agenda?" asked Matt.

"A really quick shower, followed by hobnobbing at the symposium breakfast, and then the presentations."

"Have fun with that. I think I'll stick with security. At least it sounds more interesting. Let me know if you learn something."

"Well, hopefully we won't need you. There's a lot of tension with that enormous research grant Enertech is giving out. All those nerds are going for one-upmanship in their presentations. The biggest nerd wins the jackpot, at least it seems that way. Enertech is looking to put out a new collector plate grid design in another couple of years that will be fifty percent more efficient than the current one." They stopped at the ornate gold fish pool at the base of the waterfall. The fish were schooling by the automatic feeder at the side rockery, inhaling the food. Dean propped his foot against the edge of a park bench and tightened his shoelace before continuing. "Of course, Eurasia Cosmic Nuclear of the Earth Nuclear Corporation is trying to get a new particle accelerator out of it."

"I doubt ECN will get the grant with the new particle accelerator laboratory on the Lyra Base Station that's all over the news," Matt added. "Isn't it a done deal?"

"Probably, but it's too bad since ECN was the pioneer in the development of collector plate technology to harness vacuum particle energy for power. The Lyra atom smasher has generated some cutting edge research lately. If ECN ends up shutting down, it will be sad, in a nostalgic sort of way."

"Whatever you say. As long as my water's hot, I'm happy." Matt waved a hand in the air.

"I'll catch up with you later." Dean reared off to the right and jogged in the direction of home.

* * * *

Dean stood in his walk-in closet with a towel wrapped around his waist riffling for some clothes. Costello took up residence in yesterday's pile and lay down with her tail snaked across her paws and a lipless grin on her face. Her eyes batted sleepily. After staring at his wardrobe for a couple of minutes, Dean started to feel like he was acting like a chick and made a snap decision: black dress pants, gray dress shirt, and sports jacket. He thought he'd skip the tie in favor of the more casual look and left the top button of his shirt undone. "Hold down the fort," he yelled to Costello as he left the apartment.

Since the roadways would be crowded with pedestrian traffic, he decided to give up the convenience of his personal golf cart style shuttle and started the ten-minute walk to the monorail station. The symposium was being held at the Eagle Hilton, a twenty-minute ride away. Only top executives and high-level security had the luxury of having their own shuttle, and most wouldn't be caught dead riding the public transit. Dean found it relaxing.

Dean watched the news broadcast on the monorail. The first story announced the completion of the three-year project to re-sculpt the faces on Mt. Rushmore. It gave him a chuckle as he remembered visiting the site as a kid; he had referred to the sculptures as pancake people. Four centuries of wind erosion can take its toll. The broadcast moved to a cave-in in one of the deeper shafts at the Sparling Nickel Mine on Draco that trapped six miners, and then on a happier front, the sixteen-year-old girl who went missing during a school trip to the Harvest Festival had finally shown up unharmed.

"Hilton Station." After the monorail came to a stop, Dean exited and headed straight across the platform to the first set of stairs. "Clear doors." The hum of the monorail grew quieter as it torpedoed off.

Moments later, he made his entrance into the Constellation Ballroom where breakfast was being served. At the door, a man greeted him and handed him a schedule of the day's presentations. "Good morning Mr. Weston."

Dean returned his smile. "Morning."

The furnishings in the immense room looked like they belonged in an old castle—five star ambiance, but about as far from space age as you could get. Ornate paintings of celestial constellations decorated the arched ceiling, and a series of large chandeliers hung along its centerline. Dean imagined the paintings looked like something Leonardo da Vinci would have created.

The aroma of freshly brewed coffee and crisp bacon filled the air, causing his mouth to water. Dean scanned the crowded room looking for someone he might enjoy talking to. A few steps away, Ivan Campbell stood, clutching his teacup with a royal grip; far from his first choice, but he'd do.

As Dean went to greet Ivan, he noticed Ivan looked much fitter and vibrant than the last time he'd seen him; however, Dean made a conscious decision not to compliment him. As usual, Ivan dressed as though he just stepped out of a pretentious restaurant, with his thinning hair perfectly placed. Dean decided he'd keep a measurable distance from the cloud of the drug store cologne hanging about Ivan like smog, aging him twenty years. *Aux de greasy old man!* "Ivan, rumor has it there's been some fantastic work coming out of that fancy new particle accelerator of yours."

One year earlier, Ivan took the position of Director of the new Lyra Particle Accelerator Laboratory, which at the time, had just recently opened on the Lyra Base Station. The two-kilometer long linear accelerator (linac) boasted a new design, which allowed for two collision configurations. That created a lot of excitement as rather than just accelerating a beam of particles into a stationary target, they could accelerate two particle beams, colliding with each other in the middle allowing for a higher energy collision. The Consortium funded the accelerator, and the expectations were high as the nearby Herculis

Nebula served as a virtual ocean of energetic particles such as strings, quarks, leptons, photons, and nucleons to fuel their research.

"Dean, nice to see you again; and yes, you're right, in the last six months, the work some of our scientists have been producing is extraordinary. I have every confidence we will be awarded Enertech's research grant, especially after today's sessions. I assume you will be attending some of the talks today." Ivan held his head high and took a dainty sip of tea, his Adam's apple rolling out of his tight fitted collar as he swallowed.

"That's the plan. Hey, my niece, Michelle Jenkins, was hired on as one of your co-op students. She starts in a couple of weeks. She's really excited. She's a smart kid."

"Oh, is that right? I'll have to look out for her. I'm not involved in the hiring of students as you can probably imagine." Ivan continued by giving Dean an earful of results from his recent research initiatives. He finished by stating, "Inside the accelerator, in the absence of cosmic background microwave radiation, we can measure the vacuum energy density and the oscillation frequency from the breakdown of supersymmetric particles. This can be used to confirm the field measurement in the Casimir Effect. I believe we can use these measurements to calculate the vacuum energy to within five percent, and it is quite likely the vacuum energy could be manipulated on a much larger scale, taking into account the oscillation of these particles as they decay, particularly the neutralino's. The lightest neutralino is stable and an ideal candidate for the calculation, especially since it's the eventual product in the decay chain of all other supersymmetry partners. Scientists at ECN have suggested using its supersymetric partner, the neutrino, for the calculation, but the different flavors lead to errors in measuring their oscillation frequency."

Dean stared blankly at Ivan, making a concerted effort to not let his mouth drop. Dean's minor in particle physics did not qualify him as an expert, but, as he recalled, Ivan's knowledge of it stopped at zero. He was pretty sure this old dog hadn't learned a new trick; just a well-practiced old one. Ivan loved to impress people; Dean remembered that much. What he hadn't remembered, but was coming back to him like a flash fire, were the hundred other reasons he disliked the man. "So when did you get your doctorate in particle physics?" he said sarcastically. "As I recall, you barely knew what a neutrino was."

Ivan laughed, shrugging off Dean's comment. "Yes, I remember. Well working with the best, you tend to pick things up."

"Yeah, right," Dean said.

Although thankful for having an opportunity to put in a good word for his niece, Dean started scheming as to how he could politely dodge Ivan and his shoptalk. He found the entire conversation to be a little overwhelming, not to mention odd. *Why did I decide to talk to you again?* He was pleasantly relieved when a beautiful blonde woman joined them with a pleasant, "Good morning gentlemen."

Ivan's expression perked as he looked her up and down. Dean felt embarrassed by Ivan's lack of subtly. "Laura, good morning. Oh, let me introduce the two of you. Dean, this is Dr. Laura Simmons. I'm sure you've heard of her. She's been with the ECN Division of Earth Nuclear for several years. She has numerous impressive publications. Laura, this is Mr. Dean Weston. We used to work together when I was with the Mining Authority."

Dean reached out to shake her hand. "Nice to meet you, Laura."

Laura matched the gentle firmness of Dean's handshake. "I believe I spoke with you once just over a year ago when you were working at the Texture Monitoring Center. I guess you weren't there long. Aren't you the director of this base station now? This is my first time here. It's very impressive."

Dean had no recollection of speaking with her and paused for a moment, searching for something to say. "Yeah, I was at the Monitoring Center on a three month contract before the Consortium offered me this position. And by the way, thank you. I try to run a smooth operation. They're not still running the particle accelerator at ECN are they? That thing's ancient."

"No, its last overhaul was twenty-five years ago, and it's finally been decommissioned. The plan is to build an accelerator on the moon, but there is some controversy as to whether it should be another circular accelerator or a linac similar to the Lyra Accelerator. It's a question of the on-going battle of energy loss through synchrotron radiation in the curved design, and the fact that after a collision, the remaining particles are lost in the linear design. Of course, being so close to the Herculis Nebula, that's not a concern for you, Ivan." Laura gestured in Ivan's direction. "Ivan was nice enough to allow me to come and work with him as a guest for a few months to see how the experts do it and to try and put forth some recommendations to ECN. I haven't had any hands on experience with a linac. With the quality of the work coming out of his facility, I'm very excited."

Dean cleared his throat trying to cover up the awkwardness he typically felt around attractive women, and Laura was strikingly beautiful. Her shoulder length blond hair fell in soft layers highlighting her stunning features. She possessed the natural, innocent beauty of a cheerleader with the poise of a diplomat. Her approximately five-foot-four fit and sporty figure was complemented by her professional looking black pant suit and scoop-necked silk top that displayed just the right amount of cleavage. "I heard there was some uncertainty surrounding the funding for a new Earth Nuclear accelerator. Especially, with the Lyra facility stealing so much of the limelight in recent months. The word on the street is Enertech's eighty-billion may drift to them. There's also some talk about the Consortium pouring all their research dollars into the Lyra facility rather than bailing out a sinking ship. It's too bad, considering ECN's history."

Laura looked rather stunned by Dean's comments, making him feel like he just stuffed his proverbial foot in his mouth. "We're still a thriving research facility, although I'll admit in recent months we've met some stiff competition."

Ivan set his hand on Laura's shoulder. "After breakfast, Laura is giving a presentation on her recent work on neutrinos. Dean, perhaps you may be interested in attending."

Dean sensed her discomfort with Ivan's flagrant invasion of her personal space. He glanced at his schedule and found Laura's name beside the title of her presentation: 'The Mysterious Nature of Neutrinos.' "Ivan and I were just talking about neutrinos and how neutralino's are now taking center stage."

"That's a matter of opinion. All the more reason for you to come and listen." Laura took a step back to release Ivan's grip. "If you gentlemen will excuse me, I have to prepare for my talk. Nice to meet you, Dean." With a pleasant smile, she headed for the exit.

Dean turned his attention back to Ivan. "I hear you've recruited Kevin to join your elite group."

"Yes, indeed. He's a very valuable addition to the group, and now we have our own private pilot. Perhaps you should find some time to visit us. I would be happy to show you around the facility. I'm sure you would be very impressed. We've managed to recruit some brilliant scientists. The titles on today's schedule of talks speak volumes. Our work dominates the particle physics section of the symposium. I'm afraid Dr. Simmons may find herself humbled."

Oh brother! Strategizing how to make an exit, Dean politely commented, "Sounds like you're running a very impressive facility. I'll have to make an effort to get out there sometime."

To Dean's relief, Ivan glanced at his watch and said, "Well it was nice to see you again Dean, but I would like to get to Laura's presentation early to get a front row seat. Hope to see you there."

"Say hello to Kevin for me."

Dean filled the next ten minutes with idle small talk, something he loathed, until the crowd started to disperse. He checked his schedule and by the process of elimination, decided on Laura's talk, which was set to start in Meeting Room Three in five minutes. On his way, he decided to find a seat toward the back and as far away as possible from Ivan and his over inflated ego.

The meeting room was almost full, which made his plan look less obvious. He took a seat on the aisle so he could make a clean break when the presentation ended. Laura was at the front of the room preparing all her visuals and reviewing her notes. He had a fleeting and inappropriate image of her wearing an evening gown as a model in one of those tacky game shows retired people like to watch. *A good reason to work until you drop.*

She waited a few minutes then went to the podium and stood patiently until the audience settled down. The walls of the stark room sounded like they were whispering as the last few people got to their seats. The odd cough echoed, and then the room fell quiet leaving only the faint hum, which seems to come from nowhere in places like that.

Dean attempted to get comfortable to weather out the presentation by slouching back in his seat. Annie's description of him falling asleep popped into his head, and he straightened slightly. Although he had little interest in neutrinos, Laura's eloquence stole his attention. Before he knew it, he was sitting straight-backed in his chair listening thoughtfully. Twenty minutes soon passed, and Laura addressed the audience for questions. Dean shot his hand up first. "Could you provide us with some more details on how you determined the oscillation of solar neutrinos from the mass and magnetic moment?"

Dean hated being at the podium, and it wasn't because of the public speaking jitters—he spoke confidently. It was the *god-forsaken* spotlight that blared down, showing every flaw on your face and sweating your brow to the point you look like a wax figure. He'd never seen anyone *shine* in the spotlight until now. Laura's lips stretched into a smile that rounded her rosy cheeks, and her eyes widened enough to be endowed with an unearthly twinkle. She paused in the position, seeming intrigued at such a well thought out question.

"I would be happy to provide you with the details of the measurements, equations, and calculations, but it would take a few minutes. Perhaps I can invite anyone interested in hearing more about this to come and speak with me personally at the end." She continued fielding questions and wrapped up.

As people meandered their way to the exit, Dean made his way to the front to speak to Laura. To his surprise, he was alone. He thought Ivan and his fancy suited nerds would have been there in force; their synapses firing in tandem and their business cards fanned out in their hands, each displaying a list of their degrees in bold letters. *Perhaps they didn't understand the question.* "Good talk."

"Thanks, glad you enjoyed it. Most people find this stuff dry as a bone."

"How strange."

Laura wasted no time launching into a detailed answer to Dean's question. Dean found himself getting lost at points but was careful not to show it. As their discussion seemed to be petering out, Dean looked directly into Laura's eyes and asked, "So is there a personality in there with all those brains?" Realizing he once again put his foot in his mouth, he assumed an awkward stance as he felt a cold sweat break out. *Christ I'm an idiot.*

Laura didn't hesitate with her response. "Actually, I hang with a wild bunch. At parties we drink tea and play pin the pop bottle glasses on the nerd. Then we take turns trying to solve the Hodge conjecture. You know that unsolved problem in algebraic geometry. Oh, by the way here's my business card. I'm afraid I'm all out of pocket protectors."

Now Dean had the podium jitters! There he was talking to an intelligent, beautiful woman, and he may as well have been barking like a dog. He picked up the pieces of his stomach that felt as though they'd dropped into his shoes and thought fast. "Sarcasm, I like it, and I guess I deserve it. Sorry." He sheepishly took the business card and slipped it into his jacket pocket.

Laura gave him a forgiving smile. "Don't worry about it; I'm good with stereotyping. And by the way, the people here are going to start to think you're one of them if you keep asking questions like that."

"That's a scary thought." Dean straightened himself up shaking off his embarrassment, and before he had a chance to second guess himself, he blurted. "I don't suppose you're available for dinner tonight?"

Laura looked at Dean with an expression that suggested she wasn't sure if she'd heard him correctly. After a moment of silence, she broke into a sincere smile and replied. "I would love to, but I'm on the four o'clock flight to the Lyra Base Station with Ivan."

Dean felt a deep feeling of disappointment setting in, and his gaze turned down. This was the first time he'd found the nerve to ask someone out since splitting up with Karen.

"But if you manage to get out there sometime, I would love to have dinner with you. Here, give me my card back, and I'll write my new address on it," Laura added.

Dean handed the card back to her along with one of his own.

"Call me," she said as she slipped his card into her purse.

With a soft voice and a boyish grin, Dean said, "I think I'll have to take you up on that offer. Perhaps in a couple of weeks, when things are back to normal around here after the symposium."

"Looking forward to it," she said, smiling. It was one full of anticipation, halfway between sweet and sultry.

Dean walked Laura out of the meeting room and after wishing her luck with her new job, said goodbye and winked.

Chapter Six

It had already felt like a long day by the time Annie gifted the Geology Institute's marble steps with her presence. Insufficient sleep, followed by a morning full of meetings was not a happy combination, but at last she could set her attention to some brainless lab work. She strutted into the building giving the receptionist a warm and rather elevated, "Hey," and bounced up the stairs to the lab on the second floor. Annie loved to make a pronounced entrance to the Institute as the sparkling granite walls of the cavernous lobby had fantastic acoustics.

As usual, the lab was bustling. With its operating room appeal, Annie half expected to see a body laid out every time she walked in. It brought back memories of the knee surgery she'd had just over a year ago. Several people were hard at work at various stations throughout the lab with the exception of the Hazmat Room in the back where the mass spectrometer was located. Thankfully, she'd had the foresight to book it in advance.

She couldn't be happier to have the soil analysis on her afternoon agenda as it was a quick and painless task, like baking a cake. *Dump soil in Petri dish, break up with spatula, place in spectrometer, wait for results, and bingo you're done.* She hated the three-minute wait for the results. It was like watching a pot of water boil. With the six samples, taking into account the prep and clean up time, she figured she'd be on her way home by three o'clock, and she couldn't wait.

"Annie, welcome home. How was your trip?" Sara, Annie's best friend, had started at the Institute about a month ago as an entry-level lab technician. Sara had been out of work for a while, so she was thrilled when Annie got her the job; however, Annie had some reservations about being her boss.

"It had its ups and downs. Certainly longer than expected. Anything exciting going on around here?"

"Same thing, different day. Are those your exciting soil samples?" Sara gestured to the metal container Annie carried.

"Yep, these are them. I'm going to analyze them in the Hazmat

Room and go home early. I'm exhausted. How 'bout we do lunch tomorrow. I have a craving for pizza."

"Sounds like a plan, and you can tell me about your dinner with Dean." Sara winked slowly in a suggestive sort of way.

Annie rolled her eyes at the thought of Sara trying to pry out details of her evening when there was nothing to tell. Sara enjoyed drama, and unfortunately one evening after a few steins of beer and a shot of blind stupidity, Annie had told her how she felt about Dean. She'd kicked herself ever since, having to put up with Sara constantly fishing for dirt about a relationship that didn't exist. She tried to convince Sara it was just the alcohol talking that night, but Sara knew her too well.

Annie tucked her hair behind her ears, threw on her lab coat, and begrudgingly headed toward the back room with her soil samples. *Can't wait to get out of here.*

The door clicked shut behind her, and she set the metal container on the counter. She inspected the contents to ensure they had traveled well. She'd had an awful vision in her mind of opening the container only to find the vials broken and all the soil mixed up. *Ahh, perfect, that would have been my worst nightmare.* A wide yawn told her she'd have to be extra organized, or she'd be back to Cygnus to collect new samples. She took a deep breath to kick some alertness into her. Her eyes were dry, and she rubbed absently at them before putting on her goggles and latex gloves.

She opened the operating room-gray cupboard above her workspace and located six Petri dishes and lab spatulas. She set them up in a straight row at the back of the counter. After taking a seat on the lab stool, she slid the metal case toward her and pulled out the vial labeled *Sample One*. Opening her lab book, she turned to the first blank page and scratched out *Monday, August 10, 2299* on the top right.

Finally ready. Annie took one of the dish-spatula sets and with the laser scribe mounted on the wall, etched a number *1* into the side of the glass. Next, she picked up vial one and removed the lid with a gentle twist. The rich black soil inside looked as though it should have a carrot growing out of it. Holding the vial with her left hand, she gently manipulated the contents into the dish. She used the spatula to break up the denser clumps, digging away at it like a kid in a sand box. Once it met her approval, she picked up the dish and turned to the island behind her. Annie opened the door of the spectrometer specimen chamber, placed the Petri dish on the mounting tray, and closed it.

The computer immediately prompted, "Please identify sample."

"Annie Wilson, Cygnus soil sample number one."

"Accepted."

The faint hum of the vacuum pump sounded as it pumped the air out of the specimen chamber. Above the door, the light display indicated the "chamber pressure" and "analysis time remaining." Annie watched the time countdown for a couple of seconds, *2:58, 2:57, 2:56...* before getting bored, her mind drifting to the watched pot that never boils.

One down, five to go. With some degree of satisfaction, Annie turned her attention back to the Petri dish lineup. She scribed another dish, this time with a *2* and took vial two from the container. She started to give the lid a gentle twist, but it wouldn't budge. *God, I'm a weakling.* She set the vial back down on the counter and stretched her fingers out letting them perform a little dance. *Okay, let's try this again.* This time, she thought she'd put her basketball fingers to good use. Holding the vial tightly with her left hand and the lid with her right, she started counting, *one, two...* on three, she gave the lid a firm twist to the left. After a couple seconds of brute force, the lid finally moved with a sudden jolt.

"Ouch! Crap!" The razor sharp threads on the top of the jar cut right through Annie's glove, drawing blood. She placed the vial and lid down on the counter, decorated by a couple of red drips, and ran to the sink. She whipped her gloves off, disposed of them, and washed thoroughly. *Stupid damn vial!* She wrapped her finger up in a cloth and left the room to get the first aid kit.

As Annie stormed out of the room complaining bitterly, Sara walked over to her. "What the hell happened to you?"

"God damn lid was jammed shut, and when I finally got it loose, I cut my finger on the threads. They were bloody sharp."

Sara retrieved the first aid kit. "Let's see. Oh, that's not so bad, you sissy."

"It's just a piss off. I've had enough hassles for one week."

"Are we a tad premenstrual?" Sara smiled jokingly.

"Your bedside manner sucks."

"The cut's not deep. I'll mend it for you." Annie watched impatiently as Sara pulled a mender out of the first aid kit, turned it on and held it steady with the blue arc between the electrodes over the cut. Annie's tapping foot won her a dirty look from her friend. After a few minutes, the mender had regenerated enough cells to stop the bleeding, and a thin scab had formed. "Looks pretty good. Why don't we let nature do the rest?"

"Thanks, Sara. Sorry I'm so snappy. Tomorrow's lunch will fix me."

Annie headed back to the Hazmat Room only to find the whole fiasco left her with a bit of a mess. The entire ordeal had taken at least twenty minutes. *So much for three o'clock.* Vial two had tipped over into a small pool of blood and half the soil sat in a pile on the counter as though a wee dog had left her a souvenir. The lid had rolled across the counter, leaving a trail of blood and contaminating two of the Petri dishes. She cringed as she wondered if enough uncontaminated soil remained in the vial for the analysis. The clean up came first, and she went to the sink to get a small dust pan and a damp cloth. *Crunch.* Her goggles. When she ran to the sink, they had fallen off her face. She picked them up and examined them; then she frowned and returned them to her face, lopsided.

She started her clean up by setting vial two upright and sweeping up the soil on the counter into the small pan. After wiping down the counter, she sterilized Petri number *2* and dumped the remaining soil from the vial into it. As she loosened it up with the spatula, she noticed she'd forgotten to put on new gloves. *Fuck!* Forgetting to wash her hands, she put on a new pair. The Petri sandbox was looking quite pathetic, and to top it off, she had to remove a little bit from around the edge that looked to have a bit of blood in it. With a jerky motion, she swung around to load it into the specimen chamber. She set aside sample one and closed the door. The computer prompted her again, and she responded, "Annie, sample three."

Annie continued to work diligently for another twenty minutes with drips of perspiration carving streamers down her face. Her shirt lay pasted to her back in the same way her basketball jersey did after a hard game. She had one sample left, and when she picked up the vial, she saw it was labeled number four. Panic stricken, she looked around trying to sort out what happened to vial six. The Petri dishes and vials were scattered over the counter in no particular order. Annie pounded the counter with her fist and yelled, "Shit."

* * * *

Sara popped her head up when she heard the outburst trumpet through the thick glass windows of the Hazmat Room, and she walked over and sheepishly peeked in the door. "Ya need a hand?"

Annie glared at her, her eyes looking like blood moons. "What, you want to learn how to do this now?" she wailed. "Why, so you can take my job? I know you hate me being your boss, but there's no way you're ever getting my job! Get the hell out of here, or I'll report you to Tyler." Tyler was the department head and Annie's boss.

Sara's mouth dropped. Annie's deeply disturbing petulance couldn't have been exhaustion; her hair fell lank, her cheeks were ashen, and her eyes had sunk into deep hollows. Sara shut the door and hurried away from the room, speaking quietly, "Implant...connect Tyler Cook 319."

Within seconds, Tyler responded. "Can I help you Sara?"

"Yes, I think you need to come down to the lab. Something's wrong with Annie. She looks sick, perspiring, blood shot eyes, and she's very irritated, almost irrational. I'm really worried."

"What's she doing?"

"She's in the Hazmat Room analyzing the soil samples from Cygnus."

"I'll be right there. Make sure she stays in the room." He spoke sternly.

Sara tried to look busy but watched Annie out of the corner of her eye. Annie rarely used profanities, but in the time it took her to stomp back to her lab stool, Sara heard about every flavor of cuss imaginable.

Annie finished the potty mouth rendition with the compound variety "bitch-fuck!"

Annie sat back down with a scowl on her face that seemed to stretch across the room. Her normally meticulous work habits had gone terribly awry, giving way to a mess that reminded Sara of her college days. As Annie squinted at the chaos, blood started dripping from her nose making a colorful collage on the collar of her lab coat. Sara continued to watch her. When Annie finally noticed the blood, she ran to the sink.

At the same moment, Tyler burst through the lab door, running in the direction of the Hazmat Room. Sara followed. His charge must have caught Annie's attention; she looked up, meeting his glare. Her eyes were demon red, and blood formed crusted clumps on her lashes. She blinked several times before they fully opened.

"Good God! Computer, lock down Hazmat Room Lab Three." The door to the Hazmat Room instantly bolted, locking Annie in the room, and the red light above the door started flashing. "Implant...Security," Tyler continued. "It looks like we have a possible case of Cygnoid Fever up in Lab Three. I need a medical team up here stat!"

Tyler looked like an animal on the hunt as he panned the room. "I want everyone out of here now. Clear the lab!"

Sara started to panic. She ran toward Tyler yelling, "I'm not leaving her. What's going on? How could she have Cygnoid fever, she's too careful. The samples were tested for the microbe after it was treated."

Looking like a surreal creature in a gruesome nightmare, Annie fled across the Hazmat Room and threw herself against the door. Tears of blood were paving highways down her cheeks. Her nose was smeared with blood as though she'd taken a head reeling punch, and she coughed a continuous fountain of blood. "Unlock this door," she clamored. "Let me out you bastards. What are you doing to me? You're trying to kill me so Sara can take my job. That was your plan all along. You bastards." Annie persisted in a garbled frenzy pounding both fists over and over again on the window of the door. "Let me out now!"

Tyler turned to Sara. "Did she leave the room since she started working with the soil samples?"

"Yes, she came out because she cut her finger on the rim of one of the vials. I mended it for her."

"Did you wear gloves?"

"No."

"Go wash your hands thoroughly and put gloves on and stay clear of anything she may have touched." Tyler followed her to the sink, washed his own hands, and pulled out two sets of gloves, masks, and goggles from the cupboard, handing one set to Sara. "Put these on and touch nothing."

With urgency, he made his way to the Hazmat door and hit the intercom button. The wails from inside the room became deafening. He spoke with a calm, yet stern tone. "Annie you need to listen to me. You're sick. We've called the medics. You may be contagious, so we can't open the door until they arrive. You need to stay calm. No one is trying to hurt you. We're going to help you, but you need to calm down."

Sara thought she may be able to reach Annie. She swallowed hard to try to clear the knot from her throat and said, "Annie, honey, Tyler's telling the truth. You're sick, and it's making you confused and paranoid." Her words came out stuttered, and she took a deep breath to try to gain some composure. It did little for her. "No one's trying to hurt you. We love you. You need to calm down, and we'll get you to the hospital."

Sara was mistaken. Her attempt to rationalize with Annie unleashed her fury and sent her further off the deep end. "Don't tell me what to think. I know your plan. I thought you were my friend. God damn you for this!" Annie was beyond reasoning. Her shrieks had become earth-shattering, and her fists had started bleeding from her incessant pounding. "I hate you. I hate you both! Let me out of here."

An agonizing ten minutes passed before her pounding finally stopped. Sara could hear the medics coming down the hall, but her churning stomach told her the situation was shadowed with gloom. Grimacing, Annie spread her wounded hands out on the window like slabs of raw meat. She fell toward the window; her face pressed against the glass. The weight of her body pulled her to the floor leaving an almost opaque layer of blood behind. Tyler and Sara watched in horror as the last image of Annie's bloodied contorted face sank out of sight. Seconds later she fell silent.

The silence was broken by the sound of five people in hazmat suits storming the lab. Tyler gave them a bleak look. "It's too late, but there's nothing that could have been done anyway."

One of the men addressed Tyler. "I'm sorry sir. You'll both have to come with us for decontamination. We've locked down the building until we determine the extent of the outbreak."

As the truth registered in Sara's head, she cried. "No, she can't be dead! Do something; please do something." Tyler took her in his arms. Her cries started to ease into babble. "How could this have happened? She had the samples tested; she's so careful."

Tyler pulled away and spoke with broken words. Tears welled up in his eyes. "I don't know Sara, but I promise you, there'll be an investigation." Nodding ruefully to the medic, he escorted Sara out of the room.

Chapter Seven

The Lyra Accelerator Laboratory owned a number of apartments for visiting scientists, and Ivan had insisted Laura take one during her sabbatical. "The apartments are quite lovely," he'd said. "And I'm right around the corner."

This is lovely? Laura thought as she walked through the door. Perhaps, she had a silver spoon stuck in her mouth. As she toured the place, she thought it would loosen, and she could pull it out but not so. The tacky roadside motel décor and zany, tapestry style wall hangings were blatant relics from the new wave period twenty odd years ago that left her cold. As a kid, she remembered thinking the tapestries with their crazed faces and pseudo-real grins were hilarious. Now they reminded her of strange Picassos and did nothing other than frighten her. As she traveled from room to room, she counted five of them; that meant ten eyes watching her every move.

By the time she finished her work term, maybe she'd have names for her creepy new friends, but for now she had to make the best of it. Admittedly, she was spoiled, and that silver spoon may accompany her to the grave. And yes, the apartment lacked the European flair of her chalet in Switzerland near ECN, but it was clean and comfortable. Fortunately, she'd given herself a day to get settled and being a light packer, the place started to feel like home in under an hour.

She'd brought a picture of her family at their California beach house taken during a recent reunion in celebration of her father's retirement. As she looked at the photo, it seemed to come alive; and for a moment, she felt as though she could jump right into it, like something you'd read in a children's story. The early morning sky was the deepest of blue, the color of sapphire. The five of them, in their shorts and T-shirts, stood on the beach with the surf just wetting their toes. The sun, still low in the sky, cast its radiance, turning the white sand into a bed of sparkling crystals and the gentle tide into a shimmering glass blanket.

A close family friend made the trek all the way from Draco for the week and took the job of photographer. Of the many photos he shot, Laura decided to frame the one with her dad making rabbit ears over her head. It captured the quirky sense of humor they shared. Laura loved visiting with her family, but it was always a question of having the time to escape her busy job.

She put the picture on the wood veneer cabinet in the living room, took a step back, and gave it a nod. Her moment of reminiscing tweaked her memory to call John, the man behind the camera. She was very fond of him, and although he wasn't an actual relative, she referred to him as Uncle John. He lived on the nearby planet Draco, and he'd been hounding Laura to come and spend a weekend with him while she was in the area. They hadn't picked a date, but she was looking forward to seeing him.

* * * *

Laura's *settle in* day seemed to have whizzed by. She checked the clock and ran to get her briefcase. With her efficiency in finding a place for everything, she'd forgotten where she'd put her notebook. She hated being late, and on her first day… She cringed and started to search. It took two minutes to scour the apartment, and when she found it, she slipped it into her briefcase. She swigged back her last bit of coffee and was off.

The accelerator complex ran along one end of the base station. As she started the fifteen-minute walk, she thanked herself for wearing flats. *Comfort before looks.* Besides, she wanted to look professional. Plain black pants and a fitted white blouse buttoned almost to the top fit the bill perfectly.

The Lyra Base Station was half the size of Eagle and a bit of a disappointment; however, Laura was confident the Particle Accelerator Laboratory would more than compensate. As she entered the neighborhood concourse, she spied Ivan's street up ahead on the right. She made a point not to look too carefully, for fear of bumping into him. During their flight to the Lyra Base Station, Ivan suggested they have breakfast together on the morning of her first day of work. Fortunately, she had a library of convenient excuses to dodge that bullet. When the flight had arrived, he'd invited her to join him for a *business* dinner. She looked at it as an opportunity to make a good professional impression and accepted. As much as she denied it, in recent months ECN had become outranked by the Lyra Accelerator. The timing of decommissioning of the ECN accelerator couldn't have been worse, coinciding exactly with a rush of the most revolutionary research in centuries from the Lyra facility. To top it off was the highly publicized grant, and Enertech's goal to take energetic particle collectors to the next level. Secretly, part of the reason she'd volunteered to come to the Lyra Accelerator for the work term was out of self-interest. She figured it would give her a leg up in acquiring a job there if ECN was disbanded.

Unfortunately, the business dinner did not turn out as she'd planned. Ivan took her to a quiet, romantic restaurant and filled the evening with inappropriate personal questions. Then there was his goodbye. He gave her a kiss on the cheek that left behind an off-putting residue of oil and cologne. While he could be a very pleasant and well-spoken man, he was definitely not a person she wanted to become too friendly with. He reminded her of the James Bond remakes. *Shaken, not stirred;* his counterfeit *savoir faire* left her both shaken and stirred.

As Laura continued her walk, her mind drifted to the cute guy who'd asked her out after her talk. Her long, dry academic career had a way of scaring men off, at least the ones she'd ever consider dating. Although she hated being single, she hated bad dates even more. Especially those with men who shared her technical interests and enjoyed talking shop in lieu of having fun. Dean had come across as an unusual guy: cute, awkwardly shy, and to the point. She wasn't sure in what category he belonged, but something told her he had an interesting spark. She hoped he'd call her.

The entrance to the accelerator complex was an impressive trip down memory lane with an exciting line-up of holographic displays paying tribute to all the greats in the world of particle physics, Einstein, Charpak, Cooper, Kolavich…they were all there. Laura made her way to the receptionist who sat at a polished marble topped desk with a brushed brass sign mounted above it beaming LYRA PARTICLE ACCELERATOR LABORATORY.

"Hi, I'm Laura Simmons...here to see Ivan Campbell."

"Good morning, Dr. Simmons, we've been expecting you, and welcome to the Lyra Accelerator. I'll let Ivan know you're here."

"Thank you." Laura made her way over to the displays to pass the time. Far too quickly, she heard the familiar drawl.

"Good morning, Laura. Don't you look lovely today? Did you manage to get settled in yesterday?"

"Yes, thank you." The discomfort she'd felt during their dinner returned like a bad toothache, and she decided she would make her best attempt to be standoffish without being rude. As he approached her, she immediately caught a whiff of his offensive cologne.

"Well, I've got a busy day planned for you. I thought you could take a few moments to get settled into your office, and then I'll give you a tour and make some introductions. Of course, you met a few of my colleagues at the symposium already." Ivan gestured toward the door behind him. "Shall we?"

Laura smiled politely and followed. "Unfortunately, things were very rushed at the symposium. I'm looking forward to having the time to continue discussions with a couple of the people I met. Their work is brilliant. I find it quite humbling."

Laura followed Ivan through the door and down a long hallway. They soon arrived at the central support staff area. Individual offices lined its perimeter, and there was a coffee lounge at the far end. Ivan continued past half a dozen offices and made an immediate right.

"Here we are. This is your new home. My office is only two doors down next to the coffee lounge."

Laura gave Ivan an approving smile. "What a view! I didn't think you'd be able to see the Herculis Nebula from here."

"You can't see the whole thing, but it is breathtaking. We tried to match the carpeting to the blue-green of its center. It was a bit of a challenge given the way the colors change. We've found the edge of the nebula in the darker red region to be a good source of leptons and quarks for the accelerator."

After admiring the view, Laura took a few seconds to survey the room. The office was nicely appointed with oak furnishings. Laura set her briefcase down on the desk next to the computer monitor and turned to Ivan. "Well this is great, and I'm glad to hear the coffee's only a few steps away."

"Let's get some java. I can show you my office on the way." Ivan put his hand on her shoulder and gave her a gentle nudge in the direction of the door. Laura took a few large steps to get a head start.

As promised, the first stop was his office. Ivan's assistant occupied the office directly off the central area, and a door adjacent to her desk provided access to his. "I'd like you to meet my assistant, Pam." Pam was a very attractive, tall woman with auburn hair and a Mediterranean complexion. "Pam, this is Dr. Laura Simmons, from ECN. As you know, she's going to be working with us for a few months."

Laura reached out and shook her hand. "Nice to meet you." *What a surprise…he has a hot assistant.*

A few more steps, and they were through the door into Ivan's office, which was over three times the size of the one allocated to Laura. The mahogany desk looked as though it had been purchased at an estate auction, and there was a leather couch, a large storage closest, and some very tasteful wildlife paintings. The most prominent hung above his desk and seemed to be full of negative energy—the kill or be killed kind of energy. A gnarly limb from a *haunted* white pine cast its imprint on the forest floor with lightening strike clarity. Fallen needles fought sword fights in the air and underneath them, a fox cowered in its last moments of life. The snarling wolf had the yellow-orange eyes of a demon with teeth like a jagged old fence. The fear in the fox's eyes was piercing, and it took little imagination to visualize how the scene would play out.

Ivan instantly remarked on Laura's interest in the paintings. "You look like you have some appreciation of fine art."

"I'm by no means an art critic, but I have to admit these are striking."

"Thank you. They're all Thompson's. He's by far my favorite artist. A common theme among his work is survival of the fittest. It's quite captivating, wouldn't you say?"

"Captivating and bone chilling! I don't think I'd like to be that fox."

Ivan let out a chuckle. "Yes, I think it would be better to be the wolf. Can I tempt you with a cup of our fine coffee?"

"I've never been known to refuse one."

Ivan led the way to the coffee lounge and poured a couple of cups from a large silver thermal carafe. "I prefer a thermos. It holds the rich fullness of the coffee longer." He signaled to the cream and sugar on the counter and said, "As you like it." As he prepared his coffee, he put in a call to Ron Fieldman, head of security for the Accelerator Laboratory.

"Can you meet me in Dr. Simmons' office? We need to get her set up." There was a slight pause. "Thanks."

Ivan turned and led Laura back to her office. Moments later a man shadowed the doorway. He was short, uniformed, and looked like he could operate a jackhammer. "Good morning, Dr. Simmons, I'm Ron Fieldman, head of security...call me Ron. Welcome aboard."

Laura usually found security people to be quite intimidating, but Ron's wide smile certainly did not fit that persona. "Nice to meet you, Ron." She offered her hand, and he gave it a firm, confident shake.

"Ron can explain the security in the facility and the sections you'll have access to. He'll also get you set up on the computer system. I'll be back in a few minutes." Ivan exited the room.

Ron started by holding up a DNA scanner. "Everyone who walks through the door at the Accelerator is DNA scanned so their movements can be monitored. A bit *big brother* but necessary for a high security operation. The complex is divided into five sections that extend the length of the accelerator. Section One is at one end of the complex, and Section Five is at the other. We are in Section Two right now. All the offices are here. The Control Room for the accelerator is located at the middle of the complex in Section Three. The sections are accessed through a central corridor. The DNA scanners in each section update every ten minutes, so if you're spending hours relaxing in the coffee lounge, I'll know it." Ron laughed. "Ivan has authorized access for you everywhere, with the exception of Section Four."

Laura interrupted. "What's in Section Four?"

Ron glared directly at Laura and spoke with a frank voice. "That's where we torture trespassers." A boisterous laugh followed. "Just kidding! It's high security stuff. Sorry, not for guest workers." He finished with a solemn expression, which left Laura regretting having asked the question.

"The DNA scanners at the doorways will permit you automatic access to all of the other sections. All you need to do is wave your hand in front of the scanner, and the door will open. They're quite sensitive. The layout of the facility is very basic. I'm sure after Ivan shows you around, you'll feel quite at home." Ron softened his look with a gentle smile as he placed the DNA scanner on the desk. "All I need you to do is place your thumb on the scanner." Laura obediently followed his instructions, and he pressed the button marked "scan."

Within seconds, the device prompted him. "Scanning complete, please provide identification."

"Dr. Laura Simmons authorization Sections One, Two, Three, and Five. Computer access approved."

"Authorization accepted."

"Good, we're done. How about you come around, and I'll show you the login procedure for the computer. I'm sure it's the same as you have at ECN." Ron walked around to the other side of the desk and angled the thin crystalline monitor toward Laura. "It couldn't be simpler. All you do is press your thumb against the scanner on the side of the screen, and you're logged on. The keyboard senses your DNA, and the voice recognition system recognizes your voice, so the computer knows if someone else is using a computer you're logged on to. If you leave your office for more than ten minutes, the section scanners will pick it up, and you'll be automatically logged off. Any questions?"

"No, you're right. This is the same system we have at ECN."

"Good, let's do the voice activation." Laura pressed her thumb on the scanner at the side of the monitor. The screen immediately displayed, 'Welcome, Laura Simmons.' Ron spoke up, "Computer voice recognition for Laura Simmons." He then turned to her and said, "Clearly say this sentence: Peter gave Sally a large delicious red apple."

Laura smirked then followed the instructions, and the mono-toned computer voice indicated, "Voice recognition accepted."

"Well, you're all set." Just as Ron made his assertion, Ivan appeared at the doorway. "Perfect timing, we've just finished. Laura, I'm sure I'll run into you later. Enjoy your tour." Ron nodded to her on his way out the door.

"He seems like a nice guy," Laura said.

"He is, but don't let his charm fool you. He's as tough as nails. Just what we need around here. We're in Section Two now, and I thought we'd start at the end of the complex with Section Five. It's a pod hangar, and the collision particles collected from the Nebula are kept there in a containment unit. That will save the best for after lunch...the Control Room in Section Three. The Detector and Hazmat Rooms are in Section One, but we can probably skip the other part of that section. There's a direct connection to the base station for deliveries and a big storage area."

"I'm just going to get my notebook to take along." Laura took the leather booklet from her briefcase. Her name was embossed in gold on the top right corner. "Okay, all set."

Ivan guided Laura out of her office, through a door at the end of the hallway and down a flight of stairs. The stairs spilled out into a large industrial corridor, which looked like a narrow runway. The metallic walls reflected the intermittent ceiling lights and seemed to continue forever in both directions, merging into two vortexes at either end. Carts carrying people and equipment motored along the sides of the corridor, and the sound echoed along its length like clanging on a pipe. "Talk about tunnel vision. I feel like a sewer rat. Are we around the middle of the accelerator? One kilometer looks very long when you're looking at it from this perspective. I'm glad I wore flat shoes."

Ivan nodded. "Actually it is very long. That's why we're going to take a cart." He signaled her to hop into the cart parked off to the side of the hallway in a small alcove.

Chapter Eight

It had been almost three hours since the tour began. Laura wasn't good with names and with the exception of the few people they had lunch with, she'd already forgotten everyone else's. She found Section Five to be quite interesting. It was a vast hangar the size of a football stadium with an airlock on one end. The Accelerator had three pods dedicated to high-energy particle collection from the nebula. However, Ivan did admit they were occasionally used for transport of senior level personnel.

A large black particle storage unit stood along the side of the hangar. The unit sat about two meters high with a long tubular design and was mounted on a series of short legs. It left Laura with the impression that one day it might morph into a giant metallic butterfly. Located along its side were two large rectangular viewports, and inside it looked like the swirling high-energy particles were performing the *hula*. There were portals located at each end of the unit. Particles collected from the nebula could be loaded through one. The other led to a particle separator, which exited to a small removable containment unit for loading particles into the accelerator for collisions.

While they were in the hangar, one of the pods arrived piloted by Kevin Cowen, who Laura learned was not only a resident pilot but also the Control Room engineer. Kevin joined them on their tour, which pleased Laura as it diluted Ivan's presence. She found Kevin to be a rather unattractive man, but she enjoyed his sense of humor. She'd decided if he didn't lose too much more hair, he would make a fine jolly old Saint Nick one day. A touch of gray had already taken root in his un-kept mop.

The well-appointed lunchroom certainly outranked the typical *grab a nasty sandwich* cafeteria at most industrial facilities. Over the course of her dinner with Ivan, Laura had coined him a foody as he had gone on at length about all the fine dining restaurants he liked to frequent. She couldn't believe he wasn't fat. His culinary obsession was clearly demonstrated by the selection in the lunchroom buffet.

Laura had the chicken cordon bleu with wild mushroom risotto and spring vegetables, which made her thankful for all the walking she'd done earlier.

* * * *

Ivan got up from the lunch table. "I hope you enjoyed your lunch, Laura. I feel good food makes for a productive afternoon."

"I'm not sure I agree. I feel like I need a nap now, but it was delicious. Thank you."

Before lunch, they'd parked their cart in the alcove by the lunchroom, and Laura had noticed the door across the corridor was boldly identified as "Section Four." The sign to the immediate right read HIGH SECURITY, RESTRICTED ACCESS, in deep red lettering. They left the lunchroom, and Laura stopped to get her notebook from the cart. At the same moment, a man wearing a suit almost as fancy as Ivan's entered the restricted section. Laura couldn't stifle her curiosity and glanced through the door to see if she could see what all the fuss was about. She saw a hallway leading to a larger room beyond. There appeared to be another small alcove off to the side of the entrance.

Ivan scowled. He made an abrupt gesture to Section Three on their left. "Well, I promised I'd leave the best for last."

As they approached the door, Ivan waved his hand in front of the scanner, and it automatically opened, revealing a compact state of the art control room. Laura glanced around, only somewhat impressed. "I was expecting the Control Room to be larger."

Ivan didn't miss the opportunity. "Bigger isn't necessarily better you know."

Laura wasn't sure which was going to make it to the finish line first: embarrassment or anger. Either way, she felt herself becoming flushed and was pretty sure it showed. "What's down there?" she asked curtly, pointing.

Fortunately, Kevin answered. "That leads to the repair module for the accelerator. Come on, I'll show you." He took a of couple steps and entered the first door on the right. The small room, not much bigger than a large closet, had two environmental suits hanging like headless bodies beside a window looking onto the accelerator. "This is just a storage room, but I guess this will be your first glimpse of the accelerator." He walked to the window and pointed at it like a game show host. "Have a look, although this view doesn't do it justice. Of course, all you can see is the radiation shielding. The particle beam is accelerated and focused inside a small diameter copper tube, which as you know conducts electricity and magnetism very well. Being in space, we have no trouble maintaining a vacuum in the tube."

Kevin's girth provided a perfect blind to the view he so happily wanted to show off. Laura set her notebook down on the small table by the door and squeezed past him to have a look. The one meter section of the large cylindrical gray tube she could see was nothing stellar. Laura never understood the awe of looking at the outside of an accelerator. It's inside the copper tube where the action is. *Wow, another big long tube, how exciting.* "What kind of detectors do you use?"

Ivan jumped to answer Laura's question. "Well, first of all, I'll tell you we use a laser to accelerate the particles, and we have a series of superconducting magnets at regular intervals along the accelerator to focus them. They're arranged with alternating poles, so the magnetic field keeps the particle beam confined and focused. As you know, the design allows for the acceleration of two beams of particles toward each other, colliding in the middle or one beam of particles into a stationary target at one end. Accordingly, we have a detector in the middle and also down in Section One, which is the end where collisions occur. As part of the detector system, we have an ion microscope that can be used to reveal the initial structure of the target. After the collision, cryogenic detectors are used to reveal the energy and path of the particles. They're made of semiconducting crystals of germanium and are cooled to within 0.1 degree above absolute zero."

"The best view by far is from within the repair module," Kevin added. With overdone enthusiasm, he turned and continued along the hall to the Utility Room.

The room was somewhat larger than the Control Room and had repair equipment littered through it. The large red toolbox centered on one wall had several of the drawers left ajar, and a pair of work overalls were carelessly slung over the rack on its side. The disheveled room looked more like a backyard workshop than a particle accelerator repair room. There was an airlock at the far end of the room, and beyond that Laura could see a repair module at the docking port.

Kevin continued on like an excited puppy. "The repair module you see runs along the entire length of the accelerator. This is the central docking port, but there's also a port across from Sections One and Five. The module's out just about every day. Usually just general maintenance, but occasionally something more. Sam, our chief repair technician, had it out this morning, and I think later on, he's planning to follow up on some signal interference problems we were having down near Section Two. I'm sure he'd be happy to take you along. He may even let you drive."

Ivan laughed. It was the kind that sounds forced. "Yeah right! You just tell the module where to go, and it takes you there."

Kevin bowed his head slightly. "Well you weren't supposed to tell her that. I thought she'd like an adventure."

As the air filled with tension, Laura decided to play along despite her lack of interest. "Would I have to wear an environmental suit?"

"No, those are only required if you have to exit the module to do a repair. The entire housing of the accelerator is space vacuum and almost as cold. Don't worry, it's all climate controlled in the module, and Sam would give you a good tour. The module scoots along its little monorail pretty quickly."

"Thanks for the offer, but I think I'll pass. I'm claustrophobic," Laura said.

"No problem." Kevin smiled and turned to lead the way back to the Control Room. "We're not running a collision until tomorrow morning, but I can give you a quick review of the system."

Laura followed them back to the Control Room and listened attentively to Kevin's summary of the system highlights. She was highly impressed by the knowledge they both possessed in the area of particle physics. Each of them seemed to have a brilliant grasp of the subject; and despite her years of devotion to the field, she felt to some extent, left in their dust. She made a gallant effort to hold her own in the discussions. When they were finished, the two of them escorted her out of the Control Room.

"Laura, is it okay if you find your own way back to the office area in Section Two? It's only a short walk. I have some business with Kevin in Section Four that will take a few minutes," Ivan said.

"That's just fine, and I could use the walk after my visit to your lunchroom. Thank you both for the tour. I'm sure I'll see you later."

Ivan gave Laura a warm smile. "I'll come by when we're finished."

Ivan and Kevin disappeared into Section Four, and Laura started off down the corridor, walking as fast as she could to burn off her lunch. She covered the distance to the staircase in just over five minutes and then realized she'd left her notebook behind. *Damn!* She made an abrupt about face and headed back to the Control Room. After waving her hand in front of the scanner, the door opened, and she went right in. "Kevin?" The room appeared to be empty, and she continued to the storage room off the hall. At the same instant, Kevin and Ivan returned to the Control Room.

"Kevin, I thought I'd better update you on Dean Weston and Karen Jenkins." Laura froze at the mention of Dean's name.

"Annie Wilson was successfully eliminated yesterday. They're investigating it as an accidental case of Cygnoid Fever. Ironically, things couldn't have worked out better for us. If you can believe it, Karen was the one who ran the safety analysis on the soil samples. Can you imagine what Weston's going to do when he hears his ex-wife screwed up? It couldn't be better."

Laura couldn't believe what she just heard and held her breath. Her head throbbed, and a cold sweat broke out on her forehead as she stood motionless, listening.

"He's probably already got the news about Annie's sad demise. Everyone's lined up for tomorrow night to finish the job. The four of them will finally be out of the way, and we'll be able to carry on worry free. I'm surprised Weston didn't wise up after talking to me at the symposium. I was talking circles around him. The man's inferior."

Kevin softly said, "It's too bad about Karen...she's nice and really pretty. I wish there was another way." His tone perked up. "She has a nice rack!"

"I believe they're called breasts, and I wish there was a way around this too...she is enchantingly beautiful. Weston didn't deserve her. It's no wonder she strayed. Half the time, the man looks like he just walked out of a high school yearbook." Ivan's callus tone suggested a severe lack of repentance. "I will say she was a bit of a know it all. It's unfortunate it had to be this way, but it's not the first time someone was sacrificed for the greater good, nor will it be the last."

"What about Roger? No one suspects anything, I hope."

"Are you kidding? It was the perfect way to get rid of a drunk. I fulfilled my moral obligation and called the family with my condolences."

"I suppose I should have done the same. Oh well, too late now. By the way, I forgot to show you how I improved the containment. The wave frequency is steady and oscillating through the proper range. Why don't we head back, and I'll go over it with you. It will only take a few minutes," Kevin said.

Laura listened carefully for their footsteps to disappear. She'd hardly taken a breath, and the minute they were gone, she gasped. Her first impulse was to get out of Section Three without being seen. Knowing Section Four was only a few steps away, she waited a moment, scooped up her notebook and ran into the corridor.

The corridor was empty except for a cart in the alcove. Thoughts were flooding her head. *I have to warn Dean. I wonder if whatever's in Section Four has something to do with all this.* She darted into the alcove to stay hidden.

As she ducked behind the cart, the same man she'd seen entering Section Four earlier came out of the lunchroom, once again heading in that direction. He didn't notice her, and as the door opened, she had a clear view of the hallway and the room beyond. Ivan and Kevin were nowhere in sight. The man wasted no time and made his way down the hallway, past the small alcove toward the larger room in the back. Fueled by adrenaline, Laura sped behind him, getting through the door to Section Four seconds before it shut. She made a sharp right into the alcove and pressed her back firmly into the wall, praying she hadn't been seen. *What the hell am I doing?* She knew she had at most ten minutes before the next DNA scan would give her away. She stood silently listening for voices. Her short pulsed breaths seemed deafening. Kevin could be heard in the distance.

"I've adjusted the magnetic field in the storage unit, and it seems to have done the trick. If you look at the monitor, you can see the pulse waves. The frequencies range from as low as 200 up to 1800 hertz with peaks at regular intervals. Very healthy!"

Laura slowly poked her head around the corner. At the back of the room, she could see a storage unit similar to the one she'd seen earlier in Section Five; however, the light show inside looked entirely different, and it wasn't just the fluorescent lighting in the room. Fine lights danced about, flickering through a broad spectrum of colors. *I've never seen energetic particles like that.* Connected to the far end of the storage unit was what appeared to be a small room approximately the size of a closet. The room was sealed off with a large oval hatch just big enough for a person to fit through. *What the hell?* Fighting her temptation to see more, Laura returned to her original position, trying to think of her next move.

"How was your last flight?" Ivan inquired.

"Rough, but better. After flying that texture a few times, it becomes quite predictable. Like riding a rollercoaster over and over again."

"Yeah, I hate rollercoasters, and as I recall you're not too fond of them either."

"That's the old me." Kevin laughed confidently. "All the more reason to leave the flying to me. Just make sure the security is running smoothly. This whole thing makes me nervous. If it ever got out… Christ!"

"Relax, Kevin. Ron's all over this and so is Larry. We have a tight circle. Just leave those worries to me and do your job. Hold on, I've got a call."

"Implant answer…yes." Ivan paused. "What do you think I'm crazy? She's not here."

Laura felt a wave of nausea come over her. *I'm dead!* In a flustered panic, she flew to the door to make her exit.

"Kevin, look around. Ron says Simmons is in here. God damn it, Ron, fix this now! Get down here." Ivan and Kevin started tearing through the Section. "Find her...damn bitch." Ivan yelled.

Chapter Nine

Laura knew escaping down the corridor and walking out the front door was futile. The timing of her explosive exit from Section Four could have been better. A cart had just passed by, but the driver didn't seem to take notice of her. She immediately ran back into Section Three. *The module!* The adrenaline had heightened her instincts to that of a hunted animal, and she quickly formulated a plan. Making a hard left, she tore into the back room and started to outfit herself in the overalls slung over the tool box. The overalls reeked of body odour and not just perspiration; it was the kind of smell that comes from personal filth, the kind deserving of its own name. As she zipped it up, she dry heaved and had to steady herself. As she did, she caught a glimpse of a pocket knife in one of the drawers of the tool box that had been left ajar. She grabbed it and stuck it in the pocket of the overalls. There was a damp tissue in the pocket. She pulled her hand out and covered her mouth, fending off her growing nausea. *Disgusting!*

As Laura made her way through the airlock to the module, she felt her hairs standing on end just like the little fox in the picture on Ivan's wall. She wondered if Ivan's conniving eyes had turned the color of the wolf's. Perhaps his teeth were bared as he hunted for her, saliva dripping from the sides of his mouth. Psyching herself, she jumped into the claustrophobic module, tossing her notebook beside her, and spoke, "Lock door, destination Section One, top speed."

The door of the module hissed shut, and it started to inch along its rail, quickly picking up speed. The intermittent lights along the side of the accelerator started to pass by in a blur providing a strobe effect, only adding to her anxiety. The only relief came from the cold outside nipping at her. Her only hope was that the DNA scans didn't include the module. It wasn't much to hang on to, as it would take little time for them to figure out her plan when they couldn't locate her anywhere else.

* * * *

Ron's voice echoing across Ivan's implant was deafening. "Check the corridor, she can't have gone far. I'll check the door scanners, and I'm setting the DNA scans to run every minute. Don't worry, we can track her, she can't possibly get out."

Ivan and Kevin arrived in the corridor just outside Section Four together. A cart had just passed heading toward Section Five; otherwise the corridor was free of activity. Kevin went to check the lunchroom. As Ivan hollered, the echo muffled his voice, "Hey, down there. Stop."

The cart came to a rolling stop, and the young man driving it poked his head out. "Yes, Mr. Campbell, is there a problem?"

It only took seconds for Ivan to catch up with the cart. "Hey, Amir, we've had a serious security violation. Did you happen to see a young woman come out of Section Four as you passed by?"

"No, sir, but I heard the door open just after I went by. I didn't look back though. Did you check in the lunchroom or Section Three?"

"We're on it. If you see an attractive blonde woman wearing a white blouse, detain her as best you can and notify me immediately."

"Yes, sir." The cart continued on.

Ivan arrived back at the lunchroom just in time to see Kevin on his way out. "She's not in there," Kevin said. They both headed toward the door of Section Three.

Ivan's implant signaled again. It was Ron. "Have you located her?" Ivan asked.

"No, I'm just waiting for the most recent scan results. Over the last ten minutes, I placed her in Section Three before moving to Section Four."

"Section Three, are you sure?"

"Yes. She left there and went immediately into Section Four," Ron asserted.

"If she was in there when we were talking...Christ!"

"Talking? Is there a problem?" Ron said.

Ivan shouted, "Yeah, a big one. We have to find her, or we're finished. Do you understand me?"

"Ivan, I have the scan results. Apparently she went back into Section Three a few minutes ago. The security team should be there any second."

"Good. We're on our way in there now."

* * * *

The journey to Section One only took a few minutes. The sound of the computer voice calmed Laura's anxiety, and her nausea subsided. "Docking...Section One." The module came to a smooth stop, but it took a couple of minutes before the locking mechanism engaged allowing the door to release. As soon as the green exit light came on, she opened the door and jumped out. A sense of relief instantly came over her, but was short lived as she now faced the difficult task of navigating her way out of the facility.

As she approached the airlock door, she could hear a man and a woman talking inside the room. *My God, I'm dead! Keep it cool!* With great repugnance, she unzipped her overalls slightly and unbuttoned her blouse a bit to display some cleavage. She took a calming breath and entered the room. With a flighty voice, she introduced herself. "Hi. I'm Laura Simmons; it's my first day. Kevin Cowan arranged for me to go with Sam for his repair work this afternoon. He said to meet him here. Have you seen him?" Laura played with her hair as she spoke.

"He's not here honey." There was a large gap in the woman's yellowed teeth, and one of them jutted out the side of her lips as she spoke. She sat in a chair, covering every inch of it; her graying, frizzy hair sitting on her head like a fright wig. "I don't know what Kevin told you, but you may want to call him and check your plans. Sam usually likes to work alone, but my guess is he wouldn't mind having you along." She cackled.

"Darn, I was pretty sure he said here. Great, mess up on my first day. Do ya mind if I look around?"

"Go right ahead." The woman turned her attention back to the man she had been talking with.

One hurdle! Laura rolled up the sleeves of the baggy overalls and pranced her way to the exit holding her head high. "Thanks, guys."

"Hey, you got some gum stuck to your ass." This time it was the coarse voice of the man.

Laura stopped and turned her head around to examine the clump for herself. "Oh, would ya look at that...ever gross. These were a loaner. I guess the first stop is the washroom." She giggled and continued toward the exit.

* * * *

It only took seconds for Ivan and Kevin to search Section Three. "What the hell! Where could she have gone?" Ivan slammed his hand against the wall.

"Jesus, the module's gone. Computer, locate the repair module ," Kevin said.

A computer voice sounded. "The repair module is docked at Section One."

"Damn it!" Ivan placed another call to Ron. "It looks like she took the module to Section One."

"Yeah, that would explain why the recent scan didn't pick her up. I have a confirmation on her location now. I'm locking her access to all the door scanners, so we should be able to trap her. I'll notify Section One security. I'm on my way there now."

* * * *

Laura entered the corridor and found it bustling with activity. With eagle eyes, she looked around to see if she could see any signs of the loading area connected to the base station. A small forklift heaped with boxes passed through a door down the corridor on the right, and she decided to check it out. Sure enough, the sign above the door read, LOADING BAY. She was about to go in when she noticed a cart heading toward her at top speed with Ron at the wheel.

Oh my God! Her few moments of relief were now overwhelmed with horror. She waved her hand in front of the door scanner, but nothing happened. *Christ, they must have locked me out!* Her hands were shaking, and she could feel the veins in her temples bulging. In a frantic move, she grabbed the tissue from her pocket then reached down and pulled the gum off the back of her overalls. It was still moist.

Sticking the gum to the tissue, she wrapped the entire mess around her hand then waved it madly in front of the scanner. The door opened.

The loading bay was quite large, but seemed stunted beside the large storage room to which it was connected. There were about a dozen people working in the area, moving equipment and supplies. A couple of people noticed her walk through the door but paid little attention. There was a small refrigeration truck with the insignia, LYRA FOOD SUPPLIERS, on its side parked at the back. A few boxes were stacked at the rear of the truck, and it looked like the driver was about to close it up. Knowing this was her only chance, Laura marched up to the man purposefully and said, "Hi, there. Mr. Campbell put a special order in for a couple dozen ducks. Do you know if they arrived in this shipment?"

"Ducks? There's no ducks in these boxes. This order's for beef, pork, and some fresh produce."

Laura glanced toward the truck and gestured to the remaining boxes inside. "You know Mr. Campbell." She rolled her eyes and flicked her hair out of the way. "He asked me to check specifically. Do you mind if I have a peek. God forbid if he doesn't get his precious ducks."

The man chortled. "Sure, but make it quick. I'm just loading these boxes onto the skid, and I'm out of here. I've got three more deliveries to make, and it's almost three o'clock."

"No problem, I'll be two secs." Laura jumped into the back of the truck as the man got to work. She waited until he was out of sight and hid behind some boxes.

A minute later she heard his voice again. "Hey, did you find your ducks?"

Laura sat motionless. *Come on, go!* The doors clunked shut leaving her in near darkness. A moment later, the sound of the engine filled the air, and the truck took off.

* * * *

Just as the truck slipped away from the loading bay, Ron burst through the door with the security team. "I want all exits locked down.

No one goes in or out!" Ron directed two security officers in the direction of the storage area and blurted, "Search the room, she can't have got far." Ron and another man set their attention on the loading bay. "A blonde woman came in here just a few moments ago. Did any of you notice where she went?"

One of the workers responded. "I saw her walk in, but that's all."

"I heard her talking to Hank. Something about ducks," remarked another.

"Who's Hank?" Ron inquired.

"The guy from Lyra Food Services. He delivers twice a week. He just pulled out."

"Damn it." Ron yelled. "Continue searching the area."

Chapter Ten

Laura sat huddled in a ball toward the front of the truck, and she could feel the tears starting to well. The last thirty minutes played out in her head like a typhoon, and she felt the nausea returning. She held out her hands. They were shaking so hard she had to ball them into fists to get them to stop. She started to whisper to herself, "Keep it together; just keep it together." Between the *eau de sour milk* hanging in the air and the reek of the overalls, she felt like she was breathing in a toxic fog. She stood up, ripped the overalls off and kicked them into the corner; the cool air being the only thing keeping her from succumbing to the head spins.

Laura sat back down for some *thinking time* as she liked to call it; time to clear her head and listen to her inner voice of reason. She wondered what it would tell her. She'd never been running for her life. To fight off the chill setting in, her mind first drifted to some warm thoughts: her family.

Laura grew up in a secure environment with her mother, father, and two siblings. She still thought of her older brother as a *pain in the neck*, but she loved him to death; and her younger sister had become one of her closest friends. Having grown up in suburban San Diego, she had decided to pursue her university education at Stanford to be close to home. She earned a doctorate in particle physics and upon graduating joined ECN where she worked for the past seven years. At thirty-three years of age, she was quite happy with her life, and she'd be damned if Ivan was going to put a kink in it.

To Laura's best recollection, the biggest fiasco of her life was the time in high school when her brother and his friends talked her into joining them on a late night excursion to toilet paper a neighbor's house. Deflecting the *wimpy girl* image, she joined in. They quietly carried out the task snickering to each other in the moonlight and then made their break. The next morning, a police officer came to the door gripping a student I.D. card belonging to none other than Laura Simmons. She'd apparently dropped it at the crime scene. Laura was held accountable while her brother sat laughing at the top of the stairs. The whole ordeal left her with a severe distaste for conflict. Since that time, she had kept herself on the straight and narrow and had never had to deal with an emergency. She always wondered how she would measure up if she did.

So far, her quick-thinking getaway had surprised her, but the adrenaline rush aftermath was just starting to hit. She took a few deep breaths to ease her queasiness and then lifted her head up to look around. The only light came through the small window on one side of the truck. As much as she tried to deny it, her inner voice told her she had to keep running.

Laura got to her feet, took the knife from the overalls, and tucked it in the pocket of her pants. *What would that little fox in the picture do now?* Stumbling slightly in the darkness, she made her way to the back of the truck, steadying herself against the boxes. The window provided minimal light, suggesting they were possibly in one of the service tunnels connecting the domes of the base station. She had been traveling for almost ten minutes, and she knew she was running out of time. She located a leaver on the back door and pulled it down firmly with both hands. *Please don't be locked.* She sighed in relief when the door flung open.

The truck was bolting through a tunnel that looked like a larger version of the main corridor at the accelerator. During the few seconds that Laura had been peering out of the back of the truck, she'd already passed a loading bay. Laura prided herself on her physical fitness, but knew it would do little to help her out of this situation. It reminded her of her brother's gutsy sky diving escapades, which he constantly bragged about. He always said, "You can't think about it. You just go." *Easy for him to say. This is for you Kyle!* Laura took one step and was out.

Thud! The landing was hard, knocking the wind out of her. The roll—flip—roll played out in slow motion, nothing like in the movies. It hurt; it hurt a lot, and she wasn't about to spring to her feet and break into a heroic run. She lay still for an instant to ascertain the extent of her injuries: achy and shook up but no sharp pain. She cautiously got to her feet and headed in the direction of the loading bay she'd just passed.

* * * *

On his way back to the security office, Ron put in the dreaded call to Ivan. "That bitch got away in the damn food truck, but don't worry. I'm on it." He tuned out the verbal backlash like it was bad static. He didn't have to listen to know what Ivan was saying.

Ivan finished his rant with, "I'll meet you there in five minutes."

And what the hell are you going to do? Ron hated people stepping onto his playing field. He knew bloody well what had to be done to get rid of this headache. The job had escalated to the level of external authorities, and he called Larry Dunn, the head marshal in charge of the Lyra Base Station security. Larry was aware of the research being carried out in Section Four. Ron and Larry saw eye to eye when it came to security matters; formal protocols were for the meek and timid. Ron briefed Larry on every detail of the situation and the repercussions if she wasn't intercepted.

"Don't worry Ron. We'll get on it right away. You can track anyone by their cochlear implant. It will just take me a few minutes to get authorization to do it. I can block her account, but if she manages to buy a ticket to get off the base station before it's blocked, at least I'll know about it. I've already blocked any communication from her implant." Larry's reassuring voice did little to calm Ron's nerves. It was Ron's fault she made it out of the facility in the first place, and as soon as Ivan arrived, he'd have to answer for it.

* * * *

Laura arrived at the loading bay only to find it was the main bay for the Base Station Mall. The doors were open, and when she went through, she was stopped by two men who appeared to be in their early twenties. "Excuse me, you can't come through here. You'll have to walk down there about five hundred meters to the mall entrance." The man pointed in the direction she had just come from. "What are you doing in a service tunnel on foot anyway? You're liable to get run down."

Laura was starting to feel like a master con artist. "I'm sorry. I was running my boyfriend's delivery route with him, and we had a fight. Bastard kicked me out of the truck. Please can I come in here?"

Both men looked her up and down then chuckled. Laura glanced down at herself. Her shirt was un-tucked, and she could only imagine what her hair looked like. "Sounds like you need to get a new boyfriend," one of them said. Laura nodded as she hurried past them through the loading dock, continuing out into the mall.

As much as she wanted to contact Dean, she knew that communication between base stations was not secure. She would have to get over to Eagle to talk to him in person, but the question forming in her mind was how to stay one step ahead of Ivan's people. She made a quick glance around for a travel kiosk. On a base station, everyone but the elite traveled by monorail, so she figured she could locate one easily. There wasn't one within eyeshot, so she picked a direction and walked as quickly as she could without sprinting.

As Laura rounded a corner, she found herself entangled in a crowd of excited teenagers loitering about a concourse surrounding a center stage. The noise of the crowd was overpowered by the announcer pumping their enthusiasm. "Come fight the ninja, choose your weapon, highest score so far is eighty-four!" At the center of the crowd, a young teenage boy with a bow attacked the holographic ninja towering over him. It took several minutes for Laura to successfully meander through the cheering crowd, and she was fortunate to come across a kiosk about twenty meters further down the mall.

She held her hand up to the scanner on the kiosk. The voice prompted her. "Welcome Laura Simmons, how can I help you?"

"I would like to purchase a ticket to the Eagle Base Station. What is the availability in the next few hours?"

"The seven o'clock flight has three seats available. The eight o'clock flight has one seat available."

"Stop," Laura paused for a moment. "I'll take the seat on the eight o'clock flight."

"Is there anything else?"

"Yes, a day monorail pass. That's all."

"Your account has been debited, printing tickets." Laura grabbed the tickets and followed the signs to the monorail station.

Once at the station, her first stop was the washroom. She looked for the handicapped one as she wanted some privacy. Once inside, she locked the door and washed her face and hands thoroughly. The soap smelled of antiseptic, and her skin tingled as it dried. Looking in the mirror, she peered into her bloodshot eyes and realized it was no surprise that the two men let her pass so easily. Her appearance had not weathered well, and within minutes, it was going to be worse. Reaching into her pocket, she pulled out the small knife. Her hand shook in anticipation of her next move. She laid some paper towel out on the counter, washed the knife, and then tucked her hair tightly behind her right ear being careful to get every strand. Locating the small bump inside her ear she held the tip of the sharp knife close to it. She hesitated a moment. "Come on focus, you can do this," she whispered. She took a deep breath and touched the tip of the knife to her skin.

The door handle rattled interrupting her little pep talk. A knock followed. "Hey you gonna be long? I gotta go."

"Just a minute, please." *Christ just what I need!*

Laura's hand continued to shake. She leaned over the counter and with the knife made a small incision in her skin. She winced with pain as the warm blood started to trickle down her hand and cheek. She dug into the wound with her fingernails, trying to get a grip on the miniature implant. The knocking continued. "Just a minute," she barked. Finally, Laura was successful and retrieved the device sandwiched between her manicured index finger and thumb nails.

Without delay, she set the device down on the towel and applied pressure to the wound. Two drops of blood had already soiled her white blouse, and her hair was becoming streaked. She washed away what she could and packaged the implant carefully in a piece of towel and then slipped it into her pocket. Concealing the injury to the best of her ability, she cleaned up and left.

"You're not even handicapped, you jerk!" The middle aged woman wore a vicious scowl and wheeled her way through the door, almost running Laura over.

Laura made her way to the monorail map. There were three main monorail lines running from one end of the base station to the other. Two of the lines followed along the perimeter of the base station, and the third went directly through the middle and was the shortest. She was presently at the bottom of the map at Mall Station. The spaceport was at the opposite end of the base station, and her apartment was one station to the right, on the map. She headed in the direction of the monorail traveling to the left, away from her apartment.

She stood on the platform for a few minutes fielding a few stares before the monorail arrived. Hustling to the opening doors, she pulled the implant out of her pocket, threw it in and then darted off in the opposite direction. She was hoping her plan would mislead Ivan long enough for her to retrieve her travel documentation from her apartment and get to the spaceport via the more direct route. The key factor in the plan was to be able to change her ticket to the seven o'clock flight at the last minute. If all three seats were gone, she was doomed.

Chapter Eleven

It was only a day after the symposium had wound up, and Dean was overloaded with a sizeable backlog of work. It took him most of the morning to sort through his emails and prioritize his long *to do* list. He took the time for a quick bite and returned to his office fully motivated. As he walked in, he noticed steam billowing from the coffee maker. "Oh Shannon, you know the way into a man's heart." His assistant was busy knitting at her desk and smiled some happy lines into her face.

He held the cup at face level as he poured so he could admire the kayaking moose hand painted on its side. He had purchased the cup as a souvenir at a gift shop in Banff, Canada on his latest kayaking adventure. He wasn't the souvenir type, but he was spurred on by his two friends who each bought one. In hind sight, it was a good purchase as no matter how stressed he was, the moose always made him laugh.

"I don't know how you get a minute's sleep at night." Shannon's heavy Scottish accent bounced off the walls and broke Dean's concentration on the moose. She started to put her lunch hour knitting away, but first held it up for Dean to see. "Little Emily's two months today." The tiny pink sweater with her granddaughter's name on it disappeared into a plastic bag.

"And when do I get to see some more pictures?" Dean couldn't care less about seeing pictures of strangers' babies, but he knew Shannon loved to show them.

"Tomorrow, I promise." Her beaming eyes made Dean glad he'd asked.

Dean added a small amount of milk to his coffee and after setting it down, reached for another cup, placed a bag of mint tea in it, and filled it up with boiling water from the machine. A minty fragrance quickly filled the room. "Ahh, you're a good man, Dean."

Dean formed a grin that mimicked the expression on the moose, and he handed the tea to Shannon. "You may as well join the party." The two had only worked together for a few months, but he'd become quite fond of her. She was very motherly toward him and constantly fussed over him, making sure he looked well turned out. One day she went as far as to catch up with him on his way into his office and stuff the back of his shirt into his pants complaining that it was billowing out too much. "You need a woman in your life to keep you tailored. You're a handsome young man, get out there," she ordered. As soon as he was back in his office, he'd pulled it out again.

"Oh, by the way, Lilly from the Utilities Department wants you to call her. She says it's urgent," Shannon said.

"Well this can't be good. I wonder if I'm going to get any work done today." Dean disappeared into his office with his coffee and sat down at his rustic pine desk. He immediately placed a call to Lilly.

"Hey, Lilly...Dean. What's up?"

"Thanks for getting back to me so quickly. We have what I hope is a temporary power shortage, and I'd like to schedule some rotating brownouts to compensate. I just wanted to clear it with you."

"Power shortage? What's the cosmic particle density like around the grid?" The base station was powered by an immense network of particle collector plates mounted on a power grid adjacent to it.

"It's down by fifteen percent. Probably from all the extra space traffic from the symposium," Lilly said.

"That'll do it. Traffic's back to normal, but it will likely take a couple of days to get the grid back to acceptable levels. If it's down by fifteen percent, rotating brownouts won't be enough. We should lower the lights to emergency levels throughout the station from eleven o'clock tonight until six tomorrow morning. I'll make a public announcement. My guess is there will be a bit of an uproar about the brownouts. Keep me posted on the levels."

Dean ended the call, sent out the announcement, and turned his attention to the pile of work on his desk. Before he had a chance to make much headway, he found himself fielding complaints from all over the station. They were all the same. Everyone had an urgent matter requiring full power. He could have put Shannon on the calls, but he thought that would be cruel. Her temperament did not handle stress well.

Dean's implant signaled yet again. *For God's sake!* "Yes, Weston here." He didn't mean to sound exasperated, but enough was enough. He started to delve into his explanation for the power outages when a weak and disjointed voice interrupted him.

"Hi, Dean, my name's Sara. I'm a close friend of Annie Wilson. She's told me lots about you. Everything good."

Dean relaxed in his chair for a moment. "Hi, Sara. Annie was going on about you the other night. I hear the two of you are working together now, that's great. What can I do for you?" There was a pause. "Sara…are you still there?"

"Yes, sorry, I can hardly talk. Something's happened." Sara's voice wavered as she started to cry. "Sorry, I'll try to…um…get this out. It's not easy, but I know you two were really good friends, and I wanted to tell you myself."

"Tell me what? What's happened?" Dean had an ominous feeling come over him. All he could make out from Sara were sniffing noises. "Please what's wrong? Is something wrong with Annie?"

"The soil samples. One of them was contaminated, and she got infected. Dean, she's gone. I watched it happen…my God." Sara started to cry harder.

"What are you telling me? She's dead?" Dean, sure he'd heard her wrong, asked, "What happened?"

"It was Cygnoid Fever. She died in the lab. It was very fast; nothing could have been done. I just can't make any sense of it. She was so careful. She knew what she was dealing with. She had it tested." Sara's whimpering sounded like it was easing off.

Dean felt a sickening knot forming in his stomach and broke out in a cold sweat. His hands started to tremble. "I'm so sorry. I don't understand. I can't believe this." There was silence for a moment. "What are the authorities saying? Someone screwed up, and I doubt it was Annie."

"They're looking into it. The area was thoroughly sprayed, and Cygnus' laws don't allow you to take samples off the planet unless they've been tested for the microbe. She took two samples at each location and sent one off in hazmat containers to be cleared. They all passed and so the question is…" Sara's voice trailed off. "I don't know how to tell you this."

"What tell me what?"

"Your ex-wife, Karen, was the Bio Foundation rep who ran the analysis of the samples and cleared them as safe."

Dean sank further down into his chair, his mind now spinning in deeper confusion and disbelief. "Karen? Are you sure?"

"Yes, her name's on the lab report. She signed off on the samples. I don't know what to say. I'm so sorry to tell you all this. I've been talking with Annie's family. I'll let you know the funeral arrangements as soon as I find out."

Dean was at a loss for words, and when he finally spoke, his voice cracked. "Thanks, Sara… Please keep me posted. God, I just had dinner with her. Someone's got to answer for this. Let me know if there's anything I can do. I'll speak to you soon."

"Yeah, I'll be in touch."

Dean leaned forward in his chair and buried his head in his arms on top of his desk. He shut his eyes, and Annie appeared, just as he'd last seen her sitting across from him in the restaurant: her happy freckled face beaming, and her silly little laugh playing like music. She even tucked her hair behind her ears, as she always did. She was there with perfect clarity. He'd first met her at a party, and she gained his immediate respect showing off her billiard skills. He watched from the sidelines as she slaughtered Matt before deciding to challenge her himself. He just managed to scrape by with his male pride intact, and in the course of conversation during the round, they'd discovered they were assigned to the same mining exploration team. They became fast friends, and she was someone he'd always been comfortable confiding in. During his divorce, she kept him sane.

His implant signaled again, breaking his trance. "Implant, do not disturb." The tingling stopped, and he sat up, staring blankly into space.

Five minutes later, Shannon marched into the room, speaking along the way. "Dean, I've had a couple of calls for you out here. What's going…" She always had a sixth sense for reading his mood; however, his melancholy expression would have been hard for anyone to miss. "What's wrong? Are you okay?"

"No, actually." Dean looked into her eyes. "I just got a call. My friend Annie...she's dead. Shannon, I can't believe it. I just had dinner with her. Look, I hate to ask you this, but you're going to have to hold down the fort. I gotta go. I'm no good here right now." Dean stood up from his desk. "I'll check in with you later. Just ignore the calls if you want. You can set up a message that I've had an emergency, and the power outages will be addressed as quickly as possible."

Shannon's worry lines deepened, and her eyes whispered tenderness. She came closer and put a soft hand on Dean's shoulder. "I'm so sorry Dean. She must have been a good friend. I can see it in your eyes. Don't worry about a thing here. I'll take care of it. You just go home and feel better. If you want to talk, I'm a good listener."

"Thanks, I'll call you later." Dean grabbed a couple of files off his desk and placed them in his briefcase, then took his sports jacket from the back of his chair, and left the room.

Chapter Twelve

It was six-twenty, and Laura had spent the last hour and a half hiding in the women's washroom at the spaceport. So far her plan had worked. She'd gone to her apartment and changed into a black turtleneck, washed the blood out of her hair, and picked up her purse with her travel documentation in it. Her creepy tapestry friends fueled her fear as they watched her with their twisted psycho eyes and sinister grins. *I've got you now!* They served her well, chasing her out of the apartment in less than five minutes. She caught the monorail to the spaceport, taking the most direct route. Regardless of her seemingly endless string of good luck, she knew her plan was a long shot.

It was time to make her move. She pulled a brush and a compact out of her purse and tried to make herself presentable. Her hair had dried nicely, but a layer of blood crusted the inside of her ear. She decided to leave it alone as it was sore and inflamed, and she pushed her hair forward to cover it. She left the stall and walked out to the sink. As she washed her hands, she had an eerie feeling like someone was about to grab her from behind. She glanced around for security cameras. There were none. Keeping her wits about her she left the room.

Fortunately, the gate for the seven o'clock flight was at the opposite end of the terminal from the one for the eight o'clock flight. Laura arrived at the gate to find a line of people preparing to board. She buried her anxiety as best she could and approached the young woman at the desk. "I wonder if you can help me. I have a ticket for the eight o'clock flight and was hoping to change it to this one. Are there any seats left?"

"I'm sorry, this flight's fully booked," the woman responded.

The crushing words shot through Laura like a hot poker. She blinked back the tears and fought to maintain her composure. "Are you sure there's nothing you can do? I have a family emergency."

"Well, there's one person who hasn't checked in yet. You can go on standby and take the seat if he hasn't shown up by the time we're closing the gate."

"Yes, please, I'd like to do that." Laura stepped aside and tried to mix in with the crowd of boarding passengers. As she waited, she observed two security guards walking past the gate. They paused and looked over. Laura looked away and initiated a conversation with the passenger standing next to her. "Do you travel often? I hate space flight."

The man had a wandering eye, which Laura found distracting. "Oh, my job keeps me traveling all the time. Don't worry, it's perfectly safe," he said.

"I find it claustrophobic." She continued to make small talk with the man until the guards went by.

The line of passengers was thinning, and the woman at the desk made an announcement. "Would Mr. Brad Anderson report to Gate Two immediately." A minute passed, and she repeated the message again.

Laura's anxiety had managed to dig itself out of the hole she'd put it in. She felt blood flooding into her head, warming her face, and throbbing her temples. The headache arriving with it was sure to be a doozy. She was now the only person standing at the desk, and the term *sitting duck* started hammering at her.

"Are you okay?" the woman asked.

"I'm just anxious about flying, but I also really want to get on that flight. It's a bad combination."

"Well, we're closing up now, so at least I can solve one of those problems for you." The woman took Laura's ticket from her, checked her passport and sent her through the gate. "You better hurry, they're about to close off the airlock." Laura thanked her profusely as she ran through the doors.

Chapter Thirteen

"Marshal Dunn, there's still no sign of Simmons, but we have two security teams scouring the terminal. Her flight boards in half an hour; at the worst, we'll pick her up then." The voice belonged to one of Larry Dunn's officers.

"Thanks, keep me posted." Larry ended the call and pulled up a seat in the spaceport security office next to another officer. Ron's idiocy boggled his mind. How the hell could he have let some nerdy woman escape from right under his nose? If it hadn't become his problem, he would have had a good chuckle at the expense of the balding little fool. In Larry's five years as head of security for the Lyra Base Station, he could never remember being so negligent. If he had, the Consortium would have had him out on his ass, and rightly so; his was an important job. Every year, the base station became infested with senior level politicians from Earth, Lyra, Cygnus, and Draco for the annual Lyra Summit for the Consortium of Planets, demanding high security. Adding to this was the black market trade of precious gems coming from the mining planet Draco. The Lyra station was close by and seemed to get more than its fair share of contraband shipments. To make matters worse, Draco was home to the Consortium Penitentiary, a high security facility that housed hardened criminals, all of whom were channeled through his station on route to prison. Larry, a burly man in his early forties, had learned very quickly to take his job seriously.

The problem had grown beyond finger pointing blame. Ron had no authority outside the accelerator, and the capture of Laura Simmons rested on Larry's shoulders. He had a close working relationship with both Ron and Ivan and understood the gravity of the situation in its entirety. So far, the cunningness of the young particle physicist impressed him, especially her little trick with the implant. He never anticipated she'd be so gutsy, and the maneuver had managed to throw them off her trail for the better part of an hour. Working in Larry's favor was the fact the spaceport was the only way off the base station, and her ticket purchase had simplified things. He'd grown tired of the little game of cat and mouse she played and just wanted her apprehended. Ivan's evidence showed she was blatantly guilty of corporate espionage and needed to be taken into custody. The exhilaration of the hunt surged through his veins as he waited for his prey to fall into the trap.

Larry was sitting back in his chair when he noticed Laura Simmons' name show up on the manifest for Flight Ninety-Three. He leaned forward and shouted to the officer at the computer. "What the hell! Stop that flight from departing. Relocate the security team to gate two."

Seconds after the security officer had implemented Larry's commands, the departure information updated on his screen. "I'm sorry, sir; Flight Ninety-Three has departed, and there's another flight docking at the gate. We can't bring it back. It shouldn't be a problem though. After all, she's trapped, and you can have the marshals at Eagle meet her when she arrives."

If only it were that easy! If Matt Jenkins apprehended Simmons, it would take her seconds to fill him in on what she heard. This was a matter he had to follow through personally. That bitch had turned *him* into a negligent fool, and it left him charged with vengeance. Larry stormed out of the security office and conferenced with Ron and Ivan. "I underestimated that God damn woman, and we've lost her. However, don't worry, I have a plan, and I believe we can use Dr. Simmons to our advantage. There's no doubt she's heading to Weston's apartment. We're moving our plans up to tonight. The men are already in place at Eagle. I'll advise them of the details. Don't worry. Things always have a way of working themselves out. By the way, tell Kevin to get a pod ready. We're leaving for Eagle as soon as I get there."

Chapter Fourteen

Just after seven o'clock, Dean started to regret his decision to leave work early. It was impulsive but under the circumstances understandable. Since receiving the news, he had only started his struggle through the all too familiar stages of psychological trauma: shock, disbelief, and finally acceptance.

After losing his mother, Dean had gone through a very difficult period. She'd fallen down a flight of stairs and hit her head on the ceramic floor at the bottom. Dean heard the echo of each thunderous thud and was the first to arrive at her side, kneeling in the pool of blood pouring from her twisted body. He rushed her to the hospital, but her head injury was severe. She died the next morning. Since it happened, the entire event had played itself over in his mind countless times, each thud tightening the guilt knot in his gut. For Dean, the most difficult part was coming to terms with the senselessness of it all. He felt she had died for nothing and blamed himself for not being there to prevent the fall.

Annie's death started to haunt him in the same way, and he couldn't escape it. He'd seen her hours before she died. They'd discussed the contaminated soil, but he thought nothing of it. He craved distraction and realized solitude was not the answer. He unsuccessfully attempted to complete some of the work he had brought home. Playing with Costello provided some entertainment until the cat settled down beside him for a snooze. Some degree of comfort was rewarded when he picked up his guitar. Despite his efforts to divert his thoughts away from Annie, one question continued to torment him: How was the sample contaminated? The more he thought about it, the more he became convinced Karen was at fault. While playing his guitar, his grief turned to anger. It quickly escalated, and he left his apartment.

Karen's apartment was three domes away, and he decided to take his cart to avoid public places. As the head of the base station, strangers easily recognized Dean and often engaged him in conversation, which he presently was in no mood for. It took just over fifteen minutes for him to arrive at her front door.

Dean pressed the doorbell, and as he waited for a response, he could faintly hear the computer announcing his arrival. "Dean Weston is at the door."

* * * *

Karen was sitting in her living room watching the news and enjoying a club sandwich when she heard the announcement. *Oh great. Go away!* She took another bite, aggressively chewed it, and chased it back with a mouthful of water. As she swallowed, the message sounded again almost making her choke. She'd had a bad enough day, and the last thing she needed was a confrontation with Dean. "Computer, open door."

* * * *

Dean watched as the door inched open and wasn't surprised Karen had decided not to greet him. Her steamy affair with the jerk with the surging bare butt led to a divorce churning with animosity, and he was sure she knew the reason for his visit. "Karen?"

"In here," she grumbled.

Karen's apartment was about half the size of Dean's. The front door opened to a small, but nicely appointed foyer, which prominently displayed the large stone Eskimo carving Matt and Sue gave them for a wedding present. The carving depicted a man squatting down to pull a large fish out of a lake. Dean loved the way it captured the excitement in the man's eyes and every time he saw it, it brought to mind his own kayaking adventures. Karen thought of it as a rustic hunk of rock, and during their marriage, agreed to display it only to spare her brother's feelings. Out of spite, she insisted on keeping it as part of the divorce settlement.

Beyond the foyer lay a spacious open concept living area. The kitchen and dining area were immediately to the right and flowed into a bright living room with a vaulted ceiling. To the left, a short hallway trimmed with oak wainscoting lead to two bedrooms. As Dean walked in, he sneered at the *five star* presentation of the apartment with not so much as one speck of dust sitting on the ostentatious furnishings. Karen was very particular about the way she kept her home, and her nagging used to drive him crazy.

Karen looked up from her sandwich. "Don't sit on my couch. You have cat fur on your jeans."

"For crying out loud, Karen. Annie's dead, and you're worried about cat fur? Do you want to explain to me how the hell the soil samples were contaminated? *You* signed off on them."

Karen stood up and raised her voice. "Yes, that's right. I signed off on them because they were clean. That's what I told the authorities repeatedly today, and I sure as hell don't see why I should have to explain myself to you. I did nothing wrong!"

Dean stormed over to her, his face reeling with anger; his voice was on the verge of yelling. During their marriage Karen had a habit of throwing blame. It was always his fault; it was his fault she fucked that guy. She was the master of deception, but not this time. Karen's self-righteous attitude had his adrenaline on overdrive. "Nothing wrong, nothing wrong! Annie's dead. Do you know what happens to you when you get Cygnoid Fever? Damn it, Karen, the soil was contaminated, and you're the one who cleared it. It seems pretty damn obvious to me. You screwed up!"

"Don't you talk to me like that! I know what I did, and how dare you storm in here questioning me about it. Besides, this is not a matter of your concern. I am dealing with the authorities, so why don't you mind your own business. You can ask them the outcome of their investigation when—"

"Ask them? You're not going to blow this off that easily. She was my friend, and I deserve, no I demand an explanation. Your clean soil sample had her hemorrhaging to death in her lab. I called the coroner today. Do you know she pounded so hard on the door of the lab that she broke her hand. I bet you haven't even stopped to think about what she went through. You're too concerned with deflecting the blame from yourself."

"What blame? I did nothing wrong! How many times do I have to tell you that before you get it through your thick head?"

"Okay, then prove it. Right now...let's go down to your lab and retest the samples." Dean insisted.

"They're gone. We don't keep samples after they've been cleared, otherwise your whole precious base station would be full of them." Karen started picking at her fingernails, which barely showed a millimeter of white.

"So you can't prove it? Great! I'm not sure how you're going to live with yourself."

"Dean, just get the hell out. Get out now, or I'll call Matt and have you thrown out."

Dean let out a sarcastic bellow. "Oh yeah, I'd like to see that one. I promise you, Karen, whoever is at fault is going to answer for it!"

"Really. Is that a threat?"

"Only if you're guilty, so you tell me." Dean always liked to get the last word and turned and stormed out. His head pounded, and yelling had left his throat feeling like raw meat.

As he passed the kitchen, he heard an enormous crash to his left and turned just in time to see a glass ricochet off the wall. The refreshing droplets of Karen's water showered his face as the glass exploded into a spray of crystals on the marble floor. Dean turned back to Karen and laughed at her. "You missed! You better clean that up before your Persian carpet gets moldy." He scoffed and headed to the door.

Dean heaved the door open, hoping to chip Karen's designer paint or shake a picture askew and ran out, just about bowling over Karen's neighbor who was hobbling along with her cane clutching a potted orchid. The woman looked up at him with hollowed, mousey eyes, her thin lips starting to form a word. Dean bolted past her before she had time to get it out.

* * * *

"Karen, dear, are you okay?"

Karen wiped away her tears and forced herself to stop crying. She could hear the click of Mrs. Burton's cane against the marble and hurried to the door, knowing her neighbor could have a bad fall on the wet floor. "Hi, Mrs. Burton; I'm fine. I was married to a jerk, but I'll be okay."

The lady shook her head at the broken glass. "Do you want me to help you clean up that terrible mess?"

"No, it's all right. But thanks for offering."

"You poor dear. You deserve better. Well, I brought you this orchid. They were on sale today, and I know how much you love them. Maybe it will cheer you up." She handed Karen the flower.

"Oh, you're so sweet, it's beautiful. What would I do without you? Thank you." Karen forced a smile.

"There's lots of fish in the sea you know. You call me if you need anything. I've had lots of men in my life, and I give free advice." She smiled as wide as her narrowed face would allow. It was a loving smile, and Karen decided she'd plant it in the valley of her heart right next to the orchid.

"Perhaps next week I'll find some time, and we can have tea."

"I'd like that, dear, and you remember what I said." The woman left.

Chapter Fifteen

"Spruce Station." The announcement on the monorail was music to Laura's ears. She got up from her seat and waited by one of the doors, taking care to steady herself as the monorail ground to a stop. As she stepped onto the platform, she checked her watch. *Ten after ten, I hope he's not asleep.* Laura picked up her pace as she made for the station exit. She'd tried to sleep on the flight, but Ivan and Kevin's conversation kept swimming through her mind, tormenting her. When she arrived at the bright, lush atrium of Dean's neighborhood, she found a renewed energy. Relief was only steps away. She laughed at herself putting such confidence in someone who was essentially a complete stranger. Dean had left her with an interesting first impression, and she'd felt very comfortable with him. She had confidence he would know what to do.

As she made her way down Spruce Road, she checked the address she had written down at the spaceport. *Number eight.* Surprisingly, there were two Dean Westons listed in the directory. Unfortunately, his business card was in her briefcase at the accelerator lab, so she assumed her Dean resided in the nicer of the two neighborhoods. As she approached the apartment, she could see a management cart parked in front, confirming she'd guessed correctly. Seconds later, she waited on his doorstep, impatiently awaiting a response.

* * * *

Dean just opened his second beer when the announcement sounded. "You have an unidentified visitor."

Unidentified? He was in no mood for a visitor but it struck him as odd how someone could be unidentified. He put his beer down and went to the door.

His brow furrowed as he caught his first glimpse of Laura. *What the hell?* He stood motionless for a moment before shaking it off. "Laura, I'm surprised to see you. Don't take this the wrong way, but what are you doing here? I thought you were at the Lyra Base Station."

"Please...Dean...can I come in?" She spoke in a whisper.

"Sure, of course."

Laura took a few steps into his apartment and then wrapped her arms around herself and looked up at him. The tears started to pool in her eyes.

"My God, what's wrong? What's happened? Come in and sit down." Dean placed a gentle hand on her shoulder and led her to his living room, signaling her to sit on the couch. "Here, let me get you some water and a tissue." As he returned, he looked around at his bachelor-pad and cringed to himself. "Please excuse the mess. I've had a really bad day."

There's nothing like first impressions, he thought as he shoveled aside the heap of guitar music and dirty dishes that cluttered the coffee table. He sat down beside her and covered a pile of crumbs with a magazine. "Now tell me what's wrong?"

Dean had seen lots of women's tears in his time, the dam usually bursting from anger or grief. Behind Laura's warm salt water pools were eyes encased in something entirely different. It took him a moment to recognize it, and when he did, it gave him pause. Confusion and fear were written into her eyes like words on a page.

"I'm sorry..." Laura's voice sounded weak. She took a drink and continued. "I'm sorry for coming here like this. Something happened at work today. I hardly know how to explain it. Honestly, I think it's a miracle I'm even alive."

"Alive? What are you talking about?"

Laura wiped her eyes with the tissue, soaking it through. "Sorry, I'm just overwhelmed. I've been running on adrenaline." She took a deep breath and straightened up. "Dean, this afternoon I accidently overheard Ivan Campbell and Kevin Cowen having a conversation. They said that some girl named Annie was out of the way. Dean, I think they killed her. Made it look like an accident...Cygnoid Fever or something. They also said something about getting rid of a drunk named Roger. They said that you and your ex-wife were next."

Dean fell back holding both hands to his head. "Oh my God," he whispered. His thoughts were swept away in confusion. *Why would*

Ivan want them dead? "Laura, are you sure you heard right?"

"Heard right? I've been running for my life ever since. After I heard it, I followed them into an unauthorized area and got caught. It's all a blur after that. I'm still not sure how I managed to escape. Why would they want to kill you and your ex-wife and that girl, Annie, and Roger? I don't understand. They're scientists for Christ's sake!"

Staring at Laura in disbelief, Dean leaned over and put his trembling hand over hers. "Laura, I just got word that my friend Annie Wilson died of Cygnoid Fever yesterday. Roger died recently...he threw up in his sleep after a night of drinking. He had a problem so I never thought anything of it. This is very real." He gave her hand a gentle squeeze. "Please, you need to tell me everything you remember word for word."

Laura returned the squeeze and sighed. It sounded like it came from sheer exhaustion. The tears had stopped. "Ivan did most of the talking. He said Annie Wilson had been eliminated, and her death was being investigated as an accidental case of Cygnoid Fever. Then he said plans were in place for you and Karen tomorrow night; and after that, everyone would be out of the way, and they could carry on worry free."

"Carry on...doing what? What were they doing in the unauthorized area?"

"I'm not sure. They were talking about containment of whatever was in the particle storage unit in that section. I had seen one of those units earlier full of particles from the nebula, but the one in this section had weird looking particles in it like I've never seen before. They were large and colorful. You could see them individually moving around. Kevin was explaining something about wave—"

"Wave frequencies!" Dean interrupted. He stood up and started pacing the room. "Jesus Laura, please think carefully. Did they mention any other names, anyone else who could be involved?"

"They talked about security. Ivan mentioned Ron Fieldman, the head of security at the lab and someone named Larry. I didn't get the last name."

"Likely Larry Dunn, he's head marshal for the Lyra Base Station."

"Dean, do you know what's going on here."

"Yes, I'm afraid I do know and…" Laura loosened some hair from inside her turtleneck, and Dean noticed her swollen, bloodied wound. "What the hell happened to your ear?"

"I removed my implant. They were tracking me."

He cringed. "You can't be serious. Come on let's get you to the washroom." Dean led the way down the hall. Costello sprang from under the dining room table and followed with a trotting gait.

"You have a cat."

"Yeah, sorry."

"Don't apologize. I love them."

In the washroom, Dean sat Laura down on the countertop, retrieved his first aid kit, and mended her wound. "I can't believe you did this. What did you use, your fingernails?" He shook his head at the gruesome thought.

"I had a knife, but my nails came in handy, too." She fell silent while he finished the job and smiled when Costello joined her on the counter for a little scratch.

Once her wound met Dean's approval, he handed her a damp cloth to clean it off. "It's still pretty swollen. I can't believe you did this."

"I had no choice. Trust me it wasn't fun. Anyway, thanks. I guess this is almost as good as dinner." Laura cracked a smile.

"Indeed. You have a nice ear." She was a good patient; deserving of a lollypop. He didn't have one to give her, but he had a rewarding and affectionate smile. It rounded the sides of his face, but was unfortunately short lived. "Ivan's going to rot in hell for what he's done. Laura, I'm going to tell you something highly confidential. I could get hung out to dry for this."

Dean took her through the events that transpired during their mining expedition to Spectra. About halfway through the story, they returned to the living room. Laura seemed fascinated to learn about the entities.

"Laura, to be honest with you, I'd have to say it was the most incredible experience I've ever had in my life. The effects those life forms had on us were indescribable. I was brilliant; my senses were heightened. I could hold my hand near something electrical and literally feel the power. I felt great."

"How long did it last?"

"About three weeks. It took a while to adjust to being normal again. For me, the worst part was my guitar. I wrote the most complex solos and played them perfectly as though I could sense the vibration of each string. I play them now and rarely get them right."

"What do you think they were?" Laura asked.

"Karen and Annie concocted some sort of theory that they were like souls or spirits without a body or some damn thing. Karen went on and on about human energy fields and auras. She's always been into that mystical crap and going on about all the yin yang mumbo jumbo. I don't know if I bought into their theory, but I'd have to admit after hearing about Annie today, my mind did drift to those entities. I guess we all like to hold onto some belief there's something more than this life at the end of the day."

"Do you think that's what Ivan's after? Some answer to what we are, some philosophical thing."

"Hell no! I know Ivan. The quest for knowledge comes honestly to him, but he's driven by self-interest. He loved the effects the entities had on that tic-tac-toe mind of his. All of a sudden, he was the smartest kid on the block; something which I can assure you was new to him. We designated the existence of the entities as a Code Fourteen...that's highly classified. Since exposure to us was killing them, it had to be that way in order to protect them. None of us could talk about what happened, except to each other. About a week after being exposed to them, Ivan called me, obsessed with his new found talents and abilities. He was a little over the top, which worried me a bit. It was almost as though he was a different person. All of us admitted the effects were great while they lasted, but then they were gone, end of story.

"Ivan didn't handle it very well. He was back to having only his charm to rely on. He went into a deep depression, took a leave of absence from work and became withdrawn. I tried calling him several times, but he wouldn't answer and didn't return my messages. I could see him harvesting those entities to get it all back."

"Do you really think he's that immoral?"

"I know he is. You should have seen his face when he was outvoted. He didn't give a rat's ass for the well-being of those entities, which sickened me. I don't pretend to know what they were exactly, but I can tell you this: they were intelligent living beings. They had individual personalities, and they were peaceful and pure. If there is a heaven out there, they're in it. A community of intelligent energy void of the negative emotions that have driven people to do horrific things. When we were on Spectra communicating with them, they felt our tension, anxiety, conflict, greed. They didn't understand it." Dean let out a disheartened sigh. "It all makes sense now. Ivan's energized appearance and all the cutting edge research coming out of the accelerator lab. And you should have heard him go on about neutrinos. I'd be surprised if he could even have spelled the word before. I thought it was weird at the time, but I never imagined. They're a bunch of succubus, you know, soul eaters. They're killing those poor helpless entities, so they can have their God damn cognitive superpowers."

"Actually, Ivan said something...what was it?" A look of concentration crossed Laura's face. "When they were talking about you and Karen, he said something about sacrificing for the greater good. Dean, Kevin was nervous about the security. They're not going to stop what they're doing. They've already killed two people who know about this. We need to stop them, or we're dead."

"I'll call Matt and get him on it. I need to talk to..." Dean stopped mid-sentence and hunched over throwing his head in his hands. "Oh my God, what have I done?"

"What?"

"It's Karen, she tested the—"

"Soil samples." Laura finished his sentence. "Ivan was telling Kevin about that."

"I went over there this afternoon and tore a strip off her. I've got to call her." Dean stood up and resumed his pacing. "Implant...Karen Jenkins." He paused. "Implant...Karen Jenkins."

"Maybe she has you on her do not answer list," Laura said.

"Yeah, maybe. Implant...Matt Jenkins." A disturbing thought crossed his mind. "Implant...what time is it?" There was no response. "Damn it Laura, my implant's been deactivated. I've got to get over to

Karen's now."

Laura got up from the couch. "I'm coming, too."

"No way! You're safer here, come on." Dean took Laura by the hand and led her to his bedroom. The bed was poorly made and his boxers from the night before were sprawled on the floor. Costello jumped onto the bed, curling up in a ball near Dean's pillow. Dean opened his closet and retrieved a laser pistol from the top shelf.

"Dean what are you going to do?"

"I'm going to bring Karen back here, and then we're going to Matt."

"I'm scared. Please let me come!"

Dean gently placed his hands on the sides of Laura's face and began to softly stroke her cheeks. "Look at me." Laura glanced up at him, fear etched across her face. "I don't want anything happening to you. I'll be back in about half an hour. When I leave, I want you to lock the bedroom door. Costello here will keep you company. Everything will be okay. Are you with me on this?"

Laura nodded as the tears started to well again. "Hurry, Dean," she whispered.

"I'll be right back." He reassured her with a wink and left the room, closing the door behind him.

Chapter Sixteen

The emergency lighting thinned the pedestrian traffic to a few rebel partiers and die hard workers straggling their way home, and Dean arrived at Karen's apartment in record time, most certainly deserving a speeding ticket. His reception was a replay of the one earlier in the evening, only this time the door didn't open. *She must hate me!* Deciding to take matters into his own hands, he pressed the doorbell twice quickly, holding it down the second time. "Computer, override door lock, voice authorization Dean Weston." The door inched open.

Dean burst his way in. "Karen, we need to talk. I was wrong, please!" There was no response. A light shone from down the hall. And as he headed in that direction, he noticed something was different. The stone carving was missing. "Karen!" He pushed the bedroom door open. A large porcelain lamp, embellished with designs of Chinese writings and pictures sat elegantly on the bedside table illuminating the room. The red duvet was puffed into a rich cloud, and accented by an assortment of floral pillow shams. *Where the hell is she? It's almost midnight.*

Dean rushed back down the hallway. "Kitchen lights on." A network of pot lights beamed down onto the gleaming black granite countertop. Nothing was out of place. Dean gazed toward the living room past the fat shadow cast by the Ming vase centering the dining room table. It took a moment for his eyes to adjust to the light. The sparkle of the distant stars danced through the window. Dean's gaze slowly drifted downward. There was something there, on the floor. A feeling of horror suddenly overcame him.

"All lights on!" The apartment brightened to high noon as Dean raced toward the living room. As he descended the single step from the dining room, he slipped on the marble floor and went sliding toward Karen's prized Persian. He broke his fall with his hands as he slid to a stop on the moist carpet. He jerked around and scurried over to the gruesome body. He looked at the pallid corpse that was once his wife and felt a knot tighten in his throat and spiral down to his heart, where it threatened to crush the blood from its arteries. The kill was fresh enough to leave her limp. One of the ceiling pot lights cast its glow on her face, filling the abyss of her mouth with a murky redness that made her look like she could spout lava. Her wide eyes held an abysmal, helpless stare.

"Karen, Karen!" Dean grabbed her shoulders and pulled her toward him. Her head slung to the side revealing a gaping hole in her skull. The carving sat a short distance away with shreds of skin, and hair hanging from its edge. A large kitchen knife rested beside it streaked in blood from the wounds in her chest. "No!"

Dean's screams were interrupted. Footsteps thundered through the dining room, and he looked up to see Laura and two men in ski masks, one with a knife to her throat. Karen's slippery body left his grip, and as her head fell to the floor, a splash of blood splattered his face. The taste of it oozed past his lips. He struggled to his feet, his clothes soaked. "What the hell are you doing? Leave her alone!"

The man held Laura firmly with his hand over her mouth. Her attempts to squirm were met by a tightening grip. He shook her and spoke with a harsh tone. "Stop it, or I'll slit your throat right here and now!" Laura stopped struggling, yet her eyes continued to shout anguish.

"Let her go!" Dean's adrenaline launched him toward the men.

The other man started. "Not so fast, Weston. Back off, or she's dead." He pulled out a laser pistol and pointed it at Dean. Dean thought about grabbing his own, but it had fallen out of the back of his jeans when he fell. "Here's how things are going to play out if you want this woman to live. You're going to take the hit for that lovely woman's murder. Remember how she cheated on you. I understand the two of you aren't on the best of terms. You're going to follow our instructions to the letter, or Laura dies."

Dean inched toward the man. "Let her go!"

"Don't screw with us, Weston." This time it was the man holding Laura who spoke. He dug the sharp tip of the blade into the crease of Laura's neck piercing a tiny section of skin. Several droplets of blood trickled down her neck and disappeared into the fabric of her turtleneck.

Laura winced. "No, please, no," she whimpered. Dean watched as her face contorted with fear.

"Leave her alone! What do you want?" Dean desperately scanned for a way out of the situation.

"Back there!" The man motioned with his pistol. "Go back by the woman, get on your knees and grab the statue." Dean froze in disbelief until the man raised his voice. "Do it!"

Fighting off a wave of nausea, Dean approached Karen to follow the instructions. His hand trembled as he searched for the strength to lift the carving. The thick liquid underneath it was still warm and pasted his fingers. He quickly returned it to its position. As he set it down the man spoke again. "Good, now the knife, with both hands."

Dean reached for the knife, and the second he got it in his grip, the man with the pistol descended on him taking his hands and jabbing the knife into Karen's chest. Blood splattered across Dean's face and torso; and as he threw himself back from the attack, the knife dropped, and he hit his head on the side of the coffee table. Paralyzed by the shock of the impact, Dean watched the man take Karen's hand and form it into a claw. Before he could find the strength to fend the man off, Dean felt Karen's nails scratch four deep groves into his face.

"No!" Laura screamed as she struggled to break free. Her reaction was met with a jab of the knife edge against her throat.

Without hesitating, the man pulled out a syringe filled with a clear fluid and jammed it into Dean's leg. Dean immediately felt violently sick as his alcohol level shot up. He threw up in the congealing, red pool and tried to steady himself, attempting to focus on something. Everything in the room started to spin out of control as though he'd been sucked into a tornado. His head fell to one side, and as he collapsed, he could just make out the faint blurred image of Karen's dead body. "Karen," he murmured before his eyes rolled back and closed.

* * * *

The man pulled a small bottle of fine Scotch from his pocket and sprinkled some in the pool of vomit. *Looks like he's a beer drinker* he thought to himself, picking up a faint aroma. The man straightened himself up. "We're finished here. Let's get her to Larry."

Chapter Seventeen

Matt was fast asleep when the call came in. At first he thought he was just fighting off an itch, and like a dog, scratched at his ear a few times with no satisfaction. *Damn.* He rolled over, heaving the blankets off Sue and glanced at the clock. *One o'clock, great!* Irritated by the continuous tingle, he leaped up and hurried out of the room so he wouldn't wake Sue up. The puppy clutched its stuffed squirrel in its mouth and joined him.

Standing in the darkness wearing only his boxers he spoke with a yawn. "Implant...Answer."

"Hi, Matt, sorry to disturb you this late. We've had a complaint of a disturbance, and I think it requires your attention." The voice belonged to Bruce, Matt's second in command.

"Bruce, its one o'clock in the morning. Why aren't you dealing with it?"

"It's at your sister's place. I thought you may want to check it out yourself."

"Did you try calling her?" Matt asked.

"Yes, of course, but she didn't answer."

"Yeah, okay, thanks Bruce...I'll head out there now. What was reported?"

"No details; it was an anonymous call."

Matt returned to the bedroom, put on the closet light and quickly dressed. Given the time, and the fact that he was going to his sister's, he chose the comfort of jeans and a T-shirt over his uniform. He tucked his pistol in the back of his jeans just to be safe. Sue peered at him through her tangled mess of hair and grumbled. "Turn that off. What are you doing?"

"We got a complaint about something going on at Karen's. I'm going to check it out. Go back to sleep." The minute he left the bedroom, he heard the puppy jumping on the bed with Sue.

Matt hopped into his cart and started driving toward Karen's. *Damn power outage.* He shook his head several times to keep himself from falling back to sleep in the dim light. As he drove, he wondered if she had another fight with Dean. He thought they'd passed that stage, but perhaps he was mistaken. As he pulled in front he found himself parking beside Dean's cart. *Oh for God's sake!*

As he made his way to the front door, his tiredness turned to anger over being called out in the middle of the night for what was likely to be another one of their lover's quarrels; and once again, he would be caught in the middle. He loved both his sister and Dean but had had a belly full of their *heartbreak hill* bull crap. The door was open slightly, and he went in. The place looked like it was lit up for a party. "Karen! Dean!" *Maybe they were having loud makeup sex.* He snickered at the thought. Everything looked quiet down the hall so he headed to the living room.

The sight he encountered was beyond anything he had ever seen. As he rushed over to Karen he put a call into Bruce. "I need a full security team here now and medics! Hurry!"

"My god, Karen!" Wedged between disbelief and panic, he went to feel her pulse, but there was nothing. He froze for a moment as the gravity of the situation descended upon him like a lead blanket. He placed his fingers on Dean's pulse having difficulty keeping them steady. As he increased the pressure, Dean groaned and rolled his head to the other side. His pulse was strong, and he attempted to rouse him by tapping his face.

"Dean, wake up!" The strong smell of alcohol and vomit hung like a heavy fog. As he glanced around the morbid scene, he became overwhelmed by a shocking realization. He got to his feet, hunched over like a man three times his age and slowly inched away as he captured the full extent of the horror.

He stiffened as a cold chill ran up his spine. The scratches on Dean's face were deep and just starting to crust over. A large knife lay within inches of his fingers. His hands were bathed in thick red blood, and the Eskimo carving he'd given them rested to the side of Karen's contorted head. Her eyes painted a picture of her last few moments of life, and her silky black hair formed a mat in the red congealed sludge. Matt stood silently in shock, unable to move.

His trance was interrupted by Bruce's voice. "Jesus, get him the hell out of here!" One of the security officers whisked Matt out of the room. "Get the medics in here now!"

* * * *

Just over an hour had passed when Matt heard the coroner wheel out the gurney with his dead sister's body, his little sister; the wee, pink bundle his mother placed in his arms on that warm June day. He still remembered her funny toothless grin and the softness of the fresh skin atop her tiny, bald head. Despite all the trials and tribulations of sibling rivalry, the bundle grew into the beautiful young woman he considered to be one of his best friends. And now she was gone. The truth was written in her blood. Dean had taken her from him.

The sound of the creaky gurney wheel faded to the rustling of Matt's security people dragging Dean, still blacked out in a drunken stupor, into custody. *Innocent until proven guilty:* the words of the law engrained into Matt when he took his oath to serve and protect. Well he didn't manage to protect his sister, and now those words seemed as lifeless as her body. He seethed for retribution.

The noise diminished as only a few people remained to collect evidence and clean up. Matt continued to listen from Karen's bedroom. The calamity seemed surreal as though he'd been listening to an old radio show like the War of the Worlds; only this one was called *Dean killed Karen.* He tried to distance himself from it, but it was impossible. The ordeal left him soaked in perspiration, yet chilled from shock and mind numbing confusion.

The coroner returned briefly to give Bruce his report, and Matt listened carefully. "The victim exhibited multiple stab wounds to the chest and abdomen, the sizes of which match the weapon found on the scene. The skull fracture was consistent with the base of a carving also found on the scene with traces of blood and hair on it. The cause of death appears to be blunt trauma coupled with severe subdural hematoma." The daunting truth of what transpired stabbed at him. Karen was murdered, and Dean was the assailant. The horrific images continued to clutter his mind as he struggled to make sense of the event.

127

Bruce had made him promise to stay out of the way, at least until he had settled down emotionally. When he heard the voice of Mrs. Burton, Karen's adorable elderly neighbor, he decided it was time to break his promise.

"Excuse me, what's happening here. All the ruckus woke me up. Is Karen all right?"

"I'm sorry, you can't come in here," a security officer said.

"Karen?" Mrs. Burton called, her voice crackly.

Matt dragged himself to the foyer, distraught, and emotionally exhausted. "Hi, Mrs. Burton."

Bruce ran over to Matt. "Matt, you're in no shape."

"I'm fine. I need to deal with this. I need to know what happened." Bruce backed down.

Matt steadied the old lady, led her to Karen's bedroom, and sat down beside her on the loveseat, which angled the far corner. "Mrs. Burton, I have something terrible to tell you. Karen was murdered tonight, and from the crime scene it appears that her ex-husband, my best friend, did it." Matt's composure surprised him. His years of training had apparently given him some ability to disconnect with the situation after all. "I know this comes as a shock to you, but I need to know if you heard or saw anything tonight. Any information would help us with our investigation."

"Oh dear, I'm so sorry, Matt," she said with tears in her eyes. "She's such a sweet girl. Please can you get me a tissue?" Matt passed the tissue box from the side table. "I went to bed at nine tonight. You know when you get older, you tire quickly." The woman spoke slowly. "This afternoon when I stopped by to give Karen an orchid, I overheard her and Dean fighting. He threw a glass at her you know. It was everywhere. She seemed very upset."

"Do you know what they were fighting about? Did you hear what they were saying?"

"It sounded like he was threatening her, but that's all I heard. She said he was a jerk. I'm sorry I don't remember more. That happens when you're old."

"Thanks, Mrs. Burton, I don't want to push you. Perhaps you'll remember more in the morning. You know how to get me. I'm so sorry to have disturbed you with this. We're all in a state of shock."

Mrs. Burton stood up to leave. "Give my condolences to your family. You have a brother, too, don't you?"

"Yes, he and his wife and daughter were close with both Karen and Dean." Matt escorted the woman out.

"You take care," she uttered as she left.

Matt took a deep breath to clear his head and find the courage to confront the carnage in the living room. He stopped at the top of the step in the dining room. He'd been to crime scenes countless times before but never one this personal. The imprints where Karen and Dean were found were mapped out with precision along with the location of the knife, laser pistol and stone carving. Dean's drunken footprints were stamped out in blood. Off to the side lay the remnants of what was once a beautiful pink orchid.

Chapter Eighteen

Dean opened his eyes a crack, but the glare from the ceiling light forced them closed. His head felt like a freight train had driven through it, and the damp chill made him feel like he'd been dumped into the icy Kicking Horse River. He rolled to one side, grinding his shoulder into the hard concrete floor. A dull ache shot through his body. *Where the hell am I?*

With his head trapped in its drunken whirlpool, it took several seconds before he could focus on anything. He found himself staring at a series of steel bars that stopped at the edge of a gray wall. A wide bench hung along the length of the wall, and he had a clear view of the collage of colorful chewing gum wads decorating the bottom of it. His short pulsed breaths helped with the gagging stench that seemed to have diffused throughout his whole body. He slowly pushed himself up to a sitting position. The jumbled events of the past night plaguing his mind became dauntingly clear as he peered down at himself. As he closed his hands, the dried blood appeared caked in the crevices of his skin.

Dean panned around the room as his consciousness returned. With a sense of dread and confusion, he knew exactly where he was. Several months earlier, he and Matt were involved in a drug bust on the base station. An enormous shipment originating from Earth and destined for Draco was intercepted at the Eagle spaceport. Several arrests were made, and Dean joined in the interrogation of the prisoners before they were shipped off to the Draco Penitentiary. There was no mistaking a cell at the Eagle Detention Center. It was a cold, harsh cage.

Dean took a moment to peer through the bars like a zoo animal before directing his attention to the metal basin in the corner. Setting his hand on the floor, he gave himself a push and got to his feet. His clothes, ridged from the dried blood, had stiffened as though they were made out of papier-mâché. As he stumbled to the corner, they crunched like hard snow. He leaned over the basin, and the contorted reflection looking back at him, frightened him. It was as though the face belonged to another person, a sinister person who held him captive. The hair on his head and stubble on his face were caked with blood, and his red sunken eyes were haloed in darkness. He turned the faucet on full and aggressively washed Karen's blood from his face, hair and arms. The red water channeled to the tip of his nose forming a sickening waterfall that pooled in the basin. He pursed his lips as hard as he could as he recalled the revolting taste from the night before. He watched what was left of his dead ex-wife escape down the drain and then with repugnance tore his soiled shirt off, dried himself with a clean corner and flung it to the floor. Overwhelming trepidation tightened the enormous knot in his stomach.

"You, Weston. Put these clothes on. Make it fast. You're wanted for questioning."

Dean looked around to see a guard passing clean clothes through the break in the bars. He wasted no time donning the orange jumpsuit, and as he finished, the guard returned with a friend. One of the men aimed a laser pistol at Dean while the other triggered the door release and cuffed him.

Dean quickly spoke up. "Please, I need to speak with Matt Jenkins; it's urgent."

The man with the pistol replied. "Oh, I'm sure you're just the person he wants to see! Ivan Campbell and Marshal Dunn are here to talk to you regarding the Simmons case. Marshal Jenkins will see you later."

"No, you don't understand, I need to speak with him now!" Dean sounded agitated.

"Sick bastards don't have the luxury of making demands. We make the rules here."

"Then I want a lawyer."

"You don't need a lawyer for this. This is not about the murder of Karen Jenkins. They want to know about your involvement with Laura Simmons. She's been accused of corporate espionage." Dean's reaction to the man's words surged to life. It felt like his emotional flesh was being torn from his body. He couldn't let Ivan and his unscrupulous followers destroy Laura.

The men led Dean past a couple of other cells and through a steel door. The interrogation room was on the right, and the men sat Dean in a chair, secured one of his arms to the armrest, and left the room. Dean sat in silence gazing around at the familiar setting. After the drug bust, he had interrogated two people in this very room. The first was a ringleader with the Draco crime syndicate. The second was a teenage kid who had somehow become heavily involved in drug trafficking. Dean knew the interrogation process far too well. Manipulation, mind games, anything to extract the required information. He did not relish sitting on the opposite side of the table, and he dreaded what Ivan might have up his sleeve. Dean underestimated him. If Ivan had been continuously exposed to the entities for a period of time there was no telling what his state of mind would be. The whole scenario left him with an overwhelming fear he was way out of his element.

After entering the room, Larry took a moment to bypass the security camera. He continued in followed by Ivan, preening with self-importance. Larry pulled up a chair while Ivan walked to the corner table and poured a glass of water, setting it down beside Dean. "Good morning Dean, did you sleep well?"

Dean's temper ignited. "You sick son of a bitch, you were always driven by self-interest but this? How many innocent people do you plan on killing? And those peaceful entities, the only intelligent life ever found, and you're slaughtering them for personal gain!"

Ivan raised a hand to silence him. "Cut it out with your holier than thou attitude. If the four of you weren't so narrow minded, all of this wouldn't have been necessary. You just don't understand the big picture, do you, Dean." Ivan started pacing the room. "Isn't it time for another great leap in the evolution of man? Think of the possibilities."

"Possibilities? What's evolution without morality? Damn it Ivan, think of what you're doing."

"Enough." Ivan pounded the wall with his fist. The eruption sent the water glass flying toward Dean, soaking his fresh clothes before tumbling to the floor.

Dean's eyes widened in astonishment, and then he realized it must have been telekinesis.

"You are a small man. Don't you see that?" Ivan yelled.

Dean slowly shook his head. "Ivan, what's happened to you? What the hell have you become?"

A wiry smile crossed Ivan's face. "Oh, Dean, I'm better than human, I'm digressing beyond man's evolutionary path. If you knew even the half of it, you'd be regretting the decision you made on Spectra. At this rate, in another six months, I'll be able to kill you by just thinking you dead." Ivan laughed arrogantly. "Anyway, I'm not here to defend my actions, least of all to you. We are laying the footings for a quintessential intellectual revolution, and I have no regrets. You said yourself how impressed you were with the research coming out of my facility. I can assure you Dean, that's just the tip of the iceberg." Ivan lowered his voice. "As for you, my friend, this is what's going to happen; and I suggest you listen very carefully."

"Where's Laura? What, did you kill her, too?"

Larry broke his silence with a stiff upper lip. "Dr. Simmons is very much alive, and after causing us much grief, I'm happy to say we now see eye to eye."

"What did you do to her?" Dean said.

Larry laughed with a frigid expression etched into his face. "Do to her? What did she do to us? Ivan's running a smooth operation here, and that bitch had to stick her nose in where it didn't belong. Ivan and Ron showed me all the evidence. Corporate espionage is a serious offense especially with an eighty billion dollar grant looming in the midst, and she's guilty as hell!"

"You son of a bitch; she's innocent. Let her go."

"You know we can't do that, but don't worry. We've had a long chat with Laura, and she fully understands the scope of her crime. She's agreed to sign a full confession," Ivan said.

"Confession? For what? Overhearing murderers conspiring?"

Larry leaned the bulk of his body over the table until he was an intimidating distance from Dean, his eyes frozen into a hard stare. "We were very fair with her. She signs the confession; she lives. We were very convincing. She didn't hesitate. There was no arguing about the evidence from the accelerator laboratory. The DNA scanners conclusively prove she was spying on sensitive conversations and trespassing into a high security area of the laboratory. The politics going on between the Lyra Accelerator and ECN is no secret. ECN could be out of business in a matter of months, and they're looking for a competitive edge. And then there's the evidence implicating her as an accessory to the murder of Karen Jenkins." Larry frowned and sat back. "It's a done deal."

"You have no evidence connecting her to Karen."

"Oh really? Laura was at your apartment last night. Forensics found her blood in your bathroom and her DNA on a pillow on your bed. The way I see it, the two of you are involved in a relationship, and your ex-wife gave you a hard time, which infuriated you. I hear she cheated on you, Dean. Laura was at the accelerator laboratory only long enough to steal the confidential information she was after and escape. She should be commended on her carefully planned and executed operation. On her way back, she decided to have a visit with you. She's jealous of any remaining affection you have for your ex-wife. You told her how livid you were about how Karen messed up the soil samples, and she fueled your fire. After having a couple of beers and some Scotch, you became further enraged at Karen, and you left. The rest is history."

"You sick bastards!" Dean yanked on his restraints. "There's plenty of evidence pointing to the truth. Matt will get to the truth."

Ivan stopped his pacing and joined them at the table, straight faced. "Why would Matt dig into this when he has a signed confession by you, stating you murdered Karen Jenkins, his loving sister?"

"I'll never sign anything like that. Have you lost your mind?"

Ivan locked eyes with Dean and scoffed. "Dean, know this: we are very good at what we do, and you will sign the confession. Arrangements for Matt and Sue are being made as we speak."

"What the hell are you talking about?"

"It's just this simple. You sign the confession, or they die. We have a tight network. If you try anything, we'll know about it. We'll be watching you and listening to everything you say, so don't think you can tip Matt off. If you want your friends to live, you will play along with us to the last detail."

"Yeah and what happens to me? A one way trip to hell."

Ivan laughed. "You could look at it that way, but why not try to be an optimist. You're alive aren't you? I thought we were pretty creative. It plays out like a good novel. Roger, Annie, Karen, you...each elimination more interesting than the last...and you're the lucky one. You live. With two signed confessions, you and your friend Laura will be on the next shuttle to the Draco Penitentiary, and that will be that. Your choice, Dean."

Dean sat silently for a moment digesting the plate of misery he'd been served. Ivan had him right where he wanted him, and the smug bastard knew it. He could never do anything that would put Matt and Sue in harm's way, no matter what the cost to him. His life was over, but at least it wasn't in vain. "If I sign, you'll give me your word you'll leave them alone."

"They'll be safe," Ivan stated. "I'm a man of my word, Dean. I can assure you, you're doing the right thing."

Dean surrendered with a defeated sigh. "Fine, you win. You're playing a dangerous game, Ivan. One day you'll get what you deserve."

"Well maybe we'll meet in hell." Ivan chortled as he got up from his seat and straightened his suit. "But I don't think so." He poked his head out the door and spoke. "Aw, Bruce you're back. We're finished in here and thank you. Mr. Weston was very cooperative. He has also informed me he wishes to sign a confession. He's quite traumatized and doesn't want to deal with a long drawn out trial. It will be nice for the Jenkins' family to have closure."

Chapter Nineteen

Dean's second night in the detention center had been a long one. For a short while, sheer exhaustion had won over the tangled mess of thoughts and images plaguing his mind, and he'd drifted off. As soon as he awoke, they were back to greet him. The visions of Karen's lifeless corpse and the terrified look in Laura's eyes had earned their own spots in the *despicable* memory box of his consciousness, right next to the image of his mother's contorted body. And then there was Ivan. He found himself becoming obsessed with hatred and anger toward the man. Dean had never considered himself vindictive; however, he found himself fantasizing his revenge.

The minutes turned to hours as he sat waiting in his cell. Any thoughts of self-pity were instantly overcome by his concern for Laura. She was a beautiful, successful woman who'd been in the wrong place at the wrong time, and her life was ruined. He couldn't escape the stabbing guilt for leaving her at his apartment, vulnerable and alone. He asked to see her, but the guard only laughed at the request.

Dean sat on the bench of his cell hunched over with his elbows resting on his knees and his right foot tapping the floor repeatedly. The noise echoed throughout the cell only to be interrupted by a clanking from down the hall, which brought him to his feet. He soon found himself in the company of Bruce and two guards.

"The prosecutor and your counsel are ready to see you. We're here to escort you back to the interrogation room," Bruce said in a cold, monotone voice.

The interrogation room was just off the main office area. As Dean turned into the room, he could see Matt over by his office talking to Larry Dunn and two distinguished looking gentlemen. Matt shot a piercing glare, and the four of them walked in Dean's direction. Dean had managed to compose himself to do what had to be done but being confronted by Matt was not part of the picture. Matt had a vindictive streak, a character trait undesirable for his position, and Dean wasn't sure how violent his reaction might be.

The guards secured Dean in the chair, the same one as before, and the men filed into the room. Bruce made the introductions. "Dean, this is Derek Zimmerman, the prosecutor for your case, and Navid Lembouchi, your counsel."

"If you don't mind, I'd just like to get this over with as quickly as possible. What's he doing here?" Dean motioned to Matt. "Under the circumstances, don't you think his presence constitutes a conflict of interest?"

Matt snapped. "Conflict of interest? You bastard! I intend to see this through to the end. Look me in the eye and tell me what you did." His voice rising. "Tell me what you did!"

Dean looked to his counsel for assistance. "I really don't think it's appropriate to have him here." Dean desperately wanted to question Larry's presence, but he didn't dare.

Navid spoke with a slight middle-eastern accent. "Marshal Jenkins is head of security for the base station, you know that. He has agreed to behave himself. Now let's get down to business."

Bruce left the room. "Let me know if you need me." The gentlemen took a seat across the table from Dean.

Dean's counsel spoke first. "Mr. Weston, as you know you have been indicted for the murder of Karen Jenkins. As per your instructions, the prosecutor has prepared a plea of guilty. I have been assigned to represent you and to assist in reaching a deal concerning sentencing. You do understand that by signing this plea you are giving up all of your rights to a trial under the laws of the Consortium of Planets?"

"Yeah, I get it. Just give it to me, and I'll sign."

"You need to review the details of the plea. My job is to go through them with you," Navid said.

"I don't care about the details. I know what happened." Dean gave Larry a smoldering glance. "It's very clear what needs to be done here."

"Well I'm going to go through this with you anyway. It's my responsibility to make sure you know what you're signing." Navid pushed the document in front of Dean and led him though the details of the crime. He labored over every aspect of the evening in great detail. It formulated a motive for the murder, highlighting Karen's infidelity, their fights, and the ugly divorce. Then there was the fight they had on the afternoon of her death regarding the soil sample. There were even a few remarks about Dean's relationship with Dr. Laura Simmons. When Navid started reading the details of the coroner's report, Dean's stomach turned, and he found himself fighting off tears. He sat in his chair with his head down, seething, trying desperately to tune him out. "Do you have any questions?"

"Yeah, where do I sign?" Dean said.

"It's just that simple for you. Where do I sign?" Matt raised his voice. "Look at me Dean!"

"Marshal Jenkins, I think—"

Matt cut Navid off. "Sorry gentlemen, I need to hear the words from his mouth. Dean you look at me, and you tell me. Did you do this to Karen? Did you kill her, slaughter her…my sister?" Matt got up from the table and marched over to Dean, looking like a rearing grizzly. He yanked Dean's chair around to face him and screamed, "Tell me."

Navid stood abruptly, keeping his hands on the table and spoke with a commanding tone. "Marshal Jenkins, this is highly inappropriate."

"I have the right to know. She was my sister, and he was my friend! Wouldn't you want a straight answer, not just a few grunts spoken with a cavalier attitude?" Navid backed down. "Tell me to my face, did you kill her Dean?" Matt wrapped his hand around Dean's jaw and locked eyes with him. "Tell me!"

Dean clamped up, gritting his teeth until his jaw ached. His face felt flushed, and the perspiration poured down his back. He wrapped his hands around the armrests of the chair until his knuckles were white. Matt was the closest friend he'd ever had, and he could see the pain in his eyes. He longed to tell him the truth and be there to help heal his wounds, but knew he couldn't risk it. Even if he tried, the evidence they had against him was tremendous, and his story would sound too farfetched for any of them to believe. Not to mention, any attempt would endanger Matt and Sue. He was powerless. Dean was running out of time as he felt the moisture start to collect in his eyes. He swallowed to clear the tight knot in his throat then spoke with a hesitant whisper. "Yes, I killed her."

Matt released his grip and stumbled backward a couple of steps, his towering frame fuming with pent up rage. "You bastard," he whispered. "You son of a bitch." His voice becoming elevated. "I called you my friend, my brother. I don't even know who you are. So help me, you'll pay for this!" Matt spit in Dean's face and backed across the room in stone cold silence.

Navid broke the tension in the room. "Marshal Jenkins, I have to ask you to take a seat. As head of security, you've been included in this meeting. If you cannot fulfill your duties with professionalism, I will have you removed."

The warm saliva started to drip down Dean's cheek meandering through the obstacle course of his stubble; the same stubble that had been caked with Karen's blood. He used the sleeve of his free arm to wipe it off.

"Very well." Matt turned abruptly to address the prosecutor. "Mr. Zimmerman, as Karen Jenkins' brother I would like to request you put in an application for the death penalty."

Dean's eyes widened as he waited for his counsel to respond. Wouldn't that just top off the depraved set of plans Ivan had for him.

Navid wasted no time. "Marshal Jenkins, your request is duly noted, but you need to be aware that Mr. Weston's sentence will be negotiated between me and the prosecution." Matt took his seat while maintaining a stabbing glare at Dean.

Dean recognized the look in Matt's eyes; it was a thirst for restitution. Matt believed in *an eye for an eye,* and Dean knew he wouldn't back down easily. His only hope of getting out of this alive was to push it through quickly. He straightened his chair as he spoke. "Can we just get this done?" As he finished his sentence he could see the hint of a sadistic grin crossing Larry's face. *You'll pay for this!*

Navid resumed the meeting. "Dean, if you don't have any questions, we can sign this up and move on to sentencing." He handed Dean a pen and indicated where he was to sign. Dean scribbled his *John Hancock* and pushed the document across the table. Navid signed as his counsel and then passed it over to the prosecutor.

After signing, Derek turned to Navid. "Taking into consideration the request by the family member present, prosecution would like to see life imprisonment at the Draco Penitentiary with no potential for parole."

"My client was clearly drunk when this occurred, and while responsible, was not fully in charge of his faculties. He has no prior record of violence," Navid said.

"Being drunk is not a defense. This was a hideously violent murder. If you prefer, I will follow the family's request and put in an application for the death penalty. They rarely approve them anymore, but this crime fits the profile."

Dean shot Navid a look to tell him to back off. Dean was a risk taker at heart, but not when he had no control. And not when his life was on the table. Navid stopped to consult with him before continuing.

"Okay, we'll take it, but I want a formal undertaking that the prosecution will not submit a death penalty application."

"Agreed." Derek flipped to the back of the plea and signed the sentencing papers and then handed a copy to Navid. "I will get Mr. Weston and Dr. Simmons' papers to the courthouse by the end of the day, and this will be finished."

"Laura, what did Laura sign?" This was Dean's first expression of concern.

"That is none of your business. Suffice it to say that you'll have company on your trip to Draco." Derek stood up to leave. "Larry, I understand you're overseeing transport tomorrow morning."

"Yes, that's correct," Larry responded.

With the bureaucracy out of the way, the guards hurried Dean back to his cell. Once inside, he wandered in an aimless panic around the small cage like a lab rat desperate to find its way out of a maze. He finally settled against the back wall, holding his head with his hands; his eyes blazed with despair. He slowly looked to the ceiling shaking his head from side to side. "No... No... No..." His whimpers turned into screams. "No...No...No..." With an ear shattering volume, he finished. "No, you Bastards!" He turned and pounded his fist against the wall repeatedly until it became too painful to continue and then fell to the floor. He sat shaking, with his knees to his chest and his head down for several hours until he finally fell asleep.

Chapter Twenty

At six o'clock the next morning, a group of security officers led by Larry Dunn came to collect Dean. He was getting used to the sour routine of being cuffed and escorted with a pistol aimed at his head. Holding his head down, he obediently walked with the men to the back door of the Detention Center where an armored truck waited to take him to the spaceport. Thankfully, Matt was nowhere in sight and on a brighter note, he anticipated seeing Laura, although he wasn't sure she would share his feelings seeing how he was responsible for ruining her life. As they entered the service tunnel, he had a clear view into the back of the truck. There were two guards present, and on a bench, Laura sat chained to the wall, wearing an orange jumpsuit like his.

"Over here, Mr. Weston." The guard signaled to the bench across from Laura. They sat him down, chaining his wrists and ankles to the wall. Dean immediately looked to Laura to make eye contact with her. The desperate look in her eyes made his heart plummet. She appeared to have cried a lifetime of tears, and he stared at her with the hope of conveying some element of strength. At least they were together.

"I'll ride in the back with them." Larry sat down on the bench along the back wall of the cab with a clear view of the two of them. Once the doors were secured, they were on their way.

Dean immediately spoke up. "Larry, you don't have to do this. You can set things right. What the hell are you doing following Ivan... the man's psychotic."

Larry chuckled and scratched methodically at his sandy-brown, *G.I. Joe* hair. "Oh, Dean..." he paused. "Already grabbing at straws are we? Actually, I was expecting you to go down with more of a fight. It was rather pathetic...your willingness to sign your life away so quickly to save your precious friends. I wonder if Matt would have done the same for you. He sure jumped at the idea of the death penalty in a hurry. And as for Ivan, let me make this clear, I follow nothing but my own agenda."

Although Dean had only met Larry in passing, Matt had kept him well apprised of his spotted history. Larry had a late start to his military career, and the two of them had completed their last year of military training together during which time Larry had become extremely disliked within their cadre. He rarely laughed unless it was at the expense of another. Using his movie star appeal, he prided himself on his one-night stands, and at one point was accused of date rape; nothing was ever proven. He enjoyed picking fights, and his weight trained physique always gave him the upper hand. The man was a bigot, and with his arsenal of fork-tongued racial slurs, used to verbally attack Matt for being half Chinese. The day eventually came when Matt had enough and snapped, taking him down to the level of a brow beaten dog thanks to his martial arts training. Matt received disciplining for the attack but bragged that "it was well worth it, putting that douche bag in his place."

Dean already loathed the man. He had a glimmer in his eye that lent him a look of innocence, but Dean knew it was just a charm in his sociopathic bracelet. "You God damn bastard, you're actually enjoying this aren't you. I wonder how long it's going to take until those entities figure out a way to make your brain liquefy and pour out your nose."

Larry scoffed. "Maybe out Ivan's but not mine. I'm plenty smart enough on my own. I didn't know you had such a vivid imagination. Anyway, I'm not in here to listen to your sci-fi predictions. We were good enough to keep the two of you alive, and you and your friends and relatives will stay that way if you continue to play ball."

"You leave my family alone. I've done everything you said." Laura's face was branded with a look of repugnance.

"What the hell else do you want from us? It seems to me we're pretty screwed already," Dean added.

Larry let out a jubilant laugh, displaying his acutely white teeth. "Yes, you are. However, you're about to enter life as an inmate. There's a social structure on the inside you know." Larry folded his arms and relaxed. "Who you are, what you did before getting there, what crime you committed, it all enters into the equation of how horrendous your life is going to be. Sure Dean, you've had some military training, but look at you, you're living as cushy a life as her."

Larry frowned as he motioned to Laura. "Here's a friendly tip.

The two of you better toughen up in a hurry, or they'll eat you alive in there. And if you think you're going to pretend to be innocent and give those people some sob story about how you were framed then, think again. Criminals aren't too receptive to crap like that and neither are we. If we hear even a hint of a recanted confession, there will be casualties. Do the two of you understand me?"

"You've made your point pretty clear," Dean muttered.

The lights shining through the small window on the back door of the truck brightened up. "Good. Well, it looks like we're here."

After the truck came to a stop, the doors released. The guards shackled Dean and Laura's hands and feet and escorted them to a pod with the words "Draco Penitentiary" ominously displayed on its side. Dean took a careful look around as he commenced his death march, catching the last glimpses of the base station he once commanded. Across the hangar, he saw a familiar figure. He thought he'd be spared this last bit of agony, but there was Matt, watching as he entered the pod. Over their years of friendship, Dean had come to know Matt better than anyone. He'd seen him with all his colors exposed, stumbling drunk, raging mad, intensely jealous, envious. The look plastered across the face at the end of the hangar was new to him. It was nothing less than shear abhorrence. Dean was sure if Matt could have, he would have shot him dead on the spot. The look stripped away a piece of Dean, a piece he felt certain he'd never get back. In the course of saving his friend, he'd lost him; a necessary trade off.

The pod had only enough room for one cell. Dean likened the small, filthy enclosure with its dim lighting to an animal den, perhaps muskrats; he always considered them to be rather vile and rat-like. The foul stench of urine fumed from the toilet and sink in the corner. The short, privacy knee wall had black mold growing on it in great patches that resembled flattened mushrooms. There was no place to sit other than the floor, and the air hung like poisoned fog. The guards removed Dean's shackles first then Laura's. They left, locking the door behind them.

"Dean what are we going to do? I can't go to prison." Laura's tears were flowing in rivers down her cheeks.

Dean sped to Laura's side and wrapped his arms around her,

holding her as tight as he could. With his left arm around her waist, he slowly inched his right hand up to her head, caressing her tangled hair. He pressed his lips softly against her ear, and with gnawing guilt, he whispered, "I'm sorry, Laura, I'm so sorry. I'm so sorry. I should never have left you. This is all my fault."

The transparent emptiness inside her brought her arms around him to bring him closer. She choked back her sobs, and her words came out choppy. "It's not your fault. I don't blame you, but what are we going to do?"

"We're going to stick together and get through this, *together*."

Laura inched away from Dean so she could see him. "This isn't something you get through! This is forever."

Dean looked deep into her distraught eyes and brought his hands around to meet the sides of her face, wiping away her tears. He barely had enough strength for himself, and although they hardly knew each other, he had to find enough to share with her. Especially since it was his insane pool of hell she was drowning in. He thought he'd try to lighten the mood. "This is one hell of a first date, huh?" He forced a smile. With everything she'd been through, she still possessed an innocent, fresh beauty. "Laura, we have to live day by day. We can't think of forever, and we can't lose hope that someone may find out the truth."

He took her back into his arms knowing her heart was shattered into a billion little pieces. "It's okay. We'll stick together and be okay," he said.

They held each other in silence for several minutes. Dean kissed the side of her cheek and softly spoke. "Come on, let's sit down and talk." With his arm around her, he led her to the wall, and they sat. Dean kept his arm around her, and she moved in close, laying her head on his chest.

Laura sheepishly peered up. "I hate this room. It's confining, like death."

"It just needs a paint job and some air freshener." He took her hand.

"My family's going to hate me. It would be better if I were dead. I'll probably never see them again."

"You close with your family?" Dean asked.

"Yeah, I have an older brother, Kyle, and a younger sister, Sam. My brother's married with two kids. My sister's on her own, and we're best friends. How about you?"

"Well, I lost my mom when I was in my twenties. No siblings. My dad and I aren't really into the calling thing, but we try to see each other when we can. I guess to a large extent Karen's family was my family. Karen's brother, Matt, is my best friend, or I guess I should say was. Her other brother, Mark, has a daughter, Michelle, who I'm pretty close with. I'm a big kayaker and talked her into giving it a whirl with me last summer. She loved it." Dean straightened up enough to look down at Laura as a realization dawned upon him. "Laura she's starting a co-op term at Ivan's lab. What the hell is he going to do to her?"

"She's a student. They'll keep her on a tight leash. You can't drive yourself crazy worrying about her." Laura squeezed his hand, and he appreciated the reassuring touch. "Have you ever been to Draco?"

"Yeah, sort of. I used to fly in there all the time, but I never really stayed. The entire planet is one big mine, and you get some pretty rough types there. The work is tough, but the pay's not bad, otherwise God only knows why anyone would live there."

"My fake uncle lives there."

Laura's remark sparked a chuckle. "What the hell's a fake uncle? Did you call rent-a-relative and ask them to send an extra person over for Thanksgiving?"

"Yeah, we get a different one every year." Laura chortled. "He's a close family friend. I've known him all my life. His name's John Becker, we call him Uncle John."

"So…what is he? A miner?"

"Are you kidding, he doesn't even like to get his hands dirty. He's a big wig in the government, Minister of Transportation and Communication. Dean, there's no way my family is going to believe I did this."

"Don't be so sure. Matt looked me right in the eye as he requested the death penalty. It was a humbling experience. It tells you a bit about people, when they can just throw away everything they know about you and pass judgment in an instant. Hopefully someone will smell a rat, but on the other side of the coin, we don't want any company."

Laura let out a discouraging grumble. "Isn't that prison a diamond mine?"

"Yeah, it was a clever way to stop theft from the mine. Years ago, it was a real problem. Workers would do anything to get the diamonds out the door, including swallowing anything that glimmered. What better way to stop it than by locking the doors? Now they have free labor and no theft, although I've heard rumours of guards on the take."

"Do we have to go in underground tunnels?"

"You've got a thing about small places don't you?" Dean tightened his arm around her. "No, the raw diamonds are found in the top half meter layer on the surface. It's really pebbly. Basically, you just dig through the pebbles. Hot work, on your hands and knees. Draco hardly gets any rain. It's hot and really dusty, and there's lots of sulfur. It used to cause me grief flying in there; the fine dust doesn't agree with the particle collector plates. It causes all sorts of problems."

"Do you think what Larry said is true. About the people in the prison?"

"Yes and no. I don't think we can expect high society types, but not all criminals are psychopathic killers. I know a bit about the place from Matt. Single cells for all, but the work areas are co-ed. It's a crap hole. They work you all day, and then you're back in your cell. There's not a lot of time for socializing."

Dean could only see a hint of blue through the lank strands of hair sitting out of place on Laura's forehead. He could still make out the concern screaming from her eyes. "So I might not even see you."

Dean brushed the hair across her forehead and met her eyes with reassurance. "Laura, we have to think positively. It's co-ed, so we won't be completely separated. But if we're not together, you have to promise you'll be strong for me." He finished his sentence with a heartfelt kiss.

She took a deep breath. "Wow; that was nice." A schoolgirl glow appeared on her face.

"So you promise," Dean said.

"Yeah, I promise."

* * * *

For the first time since the ordeal had begun, Laura felt warm and safe. She drew herself close to Dean, head to his chest, feeling the beating of his heart, and they had no trouble passing the three hour journey with conversation.

Chapter Twenty-One

"Dean, I think they're coming for us."

Laura was right. They didn't have much time. The pod had set down, and he could hear a flurry of activity outside the cell.

"Hey, come here. We probably don't have much time. You remember what I told you. No matter what, I'm here for you, and you have to be strong." Dean took Laura into his arms and looked into her eyes, their sparkle still stifled with fear. In a whisper, he said, "You're so beautiful." He brought her in close and kissed her, running his fingers through her soft hair. She kissed him back, and they held on as long as they dare. *Clunk.* The door lock disengaged. He brought her hand up to his chest and held it against his heart. "You remember."

"I will."

Dean took a step back as the door started to swing open. He felt his own sense of uneasiness but knew Laura was terrified. The pit in his stomach told him Larry's take on prison social structure was right. As the guards descended into the cell, he put his hand over his heart and gave her one last glance of encouragement.

Two male guards equipped with laser pistols escorted them out of the pod. They didn't bother to cuff them.

* * * *

One of Laura's fondest memories was of her holiday in Barbados a year earlier with her sister, Sam. Laura had reveled in the anticipation, and when the flight landed, she was beaming. Her first memory was the best. The doors flung open, and the craft filled with fresh humid air. After breathing the cool Swiss mountain air back home, she took as deep a breath as she could, savoring the flowery aroma. Exiting the pod on Draco was an entirely different experience.

As they descended the few steps into the hangar, the hot dry air smelled like a smouldering garbage dump. Laura gasped, fighting off the burning sensation at the back of her throat as it became doused with a blast of sulfur. The guard laughed. "Lots of sulfur here. Eventually you won't even notice it. Don't worry it's not toxic levels."

It looked like twilight in the hangar with the sparse ceiling lights shining like full moons; hunter's moons with the fine yellow-orange dust that hung in the air. It was as though a toxic mist had settled in a valley. *The valley of the damned.* Laura's gaze was cast down to her footprints in the dust on the floor. They looked nothing like the ones she'd left on the Barbados beach. These were shallow and the sickly color of urine. *Lots of sulfur,* were Dean's words. She didn't think much of it at the time; now she did.

The guards led them toward the large steel door centered on the far wall. They passed a group of armed guards loading boxes onto a small freighter. The pod parked next to it was under repair, and they had to detour around the pieces of shiny grid panels and tools in their path. As they approached the door, Laura could see a red glow coming from the scanner panel to its side. She was pretty certain her DNA would count for nothing when it came to opening the door. It was the gate to hell, and she had a one way ticket. One of the guards waved his hand in front of the panel. The red glow changed to green, and the door opened.

They entered a short hallway, even darker than the hangar, and quickly arrived at *The Orientation Room.* Laura felt tremendous trepidation as the guard hustled her in. This room *was* brightly lit. A chain extended from the ceiling, and at the end of it, dead center over the table, hung a single bare bulb. Laura squinted until her eyes adjusted. Larry Dunn was talking to a man in uniform. The guards signaled Dean and Laura to sit in the chairs by the table and then stepped outside and waited.

Larry spoke first. "So I hope the two of you enjoyed your flight. Since I was escorting you, there was no need to stop at the Lyra Base Station to check in. That sped things up. I would like you to meet Mr. McLean. He's the warden here. You can refer to him as God, and I suggest you do as you're told. He doesn't take kindly to people stepping out of line. I just finished briefing him on the two of you, and if you don't mind, I'll be on my way." Larry nodded to McLean and headed toward the door.

"See you in hell," Dean muttered under his breath as he went by.

McLean grabbed the Discipline Club hanging off his pants and slammed it on the table. The loud noise reverberated around the room, and Laura started backward in her chair while Dean sat glaring at the man. The bare bulb started its pendulum swing. "Perhaps Weston, the first lesson you need to learn around here is respect." As he yelled, his bushy black eyebrows came together, exaggerating the deep lines in his weathered complexion. The man had the look of a mountain hillbilly, and as he spoke, his lips revealed a row of uneven, yellowed teeth jutting from his jowl.

"No disrespect intended, sir," Dean said.

McLean glared back at Dean before starting. "It seems to me you're the one who's arrived in the land of fire and brimstone not Dunn. The sulfur and blazing sun make a delectable combination as you'll soon find out. I'm going to explain the rules around here. I'm sure you know we're operating a diamond mine. Every day is the same at the Draco Pen. The alarm sounds at six o'clock in the morning. At exactly six-twenty, you'll be dressed and standing by your cell door waiting for it to open. Every third morning is a shower morning; otherwise, when it opens, you will follow the guards in single file to breakfast, get your food when it's your turn, and sit at your group table.

"We work the mines in groups of six or eight, depending on the area. Everyone is assigned to a group, and by seven o'clock, you must be standing at your table waiting to be escorted to the dune buggies, which will take you into the field. As you get off the buggy, you will be shackled to your partner, and you'll work that way throughout the day. There will be a short lunch and periodic water breaks. You'll return for dinner at seven o'clock in the evening and be back in your cells by eight-thirty. If you're late or if you cause any problems, you will be disciplined." McLean pulled a small rounded pistol from his pocket. "Weston, you're a military man. Have you seen one of these?"

"No, sir, I haven't."

"Not surprising. They're fairly new and likely not being used for non-military applications. It's called a resonator. Tacky name but quite descriptive. The two of you are science types. I'm sure you know what happens to an object when a vibration brings it to its natural frequency.

It resonates."

"Yes, I think we're familiar with the principle," Dean said.

"Well this little gadget emits a strong energy pulse that throws the human body into resonance. Do you have any idea what that does to one's nervous system? We were fortunate enough to add these babies to our repertoire, and since then, not one person has been sent to solitary confinement. Do you catch my drift here?"

"You make your point quite clearly," Dean said.

"Miss Simmons, you are awfully quiet. Do you understand what I'm saying? I wouldn't want to see a pretty thing like you quivering on the ground in agony, wetting her pants as a result of poor communication."

Laura's mouth felt pasted closed. "I understand," she whispered. "Are we in the same work group?"

McLean laughed gleefully. "Oh, let me see." He pulled open a file from the table. "Weston, you're in Group Seven and Simmons…" The man paused as he grabbed the pen from the top of the file folder and proceeded to make a little note. "It looks like you're in Group Ten." He cracked a half smile as he looked down at Laura. "Very well, we're done here. The guards will get you set up and show you to your cell. By then, you should be just in time to join your groups for dinner."

While they had been talking, a female guard had replaced one of the men at the door. As they exited the room, she grabbed Laura's arm and ordered, "You! Come with me." Before Laura had a chance to look back at Dean, the woman whisked her through a door designated Women's Block.

* * * *

Dean followed the guard into the Men's Block. Their first stop was a change station where the man ordered him to remove his clothing and personal effects. Standing stark naked, he flicked the clasp of the watch his parents had given him when he graduated engineering. His mother had picked it out, and it was the last gift she'd ever given him. "Please, can I wear my watch?"

"Put it in the tray now!"

Dean took one last look at the silver Swiss Army watch. It kept perfect time, and he loved the GPS feature as his sense of direction was terrible. The sharp needle of the second hand ticked around as it always did, and the date glowed red in the upper right corner. *August 12, 2299, the day my life ended.* He flipped it over and ran his thumb across his initials scribed on the back then, reluctantly, set it down in the small metal tray the man held. It was like saying goodbye to his mother all over again.

"Now arms up and do a three sixty for me," the guard commanded.

As Dean followed the instructions, he thought of Laura going through the same demoralizing procedure. He hoped she had more inner courage than appeared on the surface.

The guard handed him a cloth bag full of clothing and a few toiletries. "You have two sets of clothes and one pair of shoes. There's no laundry service. You can wash them in the sink in your cell and hang them on the rack to dry. They're replaced once a year. Get dressed."

Dean put on the plain black pants and the gray T-shirt with the Draco Penitentiary insignia embossed on the top right. When he was ready, he picked up the bag and followed the guard through a door into a long dark tunnel that appeared to run over fifty meters. Leaky pipes ran the length of the arched concrete ceiling, and bare lights hung periodically casting reflections on the moisture soaked walls. A garden of mold glistening black complemented the edge of the floor. A drip from the ceiling landed on Dean's forehead and left a sticky residue when he tried to wipe it off.

They passed through another steel door and arrived in the cell block. The two rolls of cells were all on one level with a main corridor between them. Dean followed the guard almost to the end of the block. "You're in cell thirty-seven. Everything you need is in here. When you get ready each morning, you better remember to clip your cup to your pants, or you'll be damn thirsty."

The cell felt cave-like: three concrete walls with bars across the front. Perhaps a good place for a bear to curl up and hibernate but hardly big enough for one person to live. The guard accompanied Dean inside, leaving little room for moving around. Dean threw his bag on the small cot that ran along the wall. There were no bed sheets. A blanket, towel, and a metal cup lay at the foot of the bed. To the right of the bed were a toilet and a large sink. The small mirror mounted above the sink had the reflective qualities of aluminum foil. A rack hung along the remaining length of the wall. The small ceiling fixture sat in its own wire mesh cage, and it barely gave off enough light to illuminate the musty room.

"Any reading material, or do I just lie here counting sheep?" Dean said.

"Don't be smart. It won't get you far around here. Reading material is granted based on good behavior. Now let's go; dinner is about to start."

The wide door at the end of the hallway emptied out directly into the dining hall. Other prisoners were filing in, and the guard escorted Dean to Table Seven. "When everyone's seated, they will call you up by group number. There are two food stations. You go to the closer one." The guard pointed to the left. "Now sit down and behave yourself."

The large room had a hollow feel to it, and the battleship blue paint did nothing for the ambiance. The tables were clearly identified by numbers on the wall. Laura would sit across the main aisle from Dean and a couple of tables up toward the far food station. There was no sign of Laura. Seats quickly filled up one by one as the groups strolled in.

Dean sat tapping his fingers on the table catching several curious glances. *I guess I'm the new guy.* He thought of Larry's words of advice as he minded his own business, avoiding eye contact.

"Oh, look, who do we have here?"

The cheery voice with a faint British accent was the last thing Dean expected to hear. He looked up to see a man who appeared to be in his early thirties. The man stood on the shorter end of the scale and had sandy blond hair. His scruffy attempt at growing a beard stripped ten years off him. He had a happy look to him as he sat down across from Dean. "Hi, there, I take it you're new. I'm Andy Weber; nice to meet you." He reached out to Dean.

A throaty laugh sounded from down the table. "Weber, you're going to get your head lopped off one of these days with that approach."

Dean extended his arm to accept the greeting. "Dean Weston and don't worry, I'm not the head lopping type."

"Well, that's good. So what brings you to this fine hotel?"

Dean leaned back and flashed a cool smile. "A sad misunderstanding."

"Oh yeah, you're all the same. We'll get the dirt eventually."

"I know who you are." Dean was so transfixed by Andy's warm welcome, he hadn't noticed the young kid who'd sat down next to Andy, but he recognized the voice immediately. "You're one of the pricks who questioned me on the Eagle Base Station."

Dean gave the kid a good, hard look, and his memory of that day refreshed. His was a face he wouldn't soon forget, young and innocent looking with red hair and a fine collection of freckles—even more than Annie had. He had sat across the table from him in the interrogation room at the Eagle Detention Center for over an hour while they drilled him with questions. He openly accepted responsibility for his part in the drug smuggling ring. At the time, it had left Dean with an uneasy feeling about how such a young kid could have become so heavily involved in such a slimy operation. They were smuggling a new drug called anthaline, which when taken with alcohol, could cause cardiac arrest. Several young deaths had already been blamed on the narcotic.

"Yeah, I remember you. You were involved in the anthaline bust," Dean said.

"Yeah that's right, and you're one of the ass wipes who screwed me over without even looking into why I did it. It's all right, Charlie will see to it you get what's coming to you."

"What the hell are you talking about? You were trafficking a drug attributed to over ten deaths in the last year...all kids."

Andy interrupted. "I don't know what went on between the two of you; but I'll tell you, Dean, this kid doesn't belong here. And whoever put him here ought to be hung out to dry for not digging up the facts."

Andy's comment struck a nerve. "Oh, what facts are these?" Dean asked.

Andy reached over and tapped Jeff on the shoulder. "Do you mind?"

"Go right ahead, he may as well know why I'm going to kick his ass."

"Perhaps you remember the Gibbons murder in the news about five years ago. Jeff was thirteen at the time, and his sister was eleven. The two of them were in the room when their father hacked their mother to death. He turned on them next, but hero Jeff here managed to get his sister to safety. The kids had no other family. Their neighbors, kingpin Charlie and his wife, offered to take them in. Do you see where this is going?" Andy leaned toward Dean. "How'd you like to be a thirteen year old kid with the well-being of your kid sister resting on your shoulders? You'd do what you're told. Jeff has been Charlie's little puppet ever since. He took most of the heat in that bust because he had to protect his kid sister. They handed him an adult conviction, and he's going to be here till hell freezes over. So now, Dean, why don't you tell us what you did to land your rosy ass in this hell hole?"

Dean felt a cold flush come over him. There was no overcoming the guilt pit growing in his stomach. "Jeff, I'm sorry. I had no idea."

"No one did; no one questioned. That's the point. No one gives a shit about anyone else. Guilty as charged, end of story. So here I rot with the rest of these pigs. What do the French say? *C'est la vie.*"

"The guards make a point of keeping Jeff and Charlie Hopkins apart and so do we. Charlie's in Group Ten. Jeff here's a good kid. You better watch your back. 'Cause if you were involved in putting Hopkins away, you can be sure he'll be looking for an opportunity to rip you apart. Now tell us, why are you here?"

"Table Seven." The announcement sounded and without hesitation, everyone at the table stood and filed their way to the trough like a herd of cattle.

Dean picked up a metal plate heaped with unrecognizable food. "Is this edible?"

Andy laughed—the infectious kind that can get a whole crowd going. "Not to the rest of the world. Looks like its calamander today. Tastes like crap, but you better eat it, or you fry in the sun tomorrow. They put sunscreen additives in the food, and trust me, the burn is worse than the food."

Dean was too edgy to join in and only grinned. On his way back to the table, Dean took another look around for Laura. She was nowhere in sight. Everyone returned to their original seats, and as Dean grabbed his fork, he looked up at Andy and asked, "What the hell's calamander?"

"You don't know a hell of a lot about this place do you?" Andy said.

"Should I?"

Andy laughed again. "Calamander is one of the two bugs indigenous to this planet."

Dean teased the black fleshy meat with his fork. "What the hell kind of bug comes in bite size?"

"A big ugly one. They look kind of like a salamander, but they're closer to cat size. Probably wouldn't make a good pet. They're not the ones you have to worry about though. Harmless and tastes like chicken." Andy unleashed another bout of laughter. This time Dean shot him a full out smile. "It's the rainbow bugs that aren't friendly."

"What...do they bite?"

"No, you just don't want to fall into one of their nests...not dinner conversation. It's loose dirt, almost like dry quick sand. You'd fall right in if you stepped on it. Don't worry, they're marked in the areas we're working." Dean continued to play with his food and then looked back up at Andy, who alternated between chewing and smiling. "You better eat that, there's not much time."

Dean took a bite and choked it down. It was chewy like bubble gum and tasted like liver. "Got any ketchup?"

Andy laughed. Dean finally succumbed and joined in. "I have the dirt on my hands." Andy reached over and rubbed his yellowed fingers together over Dean's plate.

"Mighty obliged, you're a good man Andy."

The group finished their meal and returned to their cells. There was no sign of Laura.

Chapter Twenty-Two

Buzzzzz.

The ear piercing horn sounded, startling Laura from her fitful sleep. She shivered a little before huddling into a ball under her blanket hiding her head under the musty pillow. For a drowsy moment, her mind drifted to Barbados. *What shall we do today? Maybe a boat cruise followed by a dinner with some frosty pink umbrella drinks.* She could picture the panoramic view off the balcony with the palm lined beach and crystal clear turquoise water dotted with sailboats drifting dreamily across the horizon. And then there was Sam, her sister and best friend through thick and thin. Always cracking lame jokes, knock-knocks being her specialty, setting the pace for another off-the-wall fun adventure. There was never a dull moment with Sam. From parties to late night swims, she never faltered in fueling Laura's spark for life.

Suddenly, Laura felt the pit in her gut starting to widen, and she was afraid it would soon become so gaping that everything defining her would spill out and be lost forever. Anchored in the bottom was a desperate longing for the ones she loved. She could only imagine her families' reaction to the news—disappointment, devastation, resentment. Would she ever see them again? Would she grow old and die in this prison? All she had left to keep her together was the companionship of someone she'd just met. She valued the bond she seemed to have formed with Dean, but it was new and fragile. She feared if she rarely saw him, it would crumble. She remembered his words about how she had to be strong. He'd put on a brave face, but she'd seen through it. He'd lost even more than she had, so perhaps if he could put on a brave face, she could too.

"Ya better wake up, honey. Don't have much time." The crusty voice echoed from across the corridor.

Laura cringed. *Great. Biker chicks instead of beach babes.* She rolled over, and her eyelids slowly opened. The ceiling fixture came into focus—yet another bare bulb, but this one in its own little intimidating prison. She was pretty sure the gnawing in her stomach wasn't going away, but the nausea had passed. The evening before, her nerves caught up with her and when it was time to be escorted to dinner, she found herself bent over the foul smelling toilet. The guard cut her some slack and let her stay in her cell, but she was certain the sympathy ended here. She took a few more seconds to psyche herself and then sat up.

Peering through the bars, across the corridor, she could see three other cells. The women were busy dressing, but one took a minute to glance in her direction. The rather robust woman was putting on her bra. "Hey there, ya like what you see?"

Laura, embarrassed, got to her feet and quickly changed. She focused on the tasks at hand, trying to ignore her tight quarters. She was in the middle of rinsing out her panties when the buzzer sounded again. Having no time to finish the job, she left them dripping over the side of the sink and sped to the door just as it slid open. Several guards were herding the women to the mess hall, and Laura followed, marching down the corridor single file.

She found her way to Table Ten and took a seat with a view of Table Seven, hoping to catch Dean as he filed in. Just as she caught his eye, an attractive brunette woman plunked herself in the next seat demanding her attention.

"Oh, a new face. I hope you're not as boring as the rest of the people here."

Laura only half heard what she said. "Sorry…What?"

"I said who are you looking at?"

"My friend's over there. I was just trying to get his attention," Laura replied.

"Oh, he's cute. Just how good a friend is he?"

"Pretty good."

"My name's Sandra, and you might be?"

"Laura Simmons," Laura rested her elbow on the table with her chin against her fist and looked at Sandra. Sandra's hair had a slight wave to it as it crossed her high cheek bones flowing to just below her shoulders.

"So who's your friend?"

"Dean, Dean Weston," Laura said.

"So what are the two of you, a modern day Bonnie and Clyde?" Sandra's green eyes perked up.

Laura snickered. "Something like that."

Sandra fluffed her hair up while cracking a seductive smile and looked over toward Dean and waved. He made eye contact with Laura as he sat. "Oh, isn't this poetic justice. Two lovers torn apart by their hideous crime. So what bank did you rob?"

Laura raised her eyebrows in a matter of fact sort of way. "We murdered a nosy neighbor."

Sandra laughed. "*Touché*! I think I'm going to like you, Laura."

"Table Ten," the announcement sounded.

"Come on, that's us." Sandra grabbed Laura by the arm and headed toward the food station.

Laura continued to look back as she walked. As she waited for her plate, Dean put his hand to his chest and mouthed some words. She couldn't make them out, but she knew what he said and nodded.

She brought her food back to the table. The cold oatmeal repulsed her, but after the past night something had to fill the void. "What's his problem?" Laura signaled to the man at the end of the table shoveling his food in with a sour look on his face.

"That's Charlie. He's a weathered old dick. He thinks the world owes him something. Well, doesn't it owe us all something? It's the fun you make for yourself on the way that counts. Hey watch this." Sandra took a small piece of her napkin and rolled it up then popped it in her mouth. Two seconds later it went flying through the air landing perfectly on the side of Charlie's cheek. "Quick, look inconspicuous."

Laura, somewhat amused by Sandra's stunt directed her attention to her food and took a big bite trying not to laugh. "This is really disgusting."

Charlie pounded on the table with his fist, and shouted, "Who did that?"

A guard hurried to Charlie's side holding a resonator. "Take it easy big boy."

Charlie glared down the table, grunting something under his breath and settled back to his food.

"I call him the troll," Sandra said, smirking.

Laura approved of the name. She put him in his sixties and found him hideously ugly. He was bald of his own accord with a nose so bulbous it looked as though he'd stolen it from a cartoon character. He had a trademark *sinister* appeal.

The buzzer sounded again indicating the end of breakfast, and just as everyone started to get up, the lights went out. The emergency lights illuminated almost as fast as the guards pulled their weapons.

"Stay seated until we have full power." The guards paced the aisles for several minutes. A low level of power returned. The lighting was dim but enough to allow everyone to exit, table by table.

Laura followed Sandra to a warehouse where a series of large passenger dune buggies were parked in a row. Sandra walked straight to the one with a "10" inscribed on its back and before getting in, grabbed some knee pads from a bin. "You'll want a pair of these, or you'll have a hole worn in your pants by lunch," she said.

A multitude of armed guards were present to oversee the loading of prisoners. "Hurry along, get seated."

Laura sat on the bench beside Sandra, and before she knew it, Charlie was sitting on her other side. Once all the passengers were loaded, the buggies took off one by one, forming a Conga line as they emerged into the blazing Draco sun. The fiery orange ball was rising in the sky, making it an odd shade of green, not unlike olive oil. A yellow dust cloud erupted in their path, obstructing their view of the sparse desert landscape. As the buggy gained speed, it bounced along overtop the dunes launching small pebbles from the spinning tires.

"Ouch!" Laura caught a pebble just under her eye. The impact was not enough to draw blood, but she shielded her eyes with her hands. Squinting through the sunlight and dust, there was nothing but pebbly dunes as far as the eye could see. Laura had to speak up to be heard. "How far do we go?"

"About fifteen minutes out," Sandra replied.

"So has anyone tried jumping for it?"

"Yeah, a couple months ago. It didn't have a happy ending."

All of a sudden Charlie spoke up. "I heard someone mention Dean Weston this morning. Is that the Weston at the Eagle Base Station?"

Laura looked over. The profile of his nose was even more impressive. "What's it to you?"

"Dean Weston was involved in landing me in this shit hole, that's what." Charlie's voice was almost an octave lower than most men and seemed to be well matched with his face.

Laura inched closer to Sandra. "Well, that must be a different Dean Weston. There were two of them living on the Eagle Base Station you know."

"I'm going to kill that bastard!" Charlie grumbled.

The buggy banked the side of a hill and came to a stop beside a collection of sheds. Everyone stood up and filed off in pairs, stopping at the exit to accept their shackles. "Stick with me. Most of the people in this group are jerks." Sandra grabbed Laura's arm again and started toward the front of the buggy.

As they stepped off the buggy, a guard secured a metal clamp around each of their ankles. "Take a tray and wait over there." The man gestured to the right, and the women started their three-legged race over to the rest of their group.

Once the clanking of metal chains stopped, the guard spoke up. "This is a new area with lots of potential. Small stones go in the buckets provided. If you find anything of significance, let one of us know. Now spread out a bit and get to work."

Laura looked at Sandra. "What do we do?"

"Use your tray and dig. It's not rocket science. Look for stones that glimmer even a little. They're not exactly ready for the wedding band, but you'll know if you find one."

Laura got on her hands and knees and started digging through the endless sea of irregularly shaped pebbles. Their sizes ranged from a few millimeters to the size of a thumbnail, some smooth, some sharp, and all mixed together in a fine yellow dust. She was finally getting used to the putrid, inescapable smell of sulfur. The two women tried to segregate themselves somewhat from the group, and Laura had a clear view of Dean working about thirty meters away. His shackle partner was an Asian man who appeared to be in his early forties. Laura glanced over often. His group seemed to be sticking close together, and several conversations appeared to have sparked up.

"So what's the deal with the two of you? Are you an item?"

"Huh?"

"Mr. Suave and Debonair, you haven't taken your eyes off him."

"I'd hardly describe him as suave and debonair. He's more the rough and tumble type."

Sandra stopped her digging, her expression insistent. "Well…are you an item?"

"Well, sort of I guess."

"That doesn't sound too positive. Have you screwed him?"

"None of your business. We're close. How 'bout we leave it at that."

"I see. This sounds interesting." Sandra took a short break to look Dean up and down and give him a slow, flirty wink.

Out of habit, Laura tried to check her watch several times during the course of the morning. Perhaps it was a good thing they'd taken it from her. It would be torturous knowing how many hours were left in the day. Lunch took forever to arrive, and when it did, it was short and nasty. Laura likened her tuna sandwich to pet food. It was warmed by the sun and gave her a belly ache.

So far, only a few small gleaming stones lay in the group bucket. Laura continued to dig, doomed to spend the rest of her life looking for the proverbial needle in a haystack. Her legs were aching, and the back of her neck and arms felt like they were frying in the scorching afternoon sun. Fortunately, Sandra was an entertaining partner with a quick sense of humor and a reckless fun-loving disposition—attributes that reminded her of her sister, Sam. Sandra chatted her ear off for most of the morning, and Laura learned Sandra ended up in the Pen as a result of a drunken bar fight. A group of them were playing poker, and at the end of the game, Sandra discovered one of them was cheating. A cat fight erupted, and she ended up pushing her foe toward a stone fireplace. The woman cracked her head on the hearth as she fell. She was dead by the time she hit the floor. Laura welcomed Sandra's friendship; however, she didn't appreciate Sandra's overzealous interest in Dean.

Laura took the last sip of water from her tin cup and licked her lips. They felt dry and chapped. The mid-afternoon water break did little to sooth her parched throat. Nevertheless, she enjoyed it; sitting cross legged was a glorious change from the doggy stance she'd been frozen into for the bulk of the day. A vicious scowl from a passing guard told her the break was over, and she returned to the *ruff* position. Within seconds, something caught her eye. "Hey look, I think I found one."

Sandra stopped and looked. "Wow, that's a beaut!" She grabbed it out of her hands. "Excuse me, guard. I need to use the washroom."

The guard approached the two of them, released the clasp from Sandra's ankle, and escorted her to the shack marked "Women." Once there, she paused to talk to him and in the course of their discussion, handed him something. She returned a few minutes later.

Laura was curious. "What were you doing?"

"Nothing."

"Where's the stone?"

"Never mind, just get back to work," Sandra said.

The guard glared at the two of them, so Laura decided to let it go. Sandra's chattiness seemed to have evaporated into the heat of the afternoon sun, and Laura continued to work quietly for some time exchanging glances with Dean. Eventually, one of her glances caught him walking with a guard over to the "Men's" shack. Laura watched him until Sandra spoke up.

"Excuse me, guard, I need to use the facilities again. Too much water."

Yeah right! Laura thought to herself; her throat scorched.

The man repeated the routine as Laura looked on. Only this time, he escorted Sandra to the shack marked "Men." She disappeared inside. Laura, becoming anxious, stopped working and stared, waiting for Dean to come out the door. *What the hell is she doing?*

A minute went by before Dean flew out the door fuming. Sandra came out yelling, "Stop him. That son of a bitch tried to rape me!"

Dean stopped in his tracks and turned toward Sandra. "To hell I did, you are one messed up—"

Before Dean had a chance to finish his sentence, an ear piercing screech shot from the resonator in the guard's hand. In an instant, Dean met the ground with a scream. His hands jittered on his stomach as his

164

torso flailed five inches up and down. He continued with lips smacking until drool started trickling from the corner of his mouth.

Laura witnessed the seizure with astonishment. She got to her feet and started running toward him only to be stopped by another armed guard.

"Get back to your group, or you'll be joining him on the ground," the guard insisted.

As the man spoke, Sandra dashed by with a satisfied grin on her face. She grabbed Laura's arm. "Come on, you don't want to get involved in that."

Laura shook her arm free. "Get your hands off me, you fucking bitch."

The guard aimed his resonator at Laura again, commanding her to return to her group while another rushed over with his Discipline Club. She remained insistent she get to Dean.

"That's enough! This is none of your concern!" The man yelled as he whacked Laura on the back of the knees. She immediately fell to the ground screaming. The two guards dragged her back to the group and shackled her to Sandra. "Shut up and work."

Laura tried wiping away her tears, but the sulfur on her hands just made her eyes burn. She looked toward Dean struggling to focus, blinking repeatedly to alleviate the pain. She cringed as the sound of a wounded animal blared from his quivering body.

Charlie started to laugh. "Doing the spittin' bacon on the ground is he."

Laura wanted to give him an evil look, but the burning in her eyes was paralyzing. She closed them, waiting for the tears to cleanse them and pretended to look busy while every vein in her body boiled with rage toward Sandra. *I'll get you for this.*

It took fifteen minutes before Dean recovered enough to stumble back to his group. Once there, he fell to the ground, and the guard shackled him to his partner. When prompted to work, he dug like a cat in its litter box a few times before collapsing again. When Laura's eyes finally cleared, she didn't take them off him.

"What's with the silent treatment? No hard feelings. I was just having a little fun. By the way, your boyfriend's a great kisser," Sandra said.

"Shut the fuck up."

* * * *

Dean still felt a little shaky on his feet as he made his way to his table for dinner. As he went to sit down beside Andy, he stumbled a little.

Andy caught him. "Easy there big boy."

Dean hadn't said much since being blasted with the resonator, and what he had said, came out rather stuttered.

"You able to talk yet?" Andy said.

"Enough to tear a strip off that psychopathic bitch." Dean leaned on the table, rubbing his forehead as the pounding in his head slid a little closer to the front of his skull.

"Well, don't feel so bad; you're the third guy she's done that to. Mind you the second guy took her up on her proposal."

"Somebody ought to teach her a lesson," Dean said.

"I'll bet your girlfriend has something up her sleeve."

"I wish I could talk to her; I'm sure she won't be taking this well. I can just imagine what she's going through now, and it looks like she's burnt to a crisp." Dean could only see the back of Laura, but her arms were tomato red. He pursed his lips together, and his gaze sank to his lap. He missed her.

Jeff sat across the table from the two of them, massaging the well-defined dimple in his chin. "You know, Dean, you seem pretty fused about your hottie over there for a cold blooded killer. The shoe doesn't fit."

"Yeah, how so?"

"I've been around slime-balls all my life. My father's one, and Charlie and his friends are too. You're just like you were when you questioned me. All concerned about people. Heartless killers like our friend Sim over there just don't give a crap." Jeff motioned to the Chinese assassin at the far end of the table—Dean's shackle partner.

Dean looked at Jeff with sincerity. "Shit happens, kid."

"Table Ten." *Laura's table!* Dean launched himself from his seat, hoping he could catch her for even a second. On route to his food station, he carved a wide turn to cross paths with her line.

"Laura," he said from behind her. As she turned around, he grabbed the hand she had resting on her hip.

She had longing eyes, and he wanted to take her into his arms. "Are you o—"

"Move along, Weston. Your line's over there," a guard said.

Dean didn't dare disobey. He squeezed her hand for a brief moment, and then their fingers slid apart as the guard gave him a push. Dean put his hand to his chest, and Laura gave him a nod. He could see her eyes tearing. The guard gave him another nudge, and he joined Andy in line.

"You really care about her don't you? Jeff's got a point. You don't seem the killing type," Andy said.

Dean said nothing as he collected his food and returned to the table. Andy and Jeff swapped a few jokes about the soggy pasta they were eating, trying to lift Dean out of his funk.

"Umm, I love muckaroni," Jeff said as he took his first bite.

Dean remained distracted, while watching Laura's back. The psychotic bitch sat across from her and appeared to be full of conversation as if everything was fine. Charlie Hopkins glared at the two of them from the opposite end of the table. Laura just held her head down and ate.

"What do you make of this, Dean?" Hanging off the end of Andy's fork was what looked to be a small piece of toilet paper. The wet fibres started pulling apart under its own weight, and the piece fell back to his plate with a splat.

Dean chuckled. "You going to eat that?"

"Sure, why not; it might save me some work on the other end." Andy mixed the paper in with a bite of pasta and munched it down.

Jeff piped up. "You're one messed up dude."

Dean thought the whole thing was hilarious and looked at Andy. "You remind me a bit of my friend, Matt. Funniest guy I know."

"So who's Matt?" Andy said.

"My ex-wife's brother. He introduced us."

Jeff furrowed his brow. "And you killed her. Bull Shit. I know the drill."

"Leave it alone kid." Dean took a bite—vile, but a far cry better than the previous dinner.

"Dean, watch out!" The yell came from the bitch. Dean recognized her voice immediately after their close encounter.

He looked up from his food. Charlie Hopkins was a foot away, rearing his fork back preparing to launch an attack. Dean grabbed Charlie's arm on its way toward his chest. The fork went through the flimsy fibres of his shirt just breaking the skin. Dean stood up kicking Charlie's legs out from under him, landing him on the floor. The fork dangled from Dean's shirt, and a couple of small spots of blood appeared. Within seconds, an ear-piercing screech sounded from a resonator. Charlie's body lay quivering on the floor, and a wet circle started to grow in the crotch of his pants. Two guards dragged Charlie out of the dining hall as the others tried to maintain control.

"Settle down," several guards commanded, waving their resonators. The prisoners quickly got back to their meals.

Dean pulled the fork from his shirt and wiped it clean. The prongs had been crudely sharpened. He looked to Laura who was exchanging some words with Sandra. Only a few minutes went by before the final horn sounded for the prisoners to return to their cells.

Chapter Twenty-Three

"Ouch, that hurt, you stupid-head!"

Ivan cackled as he scooped up another handful of cold, wet snow. His mitts were soaked—ideal for smoothing his perfectly formed ammunition with a thin crust of ice on its surface. The bright sun reflected off the icy lake, narrowing his eyes to slits. It was warm, and the air smelled fresh, a sure sign of spring. He worked quickly taking pride in his creation as he formed the snow into a perfect sphere. He squeezed as hard as he could, molding his creation into a sparkling work of art. *This time you're getting it in the head!* A few finishing touches and it was ready, one of the finest of the afternoon. He wound up and took aim, releasing the icy projectile at just the right time.

The frozen ball flew through the air with the trajectory of a home run hit. Ivan stood breathless waiting for the impact.

Whack!

The sound of the exploding snowball echoed across the lake, blaring over the peaceful trickling of melting snow. Nathan grabbed at his shoulder, cursing as he struggled to regain his balance. The slick snow was too smooth. He tumbled to the ground, crashing through the crust and into the melting snow below. Jagged chunks of ice surrounded him, and he reached out for one, flinging it toward his brother with all his might.

Ivan watched as the ice shard spun at him and set his arm up for a block. The ice caught the edge of his jacket only enough to slow it down on route to his forehead, where its sharp edge sliced a perfect red gash. "You're dead you little jerk!"

Ivan launched himself at Nathan just as he had got to his feet and landed the two of them on the snowy ground. He pounded Nathan on his side as hard as he could until he broke away.

"I'm going to tell Mom, and you're gonna get it," Nathan screamed as he ran toward the lake.

"Don't be such a girl!" Ivan started after him, but in a split second, Nathan was gone.

"Nathan, Nathan!" Ivan screamed in horror as he watched the larger sheets of ice float back to the surface closing off the watery hole. With wide eyes, he searched around for help, but there was no one. "Dad, Dad!" He screamed, praying he'd be heard. The trickling of the spring melt rang in his ears as he waited for a reply. He threw himself around in the direction of his house and bellowed again. "Mom, Dad!"

Time was running out and with an impulsive charge, he lowered himself through the hole into the ice blanketed water. It was nothing like the refreshing plunges of summer. A stabbing chill instantly shot through his body paralyzing and disorienting him. Quickly, his jacket and pants filled with a crushing blast of water sending his slender body into a deep freeze. He sputtered as he tried to hold air in his burning lungs. His waterlogged clothing started to drag him downward like lead armor. He kicked and kicked trying to propel himself back to the hole, but it was nowhere in sight. As he began his descent, an infinite white ceiling appeared overhead, like the lid of an immense crystal coffin.

A torrential wave of panic set in, and then he heard it. The sound of Nathan's garbled underwater screams. "Ivan, help me, save me!" The cries were earth-shattering. As he drifted downward unable to fight the dragging burden, he frantically turned toward the shrieks. Suddenly, the lake came to life with hundreds of sparkling colorful bubbles lighting his way; and there was Nathan, illuminated, sinking away from him, screaming and flailing in immeasurable terror. Numbness set in, but his instincts sent him kicking toward Nathan as fast as his stiffening joints would take him. "Ivan, help me, help me."

Ivan reached out for him, kicking his legs hard, struggling to reach him. Just as their fingertips touched something grabbed his leg. He kicked and kicked to free himself, but the grip was tight and painful. He jerked around to release himself and came face to face with a body. He recognized the grotesque bloodied woman. Her long black hair danced majestically with the current, and blood flowed outwards from the top of her head, creating an eerie light show amongst the sparkling bubbles. She switched her grip to his throat and with a choking clutch descended with him into the abyss. The water became thicker, redder, as he descended into the approaching darkness. The sparkling lights faded into the distance as did Nathan's screams. Suddenly, her skin began to melt away, and within seconds, there was nothing but a skeleton. He struggled in horror, his lungs screaming for oxygen, but he was too weak to fight his reflex. With bulging eyes, he took a deep inhale of icy water.

* * * *

Ivan shook awake in a cold sweat and jolted to an upright position. His breathing was uneasy, and his heart pounded in his chest. He rushed to the bathroom. With shaking hands, he ran the tap and splashed his face with cool water until the visions of his nightmare started to fade. It was a long time since he'd dreamed of his brother Nathan, but somehow the image of his face had returned with immeasurable clarity as if Ivan had seen him yesterday.

Nathan was only six years old at the time of the accident. During the years preceding it, Ivan held up the big brother image, never missing a chance to torment him. The memories of that warm March day plagued his mind for years. His feelings of guilt were exacerbated by the constant reminder from his parents that somehow it was his fault Nathan drowned in the lake. After Nathan disappeared through the ice, Ivan screamed, but no one came. Being only eight years old himself, he ran to the house to get his parents, but it was too late. Nathan was gone. The fact his parents had blamed him all those years ago came as no surprise. Ivan could never win their praise. No matter how hard he tried to get their attention or impress them with his achievements, he faced criticism and indifference. He had grown to loathe them.

As Ivan dried his face, he barely recognized the reflection looking back at him. The nightmare was so vivid he half expected to see a little boy smiling back with a devilish grin. That boy was gone, but Ivan wasn't entirely unhappy with what he'd become. He straightened himself up, making a sturdy attempt to erase the memories of his nightmare, an accomplishment he had become quite adept at over the years. He admired his slim frame in the mirror then glanced down at his watch.

Five o'clock in the morning, brilliant! It had been a long three days of unexpected travel dealing with Laura and Dean. Thanks to Larry Dunn's quick thinking, the whole fiasco had a good ending, and they could rest easy. Of course, he'd have an enormous backlog of work to return to. The last thing he wanted to do was go back to bed, so he ripped off his perspiration soaked T-shirt and jumped into the shower.

The sound of the running water started to bring back the images from the dream he was trying desperately to block out, so he washed quickly. He wrapped himself in a towel and made his way through his bedroom and around the corner into the walk-in closet.

"Closet lights on."

His fine selection of custom-made suits hung meticulously on a polished, black metal rod in the wood trimmed room. Ivan quickly made his selection, enjoying the crispness of his freshly pressed white shirt. Once dressed, he returned to the bedroom to tidy up. The navy blue Egyptian cotton sheets were jumbled in a heap in the middle of the bed, intertwined with the matching duvet. He pictured himself flailing beneath the covers as Nathan drifted into the abyss of his subconscious, his lungs full of icy lake water. He fled the apartment.

Chapter Twenty-Four

It seemed like lunch time when Ivan finally heard the familiar rustling at Pam's desk. At least his early start was productive. He wasted no time in setting aside his work to greet her. "It's about time!"

Pam smiled at him and put her purse on her desk, the latest Bouchard fashion—Ivan recognized it from the advertisements. She took out her lipstick and touched it up. Ivan thought the maroon was rather bold, but as usual, it matched her outfit flawlessly, including her stiletto shoes. "What are you talking about, it's eight-thirty. I'm in at this time every morning. How was your trip? We were all shocked when we heard about Dr. Simmons. She seemed like such a sincere person."

"Nobody could be more shocked than I. I had dinner with her after returning from the symposium and would never have guessed at her agenda. Fortunately, there was no harm done. Listen Pam, there's something very important I'd like to discuss with you. Perhaps you can join me in my office."

"Do you mind if I get a coffee first? I'd be happy to make it two."

"That would be wonderful."

Pam turned and left her office; her curvy behind, all packaged up in a snug black taffeta skirt, swayed back and forth like a runway model. Ivan watched her disappear out the door and then cast his gaze down to the trail of tiny heel imprints she left in the plush blue carpet. He smiled. Unfortunately, her intelligence did not entirely measure up to her physical attributes, something he was more than willing to overlook. He had a proposal for her, one he hoped she'd accept.

Ivan made himself comfortable on the couch, and Pam returned filling the room with the intoxicating aroma of Java straight from the Indonesian Islands.

"Just as you like it." A look of surprise crossed her face. "My goodness your office is tidy. What did you do with the stack of paperwork I left for you?"

"I thought I'd come in early to catch up. Please…join me on the couch." He tapped the cushion.

Pam set the cups down on the coffee table and took a seat beside Ivan, crossing her long slender legs toward him. Her calf came to rest rubbing against the material of his pants. Ivan made no attempt to move and set his hand down next to her leg, close but not quite touching.

Pam smiled. "So what did you need to talk about?"

"I am increasing your security clearance to the highest level."

Pam lifted an eyebrow. "And why would you do that?"

"Section Four. I am going to tell you about the research that's going on there, and I am hoping you will help us with a little experiment. Your participation will be rewarded." Ivan sensed some apprehension creeping into her expression. "Please relax. This is high security, but I'd like this to be a casual conversation, and I want your full attention as you'll be amazed at what I have to say." Ivan took a minute to study her. Her socially extraverted personality did not extend into her professional world; there she seemed insecure and timid. "I'm about to open your mind to one of the most significant discoveries ever made. Intelligent life we believe may help substantiate the existence of the human soul."

Ivan knew he would hit a nerve, and the look on Pam's face confirmed it. She was quite religious and loved to participate in mind expanding discussions centered on faith, spiritualism, and humanity.

"I don't understand. How is that possible?"

"Well, it all started on a mining expedition about eighteen months ago. Let me explain." Ivan took his time filling Pam in on the events that took place on Spectra, strategically leaving out a few details. "Because our presence seemed to be adversely affecting the entities, the six of us agreed the planet could not be mined. However, we also agreed the discovery was so staggering, some amount of research had to be carried out. A limited number of entities have been taken from the planet for that purpose. They are being safely kept in particle storage. Our mandate is to study them, learn as much as we can and then return them to Spectra.

"As I mentioned, one of the positive side effects of exposure is an increase in cognitive abilities. Everyone participating in the study has experienced it. I'm significantly smarter. I have perfect memory, both visual and audio. I can make objects move with my thoughts; I heal quickly, and I'm slightly telepathic. I can even sense the energy in things. It's incredible beyond words, and the potential of what we can achieve is immeasurable. Pam, I've been sharing the results of our research with a Dr. Irena Zowski. She has an undergraduate degree in physics and is a doctor of psychology. She's a true expert in metaphysics and the paranormal and has come all the way from Moscow to meet with us. She works for the Psychology Institute of the Russian Academy of Science."

"She's scheduled to see you this afternoon," Pam said.

"Yes, you're quite correct, at one o'clock. Dr. Zowski has confirmed the electromagnetic fields measured from the entities are the same as those measured from the human energy field. Some people like to think of the human energy field as the energy aura surrounding the human body. Aura readers claim to be able to sense this energy, and some even claim to be able to see it. How much do you know about the human energy field?"

"Sorry, Ivan, but I don't even know what an electromagnetic field is. Science wasn't my strong point." Pam giggled defensively.

"That's fine. Let me give you the layman's crash course." Ivan enjoyed a taste of his coffee, contemplating how to explain electromagnetic wave theory in a way she would understand. His cognitive abilities had become so acute, he struggled explaining anything at a simple level, or an idiot's level for that matter. Ironically, if she accepted his proposal, this laborious exercise would be redundant. He buried his impatience as he wanted very much to have her on board.

There were few people who could be trusted with full disclosure. Despite Pam's religious beliefs, she was not the most morally upstanding individual he'd ever met. He was certain she was having an affair with her best friend's husband. Her friend traveled often with her job, and having on occasion been involved with married women himself, Ivan recognized the signs. The discrete calls and lunches at romantic restaurants were a telltale, but most of all, her body language when talking about him was a dead giveaway.

Ivan settled back into the cushiony leather, angled toward Pam. "Electromagnetic radiation consists of an electric and magnetic field, a field simply being anything that can emit a force. For example the magnetic field of the earth's north pole puts a force on the needle of a compass. Electromagnetic radiation travels in waves just like the waves in the ocean. Waves have an amplitude and a frequency. In the ocean, a large amplitude means the waves are big...good for surfing. A high frequency means the waves are closer together, and more pass by each second.

"There are different kinds of electromagnetic radiation, like radio waves, light waves, and microwaves. It's the frequency of the wave that tells us what kind of electromagnetic radiation it is. It's measured in hertz, abbreviated as Hz, and one hertz means one full wave passes by every second. Are you following me?"

"I think so."

Lost in his thoughts for a short moment, Ivan let out a lengthy sigh. "Good. There are more kinds of electromagnetic radiation than what I just mentioned. Our brains emit waves in a frequency range starting at around three hertz. The frequencies of visible light waves are over a billion times greater, and each color corresponds to a particular frequency in the visible light spectrum."

"So what exactly is the human energy field?" Pam had a slight look of confusion.

"I'm about to get to that. Low frequency brain waves around three hertz are emitted by the brain during deep, dreamless sleep. Brain waves around thirty-eight hertz are emitted when you're wide awake. Pam, the fascinating thing is that wave frequencies well outside the range of known brain waves can be detected from humans. Using very sensitive measuring devices, researchers have detected wave frequencies ranging from 200 to as high as 1800 hertz. It is believed that the electromagnetic fields in this frequency spectrum correspond to the human energy field."

Ivan perked up with excitement. "The wave frequencies measured from the entities fall within the same range: from 200 to 1800 hertz. Do you see what this means? On Spectra, Karen and Annie were insistent that these entities were the equivalent of a soul without a body. I'm starting to believe they were right. Dr. Zowski is coming today to help with our review of the wave readings we've measured from the entities and to help us understand why the entities have such a profound effect on humans. She told me about a study carried out in the twentieth century in which the energy fields of individuals were measured while clairvoyants observed the colors of their auras. The study concluded that each auric color corresponded to a particular wave frequency range. Our entities change color, and each individual color has been found to fall into the same wave frequency range documented in that research."

"So why can you see them? You said the frequency of visible light was a billion times greater."

"And you said science wasn't your strong point. An excellent question. The entities must emit light, or we couldn't see them. Light is emitted when a particle like an electron moves from a high energy state to a low energy state. Until we understand the nature of the entities, I can't be more specific. We're hoping Dr. Zowski can help us here."

Ivan reached out and gave Pam a gentle pat on her knee. "This is where you come in, my dear. Myself and several others involved in the research have been exposed to the entities on a limited basis. Dr. Zowski would like to measure the energy field of someone who has never been exposed, before and after exposure. I was hoping you'd be willing to do this for me. I have personally been exposed to them several times and can assure you there is no risk. To the contrary, the effects you will experience will be positive. Communicating with them is quite intriguing, and you may even decide you want to be included in the research program on a more permanent basis. A select few have been involved in continued communication."

With his most sincere expression, Ivan completed his pitch. "Would you be willing to do this for me? You could be at the forefront of answering what could be the most significant question in human evolution. Do we have a soul?"

"I don't really understand how these things could prove we have a soul."

"Well, so far Irena and I have just been tossing about some theories. We know the human body has an aura or energy field around it with the same electromagnetic frequencies as the entities. We don't know anything about this field except that it exists. The point is, coherent fields have to come from something. In this case, we don't know from what, charged atoms perhaps, who knows. The frequencies of the human energy field are higher than anything that can be generated by the physical body...by neurons firing, by nerves activating muscles or biochemical reactions. So the questions are: why do we have this field around us, and where is it coming from? We think if we can draw enough parallels between the entities, which exist on their own without a body, and the human energy field then maybe, it will be enough for us to conclude the human energy field is comprised of the same type of living energy as the entities. In that case, we could consider the human energy field to be an electromagnetic field measured from a soul or living energy. We are a physical body with a soul. The entities are souls on their own."

"Souls without a body are called spirits," Pam added. "At least that's the way I think of it."

"I didn't know the difference, but that makes sense."

"There are other distinctions based on faith."

"Anyway," Ivan said abruptly, "to answer your question, I don't know if our study of the entities will allow us to make a firm conclusion about the existence of our souls, but if we find enough parallels, it most certainly will get us closer to answering that question. So what do you think, Pam? Are you interested in participating?"

"Are you sure it's safe?" Pam asked.

"I promise; however, there is one thing I must be honest about. When communicating with them, the distress over their well-being is readily apparent. Exposure to us harms them, and I find it quite disturbing, so much so that I have come close to scrapping the entire project. But we are at the cusp of an extraordinary breakthrough, and I believe we need to continue with due care for the time being. Of course, one of the things we hope to determine here is a way of communicating with them without harming them."

"Okay." Pam hesitated a moment. "I'll do it."

"That's wonderful! I think you'll like Dr. Zowski; she's a very enlightening woman. One other point, I would rather you not mention to her the fact our exposure to the entities is causing them distress. I'm not sure how she'd react, and she is quite an asset to our research. You do understand?"

"I guess."

"Then it's settled. How about you meet us in Section Four at one-fifteen? I'll have Ron clear you for Section Four access. Oh, and Pam, while participating in the program, you'll be up to level three pay grade." Ivan gave her a warm smile.

Chapter Twenty-Five

Pam swallowed her anxiety as she walked along the corridor to Section Four. She felt nervous despite Ivan's reassurances. Communicating with aliens was not something she anticipated being in her job description. If it wasn't for the money and the compelling notion that she could learn about the soul, she would have shied away from the experiment. Maybe it would put her closer to God. She reached up, and with her manicured fingers, clutched the small gold cross hanging from her neck. Her godparents had given it to her for her first communion. Her lips formed a smile. She liked the idea of being smarter, even just a little smarter.

Pam checked her watch as she stood at the door to Section Four. *Right on time.* As she entered, she could hear the deep voice of a woman intimately engaged in conversation with Ivan and Jack Johnson, one of the other physicists at the Accelerator. Sheepishly, she followed the voices, not wishing to intrude on the conversation. She wished the room had carpeting; her clicking heels made her feel like a tap dancer.

Ivan turned, and his friendly smile set her at ease. "Ah, here she is. Irena, I'd like you to meet Pam Renolds. Pam, this is Dr. Irena Zowski."

Pam offered her hand. "It's nice to meet you, Dr. Zowski." Her fingers crunched together as Irena accepted the gesture.

"*Zdravstvujtye*. That means hello in my country. Call me Irena. I insist." She spoke with a commanding tone and ended her sentence with a hearty laugh. As she smiled, the fine lines in her forehead were forced upwards to meet the cropped blond hair silhouetting her round face. The robust woman was clad in a lab coat and spouted enthusiasm. She reminded Pam of a physical education teacher she once had. "Ivan tells me you have agreed to participate in this wonderful research. I am sure you share my excitement. The existence of a subtle body on its own? Incredible!"

"Sorry, what's a subtle body?" Pam felt her anxiety creeping back.

"Oh my!" Irena threw her hands up in the air. "Let me give you the small overview."

Irena was clearly a high-spirited person. She seemed nice enough, but Pam felt intimidated by her overbearing enthusiasm. It would have been better placed at one of her old school volleyball games. She would have been a good heckler.

"I am here to measure your energy field, no? In the spiritual sense, the human energy field is sometimes called the subtle body. It is a concept in the spiritual belief of many cultures and dates back to ancient times. We can even find early references in the writings of Plato as documented in the well-known quote 'We are imprisoned in the body, like an oyster in his shell.' Clairvoyants claim they can see the subtle body as a colorful aura surrounding the human body. I personally think of it more scientifically, as measurable wave frequencies."

Irena stopped to take a breath and then continued with inflections as though she were telling a ghost story. "In the Indian doctrine, the subtle body is called Prana." Irena rolled her 'r.' "Prana is a person's energy field and is said to be made up of seven Chakras, which are swirling helixes of energy emanating from specific points along the spine. The Chakras are located at major branches of the nervous system, and the energy flows in an ever-increasing fan shape."

Irena seemed to enjoy exaggerated body language. She fanned her arms out to emphasize her point. Pam wondered if the motion might pop the button of her man pants.

"They believe the Chakra have layers like an onion, each corresponding to a layer of the subtle body. Energy can flow into the Chakras and between the layers, and it can also flow from one Chakra to another along a channel running along the spine…"

Pam tried to look interested, but it sounded like a lot of mumbo-jumbo. She was about to ask Irena about the Christian beliefs when Irena launched into another topic.

"The Chinese refer to the subtle body as the Ch'i and believe its energy flows along natural channels in the body. Imbalances in the flow of energy are thought to be symptoms of various illnesses. In traditional Chinese medicine, acupuncture is used to improve the flow of energy, thus balancing the Ch'i. Have you ever done yoga, Pam?"

"Yes. I go once a week," Pam replied. *And maybe you wouldn't be busting out of those pants if you went.*

"*Khoroshiy*! No wonder you look so fit. Yoga focuses on balancing the flow of energy on the energetic highways."

Irena turned to Ivan. "We chatted last week about the possibility that your entities are like a soul without a body. It later reminded me of Theosophy."

"Haven't heard of it," Ivan said.

"It's a doctrine of religious philosophy and metaphysics dating back to the 1800s. According to Theosophy, the subtle body can be reincarnated. They refer to the reincarnated subtle body as the Monad, but I like to refer to it as a soul. Theosophists postulate that souls evolved through a series of seven root races. In the first root race, souls existed as pure spirit without a body. By the fifth root race, the souls were believed to have evolved into the modern human...spirit and body. It's thought the souls of humanity will continue to evolve to the sixth root race. Theosophy has a solid grounding in history, particularly Nazism. The Aryan race was considered to be people with body and soul. Non-Aryans were believed to be soulless creatures that just happened to look like human beings."

Ivan yawned. "Excuse me," he said, looking embarrassed. "I was up early."

"Well then, enough with the history of the human energy field. If I'm going to be measuring it, I should give you some scientific background. In the twentieth century, a doctor by the name of Kilner described seeing a glowing mist around the body observed through colored screens and filters. Later that century, Dr. Hunt actually recorded the frequency and amplitude of electromagnetic signals from her test subjects, while at the same time, 'aura readers' observed the colors of their energy fields. Frequencies from 200 to 1800 hertz were measured, and particular frequency bands were found to correlate to specific colors observed by the aura readers. The colors included blue, green, yellow, orange, red, violet, and white, the same color spectrum as your entities. Modern techniques for measuring the human energy field have confirmed the electromagnetic wave frequencies measured by Dr. Hunt. As for the visual perception of the aura, that has yet to be confirmed scientifically, but over the centuries clairvoyants have continually claimed to see the same configuration of colors surrounding the human body."

"Unless any of you have any questions, I suggest I get started by measuring Pam's base field."

Pam was relieved to hear her boring science lesson had finished. She tried tuning it out, but the lady's voice was too annoying and overpowering. At least she was getting a raise out of it. *Maybe she'd buy some new Rawlen Borg jeans. The ones with the embroidery.* She snapped her attention back. "How do I become exposed to the entities?"

"I'm sorry, Pam. You missed the beginning of our discussions." Ivan walked her to the containment unit.

Pam's eyes widened as she marveled at the dancing, colorful light show displayed through the line of windows on the unit.

"Beautiful aren't they," Ivan said.

"Yes, breathtaking!"

"See the chamber at the end of the unit." Ivan pointed to it. "Inside there's a seat. It's quite confining, so I hope you're not bothered by that sort of thing. Once seated, you press the button on the side wall, which opens the airlock chamber just enough to allow a few of the entities in. Then you just sit down and relax for fifteen minutes, and that's it. Jack was kind enough to wire some music in, which is quite pleasant."

Pam turned to Irena. "I'm a… quite religious. If these things are like a soul, and they seem to have an effect on people, then when I'm exposed to them, am I going to become possessed?"

"Ivan, perhaps you are the best person to answer that question having being exposed to them several times," Irena said.

"Yes, I agree." Ivan put his hands on Pam's shoulders. "Pam, this is nothing like that. They've affected my cognitive abilities, given me a gift. I heal quickly, that kind of thing. I'm still myself. You have to put superstition and ghost stories out of your head. This is science. If you're not comfortable with it, we can get someone else."

No, she wasn't entirely comfortable with it, but she wanted those jeans. "It's okay. I trust you."

"Pam, you're doing the right thing. I've been exposed, too, and I'm quite myself," Jack assured her.

"Fine then, let us get on with it," Irena said with confident overtones as if someone just scored a game point. "Please come over here, and I will do the initial measurement of your energy field. It will only take a minute. I would also like to do a baseline of your wakeful brain waves."

Pam walked over to the table off to the side of the containment unit. She looked over the fancy equipment, wondering what it was for.

"Please, just sit down here." Irena pushed Pam's thick auburn hair to the side and placed several electrodes around her head. "These will measure your brain waves. We'll leave them on for five minutes. That should do for a baseline. The scan of your energy field will take about the same length of time." Irena reached for a shiny metal wand on the table and slowly ran it down the entire length of Pam's body, head to toe.

"There; we are finished…quick, and painless." Irena removed the electrodes.

Ivan helped Pam inside the chamber and repeated his instructions and few words of reassurance. She sat in the chair feeling like she was about to start an amusement park ride, except her fear was the apprehensive kind not the exhilarating kind she loved. The door shut leaving her in near darkness, lit only by the amber glow from the button she needed to push. She decided to think positively—a *haunted ride!* Thrill rides were her favorite, and it was time to get this one started. Her heart started pounding in anticipation, only the music didn't fit. It was Ivan's symphony cello crap, and there was certainly no escaping it in the tight enclosure. She rolled her eyes and took a look around. Small spaces didn't normally bother her, but these four walls felt like the sides of a coffin.

Here goes nothing. She made the sign of the cross and reached for the button to release the entities. Instantly, the room came alive with the sparkle of life. The colors looked so much more intense than they did through the windows, and she felt as if she were inside a glass of champagne. The lights were everywhere. She smiled and tried to reach for them, but her hand passed right through them. She focused on one and as a little game, tried not to lose it. It started as red then changed to green then back to red again, but then she lost track of it.

The light show made her relax. Just as she started wondering what the big deal was, it started. It was like nothing she'd ever felt. She could hardly add two plus two, yet the mathematics flowing through her mind made perfect sense. It was complex, like an equation to life. She understood it to the finest detail. The corners of her mouth started to rise but stopped. The telepathic cries were unmistakable. They were begging her to leave. She was draining them of their life force, killing them. She looked around, uncertain what to do. If she left the room, Ivan would be mad. She'd have to explain her actions to Irena, and she'd have to say goodbye to her new jeans. The effects of the entities started to creep up subtly. Her thoughts were taking on a life of their own, something completely foreign to her. In confusion, her mind tittered between compassion and enlightenment.

What do I do? She looked around at the entities. Their brilliance was diminishing. Finally, she put her head back and shut her eyes as tight as she could and whispered, "I'm sorry."

The fifteen minutes seemed like forever, and Pam jumped out of the hatch with the prowess of a pouncing cat, very glad to be finished.

"How was that?" Ivan inquired.

"Amazing but… just amazing." Pam sounded guarded. "I must admit I feel enlightened."

"You just wait. Pam, you're going to love the new you," Ivan said.

Irena gave her a satisfied grin. "Well let me measure you again, and then we are finished...at least for now."

Pam sat back down, and Irena rechecked the brain wave measurements. "It will take me some time to analyze this data properly, and I have some business back on Earth. How about we reconvene in a few weeks time to go over the results?"

"That would be fine," Ivan said. "I have one last question before you go. Do you have any theories regarding the physical makeup of the entities? The energy field we're measuring must come from something. Not to mention, we're curious how they emit light. We're comparing them to the human energy field, but you can't see that."

"No you can't, but that doesn't necessarily mean the human energy field doesn't emit light. Maybe it's just outside the visible light spectrum and only gifted clairvoyants can resolve it. As for the physical makeup, it's been suggested the human energy field could be made up of living plasma called bioplasma. Perhaps it is a fifth state of matter, a universal energy existing between the realm of matter and energy. It could be made up of something smaller, a substance finer than what we know matter is composed of. Maybe these entities fit one of these models. Until we figure it out, we won't know how they emit light."

"What exactly is plasma?" Pam asked.

"Plasma is the fourth state of matter, the others being liquids, gases, and solids. It is just a collection of moving free electrons, free protons, and ions; ions being atoms that have lost or gained electrons. There's lots of plasma in the universe: the core of a star is plasma, and the northern lights on Earth are plasma. I recently read a paper suggesting the collective movement of particles within plasma can give it characteristics similar to a biological life form. I realize this is pretty complicated. Are you following me, Pam?"

"Completely."

"*Khoroshiy*! Maybe you will be interested to know computer simulations have suggested plasma particles can even bead together to form string-like filaments that will then twist and order themselves on their own into helical strands resembling DNA. The original research in this area dates back centuries to the work of Tsytovich who suggested that complex, self-organized plasma exhibit all the necessary properties to qualify them as candidates for inorganic living matter with a structure similar to a primitive cell, thus the name bioplasma. Perhaps the human energy field is made up of bioplasma that is united with our physical bodies as body and soul. If so, then maybe it can also exist independently, like these entities, which could possibly give substance to age old ghost stories."

"Didn't you say energy flows into Chakras in helixes?" Jack inquired with a yawn. "Sorry, I haven't been sleeping well."

"Yes, I did. It is called Kundalini energy, which literally means coiled energy."

Ivan checked his watch. "Well, we're all very excited to get some answers. Irena, thank you for being part of our research. You're an invaluable asset to the program." He smiled.

Irena packed up her equipment, and Ivan escorted her out.

* * * *

On the way back to his office, Ivan decided he deserved a pick-me-up. It had been ten days since he last sat in the exposure chamber, so he made a quick divergence and headed for the stairs to the corridor. As he arrived in Section Four, Jack had just finished his exposure. Ivan chuckled to himself as Jack awkwardly bent his tall, over-weight body to fit through the small opening, bumping his head on the steel door frame for an encore. He certainly lacked Pam's grace. He stretched his hefty body out of its knot and smoothed out his thick salt and pepper hair with a clumsy stroke of his hand.

"Great minds think alike. I'm next," Ivan said.

"Do you think Pam was okay with the exposure?"

"I'm quite confident she'll be on board, and I'm looking forward to having an assistant who is both beautiful and brilliant. Give her until tomorrow morning. I know her. She likes to feel as good as she looks...she's going to want more exposure time. Now if you'll excuse me, I have to shake the cob webs from my head."

Ivan set the music to *Carmen*, his favorite opera. He'd seen it performed countless times. The chair in the exposure chamber was small for a man, but its high back provided reasonable comfort. He sat down and leaned back in the darkness, compressing the foam cushion, and took a moment to psyche himself up in preparation for the desperate pleas for help the little buggers would inundate him with. He decided Pam should be commended for keeping silent about the entities' distress after her exposure. She had certainly earned her raise.

When Ivan first began exposing himself to the entities regularly, he found the experience reasonably enjoyable. Lately, it was becoming both disturbing and exhausting. In his mind, it had become the equivalent of spending your day in a room crowded with cold, hungry, dying toddlers. Every time he sat in the chair, the experience was more anguishing than the last as if the entities were developing a vendetta against him. The music helped as a distraction, but it hardly drowned out the entities' mathematical and telepathic screams for mercy. The silver lining was that about halfway through the exposure time, the entities had weakened to the point their annoying suffering became tolerable.

Ivan pressed the button allowing a flood of entities to enter the chamber and closed his tired eyes. The second act was his favorite, and he could picture the beautiful Carmen dancing and singing.

Gurgling noises accompanied the rhythm of the song, and the lights danced in an electrifying symphony of color. Ivan's foot twitched as he slipped into oblivion...

* * * *

"C'mon, Ivan, let's play hockey." The young boy grabbed his hockey stick and tore off onto the lake, disappearing into the thick morning fog. The rising sun gave it a daunting red hue.

Ivan clutched his stick and followed. "Nathan, where are you?" The sickly stench of the dense fog made him gag. He held his breath and slowly walked deeper into the mist. Suddenly, something struck him from behind sending him flying to the ice. He winced as the impact forced him to inhale the pungent air deep into his lungs. He wriggled around to a sitting position, straining to see who attacked him. "Nathan?"

Fear crept into him as he gazed through the redness. The color deepened, becoming thicker, impervious. As the soupy mist threatened to choke the life from him, two glowing white eyes appeared, drawing threateningly close. Ivan couldn't see who they belonged to. Fear weakened his grip, and his stick fell to the ice. "Nathan? Nathan."

There was silence for a moment, and then music reverberated through the intense fog, quiet at first then getting louder. Screams for help echoed in the background. "Nathan is that you? You're scaring me."

Ivan kicked his feet. *What is that?* A warm fluid filled his boots and started to ascend his legs. Gurgling sounds accompanied the music and screams, desperate screams. The wetness hit his hands, and he could feel the stickiness of the viscous fluid as it enveloped him. The glowing eyes shot through the red fluid like two ominous headlights on a stormy night. He started to struggle, but the fluid was thick, confining. Panic set in as it got close to his face. He held his breath and clenched his lips closed as the thick warm liquid filled his nostrils. The taste was revolting but familiar. He stared at the eyes as they changed from white to red, his lungs yearning for air. Then it happened, a fast nauseating gasp. The warmth edged past his nostrils and into his throat and lungs.

* * * *

Ivan shrieked as he jolted awake. The dancing lights blurred his vision. With a palpitating heart, he released the hatch door and leapt out. He fled Section Four and retreated to the secure surroundings of his office. He slammed the door behind him, and as he walked to his desk became unsettled by the way in which the eyes of the wolf in the picture followed him. Once seated, he put his head on his desk trying to focus on positive thoughts while fighting his fatigue. The last thing he wanted was to fall asleep, only to be haunted by more hideous images. As he sat, he had an epiphany and immediately put a call in to Kevin.

"Kevin, I have a great idea. We're trying to determine the makeup of the entities. We're running a Particle Accelerator Laboratory for God's sake. The technology at our disposal has been used to determine the basic components of all matter that exists in the universe. Do you see where I'm going with this? Let's blast the little bastards!"

Chapter Twenty-Six

Charlie Hopkins stood at the sink in his cell washing up, knowing the horn was about to sound for breakfast. He wiped the drops of water out of the creases in his turkey-skinned neckline and tossed the towel over the rack. He was seething. Weston was five cells away and seemingly untouchable. To make matters worse, the son of a bitch had become all buddy-buddy with the asshole kid who had landed him in this hellhole in the first place. The two of them along with that smiley faced shackle mate of Jeff's were spending their days digging for diamonds like kids on a beach, almost enjoying it.

Charlie had been unsuccessful on several attempts to take Jeff down to where he belonged—flat on his back on a bed of plywood. He'd hated kids ever since he was one of them. Before he even got married, he'd gone out to get a vasectomy as he wanted to make damn sure he'd never have to deal with them. The nights he listened to his sniveling wife moan about how she couldn't get pregnant parroted in his head and made him cringe. At least there was a silver lining. The woman wanted it every chance she could, and he was more than happy to comply. Then the day of the Gibbons murder arrived. "Oh, those poor children," she muttered; her forlorn eyes drawn in hopeless despair for the little bastards. They have no one. The next thing he knew, he was signing the custody papers.

The girl was quiet and fortunately grew some respectable *hooters.* They'd wink at him from her slut shirts, and he'd smile to himself. She stuck to Jeff like glue. Jeff on the other hand was an outspoken little cuss who had little regard for household rules. Although Charlie loathed being back talked to by some freckle faced know-it-all kid, it didn't take him long to realize there could be a place for Jeff in the family business. He and his sister both knew the meaning of a good beating, and Jeff's affection for the little tramp made her his Achilles heel. He quickly became an obedient employee, at least until the day he screwed up.

Charlie made Jeff join a youth group, a center for cultural

exchange between teens on Earth, Lyra, Cygnus, and Draco. Its mandate was to maintain a connection between developing teens growing up in diverse conditions, separated by unimaginable distances. The group discouraged electronic communication in favor of handwritten letters and exchanges of the arts including artwork, music, and written material depicting lifestyles and pop culture unique to their home planet. The plan was to smuggle the anthaline shipment with one of these exchanges. It sounded great until Jeff, with his big mouth, tipped off one of his friends on Draco that the shipment was on its way. Consortium security intercepted the communication, and they were caught.

Charlie smiled at himself in the mirror as a revelation came to him. *Weston also has an Achilles heel,* he thought to himself. You'd have to be blind not to notice the body language between Weston and that hot blonde, Simmons. Maybe he couldn't take him out, but he could do the next best thing.

* * * *

The day passed quickly for Charlie as he finally had something to revel over. All day long, he kept his eye on the blonde bitch, digging on all fours; her heart shaped butt wagging happily as she made conversation with her *voodoo doll* partner. He schemed about making his move until his skin tingled. The thought made him so giddy he wanted to laugh out loud.

The orange sun sat on the horizon like a mammoth pumpkin, the wind churning dusty faces into it; screaming faces, fearful faces— Laura's face. They talked to Charlie. *It's almost time,* they said. *Take your prey!* He felt a throbbing in his pants, and he wanted to take her down in the most severe way, the most demoralizing way. He could picture Weston as he looked on: the flesh on his face crunched into concern, and his lungs bellowing for him to stop as he pumped her full of venom. Sadly, he'd have to settle for the plan at hand.

Two by two, the prisoners lined up to board the buggies like damned biblical animals. Once their shackles were removed, they stepped on board. As soon as it was Charlie's turn, he pushed his way to the front where the bitch and the voodoo doll had set their fiery asses down. He sat across from them, planning the final stage of his attack. As the buggies set off, he envisioned slamming their two heads together like a couple of crash cymbals.

They accelerated over the dunes, and Charlie watched the two guards at the back of the buggy, waiting for his opportunity. They were always preoccupied with the scenery, glancing around occasionally for jumpers. He wouldn't have much time, and if he wanted to maximize the damage, he'd have to make his move the second they looked away. He knew they wouldn't shoot him with a resonator unless they had a clear shot of him alone. Ten seconds would do, especially with his pent up rage fueling him. He could feel the pressure in his head building.

The buggy rounded a hill. *Now!*

Charlie launched across the aisle like a cheetah leaping for its kill and grabbed Laura by the shoulders, slamming her to the floor. With the full force of his two-hundred-and-twenty pounds pinning her, he grabbed her by the jaw and pummeled her head into the floor with a crack. He caught a glimpse of her eyes starting to make their way to the back of her head as he balled his hand into a tight fist and reared back, connecting his knuckles with her jaw. The bellowing of the guards and the force of the buggy slowing to a stop told him his ten seconds were almost up. He followed up his first punch with a couple more, this time to her rib cage. The bitch clawed at his left eye. The burning pain drove his hand to her throat, and just as he felt her go limp underneath him, the heaving force of two guards on his back drew him off her. The screech of the resonator instantly followed.

Chapter Twenty-Seven

Bob McLean savored his morning coffee as he reviewed the most recent list of parole candidates. A call came in just as he wrapped his lips around the rim of the cup. He hated morning interruptions (he needed at least two coffees under his belt first), and slammed the cup down sending a tidal wave over its edge. *Shit!* He swooshed the puddle off his desk and wiped his hands on his pants.

"McLean here."

"Bob, how are my friends doing? It's been three weeks. I just thought I'd follow up to make sure they're keeping their mouths shut." The voice belonged to Larry Dunn—the very last person he wanted to deal with. The man liked to throw his weight around.

"They're assimilating into the prison population. Having said that, they've had an eventful few weeks. Simmons landed herself in the infirmary for a couple of days thanks to one of our more unappealing guests; and I'd have to say, we've put Weston to good use. The guy's a genius when it comes to repairing power grids. I have him out there right now. We can't tolerate power outages here, and our engineers just can't keep up."

"He better be well guarded."

"He is and don't worry, he had a taste of discipline on his first day. He's been good as gold."

"And you're keeping a close eye on their group."

"Groups, and yes," Bob said.

Larry raised his voice. "What do you mean groups? I thought we had an understanding... interactions between the two of them and the prison population were to be kept to a minimum. Do I have to spell it out for you? Get them in the same damn group, and I want a list of exactly who they've been interacting with!"

Larry's condescending, dictatorial attitude always seemed to buck up whenever he had anything to do with him, and McLean was fed up with it. He slammed his hand on his desk. "I'll run this hellhole the way I see fit. If you're so concerned, then why don't you get down here and join them."

"Look Bob. I'm not stupid, and I've become pretty good at looking the other way for you. How many prison wardens can afford a waterfront condo on Cygnus? Get them in the same group now and get me that list."

"Very well," McLean growled and cut off the call. At least he got the last word.

* * * *

It was just before lunch when Dean returned to his group. This was the fourth time McLean had called upon his expertise to help carry out repairs to the power grid, a welcome break from digging on his hands and knees.

The problems plaguing the power grid were the same he used to encounter when flying pods in the Draco atmosphere. The grid panels were made of a finely polished layer of an ultraconducting silicon polymer on a semiconductor base. To harness the vacuum energy efficiently, the panel surface had to have an emissivity of one and be defect free. Unfortunately, over time, these ideal conditions were rarely met, especially on Draco. The sulfur would coat the polished panels lowering their emissivity, and micro-defects would eventually form allowing the sulfur to find its way to the base forming inclusions between the two materials. The results could be catastrophic during flight, but in a power grid on the ground, they just meant continual power outages and repairs with which Dean had extensive experience.

The dig site had moved from the previous day, and when Dean stepped off the buggy, the guard directed him away from a collection of pylons. "What are those for?" he inquired.

"Rainbow bugs...it's a nest. The dirt's loose, keep your distance," the guard grumbled.

Dean bent over to have a look at the bugs. They were quite pretty: shaped like ladybugs, but about one-half their size with markings akin to a monarch butterfly. There were a number of them munching on the low lying shrubs in the vicinity of their nest, and Dean couldn't figure out what the big deal was. Nevertheless, he veered away from the pylons and joined his group. Once shackled, he assumed his position beside Sim, keenly digging through the pebbles without even taking a moment to look for Laura. She had only been released from the infirmary a day earlier, but he had something else on his mind.

"What did they give you this morning, milk and cookies?" Andy joked.

Dean laughed and kept working.

"For crying out loud man look around."

"Yeah, what?" Dean looked up right into Laura's eyes. Despite the painful looking bruising, the smile on her face was like a Cheshire cat.

"What the…" Dean said. He peered around. The group was the same except for the addition of Laura and Sandra. He kneeled forward and grabbed Laura's hand, squeezing it as hard as he dare. "Laura, what happened? Did they switch you?"

"Yeah, this morning, just after breakfast. I couldn't wait till you got back. I can't believe it."

"This couldn't be better." Dean stared into her eyes, only thinking about the things he wanted to say to her after their three weeks of heartfelt glances and worst of all, the incident with Hopkins. Dean hardly slept after they took her away, bloodied and just about unconscious. Despite the fact she seemed to have found some inner courage, Hopkins' attack went way beyond putting it to the test. Hopkins' ruthlessness put Dunn's words of warning to shame. His vendetta was with Dean not Laura and exacting his savage revenge on her burned a hole in Dean's heart. Dean had only managed to mouth a few words to Laura since the doctor released her from the infirmary.

"Are you okay? I was so worried about you. If only I'd been there, I would've leveled that crazy bastard." And he would have. Since the attack, every time he saw Hopkins he had an overwhelming urge to charge him like a bull, drop him to the ground, and choke the life out of him.

"I'm fine. Just a little bruised, which is more than I can say for him." Laura cocked her head in a regal poise. "Check out that patch he's wearing."

"Yeah, I'm impressed. Are you sure you're okay?" The bruising on the side of Laura's face had turned a putrid shade of yellow and extended halfway down her neck.

"Don't worry; I'm fine. I had a minor concussion and only bruising to my ribs. Quite frankly, a couple of days of R & R were nice."

Dean gave Laura a short-lived, warm smile before pointing a finger at Sandra. "What about your baggage here. Did she come along for the ride?" He gave Sandra a scathing look and continued. "How'd ya like some sulfury pebbles for lunch?"

"Hey, can't you take a joke? Besides, if it wasn't for me, the troll would have eaten your heart for dinner."

"The troll?" Dean questioned.

"Yeah, that's what Sandra calls Hopkins."

Jeff was a meter away shackled to Andy and let out a hearty laugh. "Good one!"

"Hey, keep it down. The guard's looking over here, so get to work," Sim said.

Dean smiled back at Laura and slowly let go of her hand. "When they took you away, I thought the worst." He spoke quietly and continued making eye contact with Andy and Jeff, too. "Look for sulfur. I need chunks, preferably ones you can break apart in your fingers."

"Sulfur, why?" Andy said.

"Shhh. I'll tell you later. If you find a chunk, just give it to me."

"Andy said you were out helping them fix the grid again." Laura looked at Dean as though she was studying him.

He looked back with resolution. "Yeah, I was fixing the grid for them all right." As he spoke, he held out a small packed ball of powdery sulfur he had just pulled from his tray. He gave her a wink as he carefully slipped it into his shoe. Laura squinted at him thoughtfully, and he gave her a reassuring nod and whispered, "Later."

* * * *

Dean was back in his cell after dinner. He stood barefoot by the sink wearing his boxers, diligently preparing to wash the day's work from his clothes. As usual, his shirt and pants were impregnated with yellow sulfur dust, and he gave them a gentle shake over the floor before slinging them over the sink. Once the dust settled, he knelt down, swept it up with some toilet paper, and deposited it in his shoe. After washing and dressing, he grabbed his tin cup and took a seat on the floor at the front of his cell by the steel bars. The bars had a dull gray look to them, and he started working them with the sharp edge of the handle of his cup. He ground at the metal as quietly as he could, gathering every small flake that fell in a neat little pile on the floor. He worked to exhaustion, being mindful of the guards as they strolled by. Before going to bed, he carefully assembled the filings and sulfur in the toilet paper he tucked under the insole of his shoe.

Chapter Twenty-Eight

Ivan decided he wanted to be in the hangar to personally greet Kevin when he returned from Spectra. He felt great, invigorated in fact, and thought he'd skip the cart ride in favor of a brisk walk along the length of the accelerator. He did so with arms swinging while displaying both rows of his Chiclet teeth in an elated grin.

Everything was in place for the collision with the entities, and within hours he, Ivan Campbell, could well be the first person to unlock the secrets of the human soul. If that wasn't enough on its own, he'd just received a call from the President and CEO of Enertech giving him the brilliant news that the eighty-billion dollar research grant would be given to the Lyra Particle Accelerator Laboratory. He tried to sound surprised during his conversation with the man, but he'd been completely expecting the money to fall into his elite lap.

Kevin piloted the pod in and stepped out of the hatch carrying a small portable containment unit loaded with a fresh collection of entities for their experiment. They agreed this would be prudent as the *health* of these entities would not yet be compromised.

"Mission Accomplished?" Ivan asked, beaming.

"Darn right. And I must say I'm getting to be a pro at navigating that texture. I'd put Weston to shame." Kevin gave a satisfied chuckle. "I can't believe we didn't think of this until now. And we think we're so smart!"

"Seems to me this was my idea."

"Well I'm not going to let you steal all the glory. What we could learn here is earth shattering."

"No, soul shattering." Ivan smirked.

"Funny. Let's get them loaded up and get the show on the road."

"I walked here, but there's a cart outside we can take," Ivan said.

"Walked? You hate walking that corridor."

Ivan stood tall and straightened his tie. "Yes, indeed I do, but I needed some time to gloat about my new eighty-billion dollar research grant!"

Kevin spun around to face him; his cheeks pudged out like an overstuffed squirrel's to make room for his grin. "It's official?"

"Darn right! The CEO of Enertech just called me with the decision."

"Beers at the King's Pub tonight, and you're buying."

"I'd be glad to, but it's going to be champagne at Anthony's. Their filets are mouth watering and cut like butter." Ivan's mouth watered at the thought.

"I'm looking forward to it," Kevin said.

They secured the containment unit in the cart and made their way to the Particle Injection Room in Section One. Loading the entities into the accelerator was a simple exercise of exhausting the containment unit through the accelerator loading port. A laser would then accelerate them toward the target point, directed by a series of magnets. Ivan had carefully adjusted the magnets inside the target zone to hold the entities in close proximity to maximize the number of collisions.

The collision would be configured to have a beam of particles colliding into a stationary target at one end. They would then use a beam of electrons accelerated to slightly less than the speed of light. If the entities were indeed plasma made up of protons, electrons, and ions, then the ion microscope in Section One would reveal their structure prior to the collision. After the collision, the cryogenic detectors would identify the resultant particles and their energy and path.

The containment unit hissed as it discharged the entities, and Ivan and Kevin waited for the low vibration hum of the laser coming online. As soon as Ivan heard it, he turned toward the monitor with anticipation to make sure the entities arrived in the target zone with precision. A read-out of their energy field confirmed their presence. Ivan touched the corner of the screen so he could see the poor little bastards suspended in the collision chamber safe and sound.

"I think we're done here," Kevin said. "Everything appears stable, but I think we should work quickly. They won't take kindly to the magnetic field in there. You can already see it in their wave frequencies, which are in the lower range, just like when they're exposed to us. It's a sign of distress."

"You didn't have to tell me that. You must be picking up their communication, too. It's loud and clear to me. Even from inside the accelerator, I can pick up their telepathic thoughts. Sad thing is, I think they know what we're about to do to them. If there's one thing they understand, it's energy and being bombarded with billions of electron volts has got to hurt. Poor suckers."

The two men jumped back into the cart and wasted no time getting to the Control Room. They hurried in and came face to face with a tour group.

"What's going on Samantha? We're about to run a collision." Ivan really wanted to say *get the hell out of here!* He shot her a scolding look.

"Ah, Mr. Campbell. We have a couple of co-op students who just started with us, and I was showing them around. This is Cory Westberg and Michelle Jenkins. I'm sure they would be thrilled to see a collision."

"Sorry, not today. The nature of our research is confidential, and I'm afraid I'm going to have to ask you to leave," Ivan said curtly.

"Can I just show them the—"

"Absolutely not; we want to get to work. Goodbye."

With a cowed expression, Samantha ushered the students out as quickly as possible.

The unexpected tour group dampened Ivan's mood. "I'm finding the curiosity of people around here to be far too conveniently timed. Anyone not party to this research seems to be watching, sticking their nose where it doesn't belong. I tore a strip off Ron yesterday. I want security tightened. You know who that girl was?"

"Who?"

"Weston's niece. What timing is that? His niece is in the Control Room right when we are about to run this collision. It's no coincidence is what it is." Ivan punched a hand at the air. "I don't like this one bit!"

Kevin bit down on his lip. "Do you think she knows?"

"I'm going to speak to Larry. Check on the security with Weston and Simmons. This is unacceptable. Who knows who they could have told in prison, and if anyone was released with that information we'd be back to square one. I'd feel better if they were just dead."

"Ivan, getting back to the collision, isn't Jack joining us?" Kevin said.

Ivan cupped his mouth to hide his wide yawn. "He called me this morning. He's not feeling well."

"This is a hell of a thing to miss, and it's too bad, I was going to suggest he join us for dinner. I had lunch with him yesterday, and he looked fine. Big circles under his eyes, but fine. If he was getting sick, I better not have caught it. I haven't been sleeping well, and the last thing I need is to be sick."

"Yeah, well you don't know the half of it. I haven't slept in weeks, so don't complain to me. Anyway, let's have a look at the structure of these things."

Kevin took a seat at the control console and brought the ion microscope on line. "It'll take a minute to formulate a detailed image of their particle makeup and energy."

Ivan sat down beside him and swiveled his chair around for a clear view.

"My God, would you check this out," Kevin whispered as he adjusted the focus. "This is incredible."

Ivan squinted inquisitively. "They look like tiny luminous spheres or orbs. Do you have a makeup?"

"Yeah, it's just coming up. Each sphere has an outer boundary with an internal nucleus of atoms. The boundary is made up of two layers like a living cell's lipid bilayer which appears to hold the orb together while being permeable to specific molecules. The inner layer is made up of positively charged ions, and the outer layer is made up of negatively charged electrons. There's a measureable electric field between the nucleus and boundary that is accelerating the electrons inward on a helical path. I'm measuring several wave frequencies from the individual fields with the majority ranging from 400 to 1800 hertz; not surprising."

"How big are they?" Ivan asked.

"Size varies from a few millimeters in diameter to just under one centimeter. And look at this. They're emitting electromagnetic energy that's making the atoms within other spheres vibrate at a common frequency."

"Communication! Incredible, like the vibrating diaphragm in a telephone."

"My God, Ivan, what are we looking at?"

Ivan massaged his chin as he stared at the monitor dumbfounded. "Bioplasma—a plasma based life form with the same basic structure as a living cell. Incredible, these entities are a living plasma cell. Is Irena right? My God, maybe what we're looking at is the first root race." Ivan shuddered.

"What are you talking about, root race?" Kevin asked.

"I apologize. I should have invited you to join us in our discussions with Irena Zowski; it was enlightening. She filled us in on the history of the subtle body from a spiritual viewpoint as well as from a metaphysical one, also referring to some fascinating laboratory experiments in which plasma has demonstrated the properties of a life form, like a primitive cell. These entities prove the existence of such life forms. The first root race is something from the doctrine of Theosophy. The doctrine suggests the human soul first existed on its own as living energy, and they refer to it as the first root race. It then evolved into the combined body and soul we consider to be human."

"Ivan, maybe we shouldn't be blasting them."

"These entities appear to be a form of plasma life bearing a striking resemblance to a living cell. It appears there may also be some similarities between the structure of the orbs and the historical beliefs regarding the subtle body. Take the helical flow of energy; for example, Kundalini energy in its basic form like Chakras. If this could be the base of what we are on a spiritual level, then we have an obligation to take this all the way. Maybe the human energy field is also comprised of bioplasma."

"Very well, let's do it," Kevin grumbled. "I must confess I'm curious about the results. I'll set the laser wavelength at 800 nanometers. That should accelerate the electrons to allow for a collision energy of 1×1012 electron volts. The detectors will give us a fraction of a millisecond play-by-play of the collision so we can watch it in detail after the fact and cross reference it with the collision products."

"Enough talk. I'm sure our friends are growing impatient."

Kevin charged up the electron emitters then rubbed absently at his eyes before initiating the accelerator. His brow furrowed into two nearly perfect parallel lines as he watched the five second countdown begin. Three, two, one…

In a split second, the monitor lit up with a blinding flash of light, and at the same moment the room shook with the aftershock intensity of an earthquake.

"What the hell was that?" Kevin barked with a loud, agitated voice.

The vibrations subsided quickly, and the two of them kept a keen watch on the monitor. The blinding flash eased off into the subtle twinkles of a sparkler as the entities blew apart.

Then it started.

The sparks coalesced into a mesmerizing helix of light, ordering themselves into a single bright spherical yellow-orange orb. At first it was small, but as the particles continued to swirl along the helical path into the nucleus of the orb, it grew larger and larger."

"I'm picking up power fluctuations along the length of the accelerator. The magnetic field is becoming unstable," Kevin said.

"What the hell are you talking about? Get it together. Bring the backup power online!"

"I'm trying, but there's electrical interference!"

The room shuddered again.

Ivan's implant signaled. It was Ron. "What the hell are the two of you doing down there? We have power outages all through the complex, and the place is shaking like an active volcano." There was a pause. "Damn it! Our security interface just went down. I need power restored immediately."

The power went out in the Control Room, leaving only a handful of colorful lights on the console and the brilliance of the enormous, growing, yellow-orange orb on the monitor. A quiet continuous alarm initiated in the background.

"Ivan! Are you there? Answer me!" The reception was poor and full of static.

"Kevin's on it," Ivan yelled, ending the call.

"Son of a bitch Ivan, it's gone!" Kevin yelled. The room darkened.

"What's gone? What the hell are you talking about?" Ivan, distracted by the call spun his head around to the monitor. The enormous orb was gone.

"The magnetic field went down! It was the only thing holding the large orb in the accelerator. The second the field went down, the orb disappeared off the monitor." Kevin slammed his hands in unison on the armrests of his chair. "Shit!"

"Where the hell did it go?"

"Who the hell knows!" Kevin said. "Once out of the confines of the magnetic field, it could go anywhere."

"Where the hell's the emergency power?" Ivan leapt out of his seat. With shaking hands, he started to make some adjustments to the power output controls. The alarm continued to sound. "Can you shut that God damned thing up?"

Kevin leaned over the console as much as his belly would allow. "Let me do it. We need to draw power from the station grid. It's just going to take a few minutes to do the bypass."

Ivan backed away and let Kevin take over. Kevin's appearance didn't exactly scream confidence. His hairline looked damp and rat-like, and his anguished face glistened like a beacon. His big sausage fingers worked the controls, and once he completed the bypass, he set them into action tapping incessantly against his armrests.

"Would you cut that out," Ivan insisted.

Kevin grumbled and made a tight fist.

Finally, the power returned, but only to emergency levels. "We're creating quite a draw on the grid. It will take a while to come to full power," Kevin said.

"Direct the necessary power to security and to the accelerator detectors and imaging systems. I want to know what the hell that thing was and where it went."

"Well, some good news; it looks like the detectors documented everything up to the second the magnetic field went down, letting the orb escape. Let's have a look."

Ivan stretched the nervousness out of his body before sitting back down in his seat.

"I'm starting it from the beginning, so we can see what happened from the moment the beam of electrons collided with the entities."

The play-by-play began, and Ivan leaned in closer to the monitor so he wouldn't miss anything. "Look at that. The electron beam instigated a tremendous density of collisions with the entities. Slow it down a bit."

Kevin touched the edge of the screen, and the image progression slowed. Ivan continued to watch, frame by frame. "The entities exploded on impact. Pause it a minute. Can you identify the particles?" Ivan asked.

Kevin touched the screen again, and it displayed a breathtaking freeze frame of the collision. The colors were even more intense than the entities themselves, with various hues of blue, green, yellow, red, and violet igniting against the blackness of the collision chamber.

"Magnificent," Ivan whispered.

"I'm seeing a high density of very heavy particles approximately 125 times heavier than the mass of a proton. Confirming…Yes, they're Higgs Boson's; you know, God particles. Looks like they're following the standard laws of particle physics, providing a soupy medium for the other particles and instilling them with mass."

"Yes, I know what they do. What else are you seeing?"

"Electrons obviously and positrons—in fact, I'm seeing all six flavors of leptons, some electrically charged, some neutral. There's also a high density of quarks, which makes sense, since together with the leptons they form the building blocks of all matter."

"Don't patronize me," Ivan said.

"You asked what's here; I'm just telling you."

"Fine, go on."

"There are photons, gluons, and some others. Like I said before, a soup. There's also some dark matter. The particles have supersymmetry. The products of the collision are not unusual," explained Kevin.

"Yes, but the *big* question is what happened after the collision? Continue it. I want to see the rest… Look at that. You can actually see the quarks recombining into protons and neutrons. Then they stick together to form nuclei, which attract the light leptons or electrons, leaving behind neutral neutrino leptons. This is incredible. I never imagined collision products recombining. I would have thought it was impossible."

"Oh yeah, well when was the last time you zapped a plasma life form with billions of electron volts," Kevin replied, cringing. "Maybe they have a memory mark that allowed them to recombine. Just like the memory stemming from the properties of DNA that are critical for reproduction."

"True, but this is unthinkable. As smart as I am, I can't fathom an explanation for this. It makes you wonder whether bioplasma could have had anything to do with the beginnings of organic life on Earth," Ivan postulated. "Look, there are actually two perfectly symmetric intertwined helixes of swirling particles that formed two vortexes on the orb as the particles organized themselves. They resemble strands of DNA. You can even see the transfer of particles between them along an axis between the vortexes as the orb grew. It looks like the particles ordered themselves into an outer boundary comprised of two electrostatic layers with opposite charge. It's like a membrane for the plasma cell nucleus, just like the original entities. Look at the electric field across the two layers as it formed. No wonder the particles accelerated inward so quickly. The initial inward straight filament current would have generated magnetic fields around itself in a circular loop, making the flow helical. The nucleus of the orb appears stable and is definitely luminous with a brilliant yellow-orange hue. Kevin, continue a couple more frames and pan in."

As Kevin zoomed in, the brightness of the orb intensified, soaking the room in a putrid yellow rain. The light was blinding, but Ivan forced himself to look at it. The thing was enormous—well over ten times the originals. The core of the orb looked like a pustule of molten lava, swirling and changing in intensity like a hell storm of energy. Ivan squinted as he watched the core flow into designs with contorted shapes. Two powerful helixes whirled into its center, and their vortexes skipped and frolicked about its outer membrane in an electrical dance. As Ivan watched the image, he could feel its energy crackling on his skin. It felt strange somehow, like negative energy. A wave of nausea came over him. "Pan out! Now!"

Kevin sat slouched in his seat as though he'd eaten too much food, his belly swollen and his mouth open. He didn't move.

"Turn it off," Ivan screamed.

Kevin sprung forward and turned off the monitor. The fire light in the room went out, and it fell into near darkness. He held onto the edge of the console, his chest heaving as he caught his breath. "What…What is that thing?"

"I don't know." Ivan inhaled deeply, and his nausea subsided. "But it's damn big."

"No shit!" Kevin entered a command into the computer, and the details of the collision appeared on the screen. "It's just over ten centimeters." He paused, reviewing the data. "It's like a duplicate of the original entities, but significantly bigger. Hold on a second. This is weird."

"What?" Ivan said.

"Christ, the charges in the two layers surrounding the nucleus…in fact all the charges in the large orb that formed…are the exact opposite of the original entities."

"What do you mean opposite?"

Perspiration beaded on Kevin's face. "In the structure of the original entities where there was a positive charge, there is now a negative charge and vice versa. The charge structure of the new entity is the exact opposite of the originals. I have every reason to believe this large entity is also living plasma, just like the original entities."

Ivan held his breath a moment before speaking. He brought his hand to his forehead. "Shit, what the hell is that thing?"

Chapter Twenty-Nine

After four days of hard work and scheming, Dean finally saw an opportunity to confide in Laura and the others about his plan. The Consortium approved the application for the death penalty for his partner, Sim. Andy told Dean the "reapers" would likely take Sim at dinnertime when the prisoners were in a confined environment. Dean figured the commotion of the event would serve to his advantage. On the negative side, he had the pleasure of spending the day shackled to the *soon to be dead* man.

"I was hired to do a job, and I did it," Sim reflected. "It should be the people who hired me frying in the chair, not me."

How about all of you? Dean thought but kept his mouth shut. He gave Sim some words of encouragement, all the while feeling Sim and his twisted set of morals were getting exactly what they deserved. The man held no remorse for the dozens of lives he'd taken during his cold and calculating career as an assassin. Strangely, Dean found him to be kind and an amiable partner but had no intention of involving him in his plans. It baffled Dean how Sim could kill people in the course of business, innocent people who had done nothing to him, without giving it a second thought. At the same time, he wondered what he would do if he were given an opportunity to kill Ivan.

With Sim's departure, the guard count was down by two, which meant fewer to stroll by. Dean signaled Laura, Sandra, Andy, and Jeff to one end of the table. He folded his hands on the table and whispered, "I may have found a way out of here. It's risky and may not work, but I have to try."

"How? This place is locked down like crazy. No one's ever escaped," Andy said under his breath.

"The power grid. The thing's a mess needing constant repair. They like the work I've done, and they'll be calling me back I'm sure. My fix of the latest problem was temporary. They needed to order a new power modulator. It's a matter of days until they call me back, and their engineers don't seem to have a clue what they're doing."

"So what? Did you sabotage it?" Jeff asked

"No, not yet. That's what the sulfur's for, and I've been collecting zinc and iron filings from the bars on my cell. Its galvanized steel; that's why it's not all rusted like our cots. Both zinc and iron react violently with sulfur at high temperatures. And boom."

"So, what will you do? Put it in one of the power modulators at the back of the collector plates on the grid? When that goes, it will start a chain reaction. The entire grid could blow up," Laura said.

Dean nodded. "Precisely. And when it happens, all hell will break loose. We can make a break for the hangar, steal a pod, and fly right out of here. The only problem is, I can't be sure when the collector plates will blow. The powder needs to be hot, like the temperature of a hot poker, for the reaction to occur. The number of panels operating at any time depends on power demand. If we're locked in our cells when this happens, it's all over, but the way I see it, that's not likely to happen because the power demand is lowest at night."

"How are you going to deposit the powder without being seen? I'm nervous. If they catch you, who knows what they'll do." Laura stroked Dean's leg with her foot. He smiled and took the footsy game up a notch by sandwiching her leg between his. She smiled back.

"Took a bit of biting to pull out these threads." Dean grabbed the bottom of his T-shirt where there was a small rolled up lump inside the seam. "I'll just have to be careful."

"This could actually work," Sandra said with excitement.

"Shhh, whisper. We can't trust anyone else, and I don't want to be responsible for hauling some sick, badass killer out of here."

"Isn't that what you are?" Sandra snapped.

"What I am is highly motivated to get Laura and me out of here. We have a score to settle. I'm just offering the three of you a free pass. And Jeff, when I've finished my business, I'm going to make damn sure you get a fair shake. I have some well-connected friends."

"So how did you two end up in here? You going to tell us the truth?"

Dean ignored Jeff's question.

"Well, I'm not going," Andy said with a grin so wide the scruff of his beard stood on end. "I have big news of my own. My second parole hearing is in three days. I was passed up the first time round, but they told me for sure it would go through this time. I'm walking out the front door, like in the movies. Almost ten years in this place, but I hardly deserve to be smiling."

"Cut yourself some slack. You paid for what you did," Dean said.

"Yeah, well tell that to my cousin. I'm sure he'd gladly trade places with me. Oh, but guess what? He can't; he's dead. I'm never going to drink again." Andy dropped his head with a long sigh.

Andy had a good heart, and Dean knew he was plagued with guilt. Andy and his cousin were in business together selling construction equipment. They had a big deal go through and went out to celebrate. At the end of the night, Andy made a grave decision.

"Just don't drive if you do," Dean said.

"Table Seven."

Five minutes later, the group returned with their food. A guard strolled by, and they waited until she passed before continuing their discussion.

"I can plant the powder the next time I'm called for repairs, and once it's done, we have to be ready to make our move. It could happen any time: hours or days."

"Say we make it out of here, where will we go? Won't they shoot us down?" Jeff asked.

"Damn right they will. We can't leave Draco. We'll fly to the city limits, and then I was hoping that fake relative of yours might give us a hand." Dean set his fork down and grabbed Laura's hand.

"Yeah, he'd do anything for me, but I don't know how to get to his house; and we can't exactly stop and ask for directions."

"I know Draco City, especially the seedier areas. If you have an address, I'll find it," Jeff looked over his shoulder to check for eavesdroppers.

Chapter Thirty

Ivan peeked into Jack's office. Jack stared at a journal with his elbows resting on his desk and his head cradled in his hands. The crystalline monitor displayed a warped reflection of him, and Ivan wasn't sure if he was awake. He awkwardly said, "Hey Jack…"

Jack just about shook out of his seat. He straightened up. The circles under his eyes hung like half-moons, and most of his hair stood on end. "God, Ivan, what the hell you trying to do? Kill me?"

"Sorry. That must be an exciting journal you're reading. At least you weren't snoring. I just came to tell you Irena is here. We're meeting in Section Four in ten minutes. I'm just on my way to reception to get her."

Jack swiveled his chair a quarter turn and forced his eyes to open extra wide. "Okay, I'll be there. Are you going to tell her about the collision?"

"I'd rather not, but I haven't decided. I want to see how useful she is in explaining what these entities are." Jack's office looked different. Ivan gave it a quick once over. "You moved your desk. Wouldn't you rather catch the view out the window than look at a wall?"

"Needed a change. I was finding it too distracting."

Whatever. Ivan shrugged, but he liked it better before. "Well, hang a picture there for God's sake. Maybe one of your pencil sketches."

"We'll see. Anyway, I'll be there in a few minutes." Jack slammed the journal shut and slid it away. "If I stick my nose back in this, I'll never make it."

Ivan laughed as he turned to leave.

* * * *

Ivan collected Irena, and they took a cart to Section Four, joining Jack, Pam, and Kevin. "Irena, I'd like you to meet Kevin, our resident engineer and pilot."

"It is wonderful to meet you," she responded with her familiar energetic charm.

"I understand you're here to enlighten us," Kevin said.

"And enlightened you will be, I assure you."

A wide yawn swallowed up Kevin's attempt at a smile.

"Do you people not sleep, or am I truly boring?" Irena asked.

"My apologies, Ivan must be working me too hard. I've been waking up every night with bad dreams." Kevin looked embarrassed and tried to make light of it. "I feel like a kid again...you know, monsters under the bed." He chuckled. He was the only one who seemed amused by his lame comment, and Ivan was far from it.

"What do you mean bad dreams?" Jack had a pitted concern written into his eyes.

"Why don't we get down to business?" Kevin said abruptly.

"No! I need to know. What do you mean?" Jack clamored.

Irena hugged her briefcase and gestured to the door. "Maybe I should come back later."

Jack shot his hand up to stop her. "No, please, this may be relevant. I haven't been well over the past while, plagued every night by recurring nightmares. I thought it was just me and being kind of personal, hadn't mentioned it to anyone. But Kevin, if this is happening to you, too, then maybe it has something to do with our exposure to the entities?"

"I've been having nightmares, too," Ivan admitted.

"And so have I," Pam said.

"*Panyatno*," Irena said with her hand over her mouth. "There seems to be some commonality here. I doubt this is a coincidence. Do any of you have any other issues that have arisen?" Irena paused, exchanging glances with the group. "I'm not sure this is the time to be aa... What is the word?" She furrowed her brow. "Yes, shy. You must tell me."

"Paranoia," Kevin spouted. "I've noticed it with myself, but was just writing it off to lack of sleep, but I've also noticed it with some others who have been exposed. Especially you, Ivan."

That's a hell of a thing for Kevin to say amongst my subordinates. Ivan gave him a shifty look. "Excuse me?"

"Hey, I call it as I see it." Kevin crossed his arms and jutted out his chin.

"Well maybe we should get to the bottom of this rather than swapping accusations, and yes, lack of sleep can cause paranoia. I analyzed the results of Pam's scans and have formulated some theories; however, it's odd exposure to these entities seems to be causing nightmares."

"Irena, there is something perhaps relevant to this that I didn't raise earlier," Ivan said.

"Oh…"

Ivan cleared his throat and scratched oddly at his forehead in a feeble attempt to cover up his awkwardness as if caught in a lie. "When we expose ourselves to the entities in order to communicate…learn from them…it is actually harming them. Now that I hear nightmares may be a side effect of exposure, I have to wonder if it's purposeful."

"What do you mean harming them? How do you know?"

"Ivan, you're bleeding, on your forehead," Pam stammered.

"Damn it." Ivan took a tissue from his suit pocket and dabbed at the injury, carefully thinking about what he should tell Irena. "They told us telepathically, and the electromagnetic field measurements from entities exposed to us confirmed it. The field weakened over a short period of time."

"How are you harming them? Does the exposure kill them?" Irena asked.

"Yes," Ivan whispered.

"And you continued to expose them to you? What were you thinking?" Irena said with contempt in her voice.

"We were limiting it. It's research."

"Oh, really? To what avail? How many of you have been involved in this communication…this research…and what have you learned? You made me well aware of the positive effects of exposure. Perhaps there is an ulterior motive?" The scowl on Irena's face aged her a decade as angry crow's feet stomped tattoos on the sides of her eyes. Her lips puckered with repugnance.

Ivan cut her short. "I don't appreciate that accusation! We are research scientists investigating one of life's greatest mysteries."

"Maybe you should tell her about the collision Ivan. We're already getting over our heads with this, and I'll be honest with you; if I don't get a good night's sleep soon, I don't know what I'll do. For better or for worse, we need to get some answers," Jack pleaded.

"Collision?" Irena narrowed her eyes even further.

Ivan extended Jack a scathing look before turning his attention back to Irena. "Yes, after you suggested the entities could be composed of bioplasma, we put some of them into the accelerator to try and determine their structure and particle makeup. Only a few entities were used in the experiment, and the results were astounding. I'm sure you'll agree it was a worthwhile experiment when you see the results. They should help immensely in piecing together the big picture."

Irena's mouth hung open. "I don't care what the results show! How can you justify blowing apart intelligent beings as part of an experiment. This reminds me of the Nazi war crimes. I insist no further harm come to these life forms, or I will report you to the Consortium. Furthermore, the entities you have in this containment unit should be returned to their natural environment at once."

"This facility is funding this work, and it is proprietary," Ivan stated. "I will not be dictated to and will not stand for a breach of confidentiality! Nothing is to be shared with the Consortium without my authorization."

"Well, perhaps we are finished here. I will not be involved in something of this nature." Irena stomped toward the door. "*Ya ne panimayu tebia! Do svidaniya!*"

Jack rushed ahead and turned to face her, towering over her by an entire foot. "Please, Dr. Zowski, let's be reasonable here. We've come this far, admittedly with a few mistakes in judgment, but we are at the edge of a great discovery. If the health of these entities has been compromised, let it not be in vein. How about we compile all of our results, then we can do as you say and put this whole project to rest?"

Irena responded with a firm gesture in the direction of the containment unit. "And you will assure me no more harm will come to them."

Jack looked toward Ivan for an endorsement.

"Please Irena, come back. It would be criminal to throw away our findings without a thorough analysis," Ivan said. "I will agree no further harm will come to the entities. Why don't I fill you in on the results of the collision? Despite your concerns, I'm sure you'll be intrigued."

"Fine then. I will look at your results, but I will not reserve judgment. I am disgusted," Irena said with a cross tone.

Jack escorted Irena back toward the containment unit as Ivan turned on the monitor. Ivan started in with a detailed description of the structural makeup of the entities and the results of the collision from a few days earlier. Despite Irena's continued air of antagonism, she seemed astonished by the results.

"I certainly despise how we got here, but the picture is becoming quite clear. The structure of the entities confirms the existence of self-organized plasma as an inorganic life form. It looks like bioplasma truly exists, and the resemblance of these entities to a living cell is uncanny. Plasma makes up over ninety-nine percent of the universe so conceivably, bioplasmic life could be the dominant form of life in the universe!" Irena held up a thoughtful finger. Maybe simple bioplasmic life forms such as this formed during electrical storms on Earth billions of years ago. It could have evolved and even spurred the development of organic carbon-based life. The helical energy flow observed from the entities certainly resembles DNA. Could it be, plasma life is the true origin of life? Could it have served as a template for biological life that led to what we believe to be human today: the combined harmonious union of living energy and living matter?"

"Isn't that jumping the gun a little," Jack said. "We have yet to prove we are anything more than just a fine tuned biological machine. Just because these entities are made up of bioplasma, doesn't mean the human energy field is."

"Yes that's true. However, I can't help but notice the parallels between the orb structure of the entities and the documented beliefs surrounding the subtle body, which Irena described earlier," Ivan pointed out. "Irena, with your last comment, are you suggesting the doctrine of Theosophy could be correct? That on Earth, billions of years ago, living bioplasma life forms possibly existed on their own as the first root race, and they evolved, spurred the development of organic life and united with it."

"Yes, you are absolutely right! That is exactly what may have happened. Let's consider the similarities between these orbs that are your entities and the beliefs of the subtle body. The helical energy flow you observed in the accelerator and the plasma vortexes are like Chakras. The flow of energy between the helixes along channels or meridians is similar to that described by the Ch'i and applied to acupuncture. The luminosity of the entities suggests an auric shell. And of course, the responsiveness of the human energy field to the external electromagnetic field of the entities is clearly demonstrated by the effects they had on you.

"The similarities are staggering. It all fits! The parallels certainly lead one to think that perhaps the human energy field is also made up of bioplasmic living energy. What is the expression?" Irena stared at the wall momentarily as if the answer she searched for was plastered across it. "Yes, if it looks like an apple, smells like an apple, and tastes like an apple, then maybe it is an apple." She made a firm nod, seeming very pleased with herself.

"So why have the entities had such a profound effect on us?" Pam asked.

"Yes, I believe I can explain that. The energy field I measured from you before being exposed to the entities is quite typical of a young healthy woman, being composed of balanced, coherent energy patterns across the full frequency spectrum. After exposure, your energy field exhibited a greater number of waves in the higher frequency ranges and a dramatic increase in the wave amplitude. I believe your energy field interacted with the electromagnetic field of the entities in accordance with the simple theory of superposition. When two waves align together perfectly, the amplitude of the resultant wave becomes the sum total of the amplitude of each individual wave. Just like in the ocean when two waves combine and get bigger."

"Yes, I understand the theory," Pam snapped. "So you're saying I absorbed the energy field of the entities, and that's why they died."

"Yes, that's exactly what I'm saying. What all of you did to those poor helpless entities is analogous to draining the power of a battery. Your human energy field absorbed the energy from the field of the entities until they were so weak, they weren't able to sustain themselves. You killed them," Irena added. She shook her head in disgust. "You should also know the energy of the human energy field can be transferred to matter it interacts with, meaning the body. This of course is the theory behind energy healing. A person with the gift of healing enhances the energy field of a sick person, which has a healing effect on the body. Clearly, your enhanced energy field has had a dramatic effect, giving you the gifts you have described. I cannot explain how this additional energy is affecting the brain and body exactly.

"A determination of that would require further study." Irena raised her voice. "Which I might add, we do not have the luxury of. Suffice to say, it is believed that by manipulating and directing the flow of energy in the subtle body, superhuman or miraculous powers can be achieved, and higher states of consciousness can be attained. Perhaps, once again in accordance with the doctrine of Theosophy, absorbing the energy field of the entities is evolving you into the sixth root race."

"So why can we see the entities? We can't see the human energy field," Pam continued.

"Yes that presents a difference between the characteristics of the two. Because you can't see something, doesn't mean it's not there. As I mentioned before, maybe the human energy field emits light just outside the visible spectrum, whereas the entities emit visible light. Plasma *can* emit light. For example, the northern lights of Earth are plasma. Gas molecules in the atmosphere become energized from collisions with cosmic particles from the sun. When they return to the ground state, they emit light. The color depends on the molecule...nitrogen emits red light, oxygen green. Light emission is a quantum physics question." Irena stiffened. " And would require *further* study." This time Irena's petulance came out in a yell, the gravelly kind of bellow that comes from a domineering woman. Ivan decided it wasn't just her masculine mannerisms that kept her ring finger bare. Her disconcerting attitude peeved him and left jaws hanging. How could she be excited over their results one second and then turn and be all snippety again?

He was about to wrap up the meeting when Pam spoke up. "I'm

curious Irena, do you follow a religion? Do you believe in God?"

"I am a woman of science. That is my religion. There are so many religions, all dictating what one must believe from the day we're born. We must look to science and the building blocks of the universe to find the truth, and there is only one truth. All religions point to the existence of the soul, and I do believe in that. In my opinion, the evidence is looking us in the eyes. As far as the belief in a divine being, I will not comment. Having said that, I believe the cumulative power of the life force is immense. Compare the power of one drop of rain to that of the entire ocean. Perhaps the power of prayer and positive thinking has some merits. Anyway, to answer your question, Pam...if God does exist beyond just an idea, then whatever it is, it must be manifested as something in the physical makeup of the universe. It can't be nothing."

"Do you think God could be made up of bioplasma?" Pam continued.

"Your guess is as good as mine," Irena said abruptly.

Remembering his wave of nausea after the large entity formed, Ivan regretted ever carrying out the collision. He swallowed his growing dislike for Irena and raised another issue. "That brings me to the single entity we seemingly created in the accelerator."

"Yes, playing God! Well what concerns me is not the size of the entity, but the fact its charge structure was the complete opposite of the originals. According to Einstein's theory of relativity, energy, and matter are the same. As you know, the law of conservation of energy states that in an isolated system, energy remains constant and cannot be created or destroyed; however, it can change form. You used your atom smasher to break those entities down into the basic building blocks of matter, and yet the particles managed to restructure themselves, almost like they had a memory. In your situation the question is: into what?"

"Are you suggesting we created some kind of monster?" Jack tossed his head back and combed his fingers through his hair in a way that suggested he didn't really want to know the answer.

"Who am I to speculate on what you created," Irena said. "What is it in the physical world that differentiates good and evil? Particle accelerators have demonstrated that every particle in nature has its own anti-particle. It is clearly wrong what you did, and it is possible the ramifications have yet to unfold. Has anyone seen the large entity, sensed anything unusual?"

"My mind's been playing tricks on me for weeks now. It's hard to say. Anyone else observe anything?" Ivan glanced around at the row of blank faces. They either had nothing to say, or weren't willing to say it. For him, he suspected his nightmares had worsened after the collision, but he couldn't say conclusively, so he decided to shelf the thought for now. "Well it looks like nothing specific, but it's a little unnerving having the anti-entity floating around somewhere in the ether."

"Hopefully it will not come back to haunt you, but I wouldn't blame it if it did," Irena said, glaring with enmity. "By the way, your forehead is still bleeding, Ivan. As soon as that gouge scabs over, you scratch it apart again. That's a nice suit. You wouldn't want it to get stained."

Ivan cringed with embarrassment and continued to dab at the sore with fidgety movements.

"What about the nightmares?" Jack inquired.

"I will do research into how electromagnetic radiation can affect brain waves, in particular the lower frequency waves corresponding to sleep. It is possible the entities managed to find a defense against you, your Achilles heel. Their way of fighting back. I suggest you discontinue your supposed communication with them immediately, and maybe you will be able to sleep at night. An ironic approach to instilling morals into the bunch of you. Tell me, are there any others who have been exposed?"

"Yes, three others. Ron Fieldman, our head of security, and two other research scientists," Ivan said.

"Your motives are quite clear in my mind, no?" Irena shook her head. "I will not press the issue as it will only make me angrier than I already am. Do you know if any of them have been experiencing nightmares?"

Ivan looked to the others for input. "Like Kevin mentioned earlier, it's a personal experience people don't tend to talk about."

"Well, if I am to help you with this perhaps a good starting point would be to talk with each of you individually to get details of your sleep problems. There are nightmares and sleep terrors. They have different characteristics. I need to know the details in order to make a diagnosis."

Jack looked at Irena with sincerity. "Can you please do this quickly and let us know what you find out. I can promise you I will not be back in that chamber."

"Yes. I will make it a priority to get back to you, and I expect all of you to keep your end of the bargain. And get those things home!"

"Thank you for your insightful expertise, Irena. I can assure you we will follow through, and I will be in touch. I hope you can overlook our poor mistake in judgment in the name of science," Ivan said.

"I will overlook it for now."

Ivan checked his watch. "I think we're finished for now, and it's getting late."

He escorted Irena back to reception, glad to be rid of her, and then made a detour to the men's room to assess the damage to his forehead. The bright spotlights mounted on the ceiling provided ample lighting but were quite an annoyance when looking in the mirror. One of the beams reflected back in near perfect focus into Ivan's eyes. He adjusted his angle and commenced his inspection. It had taken some persistence to stop the bleeding, and his scratch was finally starting to scab over again. He wasn't happy with the speed of healing; however, it didn't surprise him as he'd been limiting his exposure to the entities, hoping the nightmares would subside. This was the first sign he was overdue, and he shivered at the thought of it. *She better fix this problem.* He continued to examine the wound for a moment. It was surprisingly deep and strangely he had no recollection of doing it.

The lights flickered as Ivan considered his reflection. The strobe effect subsided, leaving him in the dark for a moment.

"Ivan," the voice was quiet, softer than a whisper.

"Who's there?" He stood in the dark, facing the mirror, listening to his own breathing.

Seconds later to Ivan's relief, the lights flickered back on. *What the hell...* Ivan blinked, questioning what he had just seen. It was only in the mirror for a moment, the stone-gray face of a young boy; his eyes glowed yellow-orange surrounded by a cold intangible darkness that could only be described as evil. The boy looked like death, but Ivan recognized him. It was Nathan.

Ivan vigorously ran the water until tepid and started splashing his face. Then he heard it again. Someone called his name. The voice was faintly audible over the rushing water, but this time he recognized it. He straightened himself up and flung himself around to face the stalls. One of the doors was gently swinging.

"Who's there?" he demanded in a throaty voice that sounded hollow against the glassy tile. He had no time for this nonsense. His heart sped, pumping his face full of warm blood, and he stomped over and pushed the door open. There was no one. "Son of a bitch!"

Ivan returned to the sink to turn off the water. He consciously avoided looking in the mirror, but as he turned the taps off, he caught a chilling sight out of his peripherals. For a moment, the reflection of the spotlight in the mirror looked exactly like the large yellow-orange entity in the accelerator right before it disappeared. He held his breath listening to the sound of nothing, but he was sure what he'd seen couldn't be heard, just felt. Its energy pelted his skin like hailstones.

"Go away!" he screamed, and he rushed toward the door. As he left, he heard the sound of a young laugh.

Ivan let out a sigh of relief as he hurried back to his office. *I need some sleep. My mind's playing tricks on me again.* He blanked the vision of the entity out of his mind and looked down at his silk tie covered in watermarks. *God damn it!* It was one of his favorites. It had a perfect deep blue background with a slight floral pattern of complementary colors. He held up his tie and gave his head a shake.

Kevin was waiting for him at his office.

"This is not good," Kevin said. "You better update Ron and Larry and if necessary… Hey, you okay? Looks like you just got out of the shower."

"I'm fine. Just a bit agitated by Irena's visit," Ivan stuttered.

"Well as I was saying, you better—"

"I know, I know. Trust me I'm on it, but we need her for the time being. The fact we've all been plagued with nightmares is of great concern. I've got to the point that I've spent some nights on this couch for a fresh environment. Hopefully, she can resolve this issue for us because I sure as hell don't plan on regressing back to the way I used to be. I think she's right, and those entities have found a way to exact their revenge on us. We are at the forefront of the evolution of man, and I won't let a few nightmares stop us. Once we are finished with her, as far as she's concerned, the program will be at an end. If she becomes a problem, Larry will have to deal with her."

"Ivan, what about the large entity? Do you think we could have created some kind of monster? If there's one thing we all agree on, it's the fact that those entities are good and peaceful. If they are causing the nightmares, I believe it's out of self-defense not revenge. My take on them is that they aren't even capable of deliberate revenge or violence. They are pure goodness. It's unnerving to think of what an entity with a charge structure opposite to them would be like. Pure evil perhaps? Like Irena said, who knows what defines good and evil in the physical universe. I'd have to say, I deeply regret putting those entities in the accelerator. I don't care what we've learned. Ever since then, I haven't felt myself, and I'm not talking about the nightmares and fatigue. They're separate. I can't quite put my finger on it, but it's like I feel a presence, and it's affecting me. Christ, sometimes I look in the mirror, and I have to do a second take. It's like my eyes are glowing the yellow-orange color of that entity."

Ivan froze at his words.

"Ivan, did you hear anything I said?"

"Yeah, I heard you." He paused. "I think you're reading too much into it. Get yourself a sleeping pill and a good night's sleep. That's what I'm going to do." Ivan tried desperately to believe his own words.

Chapter Thirty-One

The morning of Andy's parole hearing finally arrived, and he sat at the group table, straight backed and smug, planning his life like a school boy who just graduated. "Maybe I'll go into Real Estate."

"What about mining or gardening, working the ground?" Jeff said with a grin.

Dean dug his spoon into the last bite of *yuck* splatted on his plate. The cold oatmeal clumped like wallpaper paste, and he jammed it into his mouth. He'd mastered the art of wolfing his meals; it was like pulling off a Band-Aid—fast equaled less pain. Andy, true to his true character, enjoyed playing with his breakfast mound, proudly sculpting it into animals before torturously nibbling it away. Dean watched as Andy finished off the hindquarters of his gopher when two guards appeared from behind.

"Weber, Weston, you're coming with us," one of them commanded.

Andy didn't hesitate to pop out of his seat. "Yes, sir."

Dean looked over as if surprised. "Is there a problem sir?"

"Power grid again. We had brown outs all night. Clear your plates and let's go."

Dean and Andy walked their plates to the trays by the exit and then followed the guards through the doors leading back to the cell block. They continued along, retracing the steps Dean had made the day he arrived. Once they were back in the Orientation Room, Andy spun off with two guards toward a meeting room, while the other two escorted Dean through the hangar into the Operations Center.

The Operations Center consisted of a Control Room and a Utility Tunnel running the length of the exterior power grid. The grid had six sections, each section housing a series of particle collector plate arrays. The technology was universal. Energetic particles from the atmosphere would be absorbed by the shiny black plates and their energy harnessed for heat and electricity. Unfortunately, the sulfur dust not only served to damage the plates but was also responsible for the continuous corrosion of grid components. The last time McLean called on Dean's expertise, he'd had to bypass the flow of power to a secondary line in array two until a new power module could be installed. He deliberately bypassed it to a line also on the verge of breaking down.

When Dean entered the Control Room, the chief engineer approached him. He was a stout fellow with a reasonable sense of humor to ice his otherwise dry, no-nonsense personality. "Hey Weston, you mentioned you've had experience replacing power modules?"

"Yeah, piece of cake. Did your new unit arrive?"

"It arrived yesterday afternoon and not a minute too soon. The line you redirected the power to is giving us problems. You probably didn't notice the brownouts last night."

"Nope, sleeping like a baby."

The man made a sarcastic grunt. "I'll bet. Anyway, if you don't mind, I'll have one of our rookies tag along to give you a hand and learn the ropes. If you could explain the whole procedure to him, that would be great."

"Sure, no problem, but it takes a lot more than observation to do this properly. If the energy levels aren't exactly in sync with the remainder of the grid, it will throw out the power flow of the entire grid. I should probably sit down with him to go over some of the theory."

"There'll be time for that later. We need this operating now, so just take him along and teach him what you can."

"No problem." It was a shot in the dark, but worth a try. The last thing Dean needed was a rookie engineer breathing down his neck. *Hopefully, the kid's as thick as you.* "Before we get started, do you mind if I have a look at some of the readings coming off the grid."

"Sure go ahead." The chief engineer turned to the young man in overalls organizing some equipment in the corner. "Jake, get over here. This is Dean Weston...the person I told you about. He has years of experience with particle collector arrays. Fortunately for us, he's a murderer, too." The man snickered as he clapped Dean on the back. "Anyway, he's going to replace the module in array two this morning, and I want you to tag along and learn everything you can."

Dean took one look at Jake and figured he was barely out of

school, still sporting the odd pimple on his young complexion. "Nice to meet you, Jake. Where did you study engineering?"

"Lyra Institute"

"Great school...I went there. Miller still teaching Mechanics?"

"Yeah, I had him."

"He graduated with me. Is he still a stiff?"

"Excuse me?"

"You know, really serious. I don't think I ever saw the guy crack a smile. But smart, very smart."

"Yeah he's smart, but he's not a great teacher. I didn't do too well in his class."

That's a good thing. "Well, I have a funny story for you. Miller had a bit too much to drink at our grad party, and a bunch of us pinned him down and shaved off one of his eyebrows. You can't imagine how funny someone looks with one eyebrow." Dean took a moment to watch the kid's expression. He seemed to enjoy his story. "Anyway on a more serious note, I'll give you a quick rundown on the power levels we have to monitor while we're replacing the module. It'll be much easier having another person along to monitor the power fluctuations."

Dean walked Jake over to the elaborate and brilliantly lit control panel and gave him a quick theory lesson, making sure it was way over his head. All the while, he carefully monitored the temperatures and power readings of the active plate arrays to try and determine the order in which they might typically be brought on line.

"Now where's the module?" Dean asked.

"Over there. I just took it out of its packaging, and I've put together the equipment we need."

Dean walked over to the corner where Jake had been working and inspected the equipment. "We need four power couplings. Otherwise, it looks like you've got everything else."

Jake went to a cabinet to retrieve the couplings, and the two of them assembled the equipment.

"We'll access the array from the Utility Tunnel. I hope you don't mind if my friends come along." Dean smiled at Jake as he signaled to the two guards at the door. "It's going to be tight quarters, and it's hotter than hell in behind the grid. The temperature indicator has it at thirty-six degrees Celsius right now." Dean led the way to the door of the Utility Tunnel and turned back to the chief engineer. "This is delicate work; it can't be rushed. We'll likely be an hour or so."

The man nodded, and Dean and Jake headed through the door with the guards on their tail.

The door led to a short concrete tunnel that ended in a large steel door, at least one quarter of a meter in thickness. Dean couldn't believe some idiot had left it propped open. "What the hell is this door doing open?"

"I don't know. Maybe someone was moving equipment in," Jake said.

"I don't care who was doing what. This door should be shut at all times. It's thick for a reason. If anything happened to any part of the grid, and this door was open, anyone in the Control Room would be incinerated." Dean took a moment to return to the Control Room and speak to the chief engineer before continuing. When the grid blew, he didn't want any innocent people to get hurt.

The steel door led to the main Utility Tunnel. The thick concrete walls did a good job muffling the dull roar of the power grid, but it got louder as they progressed along the tunnel. The walk down to array two took only a couple of minutes. Each array was accessible through its own steel door, and once through the door to array two, the temperature shot up ten degrees.

"You're going to regret wearing those overalls Jake." Dean billowed out his T-shirt slightly while checking for the little packet of zinc and sulfur tucked securely in the bottom seam.

Once they were in location, Dean carefully laid out the equipment. He explained the procedure to Jake and handed him a small hand held device. "You can monitor everything with this. I'm certain you're familiar with how this works. You just toggle through the options and make your selection. Right now, it's set to give the temperature on the back surface of the collector plates. Once I've replaced the module, I'll be most concerned about the power readings as I switch the energy flow back to array two. At that point, don't take your eye off this for one second. The power factor needs to equal one when I make the switch, which means the voltage and current are in phase. If it deviates even slightly, you tell me immediately. Understand?"

Jake looked a little nervous. "Okay."

Dean looked up at the guards. "If you don't mind giving me a little extra room. It's not like I can go anywhere, and if I mess up, I'll get us all killed."

"Just get it done." The one guard anxiously replied. The man's forehead shimmered, and Dean suspected the vile smell crawling up his nostrils was radiating from the man's hefty guard uniform.

Dean got onto the floor and went straight to work. He had to lie down on his back and push himself underneath the manifold to install the module. He started by removing half a dozen screws to open the manifold. Replacing the module was a difficult and fiddly job. His hands were wet with perspiration, and he had to concentrate on keeping them steady. He explained each step and invited Jake to come down and take a look for himself. He glanced over to the guards periodically only to find them watching him like a hawk.

"Christ it's hot in here." Dean started to fidget, showing deliberate signs of frustration. He wiped his brow and continued to work. The job was close to completion, and he knew he had to make his move.

"Jake you're going to have to get up and monitor both the real and reactive power on that secondary line and don't forget what I said about the power factor. You with me?"

"Yes," Jake took a seat beside Dean in what little space was available.

"The module's installed. I'm just going to adjust the inductor slightly. Okay, I'm about to switch it over." Dean made some adjustments to the switching panel beside the module. He fidgeted again, looking as though he was trying to get comfortable. Could you please make sure that door is secure, just in case. And Jake, I need your full attention."

Dean could sense the three of them were a little uneasy, and the heat didn't help. As one of the guards turned to check the door, he made his move. He fluffed his shirt up slightly to free it from the sweat of his stomach and made sure it landed with the packet near his groin. He then reached down and gave himself a good scratch, hoping the men would respect the privacy of his itch and glance the other way. His first attempt was only half successful. When the packet started coming out of the seam, he felt the toilet paper holding it together start to lose its integrity. He folded his shirt up slightly, hoping none of them would notice.

"How's that power factor, Jake?"

"Steady at one."

Dean set his attention back to the module and adjusted the capacitance of the unit.

"The factor's fluctuating from one," Jake said.

"Damn it!" Dean squirmed and made a few adjustments. "How 'bout now?"

"It seems to be settling down."

Dean reached down for another scratch. "We're almost done here." As he finished his sentence, he successfully grabbed the packet and concealed it in his palm, bringing it up to where he was working. He made some adjustments on the panel and then deposited the powder packet on the top edge of the module, being careful it didn't spill behind. It was critical that all of the powder stay together for the reaction to be big enough to blow up the module. He quickly replaced the manifold and got up.

"Good work, Jake. You'll be able to fly solo at this before you know it. Now I don't know about you people, but I've had enough of this heat. How about we get out of here?"

Dean worked with Jake packing up the gear. The guards gave the work site a quick inspection, and they returned to the Control Room.

"How are things looking?" Dean asked the chief engineer.

"Fantastic, great work, Weston. I might just have to offer you a job." He laughed and then gave Dean a strange look. "What's in your hair?"

Dean froze for a moment. "Excuse me?" He ran his fingers through his perspiration soaked hair. They came out streaked in yellow with some fine gray particles. *Think fast!* Dean laughed. "Well, I dropped the soap in the shower this morning, and you know what they say about that. Anyway that was enough for me. I wasn't about to pick it up, so I was out of there. You can bet I won't make that mistake again." He grimaced and gave his hair a good rub then wiped his hands on his pants. "Damn sulfur! Anything else I can help you with today?"

"No, all done and thanks. Watch the soap!" The man let out a hearty laugh.

* * * *

It was noontime by the time Dean joined his group out in the diamond field. He grabbed a sandwich from the lunch bin, avoiding the tuna he considered even unfit for Costello and sat down beside his new partner, waiting for the guard to shackle them. He couldn't wait to fill everyone in on the events of the morning, but it would have to wait.

Before taking a bite of his lunch, he looked around with a grin and shook the bottom of his T-shirt loose. "Well that's a load off my chest. Mission accomplished. I replaced their power module for them. It might be a few days before they get to enjoy the benefit of it, but it's there waiting for them when they need it."

Laura gave him a quick knowing smile. "That's great news. We wouldn't want the air conditioning to stop running."

Dean took a good look at Laura in an effort to assess her mood, but her expression was impassive. He thought she'd be happier hearing his news. "How was your morning?"

"Yes, well I was just about to get to that, funny you should ask." Laura gestured toward Andy.

Dean spun around to find Andy with a very dejected look pasted on his face. "Don't tell me they turned you down?"

Laura didn't give Andy a chance to respond. "Dean, they turned him down all right, and guess who was there asking what Andy knew about us?"

"Son of a bitch," Dean said under his breath. "Larry Dunn?"

Andy piped up. "He seemed more interested in the two of you than me. It was my damn parole hearing! God damn it, I'm never going to get out of here."

"Don't bet on it," Dean quipped. "Andy, was Dunn at your last hearing?"

"Heck no! I've never seen the guy in my life."

"Keep it down over there," a guard barked.

Dean lowered his voice. "Andy, what did they ask about Laura and me?"

"They wanted to know if you'd discussed the details of your crime with me or anyone else. I told him if he wanted details of your crime, then he should ask you himself."

"So you were vague?"

"I tried to deflect the discussion back to me, my good behavior, my hearing."

"Why did they turn you down?" Dean said.

"They just did. They beat around the bush and didn't really give me a firm reason. That's what pisses me off the most. I really don't know why I was declined." Andy grabbed a fistful of stones and hurled them.

Dean sat silently for a moment staring straight into Laura's eyes. "It looks like we all have a score to settle."

Chapter Thirty-Two

Dean arrived for breakfast and took a seat beside Laura. He put his arm around her waist. "Good morning, sweetheart," he said and smiled.

Laura reached under the table and grabbed the top of his leg, gently massaging it. "You're amazing you know that," she whispered back. "It seems to me you owe me a date."

He turned and admired her brilliant eyes. They were deep blue, sunset blue. "I owe you one hell of a date." He wanted to kiss her but knew he couldn't.

"Why don't you two get a room?" Andy had just arrived and seemed in better spirits than the day before.

His question broke Dean's trance. "We're working on it," he said, grinning. Laura gave his leg a squeeze then retreated back.

One by one, the group settled at the table, everyone smiling like cats: close-lipped and mischievous. As they waited for their number to be called, two guards honed in on Dean. "Weston, you're coming with us. Another problem with the grid."

Dean grabbed Laura's hand and gave it a strong squeeze as he rose from his seat. "What's the problem this time?" *Are they on to me?* He gave her a look of apprehension.

"Something outside by the collector plates. That's all they told me. Come on," the guard commanded.

"Can't the man have some breakfast?" Andy remarked. He'd just finished crafting the fluffy cotton tail of his oatmeal rabbit.

"Now, Weston!"

As Dean turned to follow the men, he gave Laura a wink. "See you in a bit." *Just where I want to be if that array blows!*

Once again, Dean retraced his steps from the first day, only this time the guards stopped before arriving at the Operations Center and exited the complex through a back door in the hangar. There was a slight chill in the air, something unusual for Draco. The wind whistled along the side of the power grid, and Dean shielded his face from the billows of dust.

"Aren't we going to the Control Room? I need to talk to the chief engineer."

"He said he'd meet you out here. This isn't a secure area, so we're going to have to shackle and cuff you."

The guard took what he needed out of a shoulder pack he carried. As he did, Dean caught a glimpse of a rope inside the pack.

Dean's intuition told him something wasn't right. Other than cleaning off the collector plates, which you would never do when they were active, they rarely had an exterior problem. "Before I do any work on the outer grid, I need to check the power levels in the Control Room."

The guards ignored his request and then proceeded to shackle and cuff him. They resorted to force when he insisted he speak with the chief engineer. Once the guards secured him, they grabbed his arms and marched him toward the shiny black collector plate arrays mounted on the side of the Operations Building. Dean could see along the entire length of the grid. There was no one in sight. He demanded to speak with one of the engineers before getting to work. The guards shoved him along.

As they approached the grid, the temperature rose. The morning sun sat pasted to the skyline just above the horizon, and its *jack-o-lantern* glow beamed off the shiny collector plates on the Operations Building like an enormous laser, blinding Dean as he walked. They were about fifteen meters from the grid when Dean felt a sharp blow to the back of his head, bringing him to the ground. He squinted in the light trying to regain his focus. The loosely packed ground cushioned his fall, but reeked of rotting flesh. As Dean struggled in a daze to get up, one of the guards kicked him onto his stomach while the other grabbed the rope from his pack. Within a split second, his arms and legs were brought up behind him and tied together like a pig ready for a pig-roast. The muscle fibres in his neck threatened to unravel as his head was crunched to the side. In confusion, he watched as the guard tied the other end of the rope to a stake in the ground. Then it happened…a stabbing kick that tore the air from his lungs sent him flying toward a collection of small shrubs around a clearing. He rolled just over one meter disturbing the few rainbow bugs dining on the shrubs in his path before the ground swallowed him whole.

Darkness descended on Dean as he struggled to stop himself from being consumed by the loose dirt. He sank deep into the pit as though it was filled with cardboard confetti, coming to rest at the bottom. He blinked a couple of times before shutting his eyes tightly to shield them from the dirt. He held what little breath he had left while trying to orient himself. The seconds passed quickly as the scurrying of hundreds of small bugs wisped across his skin like fine sand paper. There was no escaping them. They instantly enveloped him. He was about to lose the battle with his lungs just as the insects found their way to his nose. A swarm of them entered the warm moist tunnel, making their way into the depths of Dean's chest cavity and sinuses. He couldn't hold on any longer and gasped for air.

The bugs packed his mouth, and he tried to spit them away, but it was no use. If only his lungs were filling with water, the suffocating horror would end. As the bugs made their way deeper into his body, he could feel their scurrying and the terrible burning sensation that accompanied it. He gasped and gasped, yet there was nothing but bugs to satisfy his hunger for air. Through the horror and panic, thoughts fumbled through his mind. *Just let me die. Are they going to eat me alive?* He flailed and flailed, but there was no breaking his restraints.

He fought to exhaustion and then finally gave up and lay still, twitching ever so slightly. The ropes cut into his skin, and the insects had infested every orifice of his body and enveloped him in a living cocoon. The excruciating burning sensation was too much. He begged to die. All he could do was gasp and gasp, with nothing but bugs to fill his chest. *How am I alive?* The question ran through his mind over and over. The pain was unimaginable, yet the sweet gift of unconsciousness was nowhere to end his plight.

Dean lost all sense of time, but the horrifying hours seemed countless. He'd tried to close off his mind to the pain, but it was too intense. Every second, he beckoned for air, but his lungs were restricted as though they'd been cast in concrete. He tried to picture the faces of people he cared about, all of whom he'd let down. Laura, his father, his mother, Annie, Karen, and Matt. When this was all over, there would be no place in heaven for him.

Finally, his mind drifted to the entities. If only he could have been one of them. Maybe he still could? Free from physical boundaries and all the suffering that came with it. He felt sickened that he wouldn't live to stop Ivan and desperately hoped death would come soon. Dean wasn't afraid to die, and his military training had left him believing he could take on the world. No physical or psychological barriers could ever stand in his way. As he felt himself breaking apart, through his madness, the harsh realization that he was sorely mistaken sunk in. The bugs weren't consuming his flesh. They were much more sinister. It felt as though they were consuming his soul, striping it down, bite after bite. He wondered if there'd be anything left of it in the end. A dismal thought crossed his mind: *some things are worse than death,* and with it, he became aware of the impossible—he was giving up.

Just as Dean thought he was about to pass into oblivion, he felt the heaving rope deliver him back to the surface. The guards kicked him onto his side, and he could hear them step back as the insects evacuated his limp body. His abdomen, chest, throat, and sinuses felt like they were on fire as the bugs fled, descending back into their nest, back to the Hell from where they came. He tried repeatedly to catch his breath, but it felt like his lungs had solidified. Finally, he was successful and a rush of oxygen came flowing in. Air never felt so precious to him. He struggled to breathe as his lungs remained constrained. After a period of time, he slowly opened his eyes, blinking several times to try to clear away the dirt. His focus returned enough to make out the large shadow cast by the Operations Building behind him. While Dean roasted like a pig in his festering grave, the *jack-o-lantern* sun had taken the high road; blaring down on him with its fiendish, one toothed grin and slits for eyes, laughing. *That's what ya get!*

The guards untied him, removed his cuffs and shackles and got him to his feet. He was dazed and wobbly and buckled under his own weight.

"Stand up," one of them yelled as he slapped alertness into his face.

"Go to Hell!" Dean sputtered in hardly a discernable whisper.

The men straightened him up as much as they could and dragged

234

him back to the dining hall.

"It's dinner time, Weston," one said in a cheery voice. "Enjoy it. It's one of your last."

They perched him in a seat at his table, and he collapsed with his head resting on his arms, his face lifeless. Out of the crack in his eye, he could just make out his group filing in.

* * * *

Laura and Andy walked into the dining hall side-by-side with Sandra and Jeff a few steps ahead. Sandra stopped dead, looking toward their table and turned around. "What's with Dean?"

Andy looked over and froze, his face falling blank. "Jeff, go check him out." He took Laura's arm.

"Oh my God, Dean! What's happened?" Laura shook free of Andy and tore ahead of Jeff. "Dean, what did they do?" She sat beside him and wrapped her arms around him just as Andy and Jeff arrived at her side. "Dean, Dean." He didn't respond. "Is he dead? They killed him!" She felt the pressure behind her eyes build until the tears burst free and continued to try to rouse him by rubbing some warmth into his cadaver-gray arms.

A guard rushed over. "Enough! Just leave him be and take your seats."

Sandra, Jeff, and Andy took a seat across from Dean and Laura. Laura couldn't stop crying as she caressed Dean's face, brushing the dirt out of his hair.

"Dean, talk to me, please. I love you. Please, I can't lose you," she whimpered. She took his hand from the table and squeezed it as hard as she could. "Please, Dean." She felt a weak return of her affection.

A small, colorful bug crawled out of Dean's nostril followed by a fine droplet of blood. "Oh my God," she cried.

Andy crushed the bug with his finger and placed a sympathetic hand on Laura's arm. "Laura, they must have—"

A menacing laugh droned from two tables over interrupting Andy's sentence. Charlie Hopkins' throaty holler followed, "He finally got his just dessert. You're precious boyfriend's a dead man, lady!"

His sinister laugh went on ad nauseam, leaving Laura consumed with animosity for the scum-ball bastard. She tried to tune out the cackling, but the pools in her eyes deepened. It was as though demons had possessed them, fueling them with hate, dread and worry and clouding both her vision and her ability to stay in control. And *stay in control,* she must. Dean needed her just as she needed him in the beginning. She slid closer to him, kissing his neck, holding his hand and caressing him.

"Laura," Andy's tone was consoling, and Laura looked up as she nestled into Dean's shoulder. Andy's eyes looked red, and he cleared his throat before continuing, "Laura, they must have thrown him in a rainbow bug nest. I'm so sorry. I don't know what's going on with the two of you. I don't understand why they would do such a thing."

"I don't understand. Why are the nests so dangerous? What's happened to him?"

Andy paused in thought. "I lived here for a year as a kid, and the danger of those nests was drilled into me. Basically, the only indigenous life on this rock is a few varieties of small shrubs, the rainbow bugs, and the calamanders. It's a simple ecosystem. The rainbow bugs dine on the shrubs, and the calamanders eat the rainbow bugs. But the rainbow bugs need a host to lay their eggs in. They like to lay their eggs internally in warm fleshy cavities, lungs in particular, but really anywhere they can find their way to. When Draco was settled, the nests were small, perfect for a calamander. But as people inhabited the planet, the rainbow bugs adapted. They made bigger nests, people size. Once you're in one you hardly have a chance of escaping unless you're hauled out." Andy looked solemnly at Laura.

"But I don't understand; he's alive."

"It's not the nesting that kills you. Yes, the bugs fill your lungs, burrowing deep into your alveoli to implant their eggs, but while they're doing it, they oxygenate the tissue, which keeps you alive. When they finish laying their eggs, the bugs flee the body, and other than having strained breathing, you seem perfectly fine. The real damage is done when the eggs hatch. After a couple of days, the larvae emerge. They secrete a chemical that causes agonizing pain. Few people have a high enough pain tolerance to survive it, and they either stroke out, or have a heart attack and die. There is a pain medication effective for treating victims of an infestation, but it's very expensive and requires hospitalization. I've heard of people unable to afford the proper treatment resorting to the use of a street narcotic to provide some hope of relief from the pain. Once the baby insects hatch, they evacuate the body immediately. If you're lucky enough to survive it, then a full recovery is very fast."

"So you're saying he has a couple of days. So maybe…"

"Shhh," Andy put his finger to his lips. "I don't know the answer to your question. Let's just hope he gets better for now. We need a pilot."

Chapter Thirty-Three

Dean staggered in from the cell block, and the first thing his eyes fell on was Laura, sitting at the breakfast table, her face drawn out in worry and grief. He had a vulnerable yearning for her, and when she rushed to his side, he felt something completely foreign to him: tears of desperation welling in his eyes. He also felt overwhelming love.

He brought her in close. "I heard what you said last night," he whispered in her ear, kissing her neck. "I love you, too."

He backed away to give her a kiss on the lips just as a guard approached. "Break it up and move along."

They sat down as close together as they could, and Dean took her hand in his. He held it firmly so she wouldn't feel his shakiness and spoke softly into her ear. "Don't worry."

Laura had her lips pursed together but not tightly enough to stop the tremors of concern. *Yet,* she kept a brave face; she never ceased to amaze Dean. He wanted to confide in her, but he loved her too much to flood her imagination with the horror of the day before. A squeeze of her hand and a reassuring smile would have to suffice.

"Dean is that thing going to…you know?" Laura whispered.

"I think so. I'm surprised it hasn't already, but I'm damn glad for it."

"How are you feeling?" she said with pause.

"I'm okay."

Seemingly out of nowhere, Andy and Sandra arrived at the table carrying extra plates for the two of them. Andy spoke up with his usual cheery voice. "We thought we'd save the two of you the trip. I doubt you even heard them call our number."

"No, I didn't and thanks." Laura pushed one of the plates in front of Dean and put her arm around him. "You should try to eat something."

"Your color's back," Sandra said.

Dean took one look at the pile of mush on the plate and pushed it away.

"You ate nothing yesterday. You're going to burn outside like I did if you don't eat."

Dean looked over at Laura and shrugged with indifference. "I wouldn't want to prematurely age, now would I." He listened to a few more words of Laura's encouragement before she gave up. When the buzzer sounded for them to move to the buggies, she stuck to him closely to help steady him on his feet.

* * * *

Another typical day in the diamond field—parched mouth, sore knees, revolting sandwiches and sulfur, lots of sulfur. Dean looked across the vast desert to the horizon; the heat wavering in air like some drunken green aberration. *Must be close to dinner.* He checked his shoe—*still there!* Just after lunch, he'd found his first diamond. It was a fine gem even in its uncut state, and he'd carefully held it up to the sunlight admiring the spectra of light gleaming from it. As he spun it in his fingers, the colors beamed outward. He puzzled how something so beautiful could generate such greed and evil among people. Laura looked on, seemingly, dazzled by the light show. He tucked it in his shoe and said, "This is for you."

Out of the corner of his eye, Dean caught a guard glaring at him, and he got back to digging. His burning arms told him he should have followed Laura's mealtime advice. Their color reminded him of his earlier comment. *The temperature of a hot poker and* Boom*!* The temperature inside the manifold would undoubtedly be sufficient to cause the reaction. However, the powdery cocktail was not of high quality. A large portion of the zinc and iron would have been oxidized, and who knows what the purity of the sulfur was. He had a growing fear it may never blow.

"That's enough for today. Put your trays in the bins and line up at your buggies." The guard spoke as he collected the buckets of treasure collected during the day.

Dean got to his feet, happy to be upright and able to breathe without pain. Once the prisoners were boarded, the Conga line started its return voyage. He and Laura sat at the front of the vehicle, so he

239

wouldn't feel the jarring as aggressively as they bounced over the dunes. The sun was close to kissing the horizon, and Dean could see the glow of the active collector arrays in the distance. He shielded his eyes from the dust cloud to try and make out how many arrays were active when all of a sudden, he saw a blinding flash of light. A deafening roar came seconds later.

Anticipation did nothing to prepare Dean for the scene unfolding before him—an intense wall of flames climbed into the sky, turning the horizon into a kaleidoscope of fire. The explosion was twice what he expected and left him hesitating a moment before launching into action. The pandemonium started just in time for the arrival of a wall of heat, wind, and flying yellow dust and debris. Dean lurched from his seat, pushing Laura to the floor, and elbowed the guard standing next to him in the head, seizing his laser pistol. The man went flying to the back of the buggy, and one of the other prisoners pushed him out.

The driver pulled his weapon and lost grip of the wheel, causing the vehicle to swerve. Dean grabbed the metal guardrail that separated the driver from the prisoners and hurled his weight around it. His feet hit the driver's chest, pitching the driver out the far side of the buggy. Dean jerked the wheel to the left and raced toward the warehouse, which was about fifty meters away. He heard laser fire, but fortunately there was enough dust to throw off the pistols' automatic targeting system. "Laura, stay down!"

A few moments later, the vehicle came to a skidding stop just inside the warehouse doors. Dean jumped out and ran around to find Laura and the others. Andy was at the back helping Jeff who was bleeding after taking a piece of shrapnel to the head. The guards rumbled about, trying to gain control and the screeching of resonators echoed all around.

"Laura…Laura…" Dean bellowed at the top of his lungs as he scoured the buggy looking for her. He could barely hear his own voice over the commotion let alone hear her screams for help if she was in trouble. He pushed through the mass of prisoners running to get off the buggy and found Laura on the floor hunched over Sandra. The blood surrounding the red hole in the middle of Sandra's forehead sizzled from the laser blast. "Laura, come on, there's no time."

"Dean, I can't just leave her," she yelled.

"There's nothing we can do, come on!" Dean clutched Laura's arm, brought her to her feet, and together they followed the others off the buggy. He turned to Andy and Jeff, "We have to get into the dining hall." He looked to the exit where a crowd of prisoners had already gathered. One man was heaving on the door handle, but it wouldn't open. Guards were descending on them from every direction. "Damn it!"

Dean looked around in desperation. A guard lay dead on the ground. "Come on!" He headed toward the guard with his laser pistol in hand, adjusting its setting while he ran. Once there, he bent over and preceded to sever the man's hand. Dean pulled his shirt over his nose to muffle the pungent smell of burning flesh. It only took a few moments to complete the job and when the hand fell free, he picked it up and handed the man's resonator to Andy. Dean recognized the watch that slipped off the severed limb and slipped it on his own wrist. "Now! Come on!"

The four of them headed to the door, pushing their way to the front, trying frantically to stay together. Dean fought his way to the scanner and waved the hand in front of it, praying the door was on the emergency power. Nothing happened. He waved the hand again and again. The guards herding the prisoners were getting closer. Suddenly, the door opened sending a flood of bodies flying through like dominoes.

Laura got tossed to the side and landed on the floor about to be trampled.

"It's okay; I've got her." Andy brought her to her feet with Jeff following behind.

The four of them flowed with the mass into the room and headed for the cell block exit. The dark room started to fill with smoke. Dean coughed several times as he tried to clear his airways. The door to the cell block opened easily.

Dean led the way and the second they were through, they came face to face with a guard pointing a laser pistol at Dean's head.

"That's enough. Drop your weapon and get into the cell." The man cocked his head to the left.

In a flash, Andy pulled the resonator from behind him, sending the guard to the ground.

Dean wanted to high-five Andy for his courage, but there was no time. "Let's go." He waved them forward. As they ran to the end of the cell block, the smoke became thicker. Dean grabbed at the crushing pain in his chest and wondered how he'd make it down the smoky hallway into the hangar. He did a head count. Somehow, they were all together. As they passed through the back door, he hollered, "Put your shirt over your face and take a deep breath."

The hallway was consumed in impenetrable darkness and smoke so thick Dean could feel it against his skin. He held his breath, but his compromised lungs burned. He held on to Laura, terrified of losing her. He counted his steps, trying to guess their distance. His lungs were screaming. With his shirt shielding his nose, he took only as much of a breath as he dared, for fear of asphyxiating. *It can't be much further.*

He met the end of the hallway with a thud as he walked right into the door. In the process, he dropped the hand. He hit the ground, feeling around everywhere for it. *Damn it!* He coughed and sputtered as dizziness began to set in. Finally, he found it and brought it up to the door, blindly locating the entrance scanner. He placed the hand on the scanner, and the door opened, exposing them to a burning blast of heat. The flames were encroaching as they fled into the hangar.

"Hurry, hurry over there." There was no pod in the hangar, but a small freighter sat near the far wall. "Andy, take Laura."

Jeff lagged behind, and as Dean turned back to get him, he found himself face to face with Charlie Hopkins. Before Dean had a chance to flinch, Hopkins took a powerful swing at his gut, buckling him over. The laser pistol fell to the ground, and Dean scurried to get it. Hopkins kicked it away as he launched himself at Dean. Dean jumped out of his way, landing Hopkins on the floor and then turned and drove his foot into Hopkins' jaw with a power that sent the man sliding across the floor. He stopped inches away from the laser pistol and picked it up as he got to his feet, aiming it at Dean's head.

The sound of a pistol firing blared over the crackling flames. The sizzling blood oozed out of the hole drilled by the blast, and Hopkins collapsed to the floor. Jeff's hands shook as he lowered his laser pistol.

Dean gasped for air, his head spinning. Jeff helped to steady him as they took their final steps to the waiting freighter.

Five minutes later, the freighter cleared the hangar doors.

Chapter Thirty-Four

Ivan had just returned to his office from a rather late, albeit immensely satisfying, dinner at the Accelerator cafeteria. Pork tenderloin together with some intelligent exchanges with a couple of his brighter colleagues successfully took his mind off the events of the past week. He loosened the top button of his pants on the way to his desk and took a moment to correct the crooked picture hanging behind it before sitting down. After adjusting the lumbar support, he found enough comfort to relax and take a moment to enjoy the sparkling view of the colorful nebula through his window. As far back as he could remember, his favorite color was undoubtedly the color of the lake by the house where he grew up. The water was crystal clear, and on a bright summer's day the sun would radiate downward bringing the intoxicating rich blue lake to life. The blue of the nebula was an invigorating reminder of the best days of his life, before Nathan had died.

Ivan cracked a grin as he stared out in a daze. Both he and Nathan loved the water, and during the summer months, the two of them spent every minute they could doing refreshing cannonballs off the end of their dock, trying to make a splash big enough to moisten the tree branches that hung above. One summer, his father had the brilliant idea of hanging a Tarzan swing from the sturdiest limb. Ivan, being the biggest, was able to swing out over four meters to where the blue of the water deepened as the lake bottom fell off. Distance was always the competition, and the summer before Nathan died, he had finally overtaken Ivan in his swing. Ivan never understood how the muscles in his scrawny pale body could propel him so far, and it infuriated him. His biggest fear was that one day Nathan's wiry build would set him at the head of their pack. He never had a chance to find out.

Ivan's reminiscing was cut short by his twitching foot. All of a sudden it felt wet, as if he'd stepped in a puddle. He pushed his chair back far enough to grab his foot and remove his shoe. *Dry as a bone.* He wiggled his toes a few times. *Must have been asleep.* He waited for a tingling sensation to set in, but it didn't. He shrugged off the feeling and replaced the shoe then pulled a file folder closer to him. It was the repair report Sam had submitted to him earlier in the day. After the collision with the entities, an extensive number of repairs were required, the most timely being the replacement of the particle tracking devices in the detector. It proved to be a costly exercise with the added inconvenience of setting them way behind schedule. Along with the Enertech work, there was a backlog of outside jobs requiring attention including a collision experiment requested by one of Laura Simmons' former colleagues at ECN, *a little awkward*. Ivan just knuckled down to setting the accelerator schedule for the following days when a call came in. It tickled his ear, and he gave it a scratch before responding.

"Campbell here."

"Hi Ivan, Brad Johnson here, Jack's brother. Remember we met at Jack's Christmas party last year."

"Yes, I remember you well. How are you?"

"Can't complain. Anyway I'm wondering if you can help me in locating Jack. We were expecting him for dinner almost three hours ago. I've been calling him, but he's not responding. We were supposed to sign some legal papers for Mom's estate. Do you know where he is by chance?"

"He wasn't in today, but he hasn't been feeling a hundred percent, so I didn't want to call and disturb him. Why don't you go to his apartment? Maybe he's sleeping?"

"If he's not waking up to my calls, I doubt he'd wake up to the door. Unfortunately, I don't have entry authorization. He's a private type."

Ivan felt a twinge of concern. "I can have Larry Dunn with base station security meet you there. He can get you in, and if it's acceptable, I wouldn't mind joining you to make sure Jack's okay."

"Sure, that would be great. How soon can you get security on this?"

"I'll call Larry and get back to you."

Ivan put a call in to Larry who complained about the interruption as he was working late, tightening up security in anticipation of the upcoming Summit on Lyra. Begrudgingly, he agreed to help, and an hour later, the three men were standing at the door to Jack's apartment. There was no response at the door, so Larry overrode the system, and the door swung open.

Brad led them into the apartment single file. A network of pot lights shone circles onto the slate tile of the entranceway.

Ivan knew Jack to be a particularly tidy person, one of the qualities they shared; however, the scene in his apartment suggested differently. The place was brightly lit, and Ivan cringed as he looked around at the apparent carnage—*of what?* It left him with a smoldering concern that threatened to break out into a raging fire. The place looked like a scene right out of a bad *nightmare*—just a little too close to home!

The kitchen sink overflowed with dirty dishes, and a slow trickle of water from the faucet cascaded over their rims, creating a near stagnant flow of wet bread crumbs and foul smelling meat. Clothing lay in heaps on the floor and across the furniture as if left to dry. Particularly strange was the large brass-flecked oval mirror hanging to the left of the front door. The entire reflective surface was meticulously covered with paper.

"Hey, Jack...what's up? You here?" Brad called out and waited for a response. "Hey, Jack?"

Jack's apartment had a typical space station layout: kitchen and combination living and dining room to one side of the entranceway and bedrooms to the other side. Brad spun off to the right to check the living room. Ivan glanced at the mess of the room, but the dining room table stole his attention. "What on earth?"

Ivan couldn't help but let his jaw drop. Brad and Larry hurried over. A number of elaborate pencil sketches covered the dining room table. Jack was very talented and over the years had produced countless sketches. Many of them hung in his apartment, and everyone he knew had at least one displayed prominently in their home. His favorite subjects were old buildings, especially churches. He was incredibly perceptive in bringing out the detail of the brickwork and foliage around them. Despite being black and white, the care he took when sketching church windows gave them a realness that would give even the most critical art connoisseur shivers.

The three of them stared at the table in complete silence. The collection of art must have taken hours to produce, and they were all deeply disturbing. Intense despair and madness seemed to be etched in every line drawn on the pages. Brad grabbed one of the sketches. "This looks like the church in our home town. That's where we buried Mom last month. But look how he drew the cemetery. It's more prominent than the church and the detail in the gravestone…there's a depiction of mom's face. And look what it says on the stone. *Undead*. My God! What is all this?" Brad's hand trembled, and the sketch slipped out of his fingers and drifted to the floor.

"I got it." Larry bent over and retrieved the sketch, taking a second to study it before putting it down.

"Look at the others. Brad, I know the loss of your mother devastated Jack, but these go way beyond that. Did he talk to you about it?" Ivan asked.

"No, in fact he avoided the topic. But not all of these sketches look like a reference to Mom. Look at this one." Brad picked up another. "It's a man in a coffin trying to scratch his way out as if he were buried alive. Bugs and all."

"And the man looks strikingly like Jack. Look at the horror depicted in the eyes." Ivan winced.

"It's like they're possessed," Brad murmured. "I don't understand. Why would Jack draw such a thing?"

"I'm going to have a look around." Larry headed down the hall toward the bedroom.

About a minute later, Ivan heard him talking. "I need a coroner down here immediately. The address is…"

Brad shot down the hall.

"Brad, hold on, wait a minute!" Ivan tried to call him back but ended up running to catch up.

Larry stood at the bedroom door as a human barricade. "I'm sorry Brad. I don't think you should go in there."

"What the hell's going on? He's my brother; let me in."

Ivan looked at Larry and nodded, and Larry let him pass.

"My God!" Brad stood motionless, his face looking like it was about to scream but nothing came out. A moment later, he bellowed,

"Look at his face! What the hell happened?"

Ivan glanced down at the pallid corpse that was once his friend. Jack's contorted body lay on the bed tangled in the gray sheets as if frozen in time. His terrified, milky eyes pierced through Ivan's soul, leaving Ivan with the same nauseous feeling he had in the Control Room when he gaped at the large entity's image. Jack's terrified eyes looked unnaturally wide. His mouth hung open as though he died screaming for help, and his fingers were formed into stiff claws. His position and expression bore a horrifying resemblance to his sketch of the man in the coffin. Ivan was stunned, and all of a sudden, he felt as though his own sanity was on trial.

The color drained from Brad's face, and his body swayed as if he might faint. Larry was the only one keeping it together and went to Brad's side. "Brad you really don't need to see this. The coroner's on his way."

"I don't understand. How can he be dead?" Brad took a couple of steps backward cupping his face with his hands. "He can't be dead."

"We'll get some answers," Larry assured him. "Judging by the color of his eyes, he's been dead for at least fifteen hours."

"But he's only fifty-one and never sick a day in his life."

"Is there a history of heart disease or stroke in your family?" Larry asked.

"No nothing. My God, I don't understand…Jack…those pictures…what the hell happened here? This is like a nightmare." Brad glanced toward Larry, grimacing.

"Ivan, why don't we get Brad out of here?" Larry put his hand on Brad's shoulder and nudged him to the door. "Ivan!"

Ivan heard Larry calling his name but felt like Medusa had turned him to stone. He felt if he tried to move, his limbs would shatter and crumble to the floor. Larry walked over and faced him. "Come on!"

He continued to stare at Jack's colorless pained face peering out from under the sheets. Then he spoke. "Did you hear that?"

"Hear what?" Larry said.

"That voice." Ivan's words came out shaky.

"For God's sake man, get it together. Come on!"

"You did this to me!" This time it was louder and sounded like a caw. It shot through Ivan like a spear.

Ivan gawked at Jack's contorted body, and then suddenly it sprung to a sitting position, locking eyes with him. "You did this to me!" it cawed. The milky eyes started to glow a sickly yellow-orange like the large entity.

"*No!*" Ivan screeched and started hyperventilating. He took a clumsy leap back as if dodging a charging beast and stumbled over a heap of clothes on the floor, catching himself on the edge of the dresser. A bead of sweat broke loose from his eyebrow and fell into his eye, blurring his vision.

"What the hell's wrong with you?" Larry scooped up a tweed blazer from the armchair by the closet and walked over to Jack, laying it gently over his face and chest. The outline of his protruding claws remained apparent. He turned back to Ivan raising his voice. "Get it together and have some compassion for Christ's sake!" He put his hand on Ivan's shoulder and spun him toward the door ushering him out and returning for Brad. "I'm sorry. I don't know what's got into him."

Brad numbly followed Larry's lead.

After getting the two men seated in the living room, Larry set off to the kitchen, announcing he was looking for anything with alcohol in it. He returned with some Scotch. "Here, have a drink. Hopefully it will help to clear your heads. I'm sorry for snapping at you, Ivan. I know you and Jack were close friends, but you need to stay focused."

Ivan looked up at Larry. Ivan felt the blood drain from his face, and his eyes were weighted with fear. "Something's not right here, just not right."

"What are you talking about...not right?" Brad sounded accusing.

The question snapped Ivan's attention. He'd already said too much. "I'm sorry. I'm just shaken. We were close friends. Brad, I'm sincerely sorry; I don't take death well."

Fortunately, the size of the Lyra Base Station was such that no one was ever very far away. It took only thirty minutes for the coroner to arrive, but the waiting made it seem longer. It had given Ivan more than enough time to notice signs of a disturbed man. Any object with a reflective surface had been covered in the apartment. Jack had hammered a bed sheet up to cover the view out the window. He had even gone as far as removing the glass in the display cabinet, and the picture frames inside lay face down. The expensive holographic television mounted on the wall was damaged from what appeared to be a glass shattering on it. Shards of debris extended below it in a perfect arc, and a brown stain blemished the beige carpet with striations of a finger painting.

The coroner entered the apartment carrying a medical bag and made his introductions. After extending his condolences, he made his way to the bedroom. Brad followed. Larry was about to follow course, but Ivan held him back.

"It's nightmares, Larry, nightmares." Ivan spoke in a whisper. "All of us who have been exposed have been experiencing nightmares, and since the large entity formed and escaped from the accelerator, they've been getting worse. Much worse, almost like they're becoming real. I can assure you, they're quite disturbing, terrifying in fact. And it's not just when I'm sleeping any more. I hear and see things when I'm awake. It's making me crazy. I sense something evil, and I think that's what killed Jack."

"That's ridiculous. You can't die from a nightmare, and what the hell are you talking about...a large entity?"

"I told you about it briefly, remember? It formed in the accelerator after the collision with the entities from Spectra. I'm starting to think Kevin was right, and we created something evil. Like I said, before it formed, we all had nightmares, but now, it's like they're coming alive and becoming real. I almost feel like something's possessing me. I don't think it's any coincidence that Jack's body looks just like the sketch of the man in the coffin. I bet he was having a nightmare about being buried alive, and I'm sure a nightmare killed him. One that seemed very real. Haven't you ever had a terrifying nightmare leaving you scared to death?"

"No, and I've told you several times, this entity thing doesn't sit well with me. I'm on board because you're paying me well, but personally I think you're nuts sitting in a chamber with a bunch of alien life forms. It doesn't surprise me you're having nightmares. And putting them in the accelerator. What the hell were you thinking?"

"You're not taking this seriously! I'm telling you, there's

something not right here, something beyond the nightmares. It's difficult to put words to, but I can feel it. It's like negative energy, and it's powerful."

Larry's voice became stern. "Ivan, I can assure you I'm taking this seriously. Especially when people start showing up dead on this base station. When was the last time you and Jack were exposed?"

"Yesterday, both of us."

"Well, I am telling you this as a friend. You need to stop what you're doing with these entities now, before it's too late. Look at yourself; you're agitated and paranoid. When was the last time you looked in the mirror? You're drawn, pale and the bags under your eyes...you need to take charge of yourself."

The coroner reappeared from down the hall. "Excuse me gentlemen, am I interrupting?"

Larry realized they were no longer whispering. "Of course not. Finished already?"

The coroner gave them an odd look. "Yes, and I've determined the cause of death to be cardiac arrest. The approximate time of death would have been in the early hours of the morning, around four. I've notified the funeral home. Brad is quite shaken and doesn't want a full autopsy at this point, but of course, there's time for him to change his mind. I suggest at least one of you stay here with him until they take the body."

"Yes, we will, and thank you, Dr. Albert," Ivan said. "But I don't understand. How does your heart just stop while you're sleeping? Jack had complained about having nightmares. Is it possible one actually scared him to death?"

The coroner looked puzzled, and then suddenly the pictures on the table caught his attention. "He did these?" The man scanned the table and then shifted his glances to the disheveled living room before turning to Brad. "Do you know… Did your brother have psychiatric issues?"

"He never did anything to suggest it, and if he was having nightmares, this is the first I've heard of it."

"To answer your question, Ivan, I've never heard of anyone dying from a nightmare, or a panic attack for that matter. But people can die

251

in their sleep. It's rare but can happen. It's called sudden arrhythmia death syndrome, otherwise known as SADS. In this situation, cardiac arrest occurs as a result of ventricular arrhythmia, or a disturbance in the heart's rhythm, even though the person has no structural heart disease. There is a group of rare diseases that can affect the electrical functioning of the heart without affecting the heart's structure, but they cannot be detected post-mortem. They can be familial. Brad, perhaps you should get yourself checked out. Ivan, is there anything that's been going on at work that could be pertinent to this?"

"No, business as usual. He'd just complained about having trouble sleeping because of nightmares, that's why I asked about them. Thanks, Dr. Albert. When did you say the people from the funeral home will arrive?" Ivan wanted the man to leave.

"About twenty minutes. I should be off," said Dr. Albert.

Larry escorted Dr. Albert to the door and then ushered Ivan and Brad back to the living room, trying to fill the time with awkward conversation. Ivan continued to be quite agitated and checked his watch every few minutes.

"When will they be here? I thought he said twenty minutes."

"He did; it's only been ten." Larry looked at Ivan with an accusing expression. "This shouldn't have happened."

Ivan met his glare just as Brad spoke up.

"What were you talking about back there? Something about entities. Is there something I should know about? Did something happen to Jack?"

"He told me he was dreaming about entities; like I said, he complained about nightmares. He wasn't sleeping well. It was affecting his work."

"Ivan, I get the feeling you're hiding something from me. Jack was my brother. And I can assure you, if you are, I will get to the bottom of it."

Ivan shot up from the couch. "I resent…"

Larry put a hand up to silence Ivan. "Got a call. Dunn here… It's quite all right, Bob, you're not disturbing me. What's up?" As Larry listened, an expression of shock crossed his face, which soon morphed into one of wide-eyed anger and disbelief. "If they took a freighter, surely to God you can track them quickly… Authorities, what authorities? I don't care if it's not my jurisdiction. I'm coming down there tonight. This is inexcusable. I'll call you as soon as I arrive on Draco. You better damn well find them!"

Larry locked eyes with Ivan. "I've got to go."

"What the hell was that all about, I don't like the sound of it." Ivan started pacing.

"There was an explosion at the Draco Penitentiary. Weston, Simmons, and two other prisoners are missing and so is a freighter. I've gotta get down there."

Ivan's fist hit the wall, and at the same time, one of the glasses of Scotch on the table exploded sending a crystalline fountain shooting in every direction.

Brad's horrified gaze lifted from the glass and bored straight into Ivan's.

Chapter Thirty-Five

"How's he doing?"

Andy spoke with the tone of a kid on a long car ride, and Laura half expected the next question to be, *Are we there yet?* However, they weren't even close, wherever *there* might be. In fact, here they were stuck in the freighter in the middle of nowhere. As far as Laura was concerned, they'd be better off if they'd landed in Oz. The truth was, they were lucky to have landed safely. Dean's compromised lungs suffered from smoke inhalation, leaving him gasping for air and then unconscious, shortly after setting the pod on the ground.

Laura had hardly heard Andy, but when he repeated his question, she started to shake off her daze. Her voice came out weak and monotone...partly from worry and partly from exhaustion. "Better. The oxygen's helping. His breathing is starting to improve. I think he may be coming around...Andy, he needs a hospital."

Laura shifted her weight on the unforgiving floor and rubbed her boney hip, wishing she hadn't passed up all those pieces of fudge cake over the years. She cradled Dean on her lap, and the numbness setting into her legs had her close to mistaking his head for a bowling ball. She held the oxygen mask to his face and stroked the soot out of his hair, watching him twitch every so often. She wanted to believe everything would be okay. The haggard reflection peeking at her from the shiny metal panel beside her told her otherwise. It was almost as if it spoke to her. She considered her distorted image for a moment. Her soiled face looked flushed from the heat of the fire, and it seemed like somewhere lost inside her was her self-assurance. Whether it was their horrific escape, Sandra's death, or her worry for Dean, something had thrashed her hope.

Andy sat in the pilot's seat gazing out into the endless plane of darkness. His arms were crossed lazily across his chest. He seemed impressed by the pilot's control panel, and Laura sensed he was fighting his boyhood urge to play with it. As he stared at the flashing lights, he had a glimmer in his eye as though he was swept away in some fantasy world dodging meteors with the electrifying thrill of the ride crackling under his skin.

"I wish I could fly this thing." Andy sighed. He spun his chair around toward Laura, lifting his feet up to maximize its play. "We have to get to your uncle's. Maybe he can help Dean. We're sitting ducks here."

"If they find us, they'll kill us. I'm sure of it," Laura said.

"So are you going to tell us what's going on with you two? If I didn't get my parole because of you, I think I have the right to know," Andy said.

"You're right, but I think I should wait for Dean to give you the details. We're involved in something highly classified. I don't know how much he's willing to tell you. All I can say is we were framed, and the people who did it did one hell of a thorough job. We pose an enormous threat to them, and I'm sure they're going to want us dead. I'm certain they arranged for Dean to be thrown in that nest, and no doubt I was next. And yes, I also think that's why you didn't get your parole. They probably figured we told you the truth and couldn't risk having you released. It's a huge cover up."

Jeff knelt down beside Laura. "Your uncle's address puts him at the north end of the city. I think I can find it, but unless we have ground transportation, it's going to be a hell of a trek even if we fly this thing to the city limits. Are you sure he'll help us? Even if he believes you're innocent, if he works for the government, he may be reluctant."

"Jeff, when he hears the truth, he won't hesitate. Are you sure you know exactly where Shady Meadows is?"

"Yeah, your uncle must have some coin. There are only two nice areas in Draco City: Shady Meadows in the north and Granite Heights in the south. All the wealthy people live in those areas. The crime rate's high in the city, so the neighborhood's going to be patrolled. I'm sure they're already looking for us. We need to get there before light."

"Andy, fix the bandage on Jeff's head. It looks like it might fall off. We're lucky that's the only injury from the explosion, other than Dean's lungs of course." Laura paused. "And Sandra," she added glumly.

"Right-o, Doc Laura." Andy opened up the med kit, and with the patience of a caged squirrel, slapped some more tape on Jeff's forehead and gave it a quick pat.

* * * *

Dean started coughing, clouding the plastic oxygen mask over his mouth with a fine spray of blood. "Where are…we?"

He continued to cough, and Laura rolled him onto his side when he started to choke. He pushed the mask away and repeated the question in between strained breaths.

"Don't you remember? You got us out of the hangar, and as we headed away from the prison, you started to lose consciousness. You just barely got us on the ground." Laura spoke as she inched herself from under him.

"Everyone okay?" Dean stumbled with his words.

"Yeah, we're fine but worried sick about you." Andy said. "Gotta hand it to you man. You did it. We're out of there. I don't know where we are but out of there."

Dean pushed himself up to a sitting position with Laura's help. "Take another breath of oxygen," she said.

He leaned against the wall and took several deep breaths through the mask. The heat of the fire had pasted his spit. He licked his lips, tasting sulfur and ash. "Thanks. Anyone know where we are?"

"No clue," Andy remarked. "It's dark as far as the eye can see. We're hoping you might be able to tell us where you landed this thing. The good news is if we can make it to Draco City, Jeff says he can find his way to Laura's uncle's house."

"Hey, don't forget to tell him about the diamonds," Jeff said.

"Diamonds?"

"Oh yeah, we're rich. This thing had been loaded up for transport. We found several small boxes back there full of diamonds, all ordered according to size and quality. I piled them all into one box." Andy extended a hitchhiker's thumb to the storage cupboard.

"Any water?" Dean asked.

"No," Laura said.

"Damn."

Laura took Dean's hand. "Dean, you can tell from the instruments where we are, can't you?"

"Yeah, how long have we been here?"

"Just over an hour."

"That's not good. I better have a look." With Laura's help, Dean got to his feet and wavered over to the pilot's seat. "Hey, Buck Rogers, do ya mind if I sit there?"

Andy groaned and shifted over to the co-pilot's seat.

"The satellite will give us our position." Dean worked slowly, but eventually the monitor to his right lit up with a detailed map displaying their exact location. "Looks like we're about eighty kilometers southeast of the prison." He started hacking then continued with a raspy voice, "Draco City is just less than two hundred kilometers from here in a straight line that happens to pass over the prison. I wouldn't suggest we go as the crow flies."

"Why don't we head to one of the mines east of the city?" Andy leaned forward pointing to the upper right quadrant on the map and drew an imaginary circle. "There are nickel mines in that area, several of them. It's been years since my dad worked the mines, but back then, there was virtually no security. No one would venture out there in the dark with the bug nests, and there's nothing to steal other than a few old trucks. We could set the freighter down and grab a truck to the city."

"Yeah, that could work. There's plenty of freighter traffic at night when the passenger traffic's low, so it wouldn't be odd flying in at this time. But they'll be looking for us by now." Dean started up the engines. "Unless anyone has a better idea, I suggest we go with Andy's plan."

"There used to be a copper mine east of the prison around here." Andy pointed to the location on the screen. "It's further east than we have to go, but if we head there first then up toward the nickel mines, it may be less obvious."

"Good idea. They probably think we're long gone by now anyway. Get seated. If anyone gets on our tail, it'll be a rough ride."

Andy looked very confident as he sat back and fastened the seat restraint, as though he'd done it hundreds of times before. Dean gave him a side glance. "You look quite at home."

"Yeah, he spent the last hour playing pilot." Laura just finished buckling herself into the passenger seat beside Jeff on the far side of the cabin.

Dean chuckled as he got the freighter airborne, and within seconds, he had them following Andy's suggested trajectory to the copper mine, flying at low altitude. He took a low pass over the mine, and it appeared to be out of commission.

"Damn, it's going to look like we're flying out of nowhere," Dean increased the altitude and set a course for the nickel mines. "Andy, are you sure those nickel mines are still operating? I've never flown into this area."

"As far as I know, but I was a kid when I lived here."

"Jeff, you seem to know a bit about this place. Any idea?" Dean said.

"Sorry, I was in drugs not mining."

"Well, there's no way of flying beyond satellite surveillance, so I'll just make this as natural as possible. At this speed, we'll be there in fifteen minutes."

After several minutes of silence, a signal sounded, startling the four of them.

"What the hell's that?" Jeff barked.

"I set a signal to sound if there was any other nearby traffic. I'm picking up a large craft about five kilometers to the port side on a parallel path. It could be another freighter." Dean sent out a signal to the ship.

"Did you just signal it? Are you crazy?" Andy yelled.

"Trust me. When you fly close to another ship out here, it's normal to send them a friendly signal. If you don't they… Damn it, they're contacting us. Hold on." Dean opened a channel. "Hey, Bulldog, there's some bears out tonight, already been contacted; you better back off the hammer. Ya flying a deadhead? Just head'n in myself."

"Hey, good buddy, I'll leave granny space to you. Got a hell of a cargo to pick up and some cold beers waiting. Catch ya on the flip flop."

"10-4," Dean chuckled then broke off communication. The other ship accelerated ahead of them.

Laura broke the festering tension with a hearty laugh. "Bulldog? What the heck was that?"

"Freighter lingo, sweetheart. But the son of a bitch called me gay." Dean smirked.

"Hey, look, you can see lights down there," Andy said.

"Yeah, looks like we're getting close. I'm going to hang back and see where my good buddy's going. We don't need company."

The energized glow of the other freighter soon appeared in the distance as it set up for a landing. It was a distracting show, but more lights shone from afar, and Dean passed over top his friend and headed toward them. The lights of Draco City loomed in the distance.

"Looks like another mining field all right." Dean slowed the freighter and circled the perimeter looking for a place to set down. "I'll set us down close to that domed building. It looks like there's a truck parked by the side with a couple of small dune buggies." Dean grappled with another problem. "If there's anyone down there, the minute they see us in these clothes we're in trouble. I guess there's no other clothing in here?"

"The only thing we found was the diamonds." Andy frowned. "Why don't we turn the T-shirts inside out so the insignia isn't so obvious? I'll keep this resonator close at hand once we land."

"Good idea. Do we have a laser pistol?" Dean took his hands off the controls momentarily and switched up his shirt.

"Yeah, I've got one here," Jeff said, his smile suggesting he had no regrets for drilling a hole in Charlie's head.

"Guys, you mind?" Laura grabbed at her shirt, and Jeff took his time turning away.

"Hey, give the lady some privacy," Dean said.

Moments later, they were on the ground, and Dean powered down the craft as Andy looked on with transparent envy. Dean noticed his fixation with his every move during flight and momentarily forgetting his physical condition, assured Andy that one day he'd give him a lesson.

"Hey, Andy, grab the box of diamonds. We may need them."

Dean moved about the cabin, feeling the effects of the smoke, his left eye irritated and drippy, and his breathing wheezy.

"Got 'em, and I'll grab the oxygen, too. You may need it."

Dean switched his attention to Jeff. "Hey, how about you give me the pistol. And by the way, I owe you one." He held out his hand to take the pistol and then wedged it in the back of his pants, pulling his T-shirt down to hide it. "I'll go out first. Andy, you can cover me with the resonator."

"Fine, I've got your back." Andy handed the diamonds to Laura so he'd have a free hand.

Dean exited the ship and walked with confidence toward the truck. The domed building had several spotlights mounted along its perimeter, bathing the area with an air of security, but there was no one in sight. One of the lights flickered and buzzed like static on a radio. The door of the truck was unlocked, and he opened it, cringing at the metal on metal screech.

The truck appeared to be decades old, and it reminded Dean of the collection of old jalopies his father used to collect and fix up. His dad used to say, *"If they're not at least fifty years old, they're just not worth the effort."* He had a particular affection for gasoline powered models and took pride in coming inside covered in thick black oil. When Dean reached the age of thirteen, his father decided it was time for him to participate in his passion. He'd bought him an old motorcycle for his birthday and told him, *"Dean, if you're responsible enough to get this running, then you're responsible enough to ride it."* Nothing could have put a bigger smile on Dean's face, and from that time on, their shared passion brought them closer together.

Dean inspected the inside of the old rust bucket. Despite the green glow of the ignition light, he had a wave of uncertainty about whether it would run. At another time, this would have presented a challenge that would make his skin tingle. He stepped onto the running board—rust crumbling under his feet—and pressed the ignition button. *Come on start.* The engine coughed. *Damn it!* He tried again, this time holding it down several seconds. It made the sound of an old tractor as it turned over. He hopped down and gave it a satisfied smile. He waved the others over. "Hurry, come on get in."

Once everyone was seated, Dean stepped back onto the running board to get into the driver's seat.

"Hey what the hell do you think you're doing? Get out of there!"

Startled, Dean swung his head around and jumped back to the ground. The man was only a meter away. "I have some equipment to unload from the freighter, and I thought I'd just move this truck out of the way so I could put it here," Dean said.

"We're not expecting any equip—"

Dean launched himself forward, taking hold of the man and swinging him in front of him. He wrapped his right arm firmly around the man's neck grabbed the bicep of his left arm, forcing the man's head downward with his free hand. The man's body went limp. It was the first time in years, Dean had called on his military training—the sleeper hold being his favorite maneuver. The entire takedown took seconds, but with the flickering light, it seemed to play out like a slow motion movie. Andy sprung from the far door of the truck, but by the time he got around with the resonator, Dean was halfway to the building, dragging the man along the ground.

"Stay out here and watch the truck. I'll find a place for him," Dean hollered. The man's underarms were clammy, and Dean readjusted his grip around his chest.

Jeff followed Laura out of the truck. "I'll go help Dean." He sprinted ahead.

It only took a few minutes for Dean and Jeff to return, and Andy and Laura were back inside the truck waiting. Dean sat in the driver's seat beside Laura, and she gave his leg a squeeze as he sat down. The idle of the truck was rough. When Dean hit the pedal, it lurched forward with jerked acceleration, bucking several times before evening out. He steered toward the roadway at the far side of the building creating a cloud of dust. Beyond the building, the lights dimmed leaving a towering wall of darkness. Only one of the headlights worked, and it was difficult to see the outline of the dirt road. A wedge of fear kept Dean's attention spiked. He flicked the clasp of his watch and handed it to Laura.

"There's a GPS function on this, if you set it for Draco, it should help us find our way."

Laura played with the watch. "Isn't this yours? How do you have it?"

"The guard who lent me his hand had it. Uncanny, huh?"

Laura programmed the watch, and the four of them formulated a plan. They would continue on the dirt road to Route Three, which would take them to the north end of Draco City. They'd then take the Dune Boulevard exit and continue to the edge of the industrial district and walk from there. It would leave them just over ten kilometers on foot.

Chapter Thirty-Six

The GPS function on Dean's watch had directed him out of *the maze* on several occasions—this time, it proved invaluable. It left him almost believing in fate. Either that or perhaps his mother was looking out for him from her untimely grave with the last token of her love. The sultry voice the guard programmed into the watch led them to the industrial district, where they ditched the truck behind a warehouse and set out on foot. Dean's charbroiled lungs set the pace for their walk—a strangely intimidating one, considering they were escaped convicts. The area was a nighttime cesspool of violence, gangs, and partiers. Frequent bouts of laughter coupled with the echo of smashing glass provided the sound track for their walk. One group of drunken white trash skinheads came close to picking a fight with them. "What's your fuckin' problem one shouted," as another started rattling the chains on his belt. Ironically, what saved them was a marshal's drive by. Fortunately, the mouthy kids kept the marshal's attention.

Dean took his last painstaking steps to the grayed cedar SHADY MEADOWS sign towering like a billboard across the manicured grounds. He collapsed behind it, his wheezing as steady as a high idling engine, and checked his watch. "It's...just after...twelve." Laura slapped the oxygen mask over his face, and it cleared away his dizziness enough to look around. A fence rose up in front of him to a height hardly sufficient to keep the riff-raff out. That job was left to the security lights. Fortunately, the neighborhood name was true to its word. Nothing but indigenous shrubs grew in Draco's sulfur-rich soil, but several impressive artificial trees lined the fence like reforested plastic, providing some cover from the lights. Dean took another minute to catch his breath, and then the four of them hopped the fence.

"This is Shady Meadows Boulevard. You said he's number thirty-five," Jeff said.

Laura nodded. "Yeah, thirty-five. I've never been there, but I've seen pictures. It's a white flat-roofed house." She handed Dean the oxygen mask. "Here, take another few breaths; we're almost there."

"I'm okay...we gotta...keep moving." Dean doused the fire in his chest by inhaling a couple more times. His idle wheeze eased to a gentle purr. "Come on." He waved a wide arc with his arm, just about throwing him off his feet.

Laura steadied him. "Dean you can hardly breathe. Are you light headed?"

"I'm fine. Let's go."

"Wait a minute, there's a car. Get down!" Andy pointed down the street as he made for one of the trees; an authentic looking pine, minus the stick of the sap and the powder room air freshener smell.

Just as Laura got her belly flat to the ground, she let out a yelp. A small figure scurried past her an arm's length from her head. The black skin of the creature had the sheen of the back of a leech. A couple of meters beyond her, it disappeared into the ground, leaving clear mucus pasted to the edge of the hole.

"Shhh!" Jeff held Laura down as she started to squirm backward. "Stay down."

As the car came closer, they could see the bold decaling on its side: SHADY MEADOWS SECURITY. Dean lay motionless, face down on the ground, taking short pained breaths as he waited for the car to pass. The car pulled into a small flagstone house beside the entrance to the neighborhood, and the armed guard driving the vehicle exited and went inside.

"Let's go; we have to hurry," Andy whispered.

"What was that thing? It was ugly as sin?" Laura's gaze seesawed between Andy and the creature's hole, and she gritted her teeth.

"A calamander," Andy said, grinning. "Tastes as good as it looks."

Laura put her arm around Dean, and the four of them started down the street in succession. The rustic cobblestone laneway was hardly wide enough for two cars and was dotted with ornamental lanterns about every fifteen meters. Dean cursed the unevenness of the street as he wavered on his feet, and Laura kept a tight grip on him.

The roadway lent the community the quaintness of a European village, but the widely spaced hacienda style homes looked as though they should be perched along the coast of California. The few trees they could duck behind were the plastic deciduous variety, so Dean tried his best to hurry along in fear of their security friend returning for another look-see. Jeff was right—the people in the neighborhood had some coin. Intricate landscaping compensated for the lack of foliage, but it tended to clash in a tacky sense with the architecture of the homes. The entire neighborhood, although ritzy, reminded Dean of a grade five cut and paste project.

"It's that one, across the street. I recognize it...the one with the holographic fountain in the yard." Laura's excitement had her walking in strides. Dean just about stumbled, and she slowed back down. "Sorry."

Jeff led the way across the street on a diagonal toward the impressive stucco house. The cobblestone finally got the better of Dean, and he lost his footing.

"Andy, help," Laura called.

Andy rushed to the other side of Dean taking almost all of his weight. As they walked past the fountain, the front entrance came into view. The rustic wood door was oversized and had two ornate etched glass side panels. The entire thing was centered in a gray marble alcove with some potted bushes accenting the sides, keeping with the disjointed character of the neighborhood. They propped Dean up against one of the planters as Laura went straight to the door and pushed the doorbell.

"Come on." She fidgeted in her spot, alternating her stance between feet then started insistently knocking.

"Easy there, he might just call security. It's late you know, and our implants are deactivated, so he's going to wonder who it is," Andy said.

A moment later, a light went on, and the silhouette of a tall figure came into view through the side panel. Laura stood as expectantly as a child on Halloween, waiting for the door to swing open.

* * * *

"Uncle John." Laura paused a minute, pursing her lips to keep them from trembling and fighting off tears. When she finally composed herself enough to speak, her words came out shaky. "Uncle John, I need your help. I'm in trouble." She lost her battle with the tears, and they started streaming down her cheeks.

"What in God's name? Laura, what are you doing here? I thought you were in prison. I wanted to come and see you, but they don't allow visitors." He took a step onto the marble and wrapped his arms around her, rewarding her with a big hug.

Laura took a deep, soothing breath, capturing the scent of the man who had never showed her anything but kindness. She always puzzled over the subtle smell of baby powder that surrounded him, but thoroughly enjoyed it as it reminded her of when she was little and would sit on his knee, listening to his commanding voice as he recited stories of Bingo and Beasle, the two trouble making monkeys he'd conjured up. They were entertaining stories, and she was sure he modeled them after her and her siblings. He would always finish up a story by asking her what trouble the three of them had been causing for their parents. She always whispered the answer, *"Only a little bit of trouble, Uncle John; only a little."* She'd follow with a mischievous laugh as she jumped away, heading for the door with her long ponytail wagging and banged up legs carrying her as fast as she could go. She'd turn back to wave, and he'd always be smiling.

He backed away, keeping his hands on her shoulders and looked into her watering eyes. He was of African-American descent in his late sixties. Just the right amount of gray accented his black hair, and the deep lines of his complexion only exaggerated the distinguished kindness spelled out on his face. "What happened to you? They said you were involved in corporate espionage and an accessory to murder. I just didn't believe it."

"We were framed, Dean and I. It's a long story, can we come in? I'll tell you everything."

"We?" John turned his head, and his mouth fell open. "Who are these people?"

"This is Dean, Andy, and Jeff. Uncle John, please help us. We escaped from the prison. If they catch us, they're going to kill us."

"That's crazy; who's going to kill you?"

"The people who framed Dean and me."

John glanced over at Dean who was holding the bloodied oxygen mask to his face gasping for air. "What's wrong with him? He looks like he should be in a hospital."

Andy was kneeling beside Dean and looked up at John. The concern in his eyes knocked the boyishness from them. "The guards threw him in a rainbow bug nest. Please, Mr. Becker, I know this is a terrible intrusion, but may we come in? He's not doing well, and if the security guard drives by again and sees us, he'll call the marshal's office."

John nodded; it was the slow, reluctant kind of head bob that comes from obligation, not willingness. "Fine, but I'm not sure I like the sound of all this."

Andy and Jeff got Dean to his feet and helped him inside.

"The family room's straight through, you can set him down in there." As Laura went to follow, John held her back with a gentle hand to her shoulder. "What's going on here? You know I'd do anything for you, but I'm not about to stick my neck out for a bunch of escaped convicts. I recognize that man from the news. He's the one who butchered his ex-wife and got you implicated as an accessory."

"Like I said, he was framed. I was there, I witnessed the whole thing. If it wasn't for Dean, I'd be dead. This is part of a huge cover-up. Please, Uncle John, just hear us out."

With a slow exhale, he agreed. "Fine, I'll do it for you. But no promises when it comes to them. I'm not in the business of harboring fugitives." John led the way through the lofty entranceway, past the circular staircase and into the family room. The echo of their footsteps subsided when they arrived.

"Is there any chance we could have some water?" Laura asked. Her lips felt like they were about to crumble, and she could taste blood oozing from the corner of her mouth.

"Of course." The kitchen was part of the same room, separated only by a long counter spotted with barstools. Laura followed John to a cupboard where he pulled out four tall glasses. "After we talked last, I was so looking forward to you spending a weekend with me. And then I heard the news. Laura, what happened to you? I never believed for one minute that you did those things. Look at you. You look like you've been through a war." He handed her a warm cloth. "Wipe the prettiness back into your face. God, it's good to see you."

Laura buried her face and scoured it in the soothing moisture; the white cloth turned gray from the soot tarnishing her skin. She took one look at it and decided to go to the sink to wash her hands, drying them on her pants—a bad habit she'd picked up in prison. By the time she finished, John had the four glasses filled with water, each with crushed ice slushing about the top. She took one, gulped it down and turned for more, cringing at the brain freeze throb in her temple. It was a worthy trade off to the feeling of sandpaper rubbing against the back of her throat. A renegade drip rolled its way down to her chin, and she wiped it away with the back of her hand. "We've been walking a long time. We needed this badly."

"I can see that. Well, come on then. I've got two glasses. You take one more." John took the waters and placed them on the coffee table in front of Dean and Andy then sat down on the love seat across from them. "Laura tells me you've been walking for quite some time."

Jeff was in a chair off in the corner, and Laura handed him his drink and then sat on the couch beside Dean. "You need to drink something." She pushed the mask away from his face and straightened him up enough to give him a sip. His lips were starting to look fat from dryness. He took a little of the water, most of it spilling from his mouth. He started to choke, coughing up more blood in the process. With a cringed expression, John tossed over a box of tissues. Dean took a couple of seconds for his wheezing to subside and then tried again to drink, this time going through half the glass.

"If you don't mind me asking, when was he thrown into the nest?"

"Yesterday. They tied him up and left him there all day," Laura said.

"You can't be serious! And you say the guards did this?"

Laura decided to drop the formalities. "John, Dean and a group of people stumbled across something over a year and a half ago. It was highly classified. Two of the people in the group decided they wanted to exploit what they found, and the others posed a threat to them. They killed three of them and pinned one of the murders on Dean, getting him out of the way by sending him to prison. I inadvertently stumbled across what was going on when I overheard a conversation on my first day of work at the Accelerator Laboratory. I barely escaped with my life. We're certain these people arranged for Dean and me to be killed inside the prison. I'm sure they're worried we've been talking to the other prisoners. The Consortium denied Andy his parole as a result of his association with us."

"Who's trying to kill you? Who's behind this?"

Dean cleared his throat. "It's okay, Laura; if he's going to help us, he needs to know the whole truth." His wheezing had become barely audible, and he took another sip of water before continuing.

"You okay?" Laura squeezed his hand. "Here put this pillow behind you; it might help."

"Thanks." Dean looked at John with a concentrated air of sincerity; his reddened, heavy eyes at least enough to earn a degree of sympathy. "I'm sorry to descend on you like this. Just by being here, we're putting you at risk, too. We have no one else to turn to." Dean let go of Laura's hand and leaned forward to adjust the pillow. "I used to be a navigator for the Mining Exploration Division. We'd fly to planets with potential mineral deposits and check them out. Just over a year and a half ago, our group stumbled across what was, in my opinion, the most significant discovery in human history...intelligent life. It wasn't biological. It was energy, but intelligent energy. The life forms appeared as small, colorful, flickering lights and could communicate with us telepathically. They were peaceful and as fascinated with us as we were with them. We picked up low frequency electromagnetic fields from them, higher than brain waves but not by much. The frequencies were the same as the field surrounding the human body, which lead my ex-wife, Karen, and my friend, Annie, to believe they were like a soul or spirit, without a body. I kind of laughed at that idea, but to tell you the truth, I just don't know. We just referred to them as entities." Dean paused to rest his voice as it was becoming hoarse. John appeared uncomfortable as Laura took his hand back.

"We were on the planet exposed to the entities for several hours while we carried out the geological analysis and very quickly discovered they were affecting us. Being exposed to them somehow made us smarter, able to heal quickly, that kind of thing. I can assure you the sum total of the effects were incredible. We also found out our presence was harming them, killing them in fact. They blatantly asked us to leave. There were six of us in the group. Four of us decided we should do as they asked: leave and never come back. We were also convinced that in order to protect them, knowledge of their existence had to be limited. Ivan Campbell, the team leader and Kevin Cowen, our pilot had an entirely different opinion. The effects of the entities lasted about three weeks, and I can tell you, Ivan wasn't too pleased when they dissipated. He was devastated, and it sent him into a deep depression."

John crossed his legs and frowned. "Ivan Campbell. He's running the Accelerator Laboratory. I talked to him after Laura was sent to prison, trying to get some details on this supposed confession she signed. He brushed me off in a hurry."

"Not surprising. John...Ivan and Kevin have been harvesting the entities and holding them in a containment unit at the Accelerator for the sole purpose of fueling themselves and no doubt a handful of others with cognitive superpowers. There's no telling what he's capable of now. Last I saw him he was telekinetic."

"What...he could move things with his mind? That's crazy!" Jeff said, his voice sounding distant from the corner.

"Yeah, no kidding. Ivan's a very dangerous man and is seriously addicted to his newfound abilities. The three other members of the crew who sided against him...Roger, Annie, and Karen have been killed; and at this point, who knows how many others. Likely, anyone with any knowledge of the entities is part of his death toll. I suppose you can add my name to the list along with countless entities."

"Don't say that. You're not going to die." Laura inched closer to Dean.

"John, none of us are safe until this man is stopped, and it's not just him. There's no way of knowing how deep this goes. Larry Dunn, whom I'm sure you've heard of, is involved," Dean said.

"Yes, he's head of security on the Lyra Base Station."

"That's right. Unfortunately, my close friend Matt Jenkins, head of security on Eagle, thinks I killed his sister; so without proof, he's not going to help me. Moreover, Ivan threatened to kill him and his wife if I talked. I just hope he's not carrying out with his threat right now, although I'm betting he's more consumed with finding us. We're fugitives now, and my hours are numbered. Quite frankly, I am at a loss on how to remedy this. Laura's an innocent victim who was in the wrong place at the wrong time. She deserves to have her life back and so does Andy. He served his time fair and square. As for Ivan and his colleagues, they need to be brought to justice. I'm sure you see my dilemma."

John caressed the deep lines in his forehead, slowly and thoughtfully. "Yes, I certainly do. Tell me, Dean, can you prove any of this?"

Laura answered first. "If we could get into the Accelerator Laboratory, I'm sure we could. I saw the entities in the containment unit and overheard Ivan and Kevin planning to eliminate Karen and Dean. If I got back in there, I'm sure I could drum up some concrete evidence. I would need to access the computer though. It wouldn't be easy."

"Easy? It would be near suicide. It sounds like they have their defenses in place, and I'm sure the security there is almost impenetrable. Not to mention they may suspect you're coming, now that you've escaped." John let out a discouraging sigh. "Well, I must admit this would be a hell of a story to make up, and it sounds like I'm getting knee deep into it by the minute. After my conversation with Ivan, it wouldn't take much for him to think you may have come to me. It looks like I'm going to have to help you get out of this mess one way or another. Dean, I'm sorry to tell you, but without hospitalization, you're chances are slim at best."

"Well then, we have to get him to a hospital," Laura insisted.

"No, that would put all of you at risk. I won't go!"

Jeff moved to the edge of his chair and leaned closer into the conversation circle. "There's a drug available on the street that could help him. It's a highly addictive narcotic, but it would give him a fighting chance. It wouldn't be hard for me to get my hands on some, and we could pay for it in diamonds."

"Diamonds?"

271

"The freighter we stole from the prison had quite the stash," Andy said with a crooked grin.

"This is getting better by the minute," John murmured. "Dean, do you think Ivan will tell the authorities about my connection to Laura? If he does, I'm guessing it won't take long for them to be pounding on my door with a search warrant, looking for the bunch of you."

"Ivan's going to want his people to catch us and eliminate us. If the authorities get to us first, he may fear we'd tell them the truth. I'd go to the authorities myself, but I don't know who exactly is involved in this, and unless I can expose Ivan's crimes quickly, I could be putting my friend Matt's life in jeopardy. I don't know who to trust."

"So you think I'm going to have visitors?"

"Without a doubt. Ivan won't stop until he's exhausted every lead."

"I'm going to have to find a place to hide you then."

"Do you have a basement? A crawl space?" Laura asked. She immediately pictured the confines of such a place and wished she hadn't.

"Not on Draco. You may as well write out an invitation for those rainbow bugs. No attic either, one of the disadvantages of a flat-roofed house. I do have a small panic room at the back of my closet in my bedroom. Even with neighborhood security, we do get periodic break-ins. It would be a hell of a squeeze, but I think the four of you would fit. You can hide your diamonds in there, too. Of course, when this is over, those will have to be returned."

Laura got butterflies listening to John's description of his *Panic* room. They'd learn the true meaning of *panic* if they shoved her in there. Her shoulders shuddered at the thought. John picked up on it and smiled. "Don't worry Laura. It's a last resort. I almost forgot how much you hate closed spaces. She wouldn't even go down tube slides when she was a kid," he said and chuckled.

Dean twisted his head toward her and grinned. "Tube slides?" He patted her knee then switched his glance over to Jeff. "About that narcotic, assuming it gets me through this, what's going to be left of me?"

"The truth is, I could probably pick the first dose up for free. It's

272

the bastard drug lord's edge for getting you hooked, then you pay through your nose for the rest of your life just to stay alive."

"What do you mean *stay alive?*" Laura asked.

"The drug was actually designed as a pain killer. The first dose is exceptional at doing the job and makes you higher than hell. It could get you through the pain of the hatching insects fleeing your body. Once they've fled your body, the pain will subside, and you'll recover very quickly. The catch is the drug causes the pain to come back after a number of hours, and you'll need to take more of it for it to go away again. You'll feel fine one minute, and the next minute you'll be experiencing the same pain as when you first took the drug. At that point in time, the only thing to get rid of the pain will be another dose of the drug. It won't make you high anymore. Only the first dose does that. It will just get rid of the pain. It's almost like the drug does something to your body so it mimics the pain. The pain will continue to come back every so often, and you'll have to take another dose to get rid of it. That's why it's addictive. At least you won't have to spend the rest of your life high. Depending on the severity of the pain, some people can tough it out and wean themselves off the drug. In the case of the pain from an infestation, that might not be so easy." Jeff sighed. "I'm sorry I can't be more positive."

John met Jeff's glance. "Dean doesn't have much time. If I take you in the morning, can you get some of that drug?"

"No problem. As long as you don't mind traveling to the shadier parts of town."

"I have a couple of meetings tomorrow, which I can cancel. I can use the upcoming Lyra Summit as an excuse."

"Summit?" Dean perked up.

"Yes, the annual Planetary Summit on Lyra. Heads of State from all four planets will be there as usual. It starts on Sunday, and I'm expected to attend since one of the key issues being discussed is traffic congestion along the main texture corridors between the planets. It's a very high profile issue ever since the passenger spaceliner was lost last month."

"Excuse me?" Dean leaned forward letting his pillow fall behind the couch. "What happened?"

"Yeah, I guess you wouldn't have heard, and no doubt if you weren't behind bars, you would have been called in to assist with the investigation."

John explained the situation that led to the accident. "The texture fragment between Earth and the Eagle Base Station started to destabilize. It was only a blip, but it took them by surprise and was enough to throw them out of the fragment. The gravity forces on the texture rim crushed the ship. They're theorizing the instability arose from the volume of traffic along the corridor...hundreds of ships every day sucking up all the high energy particles inside the texture for fuel. We thought it was a limitless source of energy, but maybe not. It's a real problem. Can you imagine if that texture destabilized permanently. It would be the last any of us would see of Earth."

Dean settled back down with a dazed look on his face. "How many people were killed?"

"Three hundred and seventy five. If we had more time, I'd like to pick your brain on the topic. I know your reputation. You're one hell of a navigator as I understand it. Anyway, for now, we need to get you through this alive."

Dean shook his head slowly with his gaze cast down. "I would have loved to have been part of the investigation." He looked back up at John. "Assuming I get through this alive, is there any chance you can get me to the Lyra Base Station. If I could get into the Accelerator, we could finish this."

"If you're going there, I'm going with you," Laura said with a headstrong attitude.

"To answer your question, Dean, yes, it would be tricky, but I think I could pull it off. Being Minister of Transportation and Communication has its benefits, but the timing could be better. Even if I get you to the base station, the security will be tight there and getting into the Accelerator will be next to impossible."

"I have some ideas about that," Laura added. "It won't be easy, but it could be done."

"Well, as grand a plan as this is shaping up to be, Dean still needs to get through the next couple of days. That's one hell of a time bomb you're carrying around inside of you. I suggest you record everything you can think of which might help me in clearing your names. If things don't work out in your favor, I'm going to need it." John walked to the wall unit on the far side of the room and retrieved a digital dictation recorder out of one of the drawers. "While you do that, Laura and I can get all of you some food, and then we should get some sleep. There are two guest rooms upstairs and one down, but I suggest everyone stay upstairs in case we have visitors. You'll want to be in close proximity to my closet. You'll be comfortable. Each room has its own bathroom."

Laura followed John back to the kitchen. "Uncle John, how is everyone back home? They must think I'm a horrible person." She felt her homesick pangs return, as they rattled the door she'd locked them behind when her ordeal began.

"Laura, no one believes you did anything wrong. Trust me, we've all been trying to get more details of the crime you confessed to, and they just shut us down. I wish I could make some calls right now, tell them you're okay, but if they're not already monitoring me, they will be soon."

"I'm worried about them. Ivan threatened to kill my family if I talked. I hope Dean's right, and that he's too preoccupied with finding us to carry out his threats. I wish there was a way of warning them without putting them at risk."

John lowered his voice. "Dean and you seem pretty close."

"I love him."

"Those are pretty big words. I assume you knew him for some time before all this happened."

"Remember when we talked the day before I started at the Accelerator, I told you I met someone at the Symposium. That was Dean."

John raised a protective brow. "That's right, I remember you mentioned his name. So you haven't known him long. Does he feel the same about you?"

"Yes, he does. I've heard the best way to get close to someone is to spend time together in paradise, like a Caribbean Island. Well, they're wrong. You go to hell with someone, and in the end, you share no secrets. Don't worry, Uncle John. Dean is the most genuine person

I've ever known."

"You need to understand he's going to need you to get through this. What he has coming is nothing less than horrific. I witnessed the final results of a bug infestation several years back, and it left me with nightmares. A teenage boy from my neighborhood decided to ignore the warnings and strayed away from the city limits one night as part of a drunken dare. His friends panicked after he fell into a nest and left him. Miraculously, the boy managed to escape, but it took him a couple of days to struggle his way home. By the time he did, the incubation was over, and the hatching phase had started. There was no time to get him to the hospital, and he only managed to endure the pain for a couple of hours before having a stroke. The pain is said to be intolerable, like you're burning from the inside out. Not to mention the flurry of revolting little insects emerging from your body. You need to be ready for this, Laura." John gave her a sobering look. "Come on, I can hear your stomach from here."

They returned with a platter laden with fruit and cheeses. With the exception of Dean, everyone ate until not even a scrap remained. Laura finished with a piece of golden pineapple. It stung her lips, but was the sweetest thing she ever remembered tasting.

Half an hour later, Laura found herself lying in bed in Dean's arms. She tried to tune out John's words and enjoy Dean's warmth, but what John said haunted her. No matter what, she had to get Dean through the next days. She gave in to her fatigue and drifted off.

Chapter Thirty-Seven

Dalton Lew had been a marshal on Draco for over fourteen years. He worked the streets for nine of them until he managed to push up the ranks to detective. At the time, he thought detective work would get him away from the street scum, giving him the challenge he always wanted; but he was wrong. It was the same pile of crap, but he just smelled it from the other side of the fence. Becoming head marshal changed all that. He got to run the show the way he wanted, and the air finally smelled fresh, leaving him intolerant of people who tried to tell him how to do his job. Especially arrogant self-righteous pricks like Larry Dunn.

"I insist on being part of this investigation. Simmons was involved in a serious crime on my base station, and right now, you can't assure me she doesn't pose a threat to it. If they manage to get off Draco, that's probably the first place they'll go. And she's traveling with a savage killer! With the Summit starting on Sunday, the base station is going to be flooded with high profile government officials; any one of whom could be in danger from these people."

Lew got up from his desk and went to face Dunn; damned if he was going to let him be the alpha dog. Standing a foot away from the man, he deliberately infringed on his personal space and put a bark into his tone. "Dunn, don't shake your fist at me. You have no authority here, so why don't you just get out and let me do my job. If you're worried about the security on your base station, then maybe you should be there. I can assure you every marshal in the city is on the lookout for them."

"You know damn well the best chance we have of finding them is in the next twenty-four hours. You can at least give me that."

A young uniformed woman poked her head through the door. "Marshal Lew, there's a Matt Jenkins here insisting to see you."

"Great!" Lew let out a disgruntled growl. "What the hell's wrong with you people that you can't mind your own business? You know, I've managed to police Draco without you until now."

"And the crime rate's through the roof."

Lew scowled as he caught a glimpse of Matt strutting toward his office. "Anna, show him in."

"Looks like he's done that himself, sir."

"What can I do for you, Jenkins?"

A red-faced Matt barged into the office and took a spot beside Larry. "Good morning Dalton, sorry to intrude like this, but I heard about the escape first thing this morning and got here as fast as I could. Do you have any leads on Weston? No doubt you know my feelings about having him apprehended."

"Well, it's not just Weston that's on the loose you know, and yes we have some leads. We've been working this all night. Now, I will give you the same talk I just gave Dunn here. Why don't you mind your own business and let us do our job. You have no jurisdiction here."

"Dalton, Weston was my closest friend. I know how he thinks. I know who his friends are. I can assure you, I can be an asset to this investigation."

"Perhaps, but it's too personal for you. I won't allow it."

Matt gave Larry a side glance and said with some attitude, "What's your interest in this?"

"Simmons, she stirred up a lot of shit on my base station. She has some pretty classified information in her head that she uncovered at the Accelerator Laboratory. I'm here for the same reason as you. I want these people caught."

"Look. Can you at least fill us in on what you know? I might be able to be of some help. Like I said, I know how Weston thinks."

Lew decided Matt's argument might have some merit. Besides, he liked the man almost as much as he disliked Dunn. "Fine. I'll fill you in, but then you leave." Dalton turned to his desk and swung his computer monitor around. "As you know, Weston and Simmons escaped with two other inmates, Andy Weber who was in for manslaughter and Jeff Gibbons who was in for drug trafficking."

"I remember Gibbons," Matt interrupted. "He was just a freckle-faced kid. That bust went down on Eagle, I questioned him. So did Weston for that matter."

"Anyway, for some dumb ass reason, the Warden decided to trust Weston to help with some repair work on their power grid. It's believed he somehow sabotaged it, causing yesterday's explosion. The four of them escaped in a freighter that was found up here at the Collin's Nickel Mine." He pointed to the map on the screen. "They took out the security guard and stole a truck that was found early this morning behind a warehouse just off Dune Boulevard. We're investigating whether any of them may have a connection with a person living in an area surrounding that location. Taxi and bus drivers working in the area last night have already been questioned, but nothing suspicious was reported. We're assuming they proceeded on foot and have spread our search perimeter to a thirty kilometer radius. With the satellite surveillance, no one within that radius will so much as sneeze without me knowing it."

"They could have called someone to pick them up." Larry pointed out.

"Their implants were disabled the minute they stepped through the door of the prison. You should know that. The security guard said the truck they stole wasn't even equipped with a radio, so it's doubtful they contacted anyone. We believe they had a specific destination in mind and went there on foot. Matt, do you know if Weston had any friends in the area?"

"No, he has a few acquaintances on Draco, but no one close enough to help him, not that anyone would help him after what he did. I'm pretty sure Ben Crawford still lives here, he was in engineering with us, but he and Dean never really got along. Then there's Angie Little. Before he hooked up with Karen, he used to talk about her. He dated her for a while in high school, but they never kept in touch after that. You may want to touch base with both of them because if he does head their way, they could be in a lot of danger."

"Agreed; is there anyone else you can think of?" Lew asked, avoiding eye contact with Dunn.

"No, but I'll tell you this, Dean is smart and cunning. He's a survivor. If you don't find him soon, you may never find him, which is why I want to be involved."

Yeah so you can take him down yourself! Lew recognized the look of vengeance, a consuming emotion, and Matt was wearing it like a coat. He could hardly blame him, but there was no place for it in police business. "Sorry, I've told you everything we know. At this point in time, all the two of you are doing is slowing my investigation down. Leave, or I'll have you removed. If I have any news, you'll be the first to know."

Larry glanced at Matt with a nod, then put his hand on his shoulder, and nudged him toward the door. "Come on. You heard the man, we're done here."

* * * *

A few steps out of the office and Matt insisted, "What the hell was that? Since when did you kowtow so easily?"

Larry chuckled at the mere thought of it. "Who says I'm kowtowing. Whatta ya say we team up, work this together. We're both motivated, and like you said, if they're not found soon, they may never be. I'm on a time-line with the Summit. I have a flight to Lyra Saturday night to help with security, and if I'm not there, they'll have my head."

Matt hesitated then nodded. "Fine, we'll work this together. Sounds like we have just over twenty-four hours, so let's get on it!"

The two men stepped onto the street. The Draco marshals' building was in the heart of downtown in an area bustling with activity. All the big mining giants had their Draco headquarters in the towers surrounding the building and distinguished looking business men and women flooded the streets. The marshals' building was quite an eyesore amongst the glass skyscrapers, but it made the area the safest in the city, which more than made up for its gray stone walls.

"Matt, I'm parked over there, the black SUV. If you don't mind, I'm just going to make a quick call to my friend, Ivan Campbell. Just give me a couple of minutes, one of his colleagues passed away yesterday."

"No problem. Who did you bribe to get that parking spot?" Matt grinned and headed toward the corner coffee house.

Larry slipped into the driver's seat and locked the door before placing the call. "Ivan, how are you doing?"

"Bloody well great, what do you think? Any leads on Weston and Simmons?"

"They stole a truck. It was found at the north end of the city. It's believed they proceeded from there on foot. I'm working with Jenkins. He knows Dean well; he may be—"

"Are you out of your mind? If he finds them, Dean will tell him everything. Get rid of him. I don't care how you do it, just do it. It seems to me, he has it coming to him anyway. He can thank his buddy for this one."

"The last thing we need is a missing marshal to draw attention to this. For now, I need to be with him. We can get rid of him later if need be. Besides, as I was saying, he knows Dean well and may be of use. Don't worry, I have this under control. In another day or so, Weston will be dead."

"Where exactly in the north end did they find the truck?"

"Just off Dune Boulevard." There was a moment of silence. "You still there?"

"Yeah, I had a thought. A short time after Simmons was put away I received a call from John Becker. You know of him, I'm sure. He's the Minister of Transportation and Communication on Draco. He insisted on hearing the details of Simmons' crime and was adamant that she was innocent and a victim of foul play."

"And you never mentioned this to me?"

"He's a government official. You can't just eliminate him because he makes a call. I brushed him off and didn't hear from him again so I let it go. There's a nice neighborhood not far from Dune Boulevard that's popular with government officials. If Becker lives there, it may be worth checking it out. He sounded like he was close with Simmons."

"I'll check it out. By the way, how are things going on your end?"

"Jack's brother backed off for now, but that exploding glass sure didn't help the situation. I have Irena coming by this afternoon. Hopefully, she can help the rest of us with our little problem."

"Don't forget what I told you last night. Stay away from those entities. I'll be in touch."

Chapter Thirty-Eight

John pounded on Jeff's bedroom door repeatedly before it opened. Jeff peered out at him through a crack, his hair looking like shredded carrots and his eye lids drawn half closed.

"It's after eight," John said as he handed him a pair of sweat pants and a T-shirt. "Coffee's ready. Hurry." Jeff grunted and shut the door.

Five minutes later, Jeff appeared in the kitchen. John noticed he had twice the number of freckles than the night before thanks to the wonders of soap. He offered Jeff a coffee, which he refused in favor of a cola. John poured himself a *traveler,* scooped up the small packet of diamonds from the counter, and led the way to the garage.

As they pulled out of the driveway, John cringed at the thought of feeding Draco's crime problem; it was a ruthless animal with a thirst for the blood of both the fortunate and unfortunate. The planet's society had segregated itself into two distinct classes, the grunt-work miners and the suits running the operations, a club he proudly belonged to but for the need for his panic room. Mining was mundane, harsh, unpleasant work; and drug use and prostitution served as an escape for those who toiled in this life.

John, as a long standing member of the white collar crowd, made every effort to segregate himself from the other half, enveloping himself in a glass bubble. He traveled in influential circles, enjoying the finer things in life. He avoided the seedy parts of town as a regular course and made generous charitable contributions at Christmas, which allowed him to feel guiltless when turning a blind eye.

They were well on their way, and John decided to cut the awkward silence of the drive with some idle conversation. To his surprise, Jeff was more than receptive and very mature for his age. *Perhaps something that comes from being a hardened criminal.*

Jeff filled him in on the heart breaking loss of his mother and the worry for his sister that sent him around the wrong curve in life, changing his destiny forever. By the time they arrived at the variety store at the lower end of town, John felt a yearning to help him.

John parked across the street from the store and sat uncomfortably in his Beemer as prostitutes strolled by. He ignored the odd knock on his window. There were two motorcycles parked in front of the store, and as Jeff went in, the bikers came out. One, a heavyset fellow with tattooed arms, opened a pack of smokes and let the wrapper fall to be carried off in the breeze. It took a few flicks of his lighter before sparks flew, but soon billows of smoke puffed from his nose and mouth. The other, a tall skinny punk, had a tight grip on the arm of a woman dressed in tight shorts and long black boots. He could hear them arguing, and the bruising around her right eye, which was the color of an electrical storm, suggested it wasn't their first time. John formed a vacant smile as they roared off.

A short time later, Jeff reappeared with another man. They chatted for a while exchanging smiles before Jeff returned to the car. It left John with a feeling of reserve as he drove off.

As John pulled into his driveway, a veil of relief fell upon him. His visit to the underworld to make a drug deal left him with a dark uneasiness that had slithered up his spine, found its way inside, and stabbed at his gut. When he stepped into his garage, he left any guilt of his opulent lifestyle behind. Jeff jumped out of the car, goods in tow, and they headed for the door.

* * * *

"Laura, I think they're back, thank God!" Andy perked up to listen like a German Sheppard.

"Hurry, go check. He's in agony, *hurry*!" Laura said. Warm, fresh tears streamed from her eyes, soaking her face. "It's okay, Dean, only a little longer. Just stay with me."

Andy took off downstairs. Laura held Dean's hand tight and stroked his hair. He lay on the floor in the pool of sunlight bursting through the window, huddled in the fetal position after collapsing from the pain. Laura listened, trying to hear if they got the drug. She heard the door to the garage slam shut.

"Did you get it?" Andy said.

"Yeah, no problem," Jeff said with a cool overtone.

"Thank God," Laura whispered. "Just another minute, Dean. Hang on." She continued to listen.

"Come upstairs, hurry, he needs it!" Andy said.

"It's already started?" John asked.

"About twenty minutes after you left. The pain hit him like a storm surge. He's been buckled over on the floor ever since. He can't catch his breath long enough to scream, or I'm sure you'd hear him," Andy said.

"Any sign of the baby insects yet? They usually start to emerge about an hour after the onset of pain," John added.

"No, not yet. Come on upstairs. I left Laura with him in the bedroom. Hurry!"

The thunder of footsteps on the stairs echoed, and the three men herded into the guest bedroom.

"Don't you people know anything about hiding from the law? Keep these drapes pulled for crying out loud." John scrambled toward the window, squinting. "Damn it!"

"What, what is it?" Andy shouted.

"There are two men getting out of a black SUV parked in my driveway."

Andy ran toward the window and held up his hand as a sun visor. "Shit, that's Larry Dunn. We're screwed."

Laura sprang to her feet. She looked at the mess of the room and started to make the bed. "They'll know were here!"

"Come on get him up and into the closet. I'll stall them as long as I can. Hurry!"

Andy and Jeff carried Dean to John's bedroom while Laura and John straightened up.

"The water glasses, what do we do with them?" Laura said.

"Put them on my bedside table, come on."

Laura scooped up the glasses and followed John into his bedroom. She set the glasses down close to the edge of the table and one fell off, spilling a dark splotch onto the gray carpet. "Damn it!"

"Leave it; there's no time," John commanded.

Andy and Jeff were struggling to jam Dean into the small enclosure at the back of the closet. "John, get the drug," Jeff said.

John lifted the small canvas pouch from the floor and set it beside the box of diamonds. The doorbell sounded. "Come on, hurry! You're going to have to stay quiet." John rammed the four of them into the tiny space like cattle and slid the partition shut. Laura could hear him pushing his clothes back in place.

The enclosure was pitch black and stuffy, and the four of them together were hardly able to twitch, their limbs thrown together in a web of confusion. Andy and Jeff continued to hold Dean upright, but there was nowhere for him to fall.

"Damn it, Dean; hang on. You can't move," Andy whispered as he felt Dean's body tremor.

"Christ, I think he's starting to convulse," Jeff said. "Laura, shhh. You're hyperventilating."

"I'm sorry; small spaces panic me." She could feel the pressure of adrenaline building in her head.

"Well, shut up. You need to help Dean."

Laura shut her eyes tight and tried to zone out.

"Shhh, I hear footsteps," Jeff said.

* * * *

"You boys take your time looking around. I'm in no hurry, but excuse the mess. You know what life as a bachelor's like."

"So how do you know Laura Simmons?" Larry asked.

"I lived next door to her family for years. I remember the day they brought her home from the hospital. She was the sweetest little thing I'd ever seen. I'll tell you this, if I did hear from her, I would do anything I could to help her. Maybe I'd even finally get the truth about how she landed in that prison. I know Laura as though she was my own daughter, and there's no possible way she signed that confession of her own free will."

"Don't be so sure. Sometimes you think you know people, but there's a whole other side to them. Dean Weston was my best friend, and I found him with a knife in his hand, drunker than hell, and passed out in a pool of my sister's blood. After he said he'd sign a confession, I still couldn't believe it until he looked me in the eye and told me he killed her. I'll never forget the look on his face, uttering those words. That goes beyond betrayal."

John looked at Matt with two counts of sympathy. He'd suffered a terrible loss, but he was also walking alongside a man who was likely one of the real perpetrators. "I'm sorry for your loss, but I can assure you, Laura had nothing to do with the murder of your sister. Her confession apparently stated she was involved with Weston, and her jealousy helped fuel his fire. I know for a fact the first time they met was at the Symposium. She mentioned his name when she called to tell me she arrived safely at the Lyra Base Station. She sounded quite taken by him. She's as honest a person as there could be. I'm certain she did nothing wrong."

Larry's eyebrows shot half-way up his forehead as he sent John a peeved look. They stepped into the first guest bedroom. He looked in the closet and checked under the beds. "Maybe you should take a lesson from Matt. People sometimes have another side to them, a hidden agenda. I was there when Laura signed the confession. I can assure you, she's guilty and any attempt you make to help her will lead to your incarceration."

"Don't threaten me, Marshal Dunn. I willingly opened my door to you without a search warrant. I suggest you show me some respect. As for Laura, she is innocent. There is a rat in the midst, and I intend to find it." John stood at the door and extended his arm toward the hall. "Shall we move to the next room?" They followed him out the door.

"Did you have guests recently? This bed looks like it's been slept in?" Larry pulled back the sheets.

"What do you expect, it's a bed?"

John heard a thud. His heart skipped a beat, but he kept a cool face.

"What was that? It sounded like it came from the next room." Larry stomped toward the master bedroom and started searching the room like a cat on the prowl. He opened the door of the closet and spoke "closet lights on." He shifted some clothes around.

"Do you mind, those are expensive suits."

"This is rather a small closet for a house this size."

"There's a walk-in over there by the bathroom. I just keep my good clothes in here." As John spoke he spied a small whitish gray, almost translucent, bug crawling along the floor from the back wall. He took a step and crushed it with his foot. "Closet lights off. At this rate, we're going to be here all day."

"What happened here?" Matt said.

"Oh geez. I was wondering what that thud was. I better get a towel." John headed for the ensuite bathroom.

"You drink three glasses of water a night?" Larry asked, accusingly.

"I'm borderline diabetic," John hollered. "Would you like to know about by bowel movements, too?" He returned with the towel, dropped it on the wet spot and stepped on it.

"That's quite all right. Larry, I think we've overstayed our welcome. Let's finish up and get out of here. Mr. Becker has been more than accommodating, and if they're not here, we're just wasting precious time." Matt hastened the remainder of the search and headed for the front door. "Your planter's tipped over a bit." Matt took a couple of steps in the marble alcove and straightened it out.

"You better watch out, or I'm going to offer you a job." John gave him a friendly smile.

Matt handed him a card. "Please call me if you hear from Laura. I will listen to her story myself, and if she's innocent, I promise you I will do everything in my power to help her. Dean Weston killed my sister, and I am here because I want justice. Perhaps you should be concerned that Laura's running around with a convicted killer. He could even be a threat to you. Think about it."

"I will." John took the card out of Matt's hand and stuck it in his front pocket. Once the SUV backed out of the driveway, he waved then shut the door.

John spun around and climbed the stairs two at a time. He heaved the clothes in the closet to one side as he called out some words of relief. "They're gone." He tried to move the partition, but it was jammed shut. Several tiny bugs were crawling through his closet.

Laura started pounding. She sounded desperate. "Hurry, get us out of here."

"I can't, your weight against the door is jamming it shut. You have to back off a bit."

"There's no room. Dean's starting to convulse."

"You have to make room, push him back." John continued to struggle with the partition. "Damn it, push back!" Suddenly the door gave way and slid open.

Dean fell to the floor with the appearance of a bug infested corpse. A flurry of tiny insects were scurrying from his face and out from his clothes. His limbs shuddered as he gasped for air, his bulging eyes the color of a blood orange.

"Dear God, get him into my shower. We'll wash them down the drain. Jeff get that drug ready!"

John and Andy lifted Dean to his feet and started half dragging him to the bathroom. Partway there, he slipped out of Andy's arms, leaving John with the burden of his entire weight. John winced as a jolt of pain shot through the aging muscles of his back.

"Sorry, the bugs. They're slimy. Come on, let's get him up again."

"Wait a minute." Laura grabbed the towel off the floor and wiped Dean's arms and shoulders clear of bugs. "Okay. Go, I'll get the water running."

"Make it cool." John yelled as he struggled to get Dean back to his feet.

Laura slid the glass shower door aside, and John and Andy lifted Dean over the small lip and lay him down in a huddled position under the stream. Laura filled the space beside him, sitting on the hard stone tile, and started to strip him down to his boxers so the bugs could make an easy exit.

"I could use a towel here," she called as she tried to wipe them off his face with her hand. They crushed easily leaving a slimy milky residue.

John handed her a towel. "Where's that drug?" Dean's convulsing was becoming more pronounced. He had his head thrown back with his mouth open, and he shook as though he'd stuck his finger in an electrical outlet.

Jeff arrived with a syringe and tourniquet. "I'm here. Someone's going to have to hold him down while I do this."

"Andy, you help. I don't know if I can hold him steady enough."

Laura stood up and squeezed into the corner to make room for him.

Jeff knelt down with his feet sticking out the door. "Andy, hold him tight."

"Got it. Hurry Jeff, he's strong." Andy held him down with his weight while Jeff tied the tourniquet around Dean's large bicep. His arm broke free as he convulsed.

"Hold him tighter. I gotta get this needle in... Shit, I need a good vein." Jeff wiped away a few bugs and felt around the crook in Dean's arm. "Here we go, hold him steady." Jeff slid the needle in firmly and injected the pale yellow fluid. "Done, the effects should be almost instant." He removed the tourniquet. "Let's give him some room."

Andy and Jeff stepped out of the shower, joining John on the other side of the door frame. Laura continued to wipe away the bugs with the towel. The severity of Dean's convulsion eased off quickly. For several minutes, the four of them watched in silence as his body relaxed. He lay huddled and shaking while his breathing started to return to normal. Suddenly, he let out a shrill howl. Laura lay down beside him and held him tightly, cleaning him off every few seconds.

"Just leave us. I'll call if I need you. This may take a while." Laura seemed embarrassed for him. His ear piercing screams of pain continued.

* * * *

Several hours passed, and Laura had entertained numerous concerned visits by the three men, each time shooing them away wanting to uphold Dean's dignity. Dean's howls had subsided to moans, and he had started to shiver.

John cautiously peeked in from around the corner. "Laura, I think we can turn the water off."

"Okay, there's only been the odd one in the last while. I've kinda lost track of time, and I'm freezing."

John turned off the tap. "What's he doing?" Dean looked like a cat with a ball as he batted at the water going down the drain.

"He's been doing that for at least an hour."

Jeff stood at the door and laughed. "He's baked."

289

"Pass me a towel, and I'll dry him off. Dean, can you stand?" Laura reached out for the plush white towel in John's hand.

It didn't surprise her that Dean didn't respond. His eyes were dilated as he stared blankly at the drain.

"Dry him off, and we'll put him in my robe." John, slightly slouched, stepped aside and let Jeff and Andy get Dean to his feet. They sat him on the toilet long enough to put the robe on him. "Laura, here's a towel. I have a pair of athletic shorts and a T-shirt you can wear. That's the best I can do. Let's get Dean to the bedroom."

Laura quickly changed and ran to the bedroom. John was just shutting the door. "How is he?" she asked.

"Like Jeff said, higher than hell, but I'm pretty certain he's out of danger for now. We just have to watch for the pain to come back, so we know when to give him another dose. Come downstairs, and I'll make you some tea. You're exhausted, and he needs to rest." John pushed the soggy strands away from Laura's face. "You still look like a little girl."

Laura was reluctant to leave Dean alone, but her skin felt clammy, and she warmed up to the thought of some tea. She thanked him as they walked down the stairs, and then she whispered, "I guess I'm causing a little trouble." She paused. "But just a little."

Chapter Thirty-Nine

Ivan stepped out of his office for a moment to talk to Pam. "Irena's expected in half an hour. Would you please arrange to have a couple of extra chairs brought into my office for our meeting? There's going to be seven of us in total. I'd rather not meet in Section Four with the containment unit there. There's no sense in adding fuel to her fire."

"I'll get on it right away."

Ivan walked back to his desk only to find, yet again, his favorite picture tilting to one side. *For crying out loud!* He carefully inched his desk further out from the wall. The jarring of the heavy wood set his water glass in motion, and he took a leap to steady it before moving to the other side to repeat the procedure. *A little bit more space. That ought to do it.* With pleasure, he stood in front of his prized oil painting, taking a moment to live vicariously through the eyes of the wolf, and then he gave it a gentle nudge to level it. *Beautiful! A timeless creation.* He turned his attention to his work, but felt distracted. Lack of sleep, Jack's death, the news of the prison break—the combination overwhelmed him.

"Pam," he called. "You got a minute?" *She must not have heard me. "Pam…"*

Pam's long red nails appeared wrapped around the doorframe as she snuck a quick look beyond the opening. Ivan looked up expecting her to say *peek-a-boo*. He admired her flowing hair as it swung to one side setting her dangling earring into pendulum motion. "Yeah, what's up? I was just getting your chairs."

"Excuse me, Pam." A man's voice sounded.

Pam took a few steps into Ivan's office to make room for the two young men delivering the chairs. Her gaze followed the butt of the steed; the mule, a fellow with a beard and a greasy cow lick, Ivan felt hardly deserved her attention. "One here and one here, guys. Thanks." They placed the seats and left. "Ivan, you were calling?"

"Yes, there's not much time to get any work done before Irena arrives, and we haven't chatted in a while. I thought we could get caught up. To tell you the truth, I could use a pick-me-up. It's been tough few days."

Pam cracked an enthusiastic grin. "I'm always good for a pick-me-up."

Ivan stood up and motioned to the couch. He knew she would be agreeable—her social spark never dimmed, and at the moment, it was the perfect medicine for taking his mind off things.

"Actually, if you don't mind, there's been something I've wanted to discuss with you. Perhaps this is a good time?" Pam sat cross-legged, sinking into the middle cushion, and patted the cushion beside her. Ivan joined her.

"What's on your mind, Pam?"

"My work. It's boring. You need to give me more of a challenge. I can't believe I've spent months doing this mindless job without giving it a second thought. I suppose I didn't have a second thought to give it," Pam said as she looked to Ivan for resolution. "Seriously, Ivan, nightmares aside, I appreciate what you've done for me; and I'd like to return the favor. I am capable of so much more than I'm doing. Please give me a chance."

"I must admit I was anticipating this. I'm certain we can work something out." He smiled as he gently rubbed her knee. "I remember when I interviewed you last year. You were so keen but quite naive. I couldn't resist your charm."

Pam glanced down at his hand and gave him a sultry smile. "Why did you hire me? As I recall, I couldn't answer most of your questions, and my experience as a sales clerk hardly qualified me."

Her question sent Ivan's mind adrift for a moment. Before college during the part of his life he pleasingly referred to as *the young and foolish days*, he'd decided to take a year to travel Europe. He'd spent the summer months working on a large fishing boat in the Mediterranean and the man running the operation had his daughter on board. She would cook for the crew and do odd jobs. Every day, Ivan would watch her from afar as he went about his work. Even on the cooler days, her arms were bare to the shoulder; and her long, shimmering hair would be pulled half back with the few waves in front providing a bronzed framework for her brilliant, brown eyes. Even while doing the filthiest of tasks, she had a radiance about her. She used to look to catch his attention then tease him with her innocent body language before returning to her work. Between the hard work and the protectiveness of the captain, he never had a chance to talk to her; but Ivan never forgot her. He spent many a night dreaming about having her. Her name was Grace, and Pam was her spitting image.

Ivan broke his tranquil daze with a pleased smile. "Life's a learning curve my dear. I'm sure you know that by now. You have a very appealing personality...a people person. I thought you'd be good dealing with clients and would grow with the job. I was obviously correct."

"Don't forget where this growth came from. I don't wish this experiment to come to an end. Do you think Irena will be able to remedy our nightmares?"

"I'm counting on it. Do you mind me asking, what skeletons lay in your nighttime closet?"

Pam hesitated.

"Sorry, I don't mean to intrude on your privacy."

"No, it's okay. Perhaps talking about it would help. It's just... well, slightly embarrassing. You're going to think I'm quite vain."

"I think you're quite beautiful."

"Thanks, I like to look my best. I've been waking up at night in a panic after dreaming that I'm hideously ugly...deformed, mutilated. It's ridiculous I know, but I'll rush to the washroom and look in the mirror, and for a short moment, I'd swear a hideous monster was looking back at me. And then there's a glow. The eyes looking back at me have this strange yellow-orange glow. It's an intense frightening stare, like the eyes are looking right through me. It's almost as though it's not even my reflection looking back. I've gotten to the point that I don't even want to look in the mirror." She smirked. "I hope you'll tell me if my hair's out of place."

"Pam, have you heard any voices?"

"No... Maybe. I thought I heard someone whispering in your office yesterday, but you weren't there. It kind of scared me, especially after Jack died. I think we're all a little uneasy. I'm sure it's just that."

Kevin suddenly shadowed the door with Irena at his side. "I was dropping off a package in reception and look who I ran into. I just passed Ron and the others. They'll be here momentarily."

Ivan got up from his seat. "Irena, great to see you."

"Once again, I am so sorry to hear about Jack," Irena said, her expression solemn and her head shaking slowly. "I am still shocked. I spoke to him at length about his nightmares, but he didn't mention anything about the sketches. He was clearly devastated by the loss of his mother."

"He will be missed, I can assure you." Ivan's regrets over the loss of his friend were driven by self-interest. He didn't want to be next. It made him determined to get results from the meeting.

Ron and the two other scientists involved in the experiment arrived in the office. Ivan took the time to put faces to the voices of the three Irena had only spoken with, and after the introductions, asked everyone to be seated. He took a seat at his desk. He wanted answers and was anxious to get down to business. "Irena, the coroner who examined Jack didn't believe nightmares could cause cardiac arrest. Do you share that opinion?"

"Yes I do, but in this case… Well before getting to that we should discuss my findings regarding the experiences all of you have been having. Perhaps the best place to start is to explain the stages of sleep. There are five stages, each corresponding to a frequency of brain waves. Throughout the night, you cycle through all five stages, but when it comes to dreaming, the fifth stage is the most important. It's the rapid eye movement stage of sleep or REM sleep. It's during REM sleep that lucid dreams occur. A complete sleep cycle takes about an hour and a half, so during the night, a person will typically experience four or five full cycles. The first sleep cycles have a relatively short REM sleep interval of around ten minutes, but later in the night, they dominate and can be as long as an hour. That's when you're most likely to dream."

Irena paused for a deep breath that threatened to pop the button holding her black wool pants together. "I know you're all thirsting for knowledge, but I'll gloss over the technical jargon quickly so we can get to some answers." An accusing look passed over her face, and her voice came out sharp. "Stage one sleep is very light where you drift in and out. By stage three, you've transitioned to deep sleep, and there is no eye movement or muscular activity. It is difficult to wake someone up from deep sleep. Fast brain waves are present during the REM sleep just like when you are awake. You can get frequent bursts of eye movement and the occasional muscle twitch. The heart may beat faster, and the breathing may become rapid and shallow."

"So couldn't an increased heart rate lead to cardiac arrest?" Ron inquired.

"No, not unless there was an underlying heart condition. You must understand there are nightmares and night terrors. They are two different things and should not be confused with one another. The night terrors occur during non-REM sleep and cause screaming and violent physical movement. They are rarely remembered and typically occur during the early part of the night when the deep sleep stages are longer. Sleep walking is common with night terrors. Nightmares on the other hand are often remembered and occur during REM sleep. They cause tremendous fear, but it is rare to scream or have any significant movement. As for what causes nightmares, illness or some medications can cause them. More often they stem from stress or anxiety in people's lives. Like Jack losing his mother. The cause of night terrors is more vague. It is often genetic, implying there might be a physiological cause."

Irena glanced around at the group. "From your collective experiences, it is difficult to pinpoint exactly what you are experiencing. I have never seen this situation in my entire professional life. It seems all of you started by simply having nightmares, but then all of a sudden, they changed. Now all of you are reporting symptoms of both nightmares and night terrors, and that concerns me. Each of you reported your recent experiences to be vivid, recurring and deeply disturbing, and you remember them in detail like they were real. The nightmares seem to have a route to your past or stem from something you care deeply about in the present. You wake up sweating, heart pounding, and out of breath. That suggests they are the nightmares. However, you have also reported screams, night tables toppled over, your beds torn apart, and waking up in different rooms. Many of you have woken up early in the night from an incident. Those are symptoms of night terrors."

"And Jack, what do you think he had?" Ivan pressed.

"The coroner said the time of death was likely around four in the morning, which suggests a nightmare. The expression on his face, the positioning of his hands, and the condition of his bed sheets are more indicative of night terrors. Do you see where I'm going with this? All of you are demonstrating symptoms of both, which is extremely abnormal. There is no doubt in my mind these entities have affected your brain waves during sleep and quite possibly during wakefulness. You have all reported your haunting continues for a short while after you wake up. Some of you have even reported having possible hallucinations. Ideally, we should be running a sleep study before and after exposure to the entities, but that is not an option I am willing to consider. Do any of you have any other symptoms to report?" Irena again glanced across the disgruntled showcase of faces.

"I have found no evidence in the literature linking exposure to low frequency electromagnetic radiation with nightmares or night terrors, yet we know your experiences are a side effect of exposure. Ivan, we discussed the possibility that the entities could be doing this to you deliberately out of self-defense. They could have found a way to seriously disrupt your brainwaves, hopefully not permanently, but you were killing them after all. I know this is not the news you want to hear, but I don't have a solution to your sleep problems other than to recommend you all get your hands on a strong sedative and stay well away from those entities. Of course, the timing of all this is disturbing. Your nightmares became exasperated after you created the large entity in the accelerator. Perhaps, Ivan, you were successful at manufacturing your own fallen angel."

Ivan let out a distraught grumble. He thought her comment was absurd, but something inside him told him he shouldn't dismiss it. "Say you're correct, and the large entity that disappeared from the accelerator is responsible for making our nightmares worse, do you think it could have killed Jack?" He wanted to elaborate about his own uneasy feelings surrounding the large entity, but thought he'd refrain.

Disgust eased into Irena's expression, and her tone changed to that of a scolding parent. "I do not know why Jack is dead. I have never heard of nightmares or night terrors causing death, but as you know this is an unusual situation. Ivan, you know how I feel about what you've done. You're way outside of your league here. You tell me what killed Jack. Your guess is as good as mine. As I understand it, the coroner already explained the possibility of SADS to you. Perhaps all of you should take a vacation and get away from here. Get the entities home and then start fresh. Given what happened to Jack, that's what I would be doing."

Ivan's frustration with the *Russian Wolf Hound* had him tapping his desktop to the pace of a woodpecker—blatantly ignoring Kevin's agitated glare. He wasn't getting the answers he wanted, and he heard Irena's hostility festering in the tone of her voice. He wouldn't put it past her to hold back on them as her own way of seeking retribution for what they'd done. *Retribution,* he thought. He felt his own flavor of hostility breaking its barriers—it was black like licorice, and it was new to him. It was as though it was talking to him; telling him that if Irena didn't fix the problem, he'd have to even the score with her. He might have to call on Larry's services yet again. The thought eased his anger enough to continue on an even keel.

"Irena, I appreciate how you feel about this research, but you must understand we're all sitting on pins and needles." He sprung up from his seat and came around to get closer, leaning against the front of his desk with arms crossed and foot tapping. His face was resolute. "Our colleague is dead, and we need some assurance the rest of us aren't going to end up that way."

"It seems to me I have given you solid advice. Get away from here, well away, clear your heads. Close the lab down if you have to. Let the effects of the entities wear off. A change in scenery would be beneficial, and if the large entity is to blame for any of this, distance certainly should help. Unfortunately, we don't know the nature of what you've created in your accelerator, other than it is of opposite charge to originals. Have you scanned for any anomalous electrical fields in the lab? Perhaps you should be looking for it. A bioscanner would be useful for this."

"That would be difficult. The accelerator puts the electric fields in the entire complex through the roof. Section Four has the lowest levels, which is why we stored the entities there in the first place."

"Well a bioscanner would at least let you know if you're in close proximity to it. You could put a few in every room and wait for one to signal."

Ivan scoffed at her preposterous idea. "This is a big facility. The entity would have to be a meter or so away for a bioscanner to signal. We'd need a fifty of them!"

"Well, perhaps you should take the accelerator off line long enough to run some proper scans."

"That's not possible. We're way behind schedule as it is. Enertech would have my head. Besides, we don't even know if it's to blame. We all had nightmares before it was created. They could just be worsening over time."

"If that's what you want to believe. The thing is the opposite of your peaceful entities. If I were you, I'd be starting a full scale witch hunt. For all you know, you could all be in grave danger. I guess you're going to have to decide what's important to you. I suggest you follow my recommendations. After that if you're still having problems, we'll initiate a sleep study. I'm sorry if I'm not telling you what you want to hear, but I think we have hashed this enough. I should be on my way." Irena stood up from her chair. "Let me know what you decide."

Ivan had Pam escort Irena out. The minute they were out of earshot, he sent his fist into the wall, which shot a crushing pain through his hand and left his arm tingling. He went to the window looking for a distraction from his rage and considered his reflection. His eyes bulged as the vision of his pathetic former life came back to him, all weak and simple-minded. He quickly turned to Kevin and Ron who stood at the sidelines, watching his outburst. "Irena's full of deception, I'm sure of it." The two men looked back at him, their expressions boiling with anger and fear like his own.

"We should bring in another person to carry out a sleep study, and this time we'll make damn sure they don't find out that the exposure kills the entities," Kevin said.

Ivan walked over and clapped him on the back. "We think alike my friend."

"What about the large entity? Should we hunt it like she

suggested?" Ron asked.

"Perhaps." Ivan bobbed his head slowly. "Perhaps." He looked Ron in the eyes. "I have something else on my mind right now. I intend to have a talk with Larry. I have a score to settle with that woman, but it will have to wait until he finishes dealing with Weston and Simmons."

Ron smiled. "*We* have a score to settle."

Ron and Kevin left the room. Ivan started back to his desk. The picture hanging behind it was tilted to one side.

Chapter Forty

Dean rolled over in bed and slowly opened his eyes, blinking several times before regaining some focus. The room was dark, but a fine beam of sunlight shone through a crack in the drapes, finding its way to a toppled shoe on the floor. Something sparkled from inside it catching his attention, and he stared blankly at it. His joints ached, and the cold clammy feeling felt very familiar; but he didn't know why. His mouth was sappy, and an earthy scent hung in the air. *Where am I?*

The taint in his mouth revolted him, and he tried spitting it out. A pasty substance caked his tongue. He scraped at it with his fingernail. It was white and gelatinous and he wiped it on the sheets. He struggled to sit up and gazed down at himself. The navy blue robe he had on was damp and parted in the middle exposing his almost naked, goose bump-covered body. A chill shot through him, quivering his shoulders. He heard footsteps, and the door opened, but he didn't turn to look.

"Dean," Laura ran to his side and took his hand. "Dean, can you hear me? Do you know who I am?" She knelt in front of him, and caressed the side of his face. Her touch felt numb, like his face had been frozen. "Please answer."

Laura's voice sounded so caring. Like the voice that used to sing him to sleep. But her words seemed trapped in the whirlpool of confusion Dean was swimming in. Just when he thought he'd bob to the surface for a mind clearing breath, he'd be sucked back down, dazed and spinning. It was as though some part of his conscious was pulling him away from the truth, protecting him.

"Dean, I love you. Please say something!"

This time Laura's words set him atop calm waters. As the fog cleared across the horizon, he became afraid of what he may see; that something horrible lurked there. He looked into Laura's eyes. They were the eyes of an angel, like his mother's, and he felt safe. He cleared his throat. "Water," he barely understood his own word. "Can I…"

"Here you go." Laura took the glass from the bedside table and helped him drink.

"My throat…it's raw."

"Drink more," she said. Dean watched as tears welled up in Laura's eyes, but she was smiling, a joyful kind of smile. "Do you want something hot, soothing?"

"No… Where are we? What's happened to me?"

"We had to give you that drug yesterday and then again early this morning. It saved your life. You're going to be all right."

As Dean sipped on the water, the horrors of the past day started to return. It left him wishing he was still stuck in the whirlpool.

"Do you feel well enough to get up? It's only six-thirty, but you've been sleeping since late yesterday afternoon. Everyone's up already. It was hard for anyone to get any sleep with all the worry for you. What do you think? Do you want to try?"

"Yeah."

Laura took his hand and led him to the washroom. "I've got some clean clothes here for you. They should fit." Dean stopped just inside the door and leaned against the wall. "You okay?"

"My stomach, I…" His throat burned with the rising vomit, and he made a leap for the toilet.

There was a knock on the bedroom door. "Hey, Laura, is everything all right?"

"I think so. He's just sick."

"Who's that?"

"Andy, he's worried."

"I'd kill for a toothbrush."

"Got one right here. That sounds more like you. A shower might make you feel better too…if you're up to it."

Dean brushed his teeth aggressively, being obsessive with every crevice. He repeated the process twice. "I feel disgusting," he mumbled with a gravelly voice. He looked in the mirror. Remnants of the insects provided a clear reminder of the infestation. A fine white crust clung to the stubble on his face and stiffened his ragged hair. "Can you get the shower going for me? Hot. I'd like to try."

"Sure." She ran the water until steam billowed over the door. "I'll just wait in the bedroom."

"No, please. Stay in here with me. I don't want to be alone."

"Don't worry. I'll stay." Laura sat down on the lid of the toilet. "Take your time. I'll hand you a towel when you're done."

Dean showered in a certifiable frenzy, trying to blank out his ghastly memories. His skin still felt as though it was crawling, and he shuddered at his defenselessness. As he showered, his shudders turned to shivers of pleasure, and his thoughts drifted to disbelief that he was still alive and hope of actually getting through this. He had to make things right for Laura, especially after she stood by him through his darkest time.

After half an hour of showering, a shave, and two more sessions with the toothbrush, Dean started to feel more like himself. Laura stayed with him in the bathroom. It had been a long time since someone *took care* of him, and it felt good. She looked to the future with her words and spoke with a happy voice. "We're going to kick their butts." The comment made him laugh.

He towel dried his hair and then took Laura in his arms and held her tight, but he didn't speak. He decided he would never talk about his experience with the rainbow bugs, not ever. He'd just drown it in the whirlpool of his conscious. He didn't like Laura seeing him so vulnerable and tried to hide the emptiness in his eyes. The rainbow bugs had feasted on his soul, but with Laura in his arms he felt almost whole.

"Thank you," he whispered.

The growling of Dean's stomach got Laura moving for the stairs. "Come on. Everyone's anxious to know how you are. I'll make you some breakfast." He started slowly down the stairs, a little shaky on his feet, but picked up the pace when he smelled the coffee.

"Aw, look who's here! Good as new!" Andy's cheery voice had a way of perking up even the most damaged soul. He broke into a huge contagious smile. "You look better. Want some calamander for breakfast? You must be hungry."

John smiled and pulled a barstool out for Dean, beside Andy and Jeff. "I can't believe Andy's bugging you to eat calamander."

"Who said I was bugging him? If he doesn't want that, there's a wormy apple over there."

Dean spun himself around in the seat, plopped his elbows on the counter, and drew a smug expression, trying to look impassive.

Jeff decided to join in the fun. "Hey, Dean, if you squirm a bit in your chair, you'll find it becomes more comfortable."

"Shut up! What's with you people? Don't you have any compassion?" Laura said in a scolding tone.

"It's okay, sweetheart. Dark humor makes the world go round. One of those wormy apples would hit the spot. Andy, do you mind? And maybe a coffee. Haven't had one of those in a while." He cracked a wry smile.

Andy threw an apple from the fruit basket on the counter. "Wouldn't you just kill yourself laughing if he actually found a worm in it?"

"Wouldn't bother me in the least." Dean took a hearty bite and chewed slowly.

"You're going to need more than that. No wonder you're shaky. You've hardly eaten in three days." Laura placed a coffee down in front of Dean and turned to make him some breakfast.

"In all seriousness, Dean, how are you feeling?" John joined Laura in the kitchen across the counter from Dean. "I hate to say this, but we've got a pistol to our heads. I'm surprised we haven't had any other visitors."

"That's an understatement," Dean grumbled. Everyone waited for his answer. He took a sip of coffee. "I remember this going down better." The look on his friends' faces told him they were growing anxious. "That was a hell of a thing." He looked up from his cup. "The pain's all but gone. My throat's sore, but I can suck it up, and I'm hungrier than hell. My only concern is the drug. My head's just starting to clear. When I woke up this morning, I didn't know what planet I was on." He smirked. "Jeff, you said if I don't take it, the pain will come back."

"With vengeance."

"A hell of an incentive, I'd say. Is it going to mess up my head?"

"No, not any more. You should be back to yourself this morning," Jeff said.

"So how often am I going to have to take it?"

"You woke us all up screaming like a banshee just after midnight, and we gave you a dose. That's about twelve hours after the first dose, but I don't know if that's going to define the frequency. I've heard of people having to take it two to three times a day. What I do know is when the pain comes back, it comes back hard and fast. You shouldn't be alone, at least for now. Your body will tell you when you need it. We have enough for three months."

"Christ, three months! I can't spend my life dependent on this; I won't."

"There has to be a way to get you off it." Laura set his breakfast down in front of him.

"Oh, you know the way into a man's heart." Dean started with a forkful of eggs and then moved on to the buttered toast with raspberry jam.

"Dean, I've got a pod booked for early tomorrow morning to get me to Lyra for the morning meetings at the Summit. I was thinking if I could move it up to tonight, you could come along. If you're up to it, that is. Then of course we have to find a way of getting you into the Accelerator. It should be deserted on a Saturday night."

"I'm coming," Laura spouted.

In unison, Dean and John barked, "No."

Dean continued, "Laura it's too dangerous. I won't put you at risk."

"I know my way around the facility. I know where Ivan's and Kevin's offices are, and I know how the computer system works. If we're going to get what we need to clear our names and take down Ivan, you need me. Besides, like Jeff said, you can't be alone."

"Laura, if they catch us, they'll kill us. You know that as well as I do," Dean said.

"And if we're not successful, we're dead too, all of us. I have to go. There's no arguing the point."

John shook his head and smiled. "Dean, once this girl's made up her mind she's going to do something, there's no changing it. She's been that way since she was little. I got her a bike for her sixth birthday. She fell and fell but boy, was she determined. By the end of the day, she was a pro, bruises and all. Anyway, I don't want her to go anymore than you do, but she's right. You're going to want to get in and out of there as fast as you can, and I think you'll need Laura to do it."

Dean looked at Laura with solemn eyes. "I wish to hell you never got involved in this. I don't know what I'd do if something happened to you."

"I'll be fine. I'm a big girl. Besides, I found my way out of there once, so I can do it again. There is one thing though. Door entry is like in the prison. It's all DNA activated. We need to take someone with us who has entry authorization, or at least have some of their DNA."

"Dean seems to have that down pretty good," Andy said tapping his wrist. "By the way that's a sweet watch."

"Thanks. It was a graduation present from my parents. My mom chose it. Anyway I'm not going to lop off someone's hand. That guard was dead."

"This sounds like quite a story," John remarked. "I'm familiar with DNA scanners. They're in my office building, too. They're quite sensitive, but I'm afraid a hairbrush won't do. Like Laura says, you need to take someone with you, which I don't think is going to happen; or you need a large sample of DNA. A piece of skin would do it, or a lot of blood or saliva, but even that's iffy. If you can't get past the scanners, it would be a hell of a task getting in there, and you'd trigger the alarms immediately."

"John, what time do you think you can get us over there?" Dean asked.

"Well that's a trick on its own. I'm sure Matt and Larry are going to be watching me."

"At some point in time, Larry's going to be called over to help with security for the Summit. Maybe Matt, too. I don't know," Dean added.

"That's true, but regardless, the two of you can't exactly walk onto the pod beside me. Here's what I'm thinking…"

John started to recite the details of his plan. His position in the government gave him access to the transportation computer network and also left him with a pod at his disposal for business travel. He would book the pod for a departure of ten o'clock that night. With the Summit starting Sunday morning, space traffic would be heavier than usual. He could log onto the network around eight p.m. and designate the flight delayed until eleven-thirty p.m. The pilots wouldn't show up until just before eleven and presumably neither would Matt or Larry. The pod would be waiting there, and the three of them would arrive at the Draco Port in time for a ten o'clock departure. Once at the Port, he would log back on to the network and update the schedule back to the original departure time, so they would be allowed to take off.

"Dean, when I arrive at the terminal building for a ten o'clock departure, the pilots will not be there. You and Laura can pose as pilots and take their place. All I have to do is steal a couple of pilots' suits, and you can fly it out. Laura can be your co-pilot. There's a special terminal at the Draco Port for government officials. I'll go there to change my flight time in person. I know the terminal well. I'm hoping I can put my hands on the suits when I'm there. We'll dock at the government terminal at the base station, and you'll just walk off."

"Yeah, and how are you going to get those suits? Pretend you're the laundry boy? I don't know that I feel comfortable putting you in this position," Dean said.

"Don't worry about me." John chuckled. "I'll figure it out. People don't tend to question me much."

"Okay, your evil sinister plan sounds good, but what about the DNA?" Jeff asked while taking a bite of apple.

"Well, it seems to me you don't need a whole body part, you just need some skin," Dean said.

"Oh that sounds nice. You're going to skin someone are ya, Dean?" Andy laughed out loud.

"I won't be greedy; I just need a handful. I know where Kevin lives. We can go there after midnight and just take a sample off his back."

John blinked hard a couple of times. "You can't be serious?" he uttered.

"You got a better idea? Don't worry. From what Laura heard at the lab, the bastard's been exposing himself to the entities. He'll likely heal up before I can get a bandage on him. Anyway, I'm not a savage."

"No, of course not." Andy slapped his hands on the counter.

"As I was saying, can you, by any chance, get your hands on a local anesthesia and some bandages? A laser pistol could be used to do the job, but a sharp knife would be preferable."

John reached toward the butcher block to his left and pulled out a long carving knife and stabbed it into the cutting board beside it. The vibration left it gyrating for several seconds.

Dean looked over, wearing a devilish grin. "That ought to do just fine."

"Christ, I can't believe we're even having this conversation." Laura cringed.

"Laura, once you're in the Accelerator, how do you propose you collect the evidence?" John asked.

"I'll go to Kevin's computer. We can use the skin, so the keyboard will pick up his DNA; obviously, we can't use the voice function. We'll get into the system...I'm sure it will be loaded with evidence."

"I hope you're right." John walked over to the wall unit in the family room and pulled out a small device from the drawer. "Here's a data transfer unit. Once everything's downloaded, you can transfer it to me. I'll get a room at the hotel adjacent to the lab and wait for it. I'll book a flight to Lyra early Sunday morning in time to get me there for the meetings. I'm making a presentation on the Draco traffic congestion, and I'll present the evidence to the Heads of State at that time. It will certainly constitute a breach of protocol, but the nature of this justifies it. I'm sure they will be more than receptive to it."

"I like it!" Dean sat up straight and formed a scheming smile.

"I'll leave early this afternoon," John said. "Set the ball in motion. In the meantime, we'd better clean this place up. I'd hardly be able to claim I didn't have guests right now. And Andy, when we leave, you and Jeff are going to have to lay low and keep a keen ear out for intruders."

Chapter Forty-One

"I'll be back as quick as I can. You two should get some rest. It's going to be a long night." John went out to his car, and moments later pulled out of the driveway.

"He's right. The two of you should get some rest, especially you Dean," Andy said.

"Right-O, Mom," Dean said.

"Come on, they're right. We're going to be up all night." Laura marched Dean up the stairs into their bedroom and shut the door behind them. The room was dark. "I changed the bed sheets. They were kinda…"

Dean seized her around the waist and spun her around, meeting her lips with his. His lips were soft and sweet and made her breathless.

She brought him in close tasting the inside of his mouth. A hint of the morning apple remained, and their pent up passion melted away the inches between them. He pulled his lips away making his way to her cheek, kissing and whispering, "I love you with all my heart."

"I love you, too." Laura's voice was quiet and broken, and she gasped as she felt the soothing motion of his warm hand making its way toward her breast. A wave of passion passed through her abdomen as she felt his masculinity start to erupt. He found her lips again, pressing so hard their teeth knocked together with an awkward bump. They both giggled.

"Come here," he whispered as he led her to the side of the bed, pushing the covers aside. "I want to look at you. Feel your beauty." He pulled her shirt off and clumsily fiddled with her bra before snapping it free. "Sorry." A shy blush came over his face, making her smile. He brought his hand to her breast, and she shut her eyes and threw her head back in ecstasy. She reached for his shirt, inching it off him, not wanting to lose his touch. As she felt his bare skin against hers, her nipples became electrified. She reached for the button of his pants, but he stopped her. "Not yet." He kissed her with unearthly passion.

Her legs jittered with weakness as desire overcame her. He edged downward, tasting her firm breast, caressing her soft skin. She held his head close, looking down with eyes wide, kissing his hair. The faint fragrance of flowers sweetened her nostrils, but quickly slipped away as he descended lower loosening her pants. He gently removed them and placed his strong hands on her thighs while sensually kissing her stomach. His passion left her motionless, helpless under his spell.

"I want you," she whispered.

He returned for a kiss, and feeling delirious with desire, she went back to his pants. He inched back giving her room and shuddered at her touch. He struggled to quickly remove his pants then lay her down on the bed. They were motionless for a moment, admiring each other's silhouettes, savoring their hunger. Dean went to her side, wrapping his arms around her, parting her throbbing limbs. She pulled him on top of her, feeling his strength come down on her. He kissed her neck as her thighs parted, and she shut her eyes to heighten her senses. She soon felt overwhelming pleasure, and she made a subtle groan as they became one. They moved in unison like a well rehearsed orchestra. The piece played out to perfection, and the finale had triumphant emotion reminiscent of the end of Beethoven's "Fifth." The orchestra fell silent, and Dean rolled to the side, cuddling and holding Laura close. She made the sound of a soft purr as she nestled in with her head on his chest.

Dean decided to break their silence. "Laura, when this is over, I want us to be together. I don't care what I'm doing as long as I'm with you."

"I want that, too. We've come so far. It's like a dream, but I'm so scared. I don't want to lose you, and I'm scared about tonight. What if they catch us?"

"Shhh… We've waited so long to lie here together, let's talk about good things. Where we'll go? What we'll do? I'll go anywhere with you."

"But what about your job? I bet they'll offer it back to you," Laura said.

"They couldn't pay me enough to do that now. It's funny, all I used to care about was my career, and when my whole life went to hell, that's the last thing I thought about. It's the people in your life who matter. I had a blind set of values. No wonder Karen cheated on me. Half the time, I was never there. Off working, worrying about getting ahead. If I was half the person I am now, I bet that never would've happened. I should've been there to stop them. She's dead because of me."

"You know that's not true. You're not responsible."

"I was so angry. I never had a chance to apologize."

"Did you still love her?"

"I was too hurt to know. But I feel guilty. She's dead, and I'm passionately in love. I never felt this way with her. You and I...we're different." Dean kissed the top of her head.

"You can't feel guilty about these things. All you can do is try to remember the good things about her. That's what keeps people alive in our memories even when they're gone. Every day you have to think one happy thought about them, and they'll live on. Annie, too, and your friend, Roger. Not to mention your mom. Just one happy thought."

"You're amazing. You know that?" He gave her a squeeze. "Right now, all I want to think about is us. Going away somewhere safe. We don't need much. Just a simple life would do as long as we're together. What do you want to do?"

"I want you to meet my family. Well you've met Uncle John. I think he likes you. You'd love them, especially my brother. You remind me of him a bit. He's a thrill seeker like you. I'm really lucky; I have a great family."

"So you gonna go kayaking with me? If you can handle hours in a cold shower, you can handle that."

"Well, I'm more likely to go kayaking than sky dive with Kyle. Back home, I used to surf, but that was a long time ago. I'd give it a try. But nothing crazy to start."

"Just some three meter standing waves," he teased. Dean started to twitch. He shifted his weight, disturbing Laura's position. She pushed herself up to look at him. "Dean you're holding your breath. Are you okay?"

"I don't know… Maybe not."

Laura sprung out of bed and grabbed his boxers. "Here put these on." He fumbled a bit getting them on, and she helped him and then scrambled to get dressed. By the time she finished, he was convulsing.

"Shit!" She ran for the door. "Jeff, get up here now! It's Dean...hurry."

Seconds later, Jeff arrived with a small leather case. He sat on the side of the bed and grabbed Dean's arm. "Laura, I'll hold his arm steady. You do it."

"No, Jeff you...hurry."

"And what about tonight? What will you do then? Come on. I showed you how; just do it."

Dean's pain was escalating, and with shaky hands, Laura removed the syringe from the leather case and measured out the right amount of drug from the vial. Jeff continued to hold Dean's arm steady as she tied the tourniquet tight and got herself positioned to administer the fluid. "What if I miss the vein?"

"Just give it a second. Look right there; it's already bulging."

With great trepidation, Laura held her breath, cringing and hesitantly pushed the needle into his arm. He let out a loud moan before the pain subsided.

"There you go; you did great."

Laura took Dean's hand and with a fearful expression spoke to him. "I just want this to be over."

Dean squeezed her. "Just one more day." He spoke in a faint whisper as his head flopped to the side.

The incident seemed to have tired him out. Laura lay back down beside him, and the two of them slept.

Chapter Forty-Two

Dean finished straightening Laura's necktie for her, and she shrugged on her blazer then nudged the knot loose. "I don't know how you wear these stupid things. They're choking."

"Oh, and high heels make sense. Anyway, I might have to let you sit in the pilot's seat. You look very official," Dean said.

"How are the shoes?" John asked.

"Not bad. Good choice and not too high." Laura smiled as she smoothed out her skirt.

Once Dean was satisfied Laura looked like an official aviator, he raised his brow at John. "So you going to tell us how you got your hands on these blazers and the I.D?"

"I.D.'s fake. Don't tell anyone. As for the pilot blazers, I'm a common thief. The rest of the stuff was a quick trip to the local department store. You're lucky. I usually only go to the place for ten minutes on Christmas Eve."

Dean laughed. "Takes me five minutes."

"Let's go through this stuff and make sure you have everything." The kitchen counter was a chaotic mess cluttered with weapons, flashlights, ropes, and medical supplies.

Jeff interrupted, "Number one on your list is this." He handed Dean the small leather case. "It has a clip on it. You can attach it to your belt. Remember, you won't have me to come bounding to your rescue. Inside, there's a tourniquet, two syringes, antiseptic wipes, and two vials...enough for three days. Don't lose it!" He patted a small bag on the counter. "There's extra in here you can put in the duffle bag, and I gave some to John."

Dean clipped the small leather kit to his belt and riffled through the rest of the items. He put the data transfer unit in his pocket then John handed him two portable communication devices (PCDs).

"With your implants deactivated, you'll need these. One's for Laura. You both know my implant number. As soon as you transfer the data, get out of there. If you don't make it to my hotel room within an hour of sending the download, I'm going to assume you've been caught, and I'll go to the authorities."

"No...too risky. We don't know who's involved. Even if you called Matt, I'm sure Larry will have someone watching him after he goes to the Summit. You'd both end up dead. Stick to your original plan and get it to the Summit. I'm sure the planetary governments will be interested to know we've been slaughtering the only intelligent life ever found. What's this?" Dean lifted a blue plastic tube off the counter.

"It's a topical anesthesia, and here's an exacto knife and some bandages," John said.

"You're kidding me right? What am I supposed to do, spray this stuff on his skin then strip it off like filleting a fish?"

"Well, it was the best I could do. You were in the military. Can't you knock him out?"

"I'll figure something out." Dean cringed at the thought. "Strange I should even care after what they've done."

"Dean, how are we going to get into Kevin's apartment?" Laura asked.

"I saw Larry write down his security code when he escorted us to the prison. I know the override sequence. It's the same as on Eagle." Dean turned toward John. "Thanks for this stuff. You've put yourself at risk. Thanks for everything. Honestly, I don't know what we would've done without your help. I owe you my life."

"You're not going to get all sappy on us are ya, Dean?" Andy said.

Dean laughed as he filled up the small duffle bag. He wedged the laser pistol in the back of his pants, covering it with his jacket, then checked his watch. "We gotta go."

"As soon as we arrive at the Draco Port, I'll go on my computer and change the flight time back to ten p.m. I'll open a line of communication with you on your PCD. Just listen, and you'll know when to come in to the terminal building."

"Dean, do you think the authorities are watching John? You might be followed to the Draco Port," Andy said.

"It's possible, but the fact no one else has come by suggests Larry and Matt are operating this lead on their own. I doubt they even told the marshal's office about John. If they did, they would have had a search warrant. Larry's not going to want us apprehended unless he's present because he'll be afraid we'll talk. That's probably why he's working with Matt. Matt hates me and will be highly motivated to find me. Of course, the other thing I'm worried about is what he intends to do with Matt. Escaping from prison was likely a breach of our agreement, and Matt's life could well be in jeopardy. I have no doubt Ivan wouldn't hesitate to carry out his threat."

"Maybe Matt has another motive. Weren't the two of you best friends?" Andy asked. "Knowing you, he must question all of this."

Dean stopped what he was doing and stared across the room for a moment with a sober expression. He remembered all the good times the two of them had together. Theirs was a friendship meant to last. Even his divorce couldn't shake its *stone* foundations. They shared the same sense of humor and love of practical jokes; they had a history. He'd tried to bury the negative energy he felt when he looked Matt in the eye and told him he'd killed Karen, but the truth was a part of him died that day. He was so sure Matt would somehow see through the deception—know he could never have done such a thing. That was the kind of friend he was, or he thought he was. *The stone had crumbled to sand.* Now Matt wanted him dead, and it left him with a deep rooted feeling of betrayal. His friend had let him down, and it left him questioning his own character. How could someone so close think he was capable of such a thing?

"I tried to hint some sense into him when he was here," John uttered.

"Anyway, it doesn't matter anymore. I'm way beyond worrying about what people think of me," Dean lied. "We're just going to have to watch our asses out there. With any luck, Larry's already at the Summit, and if I run into Matt, hopefully I'll have time to tell him the truth before he burns a hole through my head." Dean zipped the bag shut with a jerked motion. "Let's get this done. You two keep a low profile."

Andy and Jeff wished them luck as they headed to the 2299 BMW M5 parked in the garage. The corners of Dean's mouth shot up like rockets as he admired the well appointed vehicle. He hopped into the driver's seat, hunkering down at the wheel.

John stood by the door. "You look like a kid in a candy store."

"How's the ride?"

"Smooth and fast, but there's nowhere to go on Draco. Really it's a waste, but we need our toys. I guess it's my kayak."

Dean had an overwhelming urge to turn on the ignition and tear out the drive, the car screeching as he took the corner. He loved toys—the bigger, the better. He looked at John and his grin soured. "Let me guess. We're riding in the trunk."

"Likely a good idea." He clapped him on the shoulder. "Come visit when this is finished, and I'll let you take it for a spin."

"I'll hold you to that."

Laura and Dean squeezed into the trunk, and they were off. John floored it, seemingly intent on turning the twenty-minute drive into fifteen. The stuffiness of the small trunk made it a daunting journey for both of them, a reminder of the skeletons that lay in their closets. "It won't take long," Dean said as he held Laura close, his own hands trembling. They traveled silently the rest of the way, and both sighed in relief when the car came to a stop.

* * * *

John was careful to park behind the government terminal building, away from any other vehicles and pulled out his computer to change the departure time back to ten p.m. He grabbed his luggage off the seat, hit the trunk release, and then placed a call to Dean's PCD. He walked to the terminal building as he spoke. "Dean, I'll keep this communication open. You'll know when it's safe to come out. There's no sign of Larry or Matt."

"Hi, Marie, they have you on the late shift do they?"

"Off at eleven," she replied with a smile. "I'm sorry Mr. Becker, your flight's delayed. You should have received a call."

"Oh, you're kidding. What's the departure time?"

She checked her screen. "Oh, that's odd. It's on time now. Ten o'clock as originally scheduled. I hope the pilots were updated." She glanced back at her monitor. "Frank Cameron and Don Weatherly are in the schedule. Maybe I should call them."

"Give them a couple of minutes. I'm sure they'll check the schedule."

The glass doors at the front of the terminal building swung open, and Dean and Laura walked in heading straight toward the desk where John was standing. "Hi, there; I'm Will Chambers. I got a call from Frank a short while ago, and he asked us to cover for his ten o'clock. Some confusion with scheduling. Anyway, as I understand it we're to fly a Mr. John Becker to the Lyra Base Station."

"I'm Becker. I was a little worried for a minute." John gestured toward the desk. "Marie here thought the pilots might not have received the update."

"You know Frank...he doesn't miss a beat. With the schedule changes, we did a little trade off. I hope you don't mind. This is my co-pilot Kim Welling."

"Nice to meet you, Kim. Well, shall we be on our way? I'm anxious to get there. I have an early morning flight to Lyra."

Marie smiled. "The pod's waiting for you. Have a nice flight, Mr. Becker."

"Thanks, Marie."

* * * *

Matt and Larry pulled up to the spaceport and took long, fast strides to the terminal building. Larry burst through the door first and called to the woman at the desk. "Has Mr. Becker taken off yet? His flight time was delayed until eleven-thirty, but now I see it's on time."

"Yes, it was, right on time. Can I help you with something?"

"Did he have anyone with him...a man about my height and a blonde woman, both around their mid thirties?" Larry asked.

"No, he was flying alone. He was on his way to the Summit."

A relief, but he still needed to find them! Ivan was on his case, and he had little time for this nonsense. Larry smiled some charm at the woman. "I need to speak to the pilot. Can you get me in touch with the pilot?"

The doors of the terminal swung open, and two pilots walked in. "Hey Marie, sorry we're late. That was quite a rollercoaster of schedule changes. We got here as fast as we could. Is Mr. Becker here yet?"

Marie stared at Frank and Don dumbfounded, her gaze alternating between them. "Becker took off fifteen minutes ago with two other pilots...a Will Chambers and Kim Welling. Chambers told me after the schedule mix-up, you called him and arranged a trade off."

"I did no such thing! I've never even heard of those people," Frank said.

"Damn it!" Matt yelled. "Those pilots, they're wanted—"

"That's enough," Larry snapped. *Leave it to Jenkins to start shooting off his half-Chinese mouth!* "Come on." He grabbed Matt's arm and pulled him toward the door, extending him a scathing look as they passed through it. "You idiot! You want them to call the marshal's office? We have no authority here. They'll have our heads for this. Don't you understand? This is over. I have a flight to Lyra in two hours, but I can call my security people and have them waiting. As soon as they dock at the spaceport, they'll take them into custody."

"You're right. They're trapped. If I catch the next flight there, I'll be right behind them," Matt said.

"My people will handle this. The Lyra Base Station is my jurisdiction. They'll be back in prison by morning."

"I'm seeing this through to the end. I'll just walk to the main terminal from here. Please call me as soon as your people have apprehended them and let them know I'm coming." Matt turned his back and was off.

With nostrils flaring, Larry reached for his pistol and aimed it at Matt. He was already some distance away, but the targeting system would ensure a clean hit. Just as he was about to pull the trigger, the pilot and co-pilot exited the terminal building. Larry concealed the weapon, ran to his vehicle, and got in the driver's seat, slamming the door behind him. He pounded his fists on the dash and screamed. "You fucking bastards!"

The ferocious animal inside him was beating its way out, making his head feel like it was splitting in two. He took a couple of deep breaths before placing a call to Ivan. "Weston and Simmons are on their way to the base station in a pod with Becker. It's ten-thirty now, and they're expected to dock at the spaceport in forty-five minutes. You've got to get Ron on this. I have no choice but to go to Lyra tonight. I can't help you, and if I have my security people apprehend them on their arrival, they'll likely tell them the truth. Our threats haven't stopped them so far. It gets worse. Jenkins is catching the next flight there. I couldn't stop him, but he has no idea what's going on. He's vindictive as hell and wants Weston dead."

"You moron! How could you have let this happen? I told you to take care of Jenkins. Do you understand what'll happen if this gets out?"

Larry's ear started to ring from the volume. "I was about to take him out, but then I had company; and I'm well aware of what will happen if he gets to Weston! Look Ivan, they have no evidence. My guess is they're heading back to the Accelerator."

"Your guess. That's a hell of a thing to go on."

"Think about it, what else could they possibly be up to? They want to expose this whole thing, and they need evidence. They'll go there, and you and Ron will be waiting. They don't have entry authorization, so they'll look for a way to break through the security and walk right into your hands. Ron's a capable man. You need to find out who they told about your operation, then blow them out an airlock, and be finished with them."

"And Becker?"

"I'll take care of Becker. He's on the attendance list for the Summit, so I'll be well positioned to keep an eye on him. It's up to you and Ron to stop Weston and Simmons from securing any evidence. Without it, Becker's story will sound crazy; but if he tries to talk, I'll take him out. Just wait with Ron and let them walk into the trap. Trust me this will work."

"I'm at the Accelerator already. I can't sleep at home. I'll call Ron and get him here stat."

Chapter Forty-Three

Dean checked over his shoulder as they made their final approach to Kevin's apartment. There were surprisingly few people around for just after twelve on a Saturday night. *A real happening neighborhood!* He worked at the door lock. "Bingo," he whispered. Before going inside, he took a moment to adjust the setting of the laser pistol for a nonfatal injury. "I'm not looking forward to this. It sounded better as a diabolical plan. I worked with Kevin for a long time. He was my friend."

Laura met his hesitation with some words of encouragement. "I heard him plotting this whole thing with Ivan. If you were there, you may not feel so—"

He gently pressed his finger to her lips. "I know, but it doesn't justify this. This is barbaric."

With foreboding anxiety, he inched the door open only enough to poke his head through. The apartment was brightly lit, and he stopped to listen. *What a mess.* There was no sound. He listened a few more seconds before deciding to continue. Once they were inside, he shut the door, leaving it slightly ajar to avoid the *heart pounding* click of the lock engaging. He put the bag down and signaled Laura to stay by the door.

With a firm grip on the pistol, he moved room to room looking for any sign of life. The apartment was a shambles and remnants of the evening's dinner lay strewn across the kitchen counter, like a dog's breakfast. It was unrecognizable but for the smell of tomato sauce. He started down the hallway toward the bedroom. As he crept something cracked under his shoe. He cringed as he looked down to find broken glass ground into the green carpet. *Damn it!*

The shards were reflective like pieces of a mirror. He froze for a moment and listened.

Nothing.

He followed the gleaming trail to the powder room on the left. The mirror appeared to have been attacked by a blunt object. The gaping hole in its middle had cracks radiating outward like a sunburst and debris blanketed the entire room like new fallen snow. *What the hell happened here?*

He continued tiptoeing across the miniature obstacle course until he was a meter from the bedroom. The door was half open, and he stayed close to the wall preparing to close in on his prey. *He better be in there.*

As he took another step, the door burst open, and there was Kevin, standing half naked, swinging a baseball bat on a path toward Dean's head. Dean instinctively ducked. The bat smashed into the wall making an enormous thud. As Dean straightened himself up, the bat was on its way back. It hit him in the side, knocking the pistol out of his hand. His body ricocheted off the wall, making the sound of a blown out tire; and then he launched himself at Kevin, tackling him at the waist. The two men crashed to the floor, crunching the bits of glass beneath them. Kevin winced.

Dean pounded his fist into Kevin's jaw, while at the same time receiving a sturdy punch to his injured side. It knocked the wind out of him, giving Kevin a chance to make for the pistol. Dean kicked it further away just as Laura rounded the corner. "The pistol...get it!"

Kevin started to leap for it, but Dean took him down with a swing across the back of his knees with the bat. Kevin landed on his belly with his hand inches away from the pistol. Laura kicked the pistol away and scooped it up, aiming it at his head with a steady hand.

Dean swung around and got to his feet and then pounded his fist into Kevin's head one more time, knocking him senseless. "Get the bag." He set his weight on Kevin's back holding his arms behind him until Laura returned. "The ropes," he uttered, razor-edged on adrenaline. She handed them to him, and he bound Kevin's arms behind him with the prowess of a rodeo cattle roper.

Dean got to his feet and dragged Kevin to the living room. One more blow to the back of his head rendered him unconscious. "Get me some gloves and the knife."

Laura started riffling through the bag, her hand shaking. "Got it." She pulled it out of the bag with a firm grip of the textured metal handle and handed it to Dean. "He's got a hairy back," she said.

"Not for long." Dean put the gloves on and then took the knife and made the incision, carving a perfect rectangle. He then worked at the flesh as if filleting a fish. He continued to work, stretching the free layer while carving the tissue underneath. The skin pulled away from the body and left a deep pink under-layer exposed to the air.

Laura backed away. "I think I'm going to be sick."

Dean finished off with surgical precision and slapped the piece of flesh on Kevin's shoulder.

"What do we do with it?" Laura asked.

"Good question." Dean scanned the room and then focused on the desk to his left. A four by six inch picture frame stood upright on the tabletop displaying a picture of Ivan and Kevin. It looked like it was shot at a New Year's Eve party. He grabbed the frame and removed its backing, tossing the picture aside. After searching through a couple of drawers, he found a stapler and stapled the skin to the backing. He reassembled the frame with the skin pressed against the glass front. "Here put this in the bag."

Laura looked at him in awe and followed his instructions.

"We need to bandage this up."

"Dean you were right. He's already showing signs of healing."

"Yeah, and I bet he'll be coming around soon. Let's bandage it up quickly and get out of here."

Laura passed him the antibiotic spray and bandages. Kevin started to stir. Dean turned his attention to the restraints. He brought Kevin's legs up to meet his hands and bound them together like a hog-tied animal, something disturbingly familiar to him.

"Isn't that a little much?" Laura murmured.

"Yeah. Well, at least he's not going to be spending eight hours in a bug nest."

Laura looked at Dean and kept silent. A minute later, Dean had the wound dressed. He ran to the powder room and scrubbed his hands. Laura followed with some gauze and the antibacterial spray.

"Dean, your forehead's bleeding from the broken glass. She dabbed at it with the gauze and gave it a quick squirt."

"Thanks; sorry, you had to see this."

"It's okay." She seemed slightly reserved. "Dean, as soon as he wakes up, he's going to call Ivan. They'll know we're coming."

"God, you're right." The relief he felt upon finishing the task instantly evaporated. "I'm going to have to remove his implant. Damn it, I feel like a butcher."

Dean returned to Kevin's side. He was starting to struggle ever so slightly. Dean gave him one more blow, shutting him down. He turned Kevin's head to one side and started inspecting his ear for a small protrusion. "If you thought his back was nasty you ought to have a look at this ear. He's like a damn hobbit. No wonder he smashed that mirror." Dean took the tip of the knife and carefully pried the implant free and then dabbed at the injury with some gauze. He returned to the powder room, flushed it, then washed up again.

Laura packed up the duffle bag, and they left.

Chapter Forty-Four

Pam's arm flung to the side knocking over the water glass. It crashed to the floor, but she didn't wake. She thrashed to one side heaving the blankets off her, exposing her long slender legs. One of them kicked as she made a squeal like a baby pig. "No." It was a garbled whisper, and her lips hardly moved. Her entire body shuddered, and an anguished look exploded on her face. "No." She struggled to say the word as if someone had their hand over her mouth. She kicked some more as she hurled the pillow to the floor. Her eyes opened, glazed over with fear. She stared as if frozen in a fit of panic then her lids fell shut. She lay peacefully for several minutes then it started.

Her fingernails met her face with a scratch. At first it was a gentle itch as if whisking away a fly, but then it intensified. Soon she was clawing at herself as though she was freeing herself from cement armor. She worked her sharp nails hard, peeling away layer after layer trying to break free of the monstrous burden. The gouges became deep as the long claws dug further into her flesh. Blood trickled down her neck staining the gold crucifix that lay delicately on her chest, but she continued to dig deeper and deeper.

* * * *

Pam woke with a shrill scream. She opened her eyes wide, stunned and panicked, and scanned the room like an animal ravaged and left for dead. Someone was whispering. She listened, but it was too faint to make out the words. Then it hit her—a stabbing, burning pain like a hot poker being rammed into her face. Terrified, she looked down at her hands. The bloodied claws had pieces of flesh trapped under the nails. She stretched out her hands and screamed.

Pam stumbled to the bathroom with legs so weak they could hardly carry her. She looked in the mirror, and a monster stared back. It was bloodied and deformed and had the yellow-orange eyes of a demon. She heard a clunk. Out of the corner of her eye, she watched as a can of hairspray rolled across the floor. She shuddered at the sound of another whisper.

"Who's there," she whimpered.

It sounded again, like a muffled echo.

She covered her ears. "Stop that! Who's there?"

"He did this to you." The whisper was barely audible.

"Leave me alone!" She shrieked. She stepped back from the mirror, but the monster didn't move. Its fucked up eyes looked at her with the intensity of a forest fire beaming from them—an all-encompassing fire, the kind that never goes out. Its piercing glow shot through her soul, and then it started to speak; this time not in a whisper. *Retribution* it told her, and she ran from the room.

She quickly dressed in some jeans, a T-shirt, and her stilettos from the day before. She ran to the kitchen and reached for the long carving knife angled in the butcher block and fled her apartment. She knew just where to find him.

Chapter Forty-Five

Ivan paced his office waiting for Ron's arrival, the intensity of his anger driving him back and forth in perpetual motion. Fatigue was setting in, and he shook some alertness back into himself like a wet dog. Stifling a yawn, he made for the washroom. *Some cool water should help.*

He went to the sink and ran the water fast, being careful to toss his silk tie around to his back. The water was invigorating, and he splashed his face several times then cupped his hands for a sip. It tasted thick and pasty, like blood. He spit it back out and watched with bewilderment as the clear fluid bubbled and swirled down the drain. *What the hell's wrong with me?*

He looked in the mirror. Except for the puffy bags protruding from the base of his eyes, he looked fine. He gave them a rub and smoothed out his few ragged brow hairs until he was satisfied. He watched as the last bit of water gathered on the tip of his nose and dripped down into the basin. A passing shadow caught his attention, and he jerked his head to the left. There was nothing. Dismissing his distraught imagination, he went for one more splash before turning off the flow.

A dark finished woodbin sat in the corner, stacked with a mountain of carefully rolled hand towels, just like you'd expect to see at a fancy country club. Ivan reached for a roll, gave it a shake, and just as he was about to bury his face in it, he heard a faint voice—a child's voice. He recognized it—it wasn't the first time it had come calling. He froze and listened. Slowly he started to scan the room. Inch by inch, sections of it entered his peripherals: the marble counter top, the white porcelain sinks, the wood framed mirrors, and the reflections of the pot lights. He squinted as he examined the stall doors for movement. "Ron, you in here?"

There was no response.

He turned his attention back to his towel, and just as he lowered his face into it, a vigorous tug to his necktie hurled him backward. The jolt pulled him off balance, and he stumbled back several steps before hitting the floor. A sharp blow to the side of his head immediately followed. The kick only startled him, and he spun around just in time to catch the blinding reflection of light off a silver blade heading toward his chest. The hand controlling the blade was dainty and discolored with long polished nails.

Ivan blocked the path of the knife, hitting the assailant mid-forearm. The knife went flying across the room before landing with the spinning motion of a twister. Ivan watched in astonishment as Pam darted for it. He barely recognized her scabbed, bloodied face as she scurried past him like a crazed animal. He jumped to his feet and spoke sternly. "Pam what happened to you? What are you doing? Have you lost your mind?"

She spun around, knife in hand, poking it toward him repeatedly like a cattle prod. "Look what you did to me you bastard!" Her high pitched screeching sounded shrill enough to shatter the mirrors on the walls. "Look!" she wailed.

Pam held her arms out for Ivan to behold; her hands were bathed in blood, and her ashen face was striated with deep fleshy groves crusted in scabs. Even more horrific were her eyes. They were eyes of the wolf in his picture, paralyzing eyes that stare right through you. The monster in front of him seemed dauntingly familiar, but he couldn't quite put his finger on why. The child's voice sound again, and it came to him from the depths of his conscious. She reminded him of the woman in his nightmares, the one with plumes of red swimming about her head, the one pulling him into the abyss. He wanted to turn and run, but Pam's eyes held him captive. "I'll kill you for this. You son of a bitch, I'll kill you!"

She launched at him, wielding the blade like a ninja. The attack shook Ivan free from his invisible chains. He retaliated with a clumsy roundhouse kick sending Pam flying to the floor, knocking the shoes off her feet. The trajectory of the knife landed it out of sight in a stall. Pam snarled as she scrambled along the floor back toward Ivan. *She wasn't the wolf—she was a hell hound.*

She arched her back as she lashed out for his leg, pulling him to the floor. Fighting her way to his face with arms flailing, she formed her hands into sharp claws and started for his eyes. Ivan exploded like a wall of flames, knocking her away before he landed his hand on one of her shoes. In a demented fit, he drove the needle sharp heel toward her head repeatedly with the power of a jackhammer. Her hair became entangled in the clasp of the shoe with each plunge. Blood inched its way up the heel to the sole until finally the crunching of bone left her motionless. Ivan's hacking slowed to a stop, and he backed off. He stared at the slaughtered beast in a demented trance. His grip on the shoe loosened, and it fell to the floor along with a web of bloodied auburn hair.

* * * *

Dean walked up to the main door to the accelerator complex inside reception. Laura was at his side, clutching his arm with a nervous grip. In the dim lighting, the reception area reminded Dean of an old museum hall, the kind with a sarcophagus laid out exactly dead center. The holographic displays of the great physicists had a ghostly appearance that made them look like they might spring to life. *Attack of the zombie physicists.* Dean checked over his shoulder to make sure his zombie friends were the only ones watching and then pulled the picture frame out of the bag. Blood oozed from the outside corner of the glass. Dean held the frame by its backing and waved it across the scanner. The door opened.

Laura pointed down the long hallway to a central office area. "This way."

They continued to a set of stairs and finally a large industrial corridor. There was a cart parked in an alcove, and they commandeered it.

"Kevin's office is in the Control Room in Section Three," Laura said. "There's another alcove across from it where you can park the cart."

Dean stepped on the accelerator with a heavy foot, and they reached their destination in just over two minutes. He whispered, motioning to Section Four, "Is that where the entities are kept?"

"Yes. They have a large containment unit in there."

Dean glanced toward the door as though he was looking across a battlefield. A sickened feeling came over him as he recalled the insistent pleading of the beautiful entities as they begged to be left alone on Spectra. Even through the doors, he could sense their presence. Dean handed the frame to Laura and put a firm hand on the laser pistol.

"You don't think there's anyone in there do you?" she whispered.

"I hope not. Let's go."

Laura waved the frame, and the door opened. The Control Room appeared deserted, but they entered with caution. Dean searched room by room to make sure it was vacant.

"His terminal is on the desk over there." Laura signaled to the right and whispered, "Hurry, Dean."

He set the bag down on the floor and put on another pair of gloves, before taking the frame from Laura. "You said the keyboard will recognize his DNA and allow us entry into the system."

"It recognizes the DNA after you're logged in. You can log in by pressing some of the skin to the side of the monitor." Laura pointed to the spot. "Work fast. Like I told you before, the security system does a DNA scan every ten minutes, and I can't remember whether or not Ron said it would signify intruders. I assume it would. Who knows whether this frame has enough DNA in it for the security system to recognize Kevin as actually being in the room."

Dean handed the data transfer unit to Laura before taking apart the frame then slipped his fingertips underneath the skin, moistening them. They came out slightly sticky and bloody. He reassembled the frame then sat down at the desk and logged in.

"It's working, look we've got access to his directory." As each file came up on the screen he scanned for anything, making reference to the entities or themselves. "There's so much here. There's got to be something that stands out." He kept searching. "Maybe it would be better if we were in Ivan's directory."

"There's got to be something. Maybe you should just download everything, and we can go through it back at the hotel. We can't be in here long."

"Good idea. Then let's head to Section Four. At a minimum, we can get some pictures."

Laura put the transfer unit in place and initiated the download. Dean slipped the frame back into the bag and removed his gloves. They both stared impatiently at the screen, waiting.

* * * *

Ivan heaved Pam's slender body over his shoulder and headed for his office. He'd taken a few minutes to clear enough room for her in his storage closest, and he figured she could accompany Dean and Laura out the airlock when the time came. His legs shook like an elderly man as he walked. She was heavier than she looked, likely from all her Yoga, but he also acknowledged the ordeal had weakened him. *Perhaps an adrenaline hangover.*

The space he cleared was just big enough, and he set her down in a sitting position with her head leaning against the back wall. Her eyes were open. The fire in them was out; he saw to that, but the coal black pupils that remained still possessed a paralyzing stare. They seemed to watch him as he set about his business, following his every move. He wanted to shut them but was afraid to get close to her, half anticipating she'd lash back at him. He kept his distance and removed his soiled shirt, changing into a crisp one from the closet. *Another tie destroyed.* He tossed the shirt on the floor of the closet beside the stiletto shoes.

As he was doing up the last few buttons on his shirt, he saw something move out of the corner of his eye. Taking a sudden leap back, he yelped. He jerked his head toward the picture of the wolf as his heart hammered in his chest. The picture slipped to an angled position and swung like a pendulum for a couple of seconds before coming to rest. His eyes narrowed to slits, as he stared in disbelief of what he was sure he'd just seen. The wolf had come alive with glowing eyes and had leaped toward the fox, sinking its jowls into its small furry neck.

"Ivan, what the hell are you doing in here? Aren't you supposed to be keeping watch for Weston and Simmons?"

Ivan jerked his head toward Ron's voice and then slammed the closet door shut with his foot.

"For Christ sake, I got here as fast as I could. What are you doing? Have there been any security alerts?"

"No, not that I know of."

Ron stomped to Ivan's desk and logged onto the security network. "You're lucky. No sign of an intrusion, but Kevin's here."

"What the hell's he doing here?"

"He arrived a short while ago. The scans are just updating. Just a second, he's in the Control Room. Wait a minute. Son of a bitch! There's one unidentified person in there with him and...Laura Simmons. Shit! Come on."

Ron took the lead tearing out of the office to the stairwell. When they arrived in the corridor, there was no cart, so the two of them sprinted at full speed. It was a seven-minute dash to Section Three, and Ron pulled his weapon, ready to fire upon entering.

* * * *

Dean checked his watch. "Damn it this is taking a long time. We can't transfer the data until it's fully downloaded. There's too many—"

The door flew open, and Ron exploded into the room with his arms fully extended and the laser pistol carefully aimed. Dean had his pistol arm already half extended by the time he heard Ron scream, "Drop it Weston! Do it, or she's dead."

Dean froze and stared at the pistol aimed at Laura's head. His pistol wavered for a moment before he loosened his grip, letting it fall to the floor. His heart seemed to stop as a pall of defeat fell over him.

Ivan scooped up the pistol from the floor and removed the data transfer unit from the side of the screen seconds before the transfer was about to begin. He turned and swung his fist into Dean's jaw, sending him flying to the floor. "Aren't you supposed to be dead? We should've just killed you when we had the chance." His voice reeked of bitterness.

"Where's Kevin? What did you do with Kevin?" Ron barked.

Dean got to his feet. "You let us go, and I'll give you Kevin."

Ron cracked a half grin. "You really think you're in a position to bargain with me; and do you really think I give a crap about him? He can rot in hell for all I care." Ron's gaze drifted to the open bag. The picture frame jutted out the top. He reached for it.

"I think it's a good picture of him wouldn't you say. He's got kind of a blank look on his face though." Dean spoke without expression.

Ron picked up the bag. "Move it." He turned toward Ivan. "We'll take them to Section Four, find out what we need to know, and then be done with them."

Chapter Forty-Six

Ron had just finished cuffing Dean and Laura to some chairs when he announced he had a call. Seconds later, he turned to Ivan. "That was the computer informing me of an impossible entry. Kevin just entered through the door at reception, but the scans already had him located here. I'll give him a call." He cupped his hands on his hips and waited. "That's weird. He's not responding?" He tried again. "I better go check. You stay here and see what you can get out of them." He disappeared out the door.

Dean panned around the room. He had a clear view of the large containment unit to his right. The colorful entities bounced around inside like children in a playground. He had felt their presence outside in the corridor, but next to their prison, it was stronger. Had he never been exposed to them before, he probably wouldn't have noticed the stifled telepathic messages and mathematical communication being transmitted from the unit. He gazed through the window at them trying to listen, clearing his head to the extent he could. Through the thick steel walls and the narrow windows, he could understand them. The cries of distress from countless numbers of condemned souls echoed as loud as a steel band. He felt sickened.

There was a large table in front of him with a computer terminal and some miscellaneous electronic equipment scattered across it. Underneath it, Dean could see a small portable containment unit, which looked to be charged. *More victims?* Laura sat to his left, her eyes wide with fright and her lips trembling.

"So Einstein, what's the tally? How many people have you killed? How much blood's on your hands, you sick son of a bitch?" He motioned his head toward the chamber at the end of the containment unit. "What's that, a gas chamber where you put the poor souls out of their misery?"

"Shut up!" Ivan's voice echoed off the smooth industrial walls. "I have no interest in listening to your *holier than thou* attitude. We've been through this already, and I feel no need to justify myself." The vacant smile he cracked was very self-assured. He walked over to Dean and grabbed him by the jaw moving in close. "Why aren't you dead?" He flung his head backward ramming it into the chair back then turned his attention to Laura. "You are beautiful. I certainly enjoyed our dinner together. You could have had quite a future here you know." He stroked the side of her face with his fingertips as his gaze inched down the length of her body.

"Keep your hands off her," Dean snarled.

"You have feelings for this woman don't you, Dean? I recognize that look. You were always the jealous type." He continued to touch Laura's face, pushing her hair to one side, seeming to enjoy the silky softness between his fingers, and then he slowly ran them across her lips. Laura held her breath, and her eyes filled.

"Get your hands off me you bastard." Her voice was monotone, yet fierce.

"Then why don't you tell me who you've told about this, hmm. How about this, you tell me, and I'll let you live. We can start with Becker. Where is he? As soon as Larry arrives on Lyra, he'll have his security people locate him from his implant, so you may as well make it easier for yourself and tell me now." Ivan pulled the data transfer unit out of his pocket and threw it on the table. "My guess is you were intending to feed everything off Kevin's terminal to him. Am I right?" Ivan took a step back, and without warning, struck Laura across the face and screamed, "Where's Becker?"

* * * *

Ron ran up the stairs to the main office area. As soon as he was through the doors, he called out. "Kevin?" He looked across the large room. He recognized the man walking toward him. The bastard had caught him off guard, and he thought of pulling his weapon but reconsidered. Jenkins was a fast draw. There was another way. "Marshal Jenkins, what are you doing here, and just how exactly did you get in?"

"Ron Fieldman right? I remember meeting you a couple of years ago. You were a security officer for the Lyra government."

"Yeah, but I gave that up in favor of this. I was offered a position as head of security when the facility opened. It's less stressful. Not too many people are interested in violating the security of a Particle Accelerator. Only the most extreme nerd would do that." He chuckled.

"You were expecting someone. You were calling for a Kevin."

"Yes, I just received a security notification that Kevin Cowen had arrived. I wouldn't have expected him here on a Saturday night, so I came to investigate. Do you want to tell me what you're doing here and how you got in?"

"There was some blood on the floor by the DNA scanner." Matt pulled a stained tissue out of his pocket. "Must belong to your Kevin. It took a lot of passes over the scanner, but I got in. Tell me something Ron. You remember the Simmons case I'm sure. I guess she's one of your extreme nerds. No doubt you've heard she escaped from prison with three others a couple of nights ago. Well Larry Dunn and I have been trying to track them down since then. One of the men she's with killed my sister. Earlier this evening, they escaped from Draco on a pod that docked at the government terminal of this base station. Dunn assured me his people would apprehend them on their arrival. I got to the spaceport shortly after them only to find Dunn's people knew nothing about it. Now Dunn isn't answering my calls. I have reason to believe Simmons and Weston were on their way here, and that pool of blood by your front door tells me I'm right. You might want to send someone over to check on your friend, Kevin."

"What makes you think they'd come here?"

"Mr. Becker insisted Simmons was innocent. If that's the case, she could be here trying to get evidence to clear her name."

Ron paused, carefully constructing his response. "Good detective work. You're right. I apprehended them a short time ago, and the Draco authorities are on their way as we speak. They'll be back in prison by morning. I appreciate you coming by to warn me, but the situation is well under control. Come on, and I'll escort you out."

"Not so fast! I promised Becker I'd talk to Simmons. I'll only be a few minutes. I would also like to see Weston onto the pod. For personal reasons, I need to see this through."

"And that is exactly why you should leave. You're personally involved in this case. You're not objective. I need to get back to the prisoners, so let's go. Now!"

"Why are you in such a hurry to get rid of me? Take me to Simmons. I insist on talking to her." Matt had the height advantage and glared down at Ron. The man looked like a Samurai in marshal's clothing. Ron wasn't easily intimidated, but he didn't want to get in a pissing match with Jenkins. He took a moment to re-evaluate the situation, massaging his chin for a moment before conceding. "Fine then. We're holding them in Section Four. Follow me."

Ron led the way to the cart, and upon their arrival at Section Four, let Matt take the lead. He had his hand ready on his pistol. The door opened. "After you my friend, they're just through the doors cuffed to some chairs."

* * * *

Once Matt was through the door, Ron pulled out his laser pistol and aimed it at the back of his head. "Ivan we have a visitor. Perhaps you could pull up another chair for him."

Ivan's eyes bulged at the unwelcomed surprise.

Matt started walking toward Dean and Laura. Dean's heart skipped a beat at the mere sight of his former friend. He knew just by entering the room, Matt was doomed.

"Not so fast, Jenkins."

Matt turned to see the pistol aimed with needle sharp precision. He took a step back. "What the hell are you doing? Put that down!"

"Throw your weapon over to me now, or I'll drill a hole right through your head."

"You've got to be kidding. Have you lost your mind?"

"Do it," he screamed as he reaffirmed his aim.

Matt slowly extracted his pistol from its holster and threw it to Ron who caught it mid air like a frog snatching a fly. He started waving the pistol toward Dean and Laura. "Move it...over there. Sit down in the chair and cuff yourself. Try anything, and it will be the last thing you ever do. Ivan, there's another pair of cuffs on the table with the cuff remote. Put them on the chair for him."

Matt walked to the chair and looped his arms around the armrests cuffing them in place. Ron followed and ensured the cuffs were secure. He took the cuff remote from Ivan and put it in his pocket and then handed him Matt's pistol.

Dean launched in. "Let him go. You son of a bitch, I did everything you asked. You gave me your word."

"Shut up!" Ivan leaped over and whacked Dean in the head with the handle of the pistol. His head flew to the side, and it took a couple of seconds for him to shake it off. Ivan grabbed him by the jaw again. "Did everything I asked? Did I ask you to break out of prison?" He lowered his voice as he turned, aiming his pistol at Matt. "You brought this on yourself."

Ron grabbed Ivan's wrist and pulled his arm down. "Have you lost your mind? We may need him."

"What the hell's going on here? Release me now," Matt ordered.

Dean started, "These people are—"

"Shut up Weston, or I'll shoot him." Ivan took aim again. "The only words I want to hear from any of you are the ones I want. Your friend here is expendable, so I suggest you answer my questions. Where's Becker, and who else have you told?"

"What's this all about?" Matt yelled.

Ivan ran to face him and grabbed a tuff of his thick black hair. "One more word out of you, and you'll be wearing a hole in the middle of your forehead. Understand?" He flung his head back as he released his grip.

Ron spoke as he came around to make eye contact with Dean and Laura then raised a brow at Ivan. "They've told you nothing?"

"No, nothing."

"Well, maybe I should take over. You're obviously not persuasive enough." Ron looked the two of them over carefully. He motioned his head toward Dean. "What's that...clipped to your belt?"

"It's my calculator."

"Smart, very smart." Ron leaned over and unclipped the leather case. He held it in his hands and unzipped it. He shook his head and started to laugh. It became more boisterous then stopped. "What you're a junkie?" He hurled the case onto the table.

"If that isn't just the icing on the cake," Matt said under his breath.

Ivan raised his weapon to shut him up.

Ron wandered toward Laura. "It seems to me when we first met I warned you not to come in here. Didn't I tell you this was where we tortured trespassers? You foolish woman, you should've listened." Ron held out his laser pistol and started playing with it. "You know these were a great invention, very versatile. They can kill, wound, sever, cut…" He gave Dean a shifty look. "Do you know what burning flesh smells like Dean? It's pungent, and it sizzles as it cauterizes." He walked over to Laura and loosened her shirt from her skirt before starting to unbutton it from the bottom up. He stopped just below her breasts then parted the fabric. Her flat stomach heaved in and out with each frightened breath. There was no hesitation. He took the laser pistol and cut a five centimeter slash straight across Laura's belly. The effects were just as he had described except they were accompanied by a shrill scream.

"Leave her alone," Dean howled.

"Don't tell him anything, Dean," Laura shrieked.

Ron straightened her sagging head with a tug of her hair. He shook the broken strands to the floor. "That's bad advice. You know the epidermis is the largest organ in the human body, and I have all night."

"What the hell do you want from them?" Matt insisted.

Ivan spun around aiming his pistol, yet again, this time screaming at the top of his lungs, "I think I told you to keep quiet."

Ron set his sights on Dean, unbuttoning his shirt and repeating the procedure. His deep groan wasn't as dramatic, but Ron smiled as he watched his face contort with pain. "Not so pleasant, is it? Now answer my questions, and I'll stop. It's very simple. Where's Becker and who have you told?"

"Go to hell," Dean grumbled.

Very well. He set his sights back to Laura and then back to Dean, repeating the horrific procedure several times before Ivan interjected.

"Enough! You're incinerating them for God's sake, and they've said nothing."

Laura's head hung to one side, her red-ringed eyes were empty and half closed. Her stomach looked like it just came off the grill—*medium rare.* Her expression yearned to tell them what they wanted, but Dean knew she would never put John at risk.

"Just kill us. We'll never tell you anything," she said in an inaudible mumble.

Her words pelted down on Dean like a hail storm. He'd failed her. Just when he thought he'd come through, he'd failed her. Their fate seemed sealed by the hands of a certifiably insane man. Despite the odds, something inside him told him he had to keep fighting. He desperately wanted to believe there was a way out.

"Laura," Dean lifted his head and rested it on the back of the chair. It flopped to one side, his hawk-like sharpness diminished to that of a fallen warrior. He whispered, "Please leave her alone."

Ron started back to her.

"I said enough," Ivan shouted. "Him," he pointed at Jenkins. "Put him in the airlock by the repair module and bleed the air out. They can watch him die on the monitor."

A depraved smile crossed Ron's face. "Good idea, but not him… Michelle Jenkins, she lives in the apartment complex adjacent to the lab. I could be back in minutes."

Both Matt and Dean shot a horrified look at Ron. Dean was the first to speak up. "She's an innocent kid! Leave her alone!"

"Implant…Mich—"

Ron tightened his hand around Matt's throat, silencing him. "Shut the fuck up, or I'll go over there and slit her throat. We seemed to have struck a nerve? Ivan you keep an eye on our friends. I'll be back." Ron took the pistol and left.

Chapter Forty-Seven

Ivan made it clear he didn't want to listen to any ranting as he held his pistol inches from Matt's head. "Just keep your mouths shut! It will give you a moment to reconsider your actions. It's not too late to tell me what I want to know." He started pacing back and forth along the length of the containment unit, his stride uneven and his movements jerked. He stood hunched over like an old man and continually checked over his shoulders as if expecting someone.

Dean watched him as he slithered back and forth, pondering what happened to the man he once knew, always well kept and articulate. It was just over three months since he'd seen him last, but he looked like he'd aged five years. Dark smudges framed his eyes, his shirt hung out the back of his pants, and Dean couldn't remember the last time he saw him wearing a shirt without a tie. *You're one fucked up dude.*

Ivan spun around toward Dean and snapped, "What did you say?"

"Nothing, I said nothing." Dean continued to study him. He seemed agitated, paranoid.

Ivan let out an exaggerated sigh that made him seem on the defense. The pacing became quicker, and he started making side glances at the containment unit. Sweat had moistened the sides of his face, and his hair lay pasted to it like a bad toupee. All of a sudden, he cupped his hands over his ears and with an ear piercing scream he yelled, "Shut up." His eyes widened to storm clouds as he slammed the containment unit with his fist.

* * * *

Ron parked the cart just outside the door of Michelle Jenkins' apartment. She lived in an apartment owned by the Accelerator similar to the one Laura was given, and Ron had access authorization. It was close to three a.m., and the area was deserted. He let himself in with undetected ease.

The apartment was dark, and after giving his eyes a moment to adjust, he walked straight to the bedroom, weapon in hand. He discretely opened the door and started in. He barely took two steps when something leaped onto his head from the top of the armoire to his right. He heard a screeching noise as he felt a set of teeth and claws jab into his neck. He flung the beast to the ground and silenced it with his weapon. Seconds later, the lights came on and there stood Michelle with ruffled hair, decked out in a baggy T-shirt and sweats; her sleepy eyes widened in confusion, disbelief, and then horror. The beast, a gray tabby cat, lay dead on the carpet. She cupped her mouth and yelled, "Costello."

Ron pointed the pistol at Michelle. "Get your shoes on; you're coming with me." His voice was no nonsense.

A pall of disbelief fell over her face as she gazed down at the scorched cat on the floor. Its body twitched as death settled in. "What are you doing here Mr. Fieldman?" She had difficulty forming her words. "Get out, or I'll call the marshal's office." Michelle cowered back a few steps as she gazed at the weapon.

"Come on. Now...move!" Ron commanded.

Michelle, threw on her runners, and Ron grabbed her arms, cuffing them behind her. He put some tape over her mouth and dragged her to the cart, sticking her in the back with a blanket over her. He drove quickly, again enjoying the solitude of the early hours. Within seven minutes, Michelle stood alone, trapped in the airlock in Section Three, her brown eyes wide with fright.

* * * *

Ron stormed into Section Four and went straight to the computer terminal on the table. He spun the monitor around so Dean, Laura, and Matt had a clear view; and he adjusted the volume. In high definition, there was Michelle, standing terrified in the airlock. Dean felt tears welling in his eyes. He remembered her shrills of joy as they navigated the rapids on their kayak adventure together. The screams coming over the monitor sounded entirely different; they were the agonizing shrieks of a young girl scared for her life. She pounded on the door insistently. "Let me out you bastard!"

"That bitch girl has quite the mouth on her. She's like a damn street rat." Ron hammered some instructions into the computer. "I'm venting the air slowly. At this rate, she'll be dead in ten minutes." He looked up from the keyboard, glancing at Dean. With an icy impassive tone, he asked, "She's your niece. You gonna sit there and watch her die, or are you going to tell us what we want to know."

"Dean, you bastard, if you don't stop this, I'll kill you I swear! Tell him what he wants to know. She's just a kid." Matt rattled his arms as if he could free himself, his complexion maroon. He screamed, "Tell him!"

Dean's eyes were blurred with tears, and he felt the veins in his temples throbbing. He watched in horror, head spinning, transfixed over what to do. As agonizing as this was to watch, they were all going to die regardless. If he talked, it would only increase the head count. He stared motionless in a horrified daze. Michelle's breathing sounded strained, and she'd backed away from pounding on the door. She held her hands to her chest as it heaved in thrusts searching for air. She fell to her knees gasping, her anguished eyes looking straight into the security camera.

Ron let out a quiet snicker as if someone had told him a knock, knock joke.

"Dean," Matt screamed.

Suddenly Ivan took a leap away from the table, his panicked gaze darting between Michelle and the containment unit.

"What the hell's wrong with you?" Ron said. "Keep it together."

"I can't be here." Ivan shook his head in psychotic bursts, covering his hands over his face. I can't watch this." He yelled in a crazed frenzy as the veins in the back of his neck bulged out.

"Well this is a hell of a time to lose your nerve. Get some backbone!"

Ivan took a couple of steps back, this time not taking his eyes off the girl. "You don't understand." He spoke with stuttered breaths. "I can't watch this. She's drowning, just like Nathan, she's drowning!" His eyes looked forced open as he stared at the screen. He turned toward Ron and screamed. "She'll die and come back to haunt me, just like Nathan did. I can't be here." He shuddered and started for the door, running.

"Get back here, Ivan! Can't you do your own dirty work? You're regressing. You're a pathetic mindless coward just like you used to be." Ron slammed his fist on the table, enraged, his expression exploding in a ball of fire. Several items flew off the table on their own from his freakish outburst. "Damn spineless bastard!" He jerked his head toward Dean, Laura, and Matt. "He's weak, a fool. But understand this, it doesn't change the fact that this girl is about to die! Tell me what I want to know now," he screamed. He calmed for a moment, seeming to savor their paralyzing fear.

Dean didn't take his eyes off Ron, his fear lifting away. He and Ivan had become certifiably insane. It had to be the entities. They were eating them alive at a conscious level. He smiled victoriously as he heard their thoughts from inside the containment unit telling him what to do. They'd found a defense, and the effects were blatantly clear.

With a firm jolt, Dean shot his chair forward and kicked the exhaust button on the side of the portable unit under the table. Instantly, a cloud of colorful entities surrounded them. At first they danced randomly, freely, but quickly they organized themselves and descended on Ron. Soon they surrounded him, enveloping him. Their colors changed in a harmonic symphony of light. Ron held his hands to his head and shrieked. "No! Stop!" He lost his balance and tumbled to the floor. The remote for the cuffs fell out of his pocket just centimeters from Dean. Dean toppled his chair and wriggled over to it until he had it in his hands. Seconds later, he was free. He sent a forceful kick into Ron's head on his way to Matt, freeing him.

"Run! Save her."

Matt grabbed Ron's pistol and flew out the door. Dean ran to Laura and set her free.

"Dean, watch it," she bellowed.

Ron lunged in their direction. Dean fired up, elbowing Ron in the jowls, sending him back to the floor. Dean spun around, kicking Ron several times in the gut. With cuffs in hand, Dean dragged him over to the containment unit and secured him to it.

"Laura, are you okay? We have to get to Ivan." Dean grabbed his leather case from the table on the way to her side.

She sounded strained from the pain, but answered clearly. "I'm okay. Can you get the bag? We'll need it. I know where his office is. He's probably there."

With a renewed source of energy, Dean and Laura ran out the door. Ivan had taken the cart, so they started sprinting back to the office area. They were halfway there when Dean collapsed on the floor.

Laura turned back. "Dean what's wrong."

Dean had the leather case in his hands, but he was too shaky to pinch the zipper. "Laura, I need help."

"Oh my God. Here, I've got it." She pulled out one of the syringes and filled it as Dean struggled to remove his blazer and pull up his sleeve. The cinders the bugs left inside him were glowing red hot, and soon the raging fire would return, stoked by the insidious drug. Laura finished pushing up his sleeve and tied the tourniquet. With her index finger, she started feeling around for a bulge. "Dean, breathe, you're not breathing."

"Drop that now!"

Dean looked up to see Matt holding a pistol aimed at his head. Michelle was tucked in behind him. Laura moved in front of Dean, shielding him. Dean wanted to call out to him, to explain, but the agonizing fire had taken hold.

"Get away from him now." Matt spoke purposefully as he reaffirmed his aim.

"You don't understand," Laura yelled.

Matt snatched the syringe and threw it across the corridor shattering it against the wall.

"No, he'll die without that!"

Matt raised his voice. "Get out of the way. The man's a monster."

Dean felt the convulsions returning. He looked at Matt, desperately wanting to tell him the truth. His head fell back as he succumbed to the blaze, the pain too intense to even scream.

"Listen to me," Laura screamed. "He didn't kill Karen. It was Ivan. He framed Dean. I was there when it happened. I knew they were going kill her. Dean went to save her, but he was too late. They told him they'd kill me if he didn't do what they said. They shot him with something. It made him drunk, sick. He's innocent. He signed the confession because they said they'd kill you and your wife if he didn't. He did it to protect you." Laura could hardly catch her breath she spoke so fast.

Dean made a garbled shriek as his back arched in spasm. He felt his face filling with blood, boiling blood.

Laura turned to help Dean. He looked up at her barely able to focus through the smoke of his internal flames. "You'll have to kill me to stop me. He'll die without this." She grabbed for the other syringe, filling it up. Matt lowered his weapon slightly, but it wavered with uncertainty. "Please, he's innocent. We can prove it." She went for Dean's arm. He tried to steady it for her, but he couldn't. It jerked right out of her grip. She grabbed it back and struggled with it for a moment. "I can't, please you have to help me," she pleaded. "Hold him down."

Matt put his weapon in its holster and held Dean down long enough for Laura to administer the drug. She put the syringe away and took Dean's hand, pushing it away from his charbroiled belly. "Come on breathe, Dean, breathe." She stroked his hair.

He caught his breath and let out a gut wrenching moan as his body started to relax. Within a minute, the fire was out; the burns on his stomach were only a meager reminder of it. With Laura's help, he pushed himself to a sitting position and looked up at Matt.

Matt had his hand on his holster. Dean knew he'd spent the last few months loathing his very existence, seething that he should be allowed to live while Karen's mutilated body lay in her grave. Despite being his former friend and brother-in-law, the coldness in Matt's eyes told Dean he'd kill him in a heartbeat. Now he had his chance, but he was hesitating. *Confused?* There was Dean, ripe for the picking—a murderer, a drug addict, unarmed, and vulnerable. Dean could only imagine the thoughts going through his head. Was Laura tricking him, or was she telling the truth? Were they scheming their next move?

The coldness in Matt's face changed to bewilderment. Dean knew he had a vindictive nature, but was also a moral man. "You kill me now, and you may never know who really killed Karen. Ivan masterminded it, but it wasn't him who did it. There were two men. They killed Annie and Roger, too." Laura helped him to his feet. "I didn't kill her, but I didn't get there on time to save her either." Dean

344

glanced down at Matt's hand with an air of resentment. "So what are you going to do? Kill me?"

Matt slowly moved his hand away from his weapon. "You can prove this?"

"Yeah, I can prove it. But we have to get to Ivan." Dean turned away from Matt and started back down the corridor. He took Laura's hand and hastened the pace. Matt and Michelle followed.

They arrived in Ivan's office only to find it vacant.

"Damn it! Laura, any idea where he could he?" Dean walked to the closet. "Where does this go?" He opened the door and took a leap back as the bloodied corpse of a woman slid out toward him. "Shit!" He glanced at Matt with a defining stare.

Laura gave a start backward. "That looks like Pam, Ivan's assistant. My God, what happened to her face?"

Michelle shuddered and cowered behind Matt, grabbing his arm.

Dean heard an ear piercing crash from out in the hall. It was repeated by another and another. They followed the noise to the men's room. Inside, Ivan smashed the mirrors one after another with a wooden bin, sending a torrent of glass showering down on the floor. Matt shielded his eyes as he pulled his weapon.

Ivan continued his attack destroying the last mirror, then hurled the bin, and cupped his hands over his ears screaming. "Stop it! Go away, leave me alone!" His eyes were glazed over in a frightful stare.

Dean kicked the bin away and took a swing deep into Ivan's gut, buckling him over. He launched his knee into Ivan's jaw and pushed him to the wall where he straightened him up and started choking him. Ivan's hollow, yet terrified eyes started to bulge as his face purpled. Dean's hatred of the man tightened his grip around Ivan's throat. Then he stopped. He released his grip and backed off slowly, shaking his head. "No, I'm not like you. I won't let you drag me down any further." He spoke in a restrained whisper, burying his vengeance.

Dean latched onto Ivan's arm and in the same motion, started pulling him out of the washroom. "It's show time. You're going to pull everything up on your computer about the entities, the people you've killed...everything. You sick son of a bitch."

Matt took the other side of him, and when they were back in his office, they slammed him into his chair. The force sent the picture behind his desk crashing to the floor.

Dean gave him a cuff in the head and pushed the chair to the desk. "Log on. I want to see everything, starting with who killed Karen."

Ivan sat in a frozen trance like his brain was half shut down, but his gaze shifted as if he was following something moving about the room. His stare landed on the window, and he grabbed the armrests of his chair with white knuckled strength as though he was about to start an amusement park ride.

"Do it," Dean screamed.

Ivan cuffed his ears and shrieked. "Tell it to stop. Shut up! It's evil. It's going to kill us all."

"Jesus Christ what have you done to yourself?" Dean slammed the chair toward the desk. "Log on, or I'll cut your hand off and do it myself!"

Michelle winced, and Laura went to her side to help comfort her.

Like a weak frightened child, Ivan started to cooperate. He chose not to speak and with shaking hands typed on the keyboard, staring blankly at the screen. Instantly, files popped up. There was documented correspondence between Ivan and a man by the name of Howard Benjamin regarding the murders of Roger, Annie, and Karen. There were numerous records of monetary transfers to the same man and to Larry Dunn. A number of other names were referred to as well. There was a file dedicated to Laura with forged evidence incriminating her as an accessory in Karen's murder. Then there were the entities. Reams of information flashed up on the screen, detailing research results and people involved in the investigation. Matt watched in silence.

Dean opened Ivan's desk drawer and searched for a data transfer unit. The drawer was a mess of papers and writing utensils and a large blue pill was sitting on its own in the front corner beside a calculator. "Let's see what the Heads of State think of all this at the Summit this morning." It took a bit of rummaging, but he found a unit buried beneath some papers. Just as he grabbed it, Ivan reached for the blue pill and popped it in his mouth.

Dean swung the chair back with the strength of an army and hurled Ivan to the floor. "What the hell was that?" He sandwiched

Ivan's head in the crook of his arm and forced his mouth open to retract the pill. It fell to the floor with hardly a hint of moisture, and Dean pitched it across the room. "You're not getting off that easily." He heaved him back to his chair, throwing him at an angle. A fine line of drool dribbled from the corner of Ivan's mouth as he attempted to straighten himself out.

"What's wrong with him?" Michelle asked.

"He's fried his brain," Dean responded. "The containment unit in Section Four...it's full of alien life forms. They're made of energy, intelligent energy. When people are exposed to them, they get cognitive superpowers. Trust me, I was exposed once. It's indescribable." Dean looked at Matt with resolution. "That's what this is all about. That's why Karen, Annie, and Roger were killed, and why he framed me. We discovered the entities on a planet during a mining expedition. There were the four of us with Ivan and Kevin. We all knew about the entities. Their existence became highly classified to protect them. Exposure to us kills them. Ivan's been harvesting them, so he and his friends can supercharge themselves. They've probably killed thousands by now along with countless people." He gestured to the closet. "There's no telling how expansive his reign of terror has become, or how many people are involved in his conspiracy. That's why I signed the confession. He said he'd kill you and Sue if I didn't, and I had no choice but to believe him." Dean placed the transfer unit on the computer and started the download.

Ivan continued to cower in the back of his chair, his face flushed and nostrils flaring. "Shut the closet," he mumbled.

Dean looked over at the mangled woman in the closet. Her legs had slid halfway out the door. Her expression was dauntingly familiar. He wondered if her last moments of life were as horrific as Karen's. He walked over to her and shut her eyes, and as he draped Ivan's soiled shirt over her face, he softly spoke, "Rest in peace." Ivan shuddered.

Dean turned his attention to Ivan. "It looks like your little friends gave you more than you bargained for. I hate to say I told you so. You better wipe that expression off your face before you get to prison. The prisoners will eat you alive."

A distraught Matt finally spoke up. "Dean, I just don't know what to say. I'm sorry."

"Well, how about you help me finish this." Dean's words came out cold. "This has to be exposed. People have to know about the massacre that's happened here. I want justice."

"Dean, the download's finished. You can start the transfer. I'll call John. He probably thinks we're dead." Laura pulled her PCD out of the bag and placed the call. It was obvious from her conversation there was a relieved voice on the other end. "Uncle John, Dean's just starting the transfer now. You should already be receiving it. Call me and let me know when the transfer's finished. There's a lot of data."

"Dean, what does he intend to do with it?" Matt asked.

"He's doing a presentation today at the Summit. He's at the hotel across the way now, but he's catching a shuttle down to Lyra in an hour. He's planning to present the evidence to the Heads of State."

"Dunn was heading to Lyra for the Summit. He's part of security. I spent the last day with him, and I can tell you he's highly motivated to keep this contained. I don't have to tell you what he's capable of. Your friend could be walking into a death trap. We need to have the authorities arrest him."

Dean shook his head. "We don't know who's involved, who we can trust. We can't assume the involvement in this is limited to the people named in Ivan's files."

Laura waved her hand in the air with an idea. "Dean, what if *we* take John to the Summit. I'm sure there's a pod in the hangar in Section Five. Matt could escort him safely and arrest Dunn himself."

"I can contact Bruce," Matt said. "They needed additional security at the Summit, and in my absence, Bruce had selected a few people to go. He could contact them and give them the heads up that I'm on my way. They can keep an eye on Dunn without raising suspicion, and I can arrest him when I get there."

"Do you trust these people?" Dean asked.

"Implicitly," Matt said with a solemn tone.

"Fine, do it."

"You're not leaving me here. You can't leave me here with it." The desperate, stuttered voice was Ivan's.

Dean shot him a piercing glare. "What the hell are you talking a—"

"It's evil! It will kill us all," Ivan shouted, cowering further into his chair.

"The only thing evil here is you, you crazy bastard," Dean barked.

"What do we do with him?" Laura said.

"Take him with us. Matt can take him into custody with Larry. That is whatever's left of him." Dean turned to Michelle. "I'm afraid you're going to have to come, too. It's not safe for you here, and I'm not taking any chances."

"Okay, Uncle Dean."

Dean smiled warmly after hearing Michelle's response. He called John and instructed him to come to the Accelerator. Matt arranged for Bruce to contact his people at the Summit, after advising him of the situation. Once John arrived, the group made their way to the pod.

Chapter Forty-Eight

The pod was small, with barely enough room for the six of them. Ivan's delirium had intensified as had his aggression, so Matt cuffed him and gave him a blunt strike to the back of the head with the handle of his pistol to knock him out. Dean watched on with pleasure. He may not have been vengeful enough to kill Ivan, but the man deserved to suffer. Dean locked the pod down, and they were off.

"Dean, the Summit's being held in the Lyra Council Chamber, which is in the building behind the Government Building. I assume you know where that is. There are several landing pads adjacent to the two buildings. If you don't mind, I think it's best if either Matt or I contact the ground authorities to advise them we'll be landing," John said. "As soon as I've presented the evidence in these files, and Dunn is in custody, I'll call for some medics. The two of you need immediate medical attention. For now, I think we should make use of whatever bandages are left in the bag to tend to your wounds."

"Go ahead Dean." Matt took control of the pod. "He's right. I can fly this thing well enough to cover for you for a few minutes, and I'll call ground control."

"Thanks." Dean dug into the duffle bag. It had become a disheveled mess of medical supplies and rope, not to mention the piece of Kevin timelessly displayed in its frame. He tossed the rope to the side and pulled out the bandages, exacto knife, antiseptic, and topical anesthesia spray; although he had little hope of that quenching the fire on their skin. Laura's stomach looked like bubbled paint, raw and blistering. He looked into her eyes. "I'm so sorry this happened." He shook his head at the sight of it. "I wish I could have done something, stopped them."

Laura took his hand. "It's not your fault." She squeezed it and let it go. He still felt responsible.

Michelle went to Dean's side and asked, "What did they do to you?"

Dean put his arm around her and rubbed her back lovingly. "It doesn't matter now. What matters is that these people pay for what they did to Karen."

"Uncle Dean, if you don't mind me asking, why did you need that drug?"

Dean opened his mouth, but then shut it again and continued to bandage Laura, ignoring the question. Matt cocked his head in their direction. Laura spoke up. "At the prison…" Her tone was guarded. "They did something awful to him. We gave him the drug. It saved his life." She looked at Michelle with an expression that told her to let it go. Dean appreciated her discreteness. Michelle didn't ask any more questions.

When Dean finished, Laura switched places with him and got to work. By the time she patted down the last bandage, Matt announced they were close to entering the atmosphere. Dean helped Laura stuff the supplies back into the bag and then got up to take the controls back. There was little cloud cover, and by the time they descended to an altitude of one kilometer, they had a clear view of Lyra City. The city, being the only settled region on the planet, covered an area of approximately six thousand square kilometers. The residential area had recently expanded into the hilly terrain to the south, and the area appeared lush with imported foliage. Dean carved a slow arc toward the flatter ground to the north where the government buildings were located. The sun lay low in the horizon, and formed a brilliant backdrop to the skyline, casting the white stonework of the government buildings with a blue hue.

Matt sprung out of his seat the moment they set down. "Dean, if the two of you show your faces outside the pod, you'll be taken into custody. So I suggest you lay low. Besides, someone needs to watch him." Ivan showed signs of coming around, and with a hint of pleasure in his face, Matt marched over and shut him down. Dean wished he got there first. "As soon as everything's finished, I'll be back. Like John said, the two of you need a hospital; and Ivan will need to be handed over to the Lyra authorities, by the looks of things, in a straight jacket. Michelle, you'll be safe with Dean and Laura. I'll get back as quickly as I can."

John scooped up his briefcase, and Matt escorted him out. Dean watched as the two men disappeared inside the Council Chamber Building and then went to shut the hatch. Just as he was about to hit the button, he heard a familiar voice. It shot through him like nails scrapping across a chalkboard. He looked over, his face frozen.

Larry leaped into the pod as if running hurdles, his laser pistol aimed and set to kill. "If I didn't need you to fly this thing, I'd kill you right now. Get this thing locked down and in the air." He threw a set of handcuffs to him. "You only need one hand free. Cuff the other to the seat." As Larry spoke, he switched his aim toward Laura and Michelle. "Do it, or I'll kill both of them. I don't need them. I only need you."

Larry's threats were not to be toyed with, and Dean followed his instructions to the letter and locked down the pod. "It will take a few minutes to get it ready for takeoff. It was barely powered down."

"Just do it!"

Dean glanced over his shoulder as Larry used the extra rope to secure Laura and Michelle's arms behind them.

"What's taking so long? Get this thing airborne," Larry yelled. "What the hell happened to him?"

"What?"

"Ivan! What the hell did you do to him?"

"His brains liquefied and poured out his nose. Didn't I tell you that would happen?"

"Don't be smart, Weston. It'll get them killed. Get this damn thing in the air."

"Where are we going?" Dean asked.

"I'll tell you once we're off the planet. Now move it, or I'll kill the girl." Larry took aim at Michelle. It wouldn't matter to him that she was a kid. The sick bastard would burn a hole through her head and probably enjoy it.

I have to stall. Dean started to edge his free hand toward the controls to look busy. "I only have one free hand. You'll have to be patient." *Where the hell is Matt?* He glanced back at Laura and Michelle. The duffle bag sat open beside Laura, and something occurred to him. The knife was the last thing to go back into the bag. He saw the glimmer of it out of the corner of his eye as he'd got up. He glared down at the bag then back up at Laura. It was easily within her reach. He just needed to distract Larry. From the looked in Laura's eyes, his message was received.

"Never mind them." Larry cuffed Dean in the head. "You've got three minutes, or the girl dies!"

Dean let his head wobble for a moment. "How do you expect me to fly this thing if you knock me senseless?" The strike barely stung, but it was all he had to play with. Dean shuddered.

"Just get us in the air." Larry watched Dean's every move. Dean reached for the launch controls with a wavering hand and then let it slip, triggering an alarm.

Larry turned his weapon toward Michelle. Laura started babbling with a pleading tone. "Please don't kill us! Dean, just do what he says."

Dean looked around to Laura and caught a glimpse of the back of her with her hands inches from the bag. He turned the alarm off. "Sorry, I'm shaky. I'm ready for takeoff. Larry, you may want to sit down."

"Just get it in the air. You're stalling."

"Well, at least, come here where there is something to hang on to." Dean pointed to the handle beside the hatch.

Larry followed Dean's suggestion and assumed a position by the hatch, glaring at him. Dean knew any more stalling, and the bastard would follow through with his threat. He didn't dare look back to see if Laura had the knife. She was resourceful and gutsy. He'd just have to have faith. He engaged the thrusters, and the pod lifted off the ground. Out the port window, the rooftops of the buildings came into view as the pod got some elevation. All of a sudden, Dean heard Laura scrambling to her feet. He turned to see her lunging at Larry, wielding the knife, and jabbing it into his shoulder.

* * * *

Security was tight inside the Council Chambers, but regardless, Matt chose to escort John to his seat. "Watch your back," he whispered to him before setting off to find Dunn.

The Council Chamber was a large round room with two doors diametrically opposite one another. There was lots of commotion as the meeting was about to begin. Matt started a fast-paced perimeter walk, respectfully dodging government officials on their way to their seats and keeping a keen eye out for Dunn. About halfway around the room, he ran into Pete Carter, one of his own men from Eagle. "Pete, where's Dunn?"

"Dunn, you mean Larry Dunn? No idea. I haven't seen him. Why?"

"What do you mean why? Didn't Bruce update you on the situation? You're supposed to be watching him. I'm here to take him into custody."

"I was talking to Bruce ten minutes ago. He didn't mention anything about Larry. What's the problem?"

Matt felt his face redden as a wave of anger and trepidation began to take hold. If it wasn't enough that he'd just about killed Dean after he'd put his life on the line for him and Sue, now his right hand man had betrayed him. No doubt Bruce was also involved in Karen's murder. He was strategically positioned for it to be cleanly executed, and it was Bruce who called him on that horrific night. The image of his sister's mutilated body returned along with the urge to belt Bruce in the head until his jaw fell loose. Matt looked Pete in the eyes and spoke sternly. "If you see Dunn, detain him and notify me immediately. In the meantime, I need you to watch John Becker. It's entirely possible someone may make an attempt on his life." Matt sped off in the direction of the security office.

Cam Potter, a black man in his late forties with an intimidating frame and the personality to go with it, was in charge of security for the Summit. When Matt burst into the security office, Cam was busy briefing several of his people on the meeting protocols. "Jenkins, is there a problem? I trust there's a good reason for this intrusion? You're not even on the security team."

"My apologies, Marshal Potter. I am here escorting Mr. John Becker. He has some very disturbing evidence of a serious crime that's been committed and intends to share it with the Heads of State at the meeting today. I believe his life is in danger. The evidence Mr. Becker has outlines a conspiracy involving several members of security including Larry Dunn, and as I just learned, my second in command,

Bruce Hartford. I can't be sure who else is involved and quite frankly, I don't know who to trust. Dunn must be apprehended. You have to heighten your security, at least until Becker has made his presentation. He's the second speaker."

"Have you seen this evidence? This is a serious accusation."

"Yes, I've seen it. It's highly incriminating, and I can assure you Becker needs to bring this to light. Please, we're running out of time. Dunn has likely been tipped off by Bruce that we're onto him. I'm going to need help apprehending him. He could be trying to run."

Potter agreed to follow Matt's requests and sent an alert out to all his people to locate Dunn. He got an immediate response. "Apparently, Dunn was just seen entering a pod on the landing pad. It was the same one that you and Mr. Becker arrived in. It just became airborne, but apparently it's been hovering for a few minutes."

"Damn it. You need to have that pod forced down now!" Matt ran out of the room heading in the direction of the landing pad.

* * * *

The knife entering Larry's shoulder sent him into a scorching rage. He staggered back a step, dropped his laser pistol, and then pulled the knife out and hurled it across the cabin. In the same motion, he struck Laura. She wobbled on her feet, but didn't go down until Larry's fist landed in her stomach. With a shrill scream, she fell to the floor holding her hands to her belly. As Larry launched at her, Dean set the pod back down on the ground. He looked over at Laura panic stricken, powerless to help her. She was struggling under Larry's weight, and he had her hands pinned. He started to haul her to her feet, and she sent her knee into his groin. Larry buckled over and hit the floor groaning.

Just as Dean got the hatch open, he caught sight of Matt charging out of the building in the direction of the pod. He looked back to Laura in desperation. Larry had gained control and had his hands wrapped around Laura's neck; her face reddening with each passing second. Dean called out, "Matt, hurry!" Michelle screamed and cowered to the back of the cabin. Matt flew through the door. In that instant, Dean watched as Laura's fingers wiggled the knife into her grip, and she rammed it deep into Larry's temple. His body fell limp on top of her with his blood draining down the side of her face. Matt heaved Larry's body aside and reached down to get the cuff remote from his pocket to release Dean.

Laura, with wide terrified eyes blurred with blood, retreated back in shock. Dean rushed to her side and lifted her up to take her into his arms. He held her tight as she shuddered. "It's over," he whispered. "It's finally over, and I love you with all my heart." The tears started flowing.

Matt released Michelle and took her into her arms as she wept.

Chapter Forty-Nine

Dean and Laura had enjoyed three weeks of freedom. Their first order of business was to check Dean into the Lyra Drug Rehabilitation Center. The Center was a high-end facility, and the government of Consortium of Planets insisted on covering the costs. Dean thought he had John to thank for that. The doctors were happy to have Laura stay with him and see him through the process. Fortunately, Dean's short exposure to the entities during their escape from Section Four had an effect that was slow to the mark, but sufficient to allow his impossible task of breaking free of the drug become a reality. He'd come to require only a miniscule amount of the drug, and the fire that had once raged inside him, barely smoldered. In another few days, it would be extinguished, and he'd be drug free.

Dean and Laura sat on the patio off their room, enjoying the afternoon sun and some company. The accommodation was well appointed with all the comforts of home. The patio had an attractive stone fence for privacy, a trickling fountain, and a fragrant assortment of plants. They sat together on the wicker loveseat, and John and Andy had made themselves comfortable on the couch across from them.

Dean put his arm around Laura and threw his legs up on the ottoman. "Laura got a call from the CEO of Enertech yesterday. Of course with everything in the news, and Ivan and Kevin in the mental hospital, they're all up in arms about the contract they awarded to the Lyra Accelerator." Dean paused. "I guess this is your news, sweetheart. I don't want to steal your glory. You tell them."

Laura formed a wide smile. "I've been offered Ivan's job running the Accelerator, and Enertech called me to sweeten the offer. They're insistent I take the position, and they were also insistent Dean join me. Strange that they should also need a new engineer and pilot."

John started to laugh. "Yes, that is a coincidence. So are the two of you taking them up on their offer."

Dean spoke up. "Let's just say it's an offer we couldn't refuse. The best part about it is we'll be working together. We have someone arranging an apartment for us as we speak."

"Congratulations!" Andy beamed. "Can I send you my resume? I'd like to apply for a position in security." His infectious laugh filled the patio, drowning out the trickle of the fountain.

"Sure send it over," Laura said, smiling. "Actually, it's going to be quite a challenge, but at least we won't be there to clean up the mess Ivan left. Apparently, they found Ron crouched on the floor beside that chamber of horrors, dead. Cardiac arrest was the cause. I bet those pretty little entities scared him to death. Good for them. And the good news is they've all been returned to Spectra."

Dean shot a glance at John. "Hey, what's the latest on Ivan and Kevin? You said you were going to follow up with the authorities."

"Yeah, they're both being held at the Hagger Mental Institution. Actually, it's only a couple of blocks from here. They're awaiting trial, but their mental capacity is greatly diminished; and they're both experiencing paranoid episodes. Apparently, Ivan's being kept in a straight jacket. They're afraid he may harm himself."

"And we're concerned about that for what reason?" Dean scoffed. "The man's evil."

"Speaking of which, what do you think he was talking about? Remember, he was going on about something evil," Laura said. "He thought it was going to kill him. He seemed scared to death."

"He was delusional," Dean responded. "There was nothing evil about those entities, I can assure you. They're pure goodness. You must have felt it even for the short time you were exposed."

"Yeah, actually I did."

"After being exposed to the entities on Spectra, I could pick up their telepathic communication even from within the containment unit. The message was weak, but they told me to release the ones in the portable unit. They sacrificed themselves to put an end to this. It looks like they found a defense by screwing with the minds of the people exposed to them. John, you mentioned several people had been exposing themselves."

"Yeah, the ones left alive are like Ivan, delusional," John said. "The Consortium has gone into the lab and sealed up all the records of Ivan's supposed research. It's classified. Apparently Ivan had been

358

working with a Russian scientist by the name of Dr. Zowski. She's an expert in psychology and the paranormal. I called her to try and find out what Ivan had been up to. She spouted off a series of what I can imagine were choice Russian words and then told me she wasn't permitted to discuss their work. I hate to think what he did to those poor entities. Anyway, I guess we'll never find out."

"That doesn't surprise me," Dean said. "It was classified before, so it stands to reason it would be classified now."

"What about your friend, Matt? How did that work out? A little awkward perhaps?" Just as the words left Andy's mouth, a voice sounded from the patio door.

Matt stepped onto the patio, carrying a large box. "Hope I'm not interrupting."

Andy blushed, something he rarely did. "Speak of the devil. No, not at all." He got to his feet and offered his hand. "Hi, I'm Andy Weber. I think I've heard every story there is to tell about you. Nice to meet you."

Matt set the box down and shook Andy's hand. "It's a pleasure, but I'm not so sure those stories do me any justice."

Andy laughed. "Have a seat. Join us, although I've got to head out shortly."

Dean stood up, politely shook Matt's hand, and directed him to the empty chair. This was the first time they had seen each other since the Summit, and they had only spoken briefly in the aftermath of John's presentation to the Consortium. Andy's perception was right—awkward.

Matt took a seat. "I wanted to come by to tell you personally that I managed to pull a few strings and get Jeff released on parole. They reviewed the evidence of the crime taking into consideration the extenuating circumstances with his sister, and they gave him his parole. I'm sure he'll be calling you himself. I believe he has the same parole officer as you have, Andy."

"Thanks, Matt. Great news!" Dean said. "You don't know how happy I am to hear it. Jeff got the raw end of the deal."

"Yes, I guess that's true," Matt said shifting uncomfortably in his seat.

"Well, on that note, I should be on my way. I'll call you two tomorrow, and we can arrange the dinner we were talking about." Andy got up from his seat and headed toward the door.

"I'm on my way, too. I'll walk out with you." John got up and joined Andy. "I'll see you at dinner, and we'll all have to get together at my place as soon as things settle down. Dean, I believe I promised you a spin in my car."

"And like I said then, I'll hold you to it." Dean pictured himself behind the wheel and smiled.

Andy and John bid their farewells and left. Dean broke the silence that followed. "So what's in the box?"

"A present." Matt smiled as he reached over and carefully delivered the package to Dean, setting it on his lap. Dean felt something moving inside it and immediately lifted the lid. Inside peering up at him with wide glassy eyes was a tiny kitten. It was hardly big enough to fit in a palm and was the spitting image of Costello—a gray tabby. "It's a boy."

Dean's grin was so wide his cheeks ached. He reached inside to grab the kitten. It made a little mew as he stroked its back.

"Oh my God! He's so cute." Laura perked up with excitement. "What should we name him?"

"How about Abbott? Seems fitting, especially since he's a boy." Dean played with the kitten for a few minutes before handing him to Laura. The little cat quickly nestled down on her lap and started purring. "Thanks man! You must have really had to psych yourself to go out and actually buy a cat." Dean looked at Laura. "He's not fond of them."

"Yes, I remember, you told me."

"Take it as a peace offering. Dean, I can't make up for what I did to you. I should have known something was wrong and investigated it further, stood behind you. It's unforgivable, especially after what you did for me."

"Matt, one way or another, we're all victims here. I'm just glad to know the men who killed Karen are in prison. Welcome to the land of fire and brimstone as they like to say. They can rot in hell."

A thoughtful silence settled between them. "Well, I don't want to take up any more of your time. I just wanted to give you the news about Jeff and of course, deliver the cat." Matt got up, and Dean escorted him to the door. "Laura seems really nice."

Glancing back at the woman who had found a place in his heart, Dean smiled. "Well, if anything good came out of this, it's Laura and me. She's great, really great. At least I have one thing to be thankful for. Hey, they're looking for a new head marshal for the Lyra Base Station. Not surprising. You should give it some thought."

"Maybe I will. I'll talk to Sue." Before stepping outside, Matt paused and looked Dean in the eye. "So, are we okay?"

"Yeah, we're okay." Dean extended his hand, and Matt gave it a solid shake and clapped Dean's shoulder.

"You be sure to call me," Matt said.

"I will and keep that position in mind. Say hi to Sue."

Matt turned and disappeared out the door.

Epilogue

"Time for your medication, Mr. Campbell."

The two men entered the padded room with caution. Ivan sat along the far back wall rocking back and forth, staring at the floor. As the men got closer, he started to squirm in a panic, babbling some barely discernible words.

"Come on, Mr. Campbell, it won't hurt," one of the men said.

Ivan scurried along on his knees as the men cornered him. The one held him steady with all his strength, while the other administered the injection. As soon as they were finished, they fled the room, locking the door behind them.

"That guy creeps me out."

"Why? He's just another nut."

"Did you see his eyes? He gave me a side glance as we left the room, and I could swear they glowed. It was eerie. Like a yellow-orange glow. There's something weird about him."

"Glowed? Yeah right! You're working too hard." The man laughed as they continued down the hall.

Works Cited

Alfred, Jay. "Bioplasma bodies." Unexplained Mysteries. http://www.unexplained-mysteries.com/column.php?id=107118 (accessed April 21, 2011).

Alfred, Jay. "Plasma life forms." Unexplained Mysteries. http://www.unexplained-mysteries.com/column.php?id=111062 (accessed April 21, 2011).

Brennan, Barbara Ann. *Hands of light: a guide to healing through the human energy field : a new paradigm for the human being in health, relationship, and disease*. Toronto: Bantam Books, 19881987.

Hunt, Dr. Valorie, Massey, W., Weinberg, R., Bryere, R., and Hahn, P., *Project Report, A Study of Structural Integration from Neuromuscular, Energy Field, and Emotional Approaches*. U.C.L.A, 1977.

Kilner, Walter J., M.D., "The Human Aura". (retitled and new edition of "The Human Atmosphere") New Hyde Park, New York, University Books, 1965.

Schmeidler, Gertrude. "Kirlian photography." The Mystica. http://www.themystica.com/mystica/articles/k/kirlian_photography.html (accessed April 21, 2011).

Tsytovich, V.N., Morfill, G.E., Gusein-Zade, N.G., Klumov, B.A., and Vladimirov, S.V., "From plasma crystals and helical structures towards inorganic living matter," New Journal of Physics, 9, 263, 2007.

About the Author

Joanne Elder was born and raised in Toronto, Ontario. She attended the University of Western Ontario where she earned a Masters degree in Engineering Science. As a Professional Engineer, she spent several years in the aeronautical industry and thereafter assumed a research position in the nuclear industry. Joanne has published numerous technical papers.

Living in King City, Ontario, Joanne spends her spare time fending off the nerd image by enjoying sports and attempting to keep her two teenagers and husband in line.

Joanne's combined passion for science and a fast-paced read has led her to her final calling: to write the next generation of science fiction thrillers, which will leave readers on the edge of their seats and their minds spinning in amazement.

Also by Joanne Elder

Entity
Coming May 2012,
MuseItUp Publishing

Energy cannot be created or destroyed, but it can be changed. The chilling question for Dean Weston is: into what? By the time Dean comes face to face with the foreboding truth, it is too late. A mad man's quest for ultimate knowledge and power has spawned true evil; an evil capable of tearing down moral barriers and leaving one thirsting for vengeance and retribution.

As this evil consumes those closest to Dean, he becomes unknowingly vulnerable, leaving him and the woman he loves in immeasurable danger. Struggling to destroy a malevolent energy life form he barely understands, Dean finds his own humanity coming into question. As his moral fibers start to unravel, Dean grasps at one last thread of hope and does the unthinkable.

MuseItUp Publishing
Where the Muse entertains readers!
https://museituppublishing.com/bookstore2/
Visit our website for more books for your reading pleasure.